A ROBERT CURTIS MYSTERY

CALLED
INTO
SERVICE

David Martyn

David Martyn

Blue Forge Press

Port Orchard ✿ Washington

Called into Service
Copyright 2019
by David Martyn

First eBook Edition
July 2019

First Print Edition
July 2019

For information about film, reprint or other subsidiary rights, contact: blueforgegroup@gmail.com

Blue Forge Press
7419 Ebbert Drive Southeast
Port Orchard, Washington 98367
360.550.2071 ph.txt

Dedicated to
Robert Curtis Martyn

My father, encourager, and supporter.

Acknowledgements

Thank you to my wife, Karen, who encouraged me to undertake a mystery series. She is my constant companion, sharing a love for history, mystery, and a good story.

Thanks also to my brother, Bob, for believing in his little brother.

A ROBERT CURTIS MYSTERY

CALLED
INTO
SERVICE

David Martyn

PROLOGUE
EUROPE 1621

In May 1620, Colonel Sir Horace Vere raised a regiment of twenty-two hundred English volunteers to fight for the Protestant Elector of the Palatinate, Frederick V. A wavering King James I permitted English participation only so long as it was not by his authorization or funding. Frederick V and his wife Countess Elizabeth, daughter of King James I, had lost their war to retain his new crown as King of Bohemia in battle to Albrecht von Wallenstein, General of Emperor Ferdinand II's Imperial Army. The Emperor now moved to take Frederick's Palatinate as well. The English regiment, funded by Frederick V and many English nobles enjoyed broad popular support. Sir Horace's volunteers sailed to the United Netherlands where Dutch cavalry escorted them to the Palatinate before returning to their long running war of independence from the Spanish Netherlands.

In Mainz on May 14, 1621, the Protestant Union, Frederick's alliance, was formally dissolved, and its army disbanded. The German protestant princes sent their soldiers home. Only the Margrave of Baden, Duke Christian of Brunswick and the Count von Mansfeld continued their struggle against the Catholic League, the King of Spain, the Emperor and the armies of the Holy Roman Empire.

The small English force was all that remained to protect the Palatinate from advancing Catholic League and Imperial Armies ordered by Ferdinand to secure the Palatinate for Duke Maximillian of Bavaria in reward for his support against Frederick V. Colonel Vere divided his force in three and garrisoned Heidelberg Castle, Mannheim, and Frankenthal.

CHAPTER 1
SECRETS

The field was silent, holding its breath, its eyes closed to the unnatural events of men. There was no sound of wind in the leaves of the trees. No song of a bird. Only a rising and falling hum of voices, moans of men in pain. A low chorus sung by the dying.

A still and broken body stirred. Bloodied eyes slowly opened but any movement was stopped by agonizing pain. His head spinning, his mind fogged, Robert Curtis closed his eyes again and waited for the spinning to stop.

Now he could smell the grass and loamy soil beneath him; now an open eye could make out the green of it. Slowly his mind began to clear. Memories, clouded at first, steadily emerged from gray, foggy dreams. Color returned to his mind's eye. He could remember being surprised by troops ahead of his column and… and nothing. Robert strained to remember more, but his thoughts were interrupted by the sound of steps and the screams of a man dying. More footsteps off towards the low sounds of moaning, again a scream, then silence. The footsteps continued. They grew louder.

An Ahlspiess, he thought. *He is spiking the wounded.* Robert listened as the footsteps grew closer. They stopped. A hand reached down and took the pistol lying beside him. After an eternity, the steps resumed and grew fainter. *Please God*, he thought, *make it dark. Send the night, please Lord. Send a dark moonless night.*

The night came but Robert, frozen in fear, waited. He listened and waited. Slowly his breathing became regular. He shifted his eyes and took in all that his frozen stillness would allow. Carefully, he lifted his head.

The field around him was covered with bodies. The moaning had stopped, nothing moved. His helmet fell from his head but landed softly on the grass. His head throbbed with pain, a hand to the crown of his head could feel blood still seeping from beneath his matted, sticky hair. He managed to lift his body on hands and knees but felt more pain from his right leg. More pain and more blood. He settled back onto his stomach and began to crawl, dragging his wounded leg as he inched his way along. Stopping to rest, he scanned the field around him. There were thick woods to the right. He started to crawl and then stopped. Sitting up, he removed his powder belt, half armor, and blue cassock. He carefully ran his hand over his leg. Blood seeped slowly from the wound. He untied the yellow and red ribbons used to gather his breeches against his gray stockings and wrapped them tightly around his leg wound and resumed crawling. He crawled towards the woods. He kept crawling, a slow but steady pace into the woods, putting distance from the field of dead behind him.

Progress through the woods was slow and painful. Thick underbrush and briars hampered his way. Robert moved slowly ahead slashing with his sword to cut open a small path before him. His battle with the underbrush soon sapped what little energy he had. As he lay on the forest floor bleeding, with his clothes shredded by the briars and about to close his eyes in sleep, a light appeared off in the darkness ahead. It shone brightly for a few seconds and was gone. It was a bright light. Not a star, not the moon, it was the light of a lantern. The adrenaline of hope coursed through his veins and he resumed his slow but sure advance towards the light. Robert crawled forward until the adrenaline had run its course. Still, he crawled until all his strength failed him.

The door to the log hut opened slightly, just enough for Wilhelm to slide inside. "There was something out there, rooting in the ground. It quieted, probably a badger, or a fox, perhaps a boar." He turned to the young woman waiting inside. "But Katharina, please be more careful with the doors and curtains," he pleaded. Wilhelm continued softly, "With so many soldiers and desperate peasants wandering about, we must take extra precaution. We must remain hidden. We can trust no one. You know that. Only your father can know we are here."

Katharina bowed her head and nodded yes. "Forgive me, Wilhelm. I shall be more careful; I promise." Looking warmly into his face she asked, "Do you think it will be safe for a fire in the morning? The soldiers have moved on. You could use a warm meal after these past several days."

Wilhelm smiled at the woman he could never hurt. "Wait until morning and then I will look again. We will see. I am sorry, Katharina, I did not mean to be cross with you. You and your father are taking a great risk on my account."

"You were not cross, Wilhelm, you are right to remind me. It is you who have risked everything to help us!" Then seeing the weariness in Wilhelm's face, she said. "If you think it safe, I shall go to bed. Should I leave the lamp on?"

"Light or dark, it does not matter. I will stay up and pray awhile. Good night. Sleep in the good blessings and protection of our Lord and Savior."

As soon as darkness turned to dawn, Wilhelm was out the door. He wore simple peasant trousers dyed in an earthy brown, a coat of mossy green and a green-brown peasant's cap. He could safely move about if he were slow and careful. He listened between slow steps, his eyes attentive to any movement or man-made color. His senses enhanced by a week of hiding, even his nose was sensitive to smoke, to fire and the smell of man.

He started in the direction of the sound he had heard the night before. The morning was quiet. He saw no new tracks. But the air, something was in the air. Something was not right. He kept moving slowly and then he saw a dark heap lying in a briar patch.

Wilhelm ventured closer. The heap did not move. Closer. It was a man. *Probably dead,* he thought. He put his hand on the knife in his belt and approached. Still, the man did not move. Clutching his knife, he nudged the body with his boot. Nothing. He touched the man's bloodstained neck. The blood was dry and hard, but the skin was still warm. He felt for a pulse. *There might be a pulse, very faint.* Wilhelm knelt and turned the man's face up. The man did not move. He placed his knife under the nose and then over the mouth.

"*Why do I bother? Why take a chance?* Then he saw condensation begin to form on the blade. *He's breathing, his pulse is weak, but he lives.*

Startled by the life before him, Wilhelm stood up straight and carefully scanned the woods. He saw nothing, heard nothing, detected nothing. *Who would know? Why risk it? I could just walk back to the hut and have a hot breakfast with Katharina. I did nothing to this man. I owe him nothing.*

Wilhelm looked down. He bent over, lifted the unconscious body over his shoulder slowly straightened up, and half carried half dragged him to the hut. As he approached the door he called in a hushed voice, straining to be quiet, "Katharina! Katharina! Light the fire and heat water. A loved one of God needs our help!"

Katharina flung open the door. Seeing Wilhelm struggling with the lifeless man, she covered her mouth with her hands and stared wide-eyed. Then coming forward and running her hands over the man's head, she said, "Quickly! Put him on the bed. I will start with the water. We must get him clean and his wounds dressed. Yes, we must light the fire. God save us all!"

Smoke arose from the small chimney. It rose only a few feet before the rocky outcropping which towered over the hut sent the curling smoke back down. The hut was well hidden; only someone far off the path catching the smell of the fire would ever find it. Even so, Wilhelm and Katharina had been unwilling to risk a fire ever since the war had come to the Neckar River valley of the Palatine.

This was different; a man's life was at stake. A stranger, yes, perhaps an enemy, yet a man. And who was the enemy? Two declared Christian armies. In both, many of the soldiers were mercenaries paid only by what they could loot. A village, a farm, a traveler, all were easier prey than castles or walled cities under siege.

Katharina carefully and gently cleaned the man and began to tend his wounds. Once clean and his wounds dressed, he lay unconscious in the bed. Wilhelm knelt beside him. After praying, he dipped his finger in a small dish of oil and made the sign of the cross on the unconscious man's forehead. He lifted a small crucifix from around his neck, hidden under his coat, and kissed it. Wilhelm crossed himself and then rose to his feet. "He is in God's hands. He appears to be a strong young man,

and we found no musket ball in his wounds. When he…"
Wilhelm's words trailed off.

"You think he will live? Do you think he is a soldier?
He had a sword but no armor or uniform," Katharina
asked.

"Yes, I think he is a soldier. But of which army, I do
not know. When he awakens, he must not know our
secret. We will show him Christian mercy, but do not
talk about us."

"He does not have the face of a soldier. I see gentleness
in his face. We must pray for him, Wilhelm. Perhaps God
has sent him here."

"Perhaps. But we must be careful none the less."

Katharina looked at the man asleep in her bed. He was
young, but his black hair already showed signs of silver
and gray emerging as ash on the edges of black coal. His
complexion was fair, though his face was burned by the
sun. He was tall, but not unusually broad in the
shoulders. His arms and his hands were not those of one
who labored.

For hours the stranger lay motionless in the bed.
Slowly his breathing grew stronger, but his eyes remained
closed. He slept, peacefully at first, but then his sleeping
body began to tremble. His fists clenched and his head
rocked back and forth, yet he slept. Again, he trembled,
sweat began to bead on his forehead. Katharina tenderly
wiped the sweat away, and the stranger slept.

After three days in the hut, Katharina glanced at the
stranger and saw an eye open. The gray-blue eye stared
straight ahead. The stranger said nothing. She walked over

to him, got down on her knees, her eyes level with his and said softly, "Wie fuhlst?"

The stranger said nothing. Both eyes now open, he continued to look straight ahead.

"Bist du hungrig?" She asked.

Robert's eyes began to move as he slowly looked around the room. He said nothing. He did not act alarmed; he just looked around and then focused on Katharina. He saw warmth, and he saw beauty. He sighed, closed his eyes and went back to sleep.

When Robert awoke again, he rubbed his eyes and said, "Eau, s'il vous plait."

Katharina looked at him, immediately got up and went for water. Bringing him a full cup, their conversations now in French, she said, "Yes drink. You have slept a long time. You should eat. Perhaps some soup and bread? And a little wine maybe?"

Robert sat up and accepted the cup. He took a long drink and smiled at his host. "Thank you. I do not know how I came here. I do not know where I am, but by the grace of God, surely you are an angel and have rescued me."

Wilhelm heard the voices and came in from outside. "You are awake; God has heard our prayers! Yes, I see color in your face. Katharina, feed our guest!" Then looking closely at Robert, he said, "Your French has an unusual accent."

Robert replied groggily, "It is not unusual in my village, but then, we are an ancient people of Normandy. Have you been to the Norman countryside?"

"No, of course, I have only heard the speech of merchants."

Robert attempted to stand but immediately fell back onto the bed. "Easy my friend," Wilhelm said. "You are gravely injured with wounds to your head and your leg."

Robert ran his hand over the back of his head. Pain shot through him as he touched the concussed area.

Wilhelm watched him wince and said, "Some skull bone was grazed, and there was much bleeding, but there was no musket ball. Your leg appears to have been crushed, stepped on, perhaps by a horse. I do not think it has broken, though some flesh has been torn."

Robert looked down at his bandaged leg and then raised his eyes to Wilhelm. "Surely a surgeon could have done no better. Thank you, sir. Thank you and your wife for your mercy to a stranger."

Katharina looked at Wilhelm. Wilhelm answered, "Any Christian would do such a thing. If you are well enough, tell us how you came to lay outside our hut?"

Robert answered with unintended honesty. "In truth, I do not know the source of my wounds. I did not see my attacker."

Wilhelm nodded. "Your wounds show your attack came from behind. It seems you crawled for some time, for brambles tore your clothes and they are covered in soil. I found a sword in your hands. Your other weapons of soldiery were not with you."

Robert snapped, "Should a man not wear a sword in these troubled times? Does a sword make me a soldier?" Then seeing Katharina with a steaming bowl, he smiled and said, "Ah, soup! Yes, thank you, Katharina was it? It smells so good! I must taste it."

His head now clear, Robert looked at Katharina, an attractive young woman, tall with light hair and blue eyes, but it was the warmth and honesty of her smile that caught his attention. Robert turned to Wilhelm, a serious young man of about his age; he was no taller than Katharina, not a tall man at all. A peasant's cap covered his brown hair, but he felt Wilhelm's inquisitive brown eyes watching him closely.

Katharina spoke. "Eat slowly, and the bread also. You must recover your strength. Enough questions Wilhelm! Let the poor man eat."

Wilhelm smiled. "Of course, Katharina. There will be time for questions later. But tell me, sir, what shall we call you?"

"I am Robert," he replied as he ate his bread and soup.

"Welcome Robert, I am Wilhelm, and this is my ... this is Katharina who looks after me."

Robert looked at Wilhelm and then at Katharina. He caught the tension in her eyes and nodding at each he said, "Wilhelm, Katharina, thank you."

A full stomach made Robert drowsy, and he begged permission to lie down again. As he did, he heard Wilhelm say quietly but sternly, "The curtains, quickly the curtains; the sun has already set."

As Katharina ran to close the curtains, Robert fell asleep.

CHAPTER 2
HOLDING BACK

When Robert awoke, he saw Wilhelm kneeling by the fireside, holding his crucifix and praying in Latin. "Lord Jesus Christ, you stretched out your arms of love on the hardwood of the cross that everyone might come within reach of your saving embrace…"

Robert completed the prayer in Latin. "…So clothe us in your Spirit that we, reaching forth our hands in love, may bring those who do not know you to the knowledge and love of you; for the honor of your Name. Amen."

Wilhelm repeated, "Amen." He turned his gaze to Robert. "That is a priestly prayer of preparation. It is not said in the congregation but normally only before mass. I thought you a soldier, Robert, but you are a priest!"

Robert smiled weakly and said, "It is a prayer that has always spoken to me. It brings both comfort and hope. Indeed, I owe my life to the saving embrace of God who sent you out to find me. Yes, as you say, I am a priest ... was a priest. Does not God's Word teach we are a Royal Priesthood, speaking of all who believe? In that regard, I remain a priest, and I would not deny my faith. But you, Wilhelm, that is Father Wilhelm, are hidden in a hut with a woman. Whether she is your wife or not, this is not proper behavior for a priest of the church. The emperor has re-established your Catholic religion in the Palatinate, so why do you hide?"

Wilhelm's smile faded. He stared at Robert, unable to answer. He grabbed a rough-hewn chair and sat down. Finally, Wilhelm replied, "If I am a priest, are you not fortunate that I brought you to refuge, that we bound up your wounds and prayed to our heavenly father that your life is saved? Surely..."

"Father Wilhelm, I believe your charity and prayers are sincere, surely Katharina is a chaste and upright woman, gifted by our God for works of mercy. So why is a good priest in hiding in a country in need of God's shepherds?"

Katharina came in with a bucket of water. She smiled brightly and said, "Good morning, Robert. You look much better today." Then seeing the concern in Wilhelm's eyes, she asked, "I hope I have not interrupted."

Wilhelm smiled, "Robert is about to tell us about himself. He has this morning revealed the most amazing things! His Latin is impeccable, and he prays perfectly as taught by the church."

Katharina was about to reply, but Wilhelm cut her off. "Please, don't bother our guest with our unfortunate circumstances, his story is so much more compelling, an educated and saintly man attacked before our very dwelling. He is a stranger to our country, yet a man of the church! He was about to tell me how a priest becomes a soldier."

Wilhelm gave his chair to Katharina and took another for himself.

Robert said, "As you say, I a man of the church. Why, brother, do you insist that I am a soldier?"

Wilhelm smiled. "Robert, you speak no German; you were found wounded by a harquebus or pistol ball not far from a field of battle the morning after a skirmish. Certainly, you fear not knowing my allegiance, for though a priest you are or once were, it is as a soldier you are here today. But I assure you, whether from the army of Flanders, the Free United Netherlands or Frederick the Fifth, Robert, you are a soldier."

Robert stared at Wilhelm. Wilhelm paused and then continued, "Be at peace, we will not turn you over to any side. We only intend to help heal you and see you safely on your way."

Robert's face showed he had no answer.

Wilhelm continued, "It is not so unusual for a priest to be a soldier, was not Saint Martin, a soldier? And even Pope Gregory? So, tell me how a priest, a man of the church, was found wounded on our doorstep?"

Robert looked intently at Wilhelm and answered, "A

man of the Church? The Church? Who speaks for the Church? Who is the Church? Isn't that why this war is more than removing Frederick from the throne of Bohemia and revoking his title in the Palatine? Isn't that why the Catholic League opposes the Protestant Union? Is the church Popes and Archbishops directing emperors, kings, and princes to do its bidding, or is the Church the very body of Christ, faithful believers desiring only to worship God and live in peace? And these armies, are they not said to defend the Church? So many soldiers called to fight for the Church. They are called to a lie! Surely no Christian is called to plunder farms, pillage peasant villages and rob innocent travelers! No Christian is called to murder the wounded left lying on the battlefield! This is what my eyes have seen in the short months I have been here."

Robert looked down and sighed. His voice softened, and he said, "Perhaps it is the will of God that takes me away from such deadly hypocrisy. But you, Father Wilhelm, you have not answered my question. Why does a priest hide in his own country with a young woman, and this priest proclaims he is unconcerned with the allegiance of the stranger, a suspected soldier, in his house? Who are you hiding from? Why are you hiding?"

Wilhelm's brow furrowed, his eyes burned into Robert's face and his response stabbed. "Robert, we have brought you into our house. We have bound up your wounds as you have noted, we do this at great risk. So, it is fair for me to ask you: Who are you, Robert? Why are you here? You say you are a man of faith. You know the prayers of a priest. You call me your brother and praise the good works and acts of mercy done in the name of our Lord, yet you speak as a man at war with himself, all rulers, and all the leaders of the church. What brings you to this battlefield? What brings you to this hut?"

Robert closed his eyes and lowered his head.

Katharina spoke softly. "Robert, I do not know why God brought you here, but please know that you are safe here with us. I have prayed, and Wilhelm as well, that you recover, that God saves your life. God can heal your body and your soul, for surely you have been troubled in spirit. We minister not for gain, not for authority but only as our Lord has commanded us. Wilhelm has a shepherd's heart for the people that is why..."

Katharina saw Wilhelm shake his head no, yet she continued, "That is why I ask you to trust us and let us help you."

Robert sighed and looking up at Katharina said, "Forgive me, Katharina, and you as well Wilhelm. I am truly grateful for the mercy and hospitality you have shown me. Surely, our Lord will reward you. Perhaps I am at war, and in truth, I know not who my attacker was or his motive. My very presence here brings risk to your house. As surely as I was attacked, you fear those who pursue you. Tell me the way to an inn or place of shelter that I may recover apart from you, that I bring no danger to your house."

Wilhelm smiled. "Brother Robert, you are in no condition to travel. And as you say, you do not know your attacker. Perhaps he believes you dead, but perhaps he knows your body was not found on the battlefield, for I believe you are a soldier, and your attacker will seek you out. You are safer here. No, Robert, remain with us. Perhaps when you trust us, you will share your secrets."

"And will you, Wilhelm, share your secret?"

Katharina looked at Wilhelm but said nothing.

Robert said softly, "I do not war with you, for surely you are a brother. I do not war with any whose desire is to walk with our Lord humbly. Our Savior does not call us to religion or doctrine; he calls us to faith. Are not those whose only desire is to love our God members of our faith and the true victims in this war? It is our so-called 'shepherds' and 'elders' that have brought upon the holy catholic Church persecution not seen since the ancient days of Rome. Is it not ironic that the Holy Roman Emperor crowned under the authority of God and the Roman Catholic Church once again pursues worldwide persecution?"

Robert laid back with his eyes to the ceiling and exhaled a long breath. "I have said too much. You have eyes to see. You have an open heart. Listen to the Holy Spirit. What does He say?"

Katharina turned her eyes from Robert to Wilhelm, hoping for a response. Wilhelm sat quietly studying Robert across from him.

Robert looked first at Katharina, then Wilhelm and said, "I must trust you. I am, as you surmise, a soldier. Though a reluctant one. I trained as a priest, but no bishop would have me. My uncle sought my commission. I come from a noble family but will inherit no title. For men like me, there is but the church or soldiering. Since I failed in the church, I was sent here."

Wilhelm looked at Robert. "Perhaps the bishops heard only your anger and did not see the man with the passion for our Lord and his Church that I see today."

"They all wanted me to take sides. They fight each other without mercy. I could not share in their merciless pursuit to martyr their opponents."

Wilhelm smiled at Robert. "And brother, do you not judge all of God's priests and clergy for the sins of some and your own perceived failures?"

Then Wilhelm's face looked puzzled. "Who would attack his fellow soldier; a priest turned soldier? Who would do that? Why?"

CHAPTER 3
THE VISITOR

There was a short rap on the door, followed by another. The door of the hut creaked open, and in shock, for a moment, Robert's heart stopped beating. A man in a brown hooded cloak entered the room. The man set the sack he carried on the dirt floor. He looked to Katharina first and then to Wilhelm. "I thought I heard a stranger's voice. One speaking French."

Katharina answered, "This is Robert. We found him wounded near the hut. We could not leave him to die."

The stranger walked up to the edge of Robert's bed and looked at him carefully before stepping back. "I know his accent. I have traded with his people. It is an old Norman French, spoken by noble families in the north of England and Scotland."

Then turning to Wilhelm, he said softly, still speaking German, "What does he know? What have you told him?"

"I have told him nothing, but he surmises I am a Catholic and a priest. He believes Katharina is a chaste woman gifted in acts of mercy. He has been here four days and has just confessed he is a soldier and a priest. He speaks as one of your protestants though a Lutheran or Calvinist I do not know."

The visitor replied, "Yes that I heard as I was about to enter."

Turning to Robert and smiling, the visitor said in French, "By the grace and mercy of God, your life was saved by the hands of Wilhelm and Katharina. You are a long way from your home in England. Or perhaps Scotland? You are fortunate indeed, for remnants of General von Mansfeld's army of the Elector Frederick and its English regiment march to garrison the walled cities and fortresses still in Protestant hands. The Army of Flanders commanded by Johann Tserclaes, Count of Tilly, pushes hard against them. Be assured you are safe here."

Robert looked surprised and then replied, "I am indeed thankful for the hospitality I have received. How is it you say I am English?"

The man spoke in English. "Your French is Anglo-Norman."

He paused, smiled and with a slight laugh said, "You Englishmen take such pride in your fine wool."

Turning serious, he continued, "I deal in tapestries, only the finest. Often, I have heard that Anglo-Norman French of an Englishman or Scotsman insisting on the

highest price for his wool. As to your soldiering, the
Scottish Regiment is to the north, and the English
regiment led by Colonel Horace Vere has recently
skirmished nearby. If Count Tilly's army is not reinforced
with the second army of Flanders and the expected army
from Spain, perhaps General von Mansfeld and your
English regiment would have better prospects. So, you
see, you are fortunate indeed to be in safe hands."

Robert looked at the man, paused and then said, "Sir, I
am Robert Curtis of Berwick-Upon-Tweed, indeed of an
old Norman family. Oddly, my father is a wool merchant.
My uncle holds the family title, Baron of Tweedbridge
and now Viscount Curtis. He secured my commission in
Colonel Vere's volunteer regiment. Who am I
addressing?"

The visitor smiled and turned to Wilhelm. "Wilhelm,
please see that I was not followed. And Katharina, some
cool water from the well would be welcome."

The visitor removed his cloak to reveal a fine
embroidered coat, tan breeches, with red and gold
ribbons gathered about rich blue stockings which were
mostly hidden by high, polished black boots. He was a
tall man and distinguished, older, with silver hair, but he
was not yet elderly. His inquisitive blue eyes seemed to
catch everything and everyone about him.

Once Wilhelm and Katharina left the hut, he bowed
slightly and continued in English. "I am Karl Schroeder,
as I said, a dealer in fine tapestries. With so many princes
and noble houses seeking my services, I stay informed. It
is a dangerous world we travel. So, Robert, Wilhelm tells

me you believe Katharina is a chaste woman and he is a priest. You have seen nothing unpriestly on his part?"

Robert was surprised by the question. "I have seen only the most Christian affection and hospitality on their part."

"I am pleased to hear that. Katharina is my daughter; a father always has worries."

Robert replied, "And you come bearing provisions and information for them. Tell me why they hide here?"

"In time," Karl said then paused. His hand stroked the silver beard on his chin, and then he turned his determined gaze on Robert. "Perhaps we may be able to help each other."

Katharina came back with the water pail. Karl smiled and said, "Should not a loving daughter give her father a hug?"

Katharina smiled and hugged Karl and said, "Papa, I am so pleased you are here. It has been frightening. The battle was so close. But now I feel safe."

"You do not feel safe with Wilhelm and now a trained soldier to defend you?" He motioned towards Robert before continuing. "It will not be much longer, Katie. Soon. Trust me. Now some cold water for a dry throat; unless you have any beer?"

"Just the water Papa, you know that."

"I understand Wilhelm carries a letter from his bishop. Has he mentioned it to you?"

"No Papa. I know nothing of such a letter. Should I ask him?"

"No, no. I'm sure he will share it with you in time."

When Wilhelm returned, Karl asked, "Did you see anyone? Was our warning snare tripped? Any sign at all?"

Wilhelm looked at Robert and said, "No, all is well."

Karl nodded. "I felt certain no one followed, but it is always best to confirm."

Then looking at Robert, he said, "I believe our English friend needs us and he may prove useful to our purposes. He is in no condition to run-off, and indeed there is no one else he can trust if he wishes to avoid capture. Let him hear our secret and upon his oath as a man of the church and a gentleman. Let him pledge never to repay our kindness with betrayal."

Katharina looked at Wilhelm, who took a deep breath and replied, "Karl, I know you to be a man of caution and discretion. Robert has shown his trust in us and in truth I can find no reason not trust him upon his word."

Katharina said. "I trust him, Papa!"

All eyes turned to Robert sitting attentively on the bed. "You have saved my life. You have shown me only kindness and goodness. You know my story, I am at your mercy. Of course, I pledge never to betray you or your secrets. Further, I give my word as a brother and a gentleman to help or aid your cause to the best of my ability, so help me God."

Karl nodded his head and spoke. "Our cause is simple. My son was taken as a prisoner to the dungeons of Mainz. He is the true and called pastor of the church in Eberbach, a free Imperial City. We seek to free him. His arrest is a direct violation of the recent Treaty of Ulm. Have you heard of this treaty?"

Robert replied, "I have heard of such a treaty. I have heard the Protestant Union will not send reinforcements."

Karl brought his hands together, fingertips touching fingertips. "No there will be no reinforcements under the Protestant Union. At Ulm, the Protestant Union pledged neutrality in Emperor Ferdinand II's war to recover Bohemia and the Palatinate from Frederick V. Sadly; the Protestant union has disbanded."

Robert looked surprised. "So, it's just the Dutch Republic, a few soldiers remaining from Frederick's Palatinate army and our small English regiment against Count Tilly and the Emperor's Army."

Karl sighed. "I'm afraid it is worse than that. A Spanish Army is to join with Count Tilly and press the Dutch. But I was speaking of the violation of the treaty. You see, in return for the neutrality of the Protestant Union, the Elector-Archbishop of Mainz, Johann Schweikhard von Kronberg, senior prelate over all of the Catholic Church in Germany, assured all of the electors that the Emperor would not seek retribution or claims of restitution by the Roman Church against protestant princes and nobles loyal to the emperor."

Robert replied, "As in all treaties, possessions and titles seem always to come first to princes, dukes, counts, and bishops."

Karl smiled. "Yes. While Eberbach lies in the Palatinate, it has for centuries been a free city. But even so, if the Emperor is not forcing conversion to Catholicism on a people freely worshipping as protestant for over one hundred years, why was my son arrested?"

Karl paused and smiled at Katharina. "My Katie has convinced Father Wilhelm Hahn, the new Catholic priest of Eberbach, a man who loves God and all of God's children, to petition an audience for her with the Elector Archbishop. I will let Father Wilhelm speak for himself but let me say he has shown himself as a man of faith who detests conversion upon the threat of death. Sadly, not all in his church are of the same charitable view. Someone is determined that Katharina and Father Wilhelm never live to speak with the Elector Archbishop."

Katharina interrupted. "There have been attempts on Father Wilhelm's life! And threats on mine as well!

Wilhelm said, "We are dealing with a most treacherous person. It is one thing to interfere with my audience with the Archbishop, but to threaten the life of an innocent woman? A virtuous young woman! As a priest and gentleman, I must support her cause."

Robert replied, "If an attempt has already been made on Wilhelm, excuse me, Father Wilhelm, and threats made against Katharina, then surely the plotter fears your message to the Elector Archbishop. Your only hope lies in an audience with him. You, Karl, believe the Archbishop, a man of his word?"

Karl nodded. "It is just as you say. We must have an audience with the Archbishop of Mainz. His reputation is one of toleration with Protestants. He is the Archchancellor and senior counselor to the Emperor, head of the Prince Electors, half of whom are Protestant. He knows there must be trust and tolerance in the empire for there to be any hope of peace."

Wilhelm added; "There are those who do not want peace. They see an opportunity to settle old grievances and see forced conversion and restitution as an opportunity for power, wealth and titles."

Robert closed his eyes in thought, then turning to Wilhelm said, "Forgive me for asking the obvious, but whoever is behind your attack and the threats against Katharina, must be someone who knows you seek an audience with the Elector Archbishop. You hide here because you know of the threat…"

Karl answered, "We have our suspicions. My son Johann was seized at night. Johann said he had business at the church and left home after supper. We never saw him again. He must have known his abductor. Of course, we asked questions, but no one could tell us who had taken him or why, not the magistrate nor the burgermeister, nor the town aldermen. It was then I first noticed a proclamation nailed to the church door. It read, "This is now the Church of The Holy Mother. Emperor Ferdinand II proclaims the return of Eberbach to the true faith of the Roman Catholic Church. Father Wilhelm Hahn, Pastor."

Robert looked surprised. "You, Father Wilhelm?"

Wilhelm continued, "I was one of a group of priests sent to accompany the Imperial Army of Count Tilly. We were sent to be priests for the Catholics of the Palatinate. We were assured there were many Catholics longing to return to the faith. I never met Pastor Johann and did not see the church until several days after he disappeared.

The proclamation was posted before I arrived."

Robert asked, "Who assigned the priests? Your name was on the proclamation. When did you learn you were assigned the church in Eberbach?"

Wilhelm answered, "Good questions! I was not informed of my assignment until the day I first visited the church and saw the proclamation already posted. I learned that it was posted the day we arrived in Eberbach with Count Tilly's army, days before I first visited the church. A deacon representative of the Elector Archbishop gave me the assignment. He was one of three men in charge of the priests and magistrates to be assigned in the recovered towns and villages of the Palatinate. It was the deacon, Maximilian von Greiffenclau; he kept the company of a papal representative, Don Lorenzo, and Don Pedro, an abbot from the Spanish Netherlands. We priests were told that if we did well, that is, if the people resumed worship in the true faith if there were peace and obedience to the church and the emperor, we would be remembered. There is a need for many Bishops in these cities. Indeed, that is what my uncle told me when he recommended me for such service."

Karl added, "My son was approached the very day the Count of Tilly marched his soldiers into the city. The city magistrate brought churchmen to meet him. They told him they expected his cooperation. But every day, one of the churchmen came. The churchman asked to see the parish records. Johann said all he wanted was the parish records. He asked nothing of the congregation."

"And you do not know which of the three was his visitor?"

Wilhelm answered, "No, nor do I know if they were of one accord. They kept to themselves, but they often argued between them."

Robert asked, "How is it Father Wilhelm, that you, a priest commissioned to return Protestant states to Catholicism, have become a champion for the Protestant pastor you have replaced?"

Katharina immediately replied, "Because I asked him, and he is a good and honest priest. He loves God, and he loves God's people. He is a good man, and noble! He loves justice. All men should be as good and noble as he!"

Wilhelm blushed and said, "Katharina is far too kind in her words. Yes, she did come to me to inquire after her brother the pastor. It has always been my intention to earn the goodwill of the people. I listened and asked a few questions. I was surprised no one could say what happened to Pastor Johann; indeed, no one acknowledged any meetings with him. Surely, if there were any charge against him, it would be recorded. An arrest would require men. Even at night, there would be orders. There would be witnesses."

Karl spoke. "And then came the threats and the attempt on Wilhelm's life. One of the priests came to him and warned him."

Wilhelm interrupted. "Yes, he said, 'Father Wilhelm, you now have a fine parish and a great opportunity in Eberbach, perhaps even a Bishopric! All these questions you ask about some heretic pastor who has run off at night, they do you no help. They have been noticed. You would be wise to stop."

Katharina said, "Wilhelm told me of his concerns. He asked if I would talk to the people. He suggested I ask everyone I know, even those I did not know. Surely someone saw who visited the pastor. Surely someone witnessed his abduction or arrest. Not long after that, I began to receive letters…"

Karl added, "Very ugly letters."

Katharina continued. "Some accused me of having an unnatural and profane relationship with Father Wilhelm. Others said Johann was a danger to our city and I would soon suffer the same fate. Others said simply, 'Leave Eberbach and never return.'"

Robert looked at Wilhelm. "And the attempt on your life?"

Wilhelm replied, "It was my first Sunday for mass. As I knew no Catholics in Eberbach, I had no helpers in the church. I did not know what to expect. Only the three Imperial clerics and several of the priests awaiting assignment came to the church. I went to ring the church bell to call the people to worship. As I finished ringing, I stepped out from under the belfry just as the bell came crashing down where I had been standing. Once the shock passed, I examined the wreckage. The support beam had been freshly cut. Of course, they said the people of Eberbach were responsible, but I remembered the warnings. It was only the first attempt on my life."

"There were others?"

"My first day at the church I was visited by the three

clerics. They said they came to bless me and support me in my new pastorate. They never did offer a blessing; they only asked if I had found the parish records. I told them the baptismal and death records appeared meticulously maintained. They asked about the transfer of estates and properties of the church from the time of the heretic Luther's unholy seizure. Well, I had not seen any such records and said so. Then the Spaniard from the Netherlands said, 'the heretic pastor had hidden them.' I repeated what I was told, that he had disappeared, run off at night. Surely, if he had run off as they said, he took them with him. Curiously, he said, 'We have reason to believe he did not take them when he fled.'"

Robert nodded and replied, "Yes, that is significant, but you said there was another attempt on your life."

"Yes, both Katharina's and mine. It was about two weeks later. I had met Katharina and had begun asking questions, as I have said. I went to the Imperial magistrate and asked for a safe conduct pass to visit the bishop of Munich, as there was talk that the Duke of Bavaria would be granted title to the Palatinate. I asked him if the road was safe to travel. He replied there were no known troop movements, but bandits were a strong possibility. He asked why I needed to see the bishop, and I foolishly told him a parishioner was concerned that her pastor was taken prisoner for religious beliefs and she sought permission of the Bishop to petition the Archbishop to attend him until the time of his examination."

"And the attempt?"

"The magistrate said he needed the name of the woman for the pass and that I was to bring her to his office the next morning. He promised not only to grant the pass but provide an escort since some soldiers would be traveling that way in the morning. I told him I only knew the woman as Katharina, but he could add her last name to the pass in the morning."

"That evening, after dark, a strange man dressed in a drab hooded cloak came to see me. He never looked me in the eye and spoke in a hushed voice. He only said that if I brought the woman, Katharina, to the magistrate, neither she nor I would ever be seen again. I told him I did not know the woman's family name or where to find her. The strange little man told me to fetch a cloak, not my priest's cassock, and follow him, so I did as he said. As we were leaving, I was about to blow out the candle, and he shook his head, 'leave it burn but lock the door,' he said. He led me to the servant's entrance in the rear of a large house. Karl was waiting for me and led us here."

Karl now spoke. "I left them here and returned to Eberbach, but not my home. I have many friends in the town. The magistrate could not find anyone willing to identify a woman named Katharina who might have run off with a priest. All he had to help identify her were the parish records. He tried to follow-up on all the Katharina's. Well, with so many displaced, moved or dead the records provided no answers. He did the next obvious thing and sent a notice that any priest and a young woman traveling together be detained for identification. First, he searched the road to Munich, and then he focused on the roads to Mainz. That is where we think Johann was taken."

Robert asked, "And now you think the road to Mainz is safe to travel?"

Karl laughed. "Of course not! But enough talk, you must begin to exercise. Let us make you a crutch and see if you can move. I promise not to push you too hard."

CHAPTER 4
THE ALARM

A well-sized crutch enabled Robert to walk. Strength was not his problem; rather, light-headed dizziness overcame him when he attempted to stand. Sitting was only mildly better. Headaches plagued him. Every morning Katharina would change the bandages on his head and around his injured leg. She applied a red, oily salve to the wounds before wrapping them with clean, washed bandages. Just the lightest touch to his head wound brought great pain, but Katharina insisted her oil was the most necessary remedy. She promised her "Hypericum Snaps" or "Saint John's Oil" as it was also known, along with earnest prayers, would protect and heal his wounds. Already she noted, the swelling on his head was going down. Robert gritted his teeth and complied with her nursing directions.

Karl encouraged Robert to stand and try a few steps; gradually the lightheadedness began to fade. Slowly his steps increased, and the dizziness started to recede. Between exercises, Robert and Wilhelm talked. Wilhelm asked, "You have heard our story. Now tell me, Robert, how you came to know the priestly prayer and speak the language of the church."

Robert lay on his bed and stared at the bare beams and crude roof above him. "My uncle arranged for my education at Cambridge where I chose theology over the law as my course of study. Law did not impress me. English law is settled and becoming a clerk recording deeds and administering petty disagreements between neighbors, I thought of little consequence. But theology, oh, the debates! The knowledge of God! The opportunity to open the Scriptures, God's very Word to all people! To enrich worship and change lives! Theology was the flame and fire that burned in the minds of the dons and students at Cambridge. We debated every dogma of the Church; every doctrine was open to discussion, every voice of professing Christianity heard."

Wilhelm replied, "Your Cambridge sounds like a cauldron of heresies brewing against the established doctrines of our faith and the Holy Father."

Robert smiled. "Yes, perhaps some of the voices were reactionary and schismatic, but God's truth can withstand challenge. First, there is His Word. It is unerring and eternal, illuminated for us by the Holy Spirit. Then there is tradition, the great Apostolic teachings of the Church through its councils, and finally, there is reason, the gift our God has given to us. It stands that as God never changes, His Word never changes. God can never contradict Himself or be other than who He is; therefore, we have confidence that His Word and His revelation can never contradict in its revelation and teaching. With these tools, men can approach the knowledge of God. With integrity, man can examine the voices of our age, whether the Pope, the Fathers, Luther, Calvin, Knox, Hooker or Cranmer, the greatest of the English reformers and the father, though not always obeyed, of our Anglican Church."

"And you are a priest of the Church of England?"

Robert lifted his head and said, "Let me try and walk once again. Please help me with the crutches."

They circled the small room once and made it nearly around the second time before Robert began to swoon. "Should I take you back to the bed?" Wilhelm asked.

"No, hold me a few moments. Perhaps the dizziness will pass."

Karl, who had been sitting and listening to the conversation quietly, now offered, "Yes. Try standing. You are getting stronger. Perhaps some fresh air? Come. I will open the door. Stand here and view the world outside this hut."

Katharina came beside Robert and said, "Wilhelm and I will walk beside you. Be careful. Small steps. Trust us. Put your arms on our shoulders, and we will support you."

Robert lifted his head, opened his eyes wide and

hobbled his way to the door. He looked at the green forest before him penetrated by shafts of golden sunlight. The tops of the trees swayed in a light breeze. His eyes brightened, his ears caught the sounds of birds singing, and he inhaled deeply of the forest fragrance.

"This is better," he said softly. "The peace. The life. The hope. Has it all been just a bad dream?"

Karl asked, "Are you ready to walk around the outside of the hut?"

Robert moved the tip of his crutch out the door and slowly took his first step outside. Wilhelm said, "Go to the right; stay on the path."

As Robert made the turn, he noticed there was no path into the woods in front of the hut, only small paths to the right and left. He went to the right and slowly made his way to the corner of the hut. The path turned right again. It led under a rocky ledge which covered the hut. He continued along the path. He could see it went on under the ledge towards a cave. At the back corner of the hut, Wilhelm said, "Keep going around the hut, you must not push too hard."

Katharina said, "You are doing so well, Robert. I am so proud of you!"

Robert made his way around the hut and back through the front door before collapsing on the bed. Breathing heavily, he stared at the familiar roof above, and a smile of accomplishment graced his face. "Let me rest a few minutes, and I will try again."

Karl nodded to Wilhelm and then said, "Robert is making good progress. I must leave. There are arrangements to be made."

As Karl was speaking a curtain fell from a rafter where it had been tethered. Karl, Wilhelm, and Katharina all watched it unfurl in shock. "The snare has been tripped!" Karl exclaimed, "An unwelcome visitor. Wilhelm, come with me. Katharina, bolt the door behind us and only open for our signal. You remember it?"

"Yes papa, two knocks then one, two knocks and then one again. Oh, please be careful!"

Robert sat up. "May I have my sword? Just in case…"

Wilhelm glanced at Karl and the then retrieved Robert's sword from a trunk. "Keep it hidden in the bed. Use it if you must."

He then took a pistol and powder horn from the trunk. He slung the strap of the horn over his cloak and slid the pistol in his belt next to his knife. Wilhelm grasped the hilt of the knife in his belt and said, "Let's go."

Karl opened his coat and removed a pistol. He nodded to Wilhelm and they both slipped out the door.

Katharina bolted the door and stood weakly against it. Her face gray with worry, the start of a tear in each eye, she closed them and said under her breath, "Please God bring them back to me safe." Opening her eyes once again and feigning a smile, she looked at Robert. He sat calmly listening. Finally, she said, "It is a good thing you are here. You remain so calm. It reassures me."

Robert smiled at Katharina and replied. "It is something a soldier learns. I would explain, but I do not wish to frighten you. Please sit down. Why don't we talk? That often helps when waiting."

Katharina sat down across from Robert, frightened and vulnerable.

Robert spoke softly. "Tell me about your life in Eberbach. You were happy and loved?"

Katharina smiled. "Yes. Very happy. Papa and mama were very loving, and Johann and I were very close. Yes, I was very happy. Happy until mama died."

Katharina lowered her head and closed her eyes. Nearly choking as she softly spoke, she said, "The one time I needed momma the most, she could not be there for me."

Robert sat silently beside her and after a sigh she continued. "But papa and Johann were always there for me. And mama loved our Lord, and we shall sing together someday our favorites hymns of praise to our precious Lord and Savior. I find comfort in knowing this."

Robert nodded. "Where would we all be without the peace our Lord sends? His grace and mercy sustain us through the darkest hour. And you are blessed with a patient, loving father."

Robert cocked his head and wrinkled his brow as he continued, "It would seem you never married. You come from a wealthy house; your father loves you; how is it a beautiful young woman is not mistress over a great house of her own?"

Katharina blushed. "Please don't call me beautiful, you hardly know me. Are all Englishmen so forward? I do not trust men who only see a woman's beauty."

Robert smiled and shook his head. "I meant no offense, and surely you will always be safe in my presence. Forgive me for appearing forward, but it is my habit to speak my mind. I always believed openness and honesty could build trust."

Katharina still annoyed, answered, "You are very free with your opinions, Robert."

Katharina sighed, then nodded and smiled. "I believe I can trust you as an honorable gentleman. But you are right in assuming my father wishes I marry. He has promised a great dowry, and several suitors have come I am sure at his urging. They were good men, men of wealth and taste. But. But I, I just couldn't..."

Robert studied Katharina, her eyes now looking down, searching. "You were seeking more than a comfortable marriage. What is it you seek, Katharina?"

Katharina looked up. "I want what my brother Johann has. His calling is clear. He has dedicated his life to serving God and God's flock. Wait until you meet him, Robert, you will understand. Such a great heart for people! All people, he would not turn away anyone, Catholic or Protestant, rich or poor, faithful or doubting. I want to know my calling. I want to give my life in service. Did not our Lord say the body is more than raiment? I want to be more than a well-dressed, handsome wife."

"And you see your brother's heart in Father Wilhelm as well."

Katharina smiled and nodded. "Yes, I never thought of it like that. But yes, Wilhelm is much like Johann. Do you think a Jesuit priest and a Calvinist pastor could be friends?"

Robert smiled. "Yes, better than friends, like brothers. Your father knows this as well. He is a wise man who can look through the outward appearance and see a man, or a daughter, for who they really are."

Katharina nodded her head and smiled, her blues eyes sparkling with new insight. "Our God has sent you to us Robert. I have seen your passion. Yes, you were sent to Wilhelm and me. You were sent to bring Wilhelm and Johann together. You were sent to help my father. He will know how you can help."

Now Robert blushed. "It is hard for me to believe our God trusts me in any calling. But you, Katharina, have God's touch of healing. My head no longer spins!"

The noise of bells broke Their conversation. Clanging bells, not ringing sweetly, clanging without rhythm or pattern. Then came the raps on the door, two quick knocks then one, and again two quick knocks followed by one.

Katharina unbolted the door and swung it open. Karl stood soberly outside. "We have captured the trespassers. Not one has escaped! Wilhelm alone leads them to our door."

Katharina looked with surprise at her father who was unable to hide his smile any longer. Running to the side of the hut she could see Wilhelm leading four goats towards the hut.

Karl called out, "We have found a flock for the new shepherd of Eberbach. Keep them together Father Wilhelm; we must keep them together!"

Katharina's look of surprise turned to amusement.

Then with a laugh, she said, "Robert you must lend Wilhelm your crutch. Every shepherd needs a crook!"

Wilhelm turned the corner waving his outstretched arms beside him in a hapless attempt to keep the goats together. The clanging bells grew louder, clearly heard over the bleating of the goats. One goat could be seen pushing his horns against Wilhelm's backside, and another had chewed through his cloak and was nibbling on his belt. The other two kept their noses at his fingertips, sniffing and licking. Wilhelm smiled. "You think this is easy? These goats have a mind of their own. Ouch! Careful! Ouch! But I think they are glad to be found. Don't! No! Ouch! Bring them water and perhaps any scraps of bread. Quickly, they're hungry; they keep biting!"

Karl laughing before turning serious said, "Yes, food is the best way to keep them together. We must get them safely back to their owner. In such hard times, they are precious and will be missed. Surely, someone is looking for them as we speak."

Robert was standing up, watching and laughing. "Father Wilhelm, are these your new bell ringers for the church?"

"Don't help, any of you just keep laughing. Ouch!"

Karl's face turned serious. He looked at Robert and said, "Do you think you will be able to travel soon?"

Robert nodded. "The spinning has stopped. Yes, I will be able to travel. But a man on crutches? I don't want to slow you down."

Karl reached out and clutched Robert's shoulder,

"Our fates are now joined together. You will not slow us down."

Turning to Katharina, he said, "A loaf of bread. After the goats have water, Wilhelm and I shall lead them out with bread. Wilhelm, you will go no farther than the entrance. After you return them, I will make the necessary arrangements for us to leave. Robert has solved our problem."

Katharina gave Karl a loaf of bread. Karl hugged her tightly and turned to leave. At the door, he told Robert, "Walk. Stay after it, man!"

As he left the hut he said, "Remember to reset the trip line. Stay vigilant."

As he walked, he said to Wilhelm, "Pray for us Father. The prayers of a righteous man can accomplish much!"

CHAPTER 5
ON THE RUN

Robert steadily regained his strength. Wilhelm and Katharina walked with him every hour on the uneven ground through the forest. He became stronger and better balanced going up and down the hillside, though he was careful not to approach the battlefield. The moans of the dying punctuated by the screams Robert heard as the wounded were murdered still haunted him. He was not ready to face his fallen comrades. He did not even ask if they were buried; the memories needed to be blocked. The only prescription for his pain was work, the work to recover.

On one walk farther down the hill, he came within view of the battlefield. Robert stopped and gazed. He stood motionless, frozen in his thoughts. Wilhelm came and stood beside him, his eyes straight ahead, reading

Robert's thoughts, he said, "They were buried. A Christian burial. Their pain is over, but you Robert, you must put this behind you. You can learn from it. What did your training as a priest teach you?"

Robert stood silent, his eyes still staring straight ahead. Wilhelm's words drowned out by the moans and screams echoing in his mind.

Wilhelm turned slowly towards Robert. "What is the duty of a priest?"

Robert pushed back against the painful memories and silently turned to Wilhelm.

Wilhelm continued. "Did not God call you into his priesthood? Does not His calling demand that you give up yourself for those you are called to serve?"

Robert silently stared back at Wilhelm.

"A priest intercedes for his people. A priest is first a shepherd; his first calling is to love and serve. You have shown a passion for knowing God. Knowing God draws you to love God, which means obeying God and loving your neighbor as yourself. Robert. Listen to me, despite your failure to find your path in the church at Cambridge, in your heart, you are still a priest who loves God and his neighbor."

Robert continued to stare straight ahead, but a tear slowly welled up at the corner of his eye. "Will you come with me and pray for my comrades and for those who loved them but will never see their homecoming."

Wilhelm nodded. "Yes brother, I am with you."

The two priests walked down to a battlefield become a cemetery. The green grass once a pleasant pasture, was broken by mounds of fresh soil. Scraps of torn clothing, the hilt of a broken sword and the waste of battle lay scattered across the field. Robert and Wilhelm walked to the center, kneeled and prayed for the dead and the living.

As they made their way back to the hillside, Robert heard the songs of birds and the chirping of crickets. The leaves of the trees added a soft and gentle rustling sound. Life had returned to the field.

That night as Robert sat at the simple table in a small hut hidden beneath a rock, he felt a new and comforting peace in his soul. He felt at home. He looked across the table at two people who saved his life. They had become his family. Three unlikely people, each loving God in a different faith tradition, but now joined in a communion of trusting love.

Robert looked at Wilhelm warmly and said, "Katharina tells me you are a Jesuit, an order dedicated to the defense of the pope. Tell me, Wilhelm, how did you become a priest, and why did you come here?"

Wilhelm replied, "I told you, I came to serve Catholics in the Palatinate…"

Robert interrupted. "Wilhelm, I have told you who I am, where I came from and my struggles. Katharina's story has been told. The question is, Wilhelm, who are you?"

Wilhelm smiled warmly. "Yes, I understand. Now we can be honest."

Wilhelm glanced at Katharina and then at his plate before looking up. "I am from Vienna. Like you, my friend, my uncle carries the family title. My grandfather was given a small estate and received the title, Baron of Hietzing in reward for his service defending Vienna against the Ottoman Turks. My father was the Bishop of Schwechat. When he was tired of my mother, brother and sisters and me, he, with my uncle the Baron, established an abbey and installed himself as Abbott *vere nullius diocese.* My older brother joined the monastery, and my sisters and mother went to a convent."

"A hard thing Wilhelm, where is the love of a father in such doings?"

"Indeed, there was no love only greed and lust. As the family supports the monastery, my brother will surely succeed my father as Abbot. It is just one more family estate. Is that a scandal? To me it is. The estate and monastery in Hietzing border the Archduke's hunting manor, Kattenberg, where my father serves the Archduke and curries his favor. Like you, my choice was the church or the army, but my father insisted I attend the University of Vienna. It is a papal institution, and the installed order of the faculty is Jesuit. So here I am a Jesuit priest."

"And the church and your flock are the better for it, my brother!"

Robert paused, then asked, "But why did you come to the Palatinate? Why march with Count Tilly's army?"

"I wanted to leave Vienna. I wanted to leave the hypocrisy of Vienna; the hypocrisy of my father, of the court, and yes, the University church. I wanted to see the Palatinate. My grandfather came from a small village near Worms, called Bensheim. It was an ancient place with an old castle. He was a soldier, a *landsknecht*. You English would call him a pikeman, but in Germany, the Landsknecht was an integrated company of highly trained pikemen with their Arquebusiers holding their flanks. They were skilled in repelling siege tunnellers. That is how grandfather was sent to Vienna."

Robert nodded. "Someone should tend the flock. I am glad it is you. It seems the counter-reformation, the Council of Trent, was slow to come to Vienna."

Wilhelm laughed. "Poor Erasmus, how he prayed and struggled to reform the church from within. The teachings of the Council were like ribbons on a pig, an appeasement which only forced the church to revise its fundraising away from indulgences."

Robert laughed. "Now you sound like me! Careful, they may draft you into the army next!"

Turning serious, Robert asked, "How did they approach the cause of the reformation at the University of Vienna?"

"They didn't. We're Jesuits; we defend the pope. They taught only what the pope wanted us to know and we were expected to obey. No, we did not ask such questions!"

Wilhelm stared beyond Robert. "The Roman Church is nearly sixteen hundred years old. It has weathered persecution and outlived empires. Yes, there have been failings. We are sinners, and we fail. But within it are those who seek to serve God. Robert, I love the Church! Yes, I am troubled when I see hypocrisy and greed. Reform has begun. No, Robert, I cannot give up on the

Roman Catholic faith. Where would works of mercy be without the church?"

Robert quickly replied, "The Roman church does its duty in works of mercy, but as you have said, 'Any Christian would do the same.' You would not deny the acts of mercy of Katharina?"

Surprised, Wilhelm turned towards Katharina and nearly shouted, "Of course not! Such a heart! She loves God and loves people!"

And in a much calmer voice, he continued. "And I begin to see the struggle of those who love Christ and His Church and are torn between following the light of His Spirit in a new way or remain a voice and a conscience from within the ancient church."

Robert nodded. "It is beyond a struggle. It tears at your heart."

After sighing, Robert smiled. "Either way, never give up on faith."

Katharina interrupted. "Both of you stop this conversation! Have you forgotten there are three of us at this table?"

Robert laughed. "My apologies Katharina. We should not bore you. I will make it up to you. I will clean up and wash the dishes! It will be my exercise."

Two days later, Karl returned. He was out of breath and without so much as a greeting said, "We have been found out! We must leave! Now! Everything is arranged. There can be no delay. Quickly, leave everything."

He turned to Robert. "Robert, can you walk? Well,

you must. Here. I will help you up. Take your crutch."

While Karl helped Robert to his feet, he turned to Wilhelm. "Give Robert his sword. You take the pistol and powder horn. And cloaks. Everyone will need a cloak."

Seeing Katharina staring, Karl stepped over and hugged her. "It will be all right, Katie. God will protect us. No need for food. We must leave at once."

In moments they were out the door. Karl grabbed a pine bough and handed it to Wilhelm. "Sweep away our tracks as we go. Just until I say it is safe."

Karl led the way down the path into the cave. Robert easily kept pace swinging his injured leg along with the help of the crutch. As the light dimmed, Robert could see the cave walls divide into two tunnels. To the left was a still pool, no telling how deep it was, the surface of the water and the silence of the cave were broken by the dripping of calcium-rich water falling from the growing stalactites. Beyond the pool was only silent, empty blackness. To the right, a tall, narrow tunnel made its way through creviced rock with a faint light beckoning ahead. The tunnel path wandered left and right, but the light was still there, growing brighter.

Robert noticed a small string running through steel rings on the end of spikes driven into cracks in the stone wall. As they came to the last turn in the tunnel path, Karl said, "Careful. Do not trip the snare line. Let any pursuer believe they provided the warning when they find the hut vacant."

Karl went first, cautiously scanning the area from behind a bush at the opening of the cave. He waved his arm and said, "Quickly, come. Make your way down the hillside to the river. Wilhelm, make sure you leave no footprints in the cave or on the path. Once we are in the brush, you can stop."

Robert carefully maneuvered his way over the trip line and went out into the daylight. The bush covered the entrance to the cave, but there was a small path going up the hill. He could see a wide carriage road at the crest. Robert gingerly negotiated his way through the forest and down the hill. He could hear the running water of a river, and he looked to see the Neckar river below. After a few steps with his eyes off the ground, his crutch slid out from beneath him, he fell onto his backside and slid several yards down the leafy slope.

Immediately, Karl was beside him. "Don't move! Quiet. Someone is on the road."

Robert slowly shifted onto his stomach and looked up. He could see Katharina behind a clump of trees. Wilhelm was not to be seen.

"Do you think they heard me," Robert whispered.

"Shhh!"

Then he heard a shout. "Here it is! The entrance to a cave just as he said. It cannot be far now."

Another voice replied, "Good. The soldiers will go first. I want them alive. They are to be taken prisoners, not killed. Understood?"

"Yes sir, taken alive. This way men."

Footsteps could be heard, then silence. Leaves began to rustle. Someone was moving down the hillside. Wilhelm appeared. He motioned for Karl, Katharina, and Robert to move down. Karl recovered Robert's crutch, and without a word, the party continued down to the riverbank.

The Neckar cut through the dense woods of Oden Wald or Oden Forest on its way to the Rhine. With the river running high and fast, there would be no fording or swimming across it. Karl led the group a few hundred yards upstream where a small tributary joined the river. In the tributary, out of sight of the main channel, tied to a tree, was a Rhine river boat. Four men were waiting on the boat and immediately helped Katharina, Karl, Wilhelm, and Robert on board.

As quickly as they were aboard, they set off pulling on oars until they reached the main channel and pointed the bow downriver. The riverbank was heavily forested with trees arching over both banks. An older man, who appeared to be the captain, unfurled a sail and they boated their oars.

Wilhelm spoke first. "It was the magistrate, his clerk, and Maximilian von Greiffenclau. I'm sure it was the clerk who led me to your house, Karl! We were betrayed! I counted six soldiers with them. They knew where they were going. They knew where to find the entrance to the cave!"

Karl replied, "Joseph Meyer, the magistrate's clerk? He was one?"

"Yes, the magistrate's clerk. He led them to the cave entrance."

Robert asked, "Karl when you arrived and told us to leave you said you feared we were found out. Why? Why did you say that? What do you know?"

"I had just returned from arranging for the boat when Joseph, Joseph Meyer, came and warned me. He said I should leave at once and that Katharina and Wilhelm's hiding place was no longer safe. I left within moments of him leaving me."

Robert looked intently at Karl. "Does Joseph know about the boat? Does he know how we travel?"

Karl turned his head then looked up. "No. I would have told him, but he spoke first. He left as soon as he warned me. I think they will still concentrate on the roads and the forest. I think they will go down from the hut into the valley and follow the trail the English army followed to Heidelberg. They know no river traffic is passing Heidelberg. The English have garrisoned the city, and its cannon from the castle make such a passage suicide. That is why the English have also garrisoned Manheim where the Neckar joins the Rhine and Frankenthal, farther down the Rhine."

Karl exhaled slowly and stood up. After looking at the progress down the river, he sat down and continued. Count Tilly will pursue and lay siege first to Heidelberg and then Manheim. We should be safe. We will spend the daylight hours in a small creek well hidden from the river on the other side from where we left. And you, Robert, you will prepare to persuade the English at Heidelberg to let us pass."

Robert's eyes widened. Of course, it was the only way. With Count Tilly controlling the countryside, the only way to Mainz was by water, through the English blockade of the river. But Count Tilly would suspect any boat venturing into the English controlled cities would be allies supporting and supplying the English. They must consider running past Tilly's army and then chancing English cannons.

Robert looked at the riverboat. It was unlike the carracks he saw in Berwick-Upon-Tweed, heavy seagoing ships designed to carry large cargo but known to be difficult to navigate. This was more of a modified Portuguese caravel, a swift, responsive, easy to navigate, shallow draft boat with limited cargo capacity. Yes, he thought, remove the sterncastle, and use only one lateen sail. Build it with a full, pear-shaped bow for increased cargo capacity and then rig it like the beamy Dutch fluyt with its sophisticated blocks and tackle to make sail handling easier. Finally, reduce the crew size for efficiency. The result is a shallow draft, and nimble boat with good cargo capacity easily handled with a small crew, a perfect ship for the Rhine and its tributaries.

The boat, about forty feet long had a large hold for cargo with narrow low decks on each side of the hold with rowing stations. Perhaps the cargo could protect against Count Tilly's arquebusiers? Yes, they must make a space in the cargo for Katharina and Wilhelm. And protection for the helmsman, the captain. He would need visibility and protection. Robert wondered, *even if we pass through Tilly's forces, how can I signal the castle before drawing their cannon fire?*

Robert was deep in thought when the boat quietly slipped into a small tributary, rounded a bend and anchored in a small bay. Karl returned from his station next to the Captain and announced, "We will wait here until dark. The captain knows the river well and wants to arrive at Heidelberg at first light."

Robert spoke. "I've been thinking. Count Tilly will likely have sentries along the river just out of range of the Heidelberg canons. We must expect fire from his Arquebusiers."

Karl answered, "Yes, that is why the hold is full. The cargo is grain, oil, and wine. You have heard an army travels on its stomach, well it is also true a garrison survives a siege with food! And we shall survive any arquebus balls by food as well—the sacks of grain line the hull with the oil and wine inside. The crew will make space for us in the center and line the stern house with the removed cargo to protect the captain. The captain and I are confident we can get past Tilly's sentries, and the supplies we bring should be most welcome. But you Robert, how are you going to signal the English? You must get us past their cannons."

"Red and white cloth. There must be some on board. I will make an English flag and hang it from a pole with a lantern. We will light the lantern and raise the flag when we sight the castle."

As Robert was speaking, the Captain walked over and joined them. "We will sew the English red cross of Saint George onto the sail. At first sight of Heidelberg, I will hoist a lantern to the top of the mast. But, you Robert, must speak for us."

CHAPTER 6
UNDER THE GUNS OF HEIDELBERG CASTLE

Robert rehearsed in his mind the best hail to the Heidelberg sentries. He knew a password would be expected and that he had no way of knowing what it could be. He would have at best one or two sentences to convince the sentry not to order the cannons to fire. The time to speak those short sentences would be used by the cannoneers to take aim at the vulnerable boat. The boat captain could use the time to bring them close to the castle wall beneath the line of fire of the cannons, but that would be provocative and only result in well-armed men being sent to the riverfront. No, he thought, *I must get this right*.

Robert's thoughts were interrupted as a crewman

quietly approached and gave a universal signal for silence. He approached each person on board, and if they hadn't acknowledged him, he gave them a soft nudge until they saw his finger across his lips. Robert looked up to see the captain and Karl crouched low on the bow of the boat staring over the bulwark.

In the intensified silence, Robert could hear the light splashes of oars in the water in cadence with the creaking of iron pins in the oarlocks. As the ordinarily soothing sound of a boat being rowed nearby crescendoed, and muffled voices could be heard on the river, adrenaline pumped through the hearts of everyone onboard. Gradually, as the sounds faded, tense muscles relaxed and in minutes that felt like hours, exhausted muffled sighs told them then danger had passed.

As most onboard drank in breaths of relief, the captain signaled to a crewman to slip overboard and go ashore for a closer look at the just passed boat. Karl watched as the man silently waded his way to shore in the shallow water of the secluded bay and was quickly out of sight.

Only then did Karl come and sit beside Robert. "There is no way of telling for certain who it was. Perhaps only locals making their way a short distance down river. Possibly, but not likely, English scouting Count Tilly's positions. Most likely Count Tilly's men patrolling the river above Heidelberg, or they could be looking for us."

"What do we do now?" Robert asked.

Karl smiled. "We rest. You prepare. We leave after dark."

Fifteen minutes later the crewman slipped back on board as silently as a smuggler. Robert did not need to hear the conversation; he could see the man shrug his shoulders while reporting to the captain. The man then returned ashore.

The captain provided bread, cheese, and wine in the early afternoon. After eating, Karl and Katharina settled back and tried to nap, and Robert could be seen talking to himself. Seeing the captain instruct a crewman to go ashore and relieve the lookout on the riverbank, Wilhelm, too nervous to rest, asked to go along. The captain looked at Wilhelm skeptically, but seeing Karl nod, he agreed, but winced, regretting his decision, when Wilhelm clumsily splashed ashore following the crewman. Wilhelm only slipped and fell once before he disappeared from sight.

Karl read the concern in the Captain's face and said, "He's a good man. God will protect him."

The captain muttered, "It's the rest of us I worry about."

About an hour before sunset, the lookout hastily returned aboard. "Quiet! The rowboat returns with four soldiers rowing and with one passenger, a man in black. Wilhelm stayed behind for a better look. He says the rider appears to wear an Abbot's cassock."

The wind picked up, and the leaves on the trees shivered, but soon the sounds of the oars splashing sloppily in the water and the groaning oar locks could be heard again. There was no talking, but grunts were heard as the oarsman struggled to row the boat slowly upstream. It seemed hours before the boat was outside of earshot but really, little more than ten minutes. Only after the passing of the rowboat was a painful memory did Wilhelm finally return to the boat, much more quietly than he left.

Karl and a crewman helped him aboard and began to speak softly between gasps for breath. "It was him. Don Pedro, the Abbott who accompanied us to Eberbach. It was him. I am certain of it!"

"The Abbott? Karl replied, "The one who traveled with Count Tilly to assign priests and magistrates?'

"Yes, the Abbot Don Pedro. I am certain."

Karl's thoughts spilled out. "Why would he be on the River? Where could he be coming from? Not Heidelberg. Perhaps Count Tilly is camped near the river. Is he preparing his assault? Has the Spanish army arrived? There must be some way to..."

The captain interrupted. "It would be a fool's errand to venture down river in less than total darkness. If Count Tilly is camped, we should clearly see his fires. Our best option is to drop the mast and drift by his camp on the far side of the river and under the forest canopy and hope he has not posted sentries across the river."

"How long will it take to raise the mast after we pass Tilly's camp?" Karl asked.

Now the Captain smiled. "With these new Dutch blocks and tackle, only minutes."

Darkness came early in the thick forest of Oden Wald. Sacks of grain and barrels were stowed around the inside of the stern house protecting the helmsman. The freshly greased oar locks and pins were found to be blessedly silent. Katharina and a crewman had sewn the large red cross of Saint George on the white sail. The mast remained on the deck, its base hinged to the mast table with hauling lines and stays at the ready and a lantern was attached to a halyard close at hand. The passengers went to the center hold where just enough cargo had been removed to accommodate them. A tarp was rolled up and ready to be unrolled over the hold if the boat encountered any river traffic.

Just as dusk was fading to darkness, the captain gave a voiceless command to the crew, and after a few short strokes of the oars, the boat had rounded the bend and entered the slow-moving Neckar River. The moon was little more than a crescent coming and going between the dark clouds of night and bright stars appearing in a flash would then dim and disappear again. No breeze stirred in the night, and the only sounds were the crickets, frogs and an occasional owl who let the boat pass unannounced.

Permitting just a few strokes at a time, the captain listened intently as they drifted downstream in silence. Robert laid down and watched as the clouds and the on again off again moon slowly slid by. The easy motion of the boat, the cadence of the rowing and the soft sound of the helm and the rudder in its pintles sang a lullaby of peace. Robert drifted off to sleep only to be nudged awake by Karl when he began to snore.

Robert's weary eyes opened wide when he heard voices. The many voices grew louder, disconnected from a single conversation. Some laughed, some sang, some argued, but all carried distinctly across the water. As the boat slowly drifted around a bend, campfires appeared along the opposite shore. A crewman came silently along the deck and pushed Robert's head down. Slowly the tarp was unrolled over the cargo hold. It was clear the captain wanted no unplanned sound or sighting of his passengers.

Sitting in the hold, Katharina buried her head in Wilhelm's shoulder and clutched his hand. Wilhelm softly rubbed her shoulder in reassurance while Karl, seated opposite silently watched. Just then, something slapped the bow of the boat. The boat slowed until a distinct twang resounded as something hit against the mast. Soon the oars were out, and the crew began gently backwatering. Footsteps on the deck alerted the passengers. The boat was still, but wordless crewmen glided silently on deck as a cat focused on its prey. Something was rolling now. Slowly, but the sound of wood on wood was clear to the passengers. Again silence. And then a soft splash of something tossed in the water. Again, there was silence and then the oars, the helm and the sound of the boat making its way down the river.

The passengers were settled in their cocoon in the cargo hold when they heard muffled voices and splashes on the river. The tarp rolled back, and the captain peered down from the deck. "You must remain quiet and do not come up from the hold. We have caught a snare line stretched across the river. We have tangled a barrel in the line and set it back in the current. We should know soon if the sentries believe our ruse or continue down river.

We are approaching a bend; once we round it, we will raise the sail. A favorable night breeze has come up, and with the sail and oars together, we shall proceed as fast as possible. I cannot rule out more sentries down river waiting for us. The evening air is fresh; if you assure me of silence, I will keep the tarp off."

The captain returned to the helm and his crew set about raising the mast and securing the stays. A few minutes later the lateen sail was raised and soon filled. The crew took their station at the oars and began to row. With each stroke, the sound of the water sliding by the hull grew louder, and the nimble boat quickly gained speed. With the mast and sail rigged, the captain steered a course down the main channel avoiding the overhanging branches of the trees near the banks. The muffled voices upriver slowly faded into silence. The reassuring sound of the boat slicing through the current was again interrupted. A bright muzzle flash immediately followed by the unmistakable thunder of an arquebus confirmed the boat was spotted. A quick glance reassured them that no one was hit. Less than a minute later another volley came from the bank the boat had been hugging, opposite the camp of Count Tilly.

The captain did not need to remind his passengers to stay below behind the shelter of the cargo as a lantern clearly could be seen, its light bouncing as the sentry ran along the bank. And then a volley from three or four arquebuses fired, the lantern fell to the ground and extinguished.

The captain shouted, "Quickly, hoist the lantern to the

top of the mast! We are in range of the cannons of Heidelberg! Robert come up here immediately!"

As Robert made his way up from the hold, the captain gave the order, "Hold water! We approach the boom tower and cannot proceed until the chain across the river is lowered."

The men stopped rowing. Slowly the dark shadow of Heidelberg with its walls to the river and castle looming on the hill above, took shape. The captain skillfully let the sail luff but kept the red cross of Saint George visible against the white sailcloth and said, "Now Robert."

Robert, surprised by how his leg stiffened while sitting in the hold, carefully hobbled onto the deck and propping the crutch under his shoulder called out, "Captain of the watch, I am Robert Curtis, Lieutenant of Cuirassiers, English Volunteers. I was wounded and left for dead not a fortnight ago. I have come with friends and food for the garrison and information for Colonel Vere. Send a lantern to where you wish us to come ashore and you may inspect us."

Robert waited for a response. No lights shone from the city wall, but Robert could hear the creaking noise of cannons being swung and elevated.

"Woe be it to the man that sends needed rations to the bottom of the river! We await your instructions before the current takes us afar."

Finally, a voice came loud from the tower casement. "And tell me, Lieutenant of Cuirassiers, Robert Curtis, know ye the man James Curtis?"

Robert replied, "Aye, he is my uncle Viscount Curtis,

Baron of Tweedbridge."

"The scoundrel of Berwick is the better title. Chasin' favor and riches off the backs of honest, hardworking men. Paid handsomely he was, collecting the Ship Tax. Put his own brother in bankruptcy and the Robert Curtis I know has been feeding at his uncle's trough his whole life. And here you are back from the dead. Easy enough score for me to right this very night."

"It is to Edward Barkley I speak then? Yes, Barkley, it is me. But you, man, know the value of a boat full of grain, oil, and wine. And there are others aboard as well. The Barkley's I knew in Berwick-Upon-Tweed would not harm a lady."

"A lady you say?" Barkley replied with surprise in his voice.

"Lieutenant of Cuirassiers you may bring your boat alongside the wharf for inspection."

The sound of a chain noisily moving through a mechanism and then a heavy door swinging open could be heard, and soon a lantern appeared on the landing. The sail was dropped, and the boat was rowed alongside. More lanterns appeared, and a company of armed men waited as the boat tied up.

Edward Barkley ordered, "Everyone out of the boat, step ashore one at a time, hands where I can see them. You will hand over your weapons when asked by one of my men. Is that understood?"

Robert asked Karl, "Does the crew understand English?"

Karl repeated the command in German as Robert

stepped out of the boat. Barkley, holding a drawn pistol said to Robert, "Your weapons sir. And stand here beside me."

Robert looked at Barkley angrily but carefully handed him his sword. "And your pistol," Barkley demanded.

"It was taken while I laid on the battlefield."

"A Lieutenant of Cuirassiers without a pistol? A right shabby officer you make, sir."

Waving his pistol towards the boat, Barkley shouted sharply, "Come on there, look lively."

Soon Karl was ashore. He was followed by Wilhelm who stopped to at the gunwale with his hand out to help Katharina step ashore. Murmuring could be heard from the guards as she stepped into the light of the lanterns.

"So, there was a woman aboard. Ain't it just like a bought commissioned officer, loses his weapon but finds a woman!"

As Karl, the captain and the crew quickly debarked, Robert said to Barkley, "Sergeant Barkley, you will escort us to Colonel Vere at once. You will set a guard detail on this boat. Nothing aboard is to be touched. Do you understand?"

Barkley held the lantern and looked closely at Robert. "Lieutenant Curtis is listed as dead or deserted. You don't look dead, sir, but if you are a deserter, you soon shall be. Colonel Vere is not here; he is in Mannheim. Our own Colonel Herbert commands this garrison. You indeed shall see him!"

Just then a guard shouted, "Sergeant, the boat carries only sacks of grain and casks of oil and wine."

Barkley replied, "Very fine then, no one goes aboard until orders from the Colonel. Jones and Smith stay and guard it. The rest of you will escort our German friends."

Inside the city walls, Barkley led the group past the stone stairway towards the iron gates of a prison. Robert commanded, "You are to take my friends and me to Colonel Herbert immediately. That is an order! The crew of the boat will be shown proper hospitality. Do you understand! I assure you there will be hell to pay if you mistreat any of our German allies!"

As Robert's voice echoed against the dark stone walls, confusion flashed across the face of the guard detail. Finally, Barkley spoke. "I must have missed the stairway up in this darkness. Another lantern to show the way, you heard me, look lively then."

CHAPTER 7
BACK FROM THE DEAD

The fugitives climbed the hard, stone stairs, slippery with the dew and humid cold air. Robert took each step one foot at a time careful that the crutch did not slip out from under him. They passed through another high iron strapped gate of heavy oak and entered the city of Heidelberg. As dawn brought the first light to the city, several of the houses shown with lantern light from their windows along the street. Merchants were setting up their stalls for the day as they passed the central market. They kept walking steadily uphill until they reached another wall and another gate. The castle looming above them turned from brown to gold as the morning sun highlighted the eastern towers. Barkley exchanged passwords with the posted sentry, the small door in the large gate creaked open, and they passed through. Ahead of them lay a winding road up the hill to the massive castle above the city. Heidelberg castle was the home of the Elector Count Palatinate and one of the strongest fortresses in the Holy Roman Empire.

Karl looked up the steep hill and long path and then looked to Robert. Robert nodded. "What are we waiting for; keep moving!"

At the base of the castle, another sentry challenged the group for a password before the man-door in the massive castle gate opened. The weary boat crew and their passengers walked through the once formidable castle gate death chamber with its archer portals and hot oil cauldrons, now made obsolete by cannon fire. Continuing through, they safely arrived in the castle keep. Inside the keep, sergeant Barkley asked Robert to wait while he went to speak with the captain of the guard. The captain of the guard, Robert's captain, and fellow cuirassier returned with Barkley. "Robert it is you! We thought you dead. The colonel is an early riser; I will take you to him at once."

"Thank you, Captain Richard. Please see that the boat captain and his crew are provided good food and quarters. These, my rescuers and friends, must come with me to see Sir Gerard. And see to it that the provisions our German allies provide are quickly unloaded and securely stowed. No telling what smugglers and thieves might venture down to the wharf," Robert said with a knowing stare at Barkley.

Captain Richard nodded. "Right away. Does your

party need refreshment before I take you into Sir
Gerard?"

Robert did not ask his friends; he quickly replied,
"Our visit is most urgent. We must see him now."

Richard nodded. "This way, his quarters are in the
bergfried, the central tower." Looking at Robert's crutch,
he said, "I'm afraid you have more stairs to climb."

Captain Charles Richard led Robert and his friends up
the ancient stone steps of the keep, Robert's crutch
pinging as he planted it on each one. The Captain
exchanged passwords with sentries at each level. At the
top, the sentry rapped lightly on the door before
entering and announcing Lieutenant of Cuirassiers,
Robert Curtis, and allies.

Robert, Karl, Wilhelm, and Katharina entered the
room to find Colonel Sir Gerard Herbert standing before
a large window gazing out upon the city and river below.
The Colonel turned, smiled stepped over and grasped
Robert's arm. "Curtis! Thought you dead. But here you
are! Splendid! Splendid indeed! Just a scratch to your
head and the leg wound, eh, should heal. Very good
indeed! And these with you?"

"Sir Gerard, these are my rescuers: Father Wilhelm
Hahn, Fraulein Katharina Schroeder and her father, Herr
Karl Schroeder."

Karl whispered to Wilhelm and Katharina as he
translated.

"Sit, please," said Colonel Gerard motioning towards
the chairs around his table. "Now, Curtis, tell me how
you came here. Your own sergeant Barkley reported you

presumed dead. Said he was standing near behind you when you fell. When the truce flag came to collect the wounded and bury the dead, they found no officers."

"Yes sir, a ball came through my helmet. Took the flesh and some bone. Afraid I can't remember being shot." Robert paused and said, "Pardon, Sir Gerard, but who saw to our wounded and dead?"

"Why it fell to Sir Geoffrey, your cousin, why do you ask?"

"He found no survivors, I'll wager."

"He found some stragglers, wounded, but ambulatory."

"I awoke after the battlefield was abandoned and I crawled off sometime during the night. I would have perished for certain had not Father Wilhelm found me and brought me to his lodging. There Katharina most mercifully tended my wounds. I owe them my life. And that is why they accompany me."

Sir Gerard glanced at Wilhelm and Katharina while Robert continued.

"Katharina's brother, Johann, is pastor of the church in Eberbach. At least he was until he was taken at night by soldiers of Count Tilly on orders of the emperor's new magistrate. We believe he is imprisoned in Mainz. I have pledged my word as a Christian gentleman to aid in his release."

Colonel Herbert answered, "I don't see how I can help. The situation in Mainz changes by the day. The combined army, remnants of General von Mansfeld's and we English volunteers, is spread thin, garrisoning many towns to slow Count Tilly's work until reinforcements arrive. I pray they come soon for it is well heard that another Spanish army is marching north."

Karl spoke up. "If I may, colonel, that is where we can be of help to each other. I am a trader in tapestries, well known in the courts and castles of the Germans, in France and Netherlands, castles of Catholics and Protestants alike. I hear things; many things. Though the treaty of Ulm calls for the neutrality of the Protestant Union, there remain some who look for ways other than soldiers to support your cause. The boatload of grain, oil, and wine we bring with us is one such way. Information is another."

"A boat loaded with provisions! Most welcome! Sergeant Barkley has charge over the wharf. He will see to their safekeeping."

Robert replied, "Begging your pardon, Colonel, but you are aware of Barkley's history as a smuggler?"

Sir Gerard laughed. "Yes, I am aware. Sometimes a man of his talents is of use. Don't fear; he is watched."

Turning serious he said, "I am also aware there is history between you and sergeant Barkley. You seem to tolerate an extraordinary amount of insolence from him. Such behavior can be dangerous to morale."

Robert was about to answer when the colonel stopped him. "We'll speak of this later."

Then focusing on Karl, the colonel asked, "Why, Herr Schroeder, do you need my help?"

Karl smiled. "I seek a meeting with your Commander, Colonel Horace Vere. I seek safe passage for myself, my daughter and father Wilhelm. And I seek the assistance of Lieutenant Curtis for our mission."

"I shall certainly send you downriver to Mannheim and Colonel Vere. Tell me, Herr Schroeder, why do you bring this papist priest? Meaning no disrespect, father."

"Father Wilhelm is an honest man of God. He has put his life at risk in seeking the fate of my son, pastor Johann. He could quietly accept his new pastorate in my son's place, but he chose the truth and Christian mercy. He is a man proven trustworthy to me and one who will support me before the Archbishop of Mainz."

Looking to Robert, Sir Gerard said, "I shall need to prepare documents for you to carry to our commander, Colonel Sir Horace Vere. You have been stricken from the rolls as dead. I fear it was easier for our Lord to raise Lazarus from the dead than it is to bring back to life an English officer gone from the rolls! And travel documents and passwords going forward will be necessary. Give me this day to prepare documents. Go, get something to eat, get some rest, and return in the morning. Good to have you back with us, Curtis."

"Thank you, sir."

"Good day, fraulein, Herr Schroeder, and you as well father. Oh, and Curtis, bring Herr Schroeder and Captain Richard with you tomorrow morning."

"Yes, sir."

As Robert was leaving, he heard Colonel Herbert call out, "And your papist priest as well."

Robert, Karl, Wilhelm, and Katharina were met at the bottom of the staircase by sergeant Barkley. "Your boat captain and crew are having their breakfast with the men. Captain Richard waits for you and your friends at the officer's mess. I'll take you there."

As they walked, Barkley turned to Robert and said, "Same as always, no one tells the soldier anything. I hear say Count Tilly's army is preparing for a siege. You come down the river Mister Curtis, is that true?"

Robert looked at Barkley and said, "The garrison will be needing the provisions we brought. Aye, Tilly's camp is just out of cannon range. It's a hard place we are in, but reinforcements should come."

Barkley kicked the dirt and said, "I hope the promises of reinforcements are better than the promises of pay. Damned ship tax got us here, but it hasn't got us paid."

As they reached the officer's mess, father Wilhelm said, "I will pray for an end of this war and the safe return to your home."

"What did he say?" Barkley bellowed

Karl patiently translated Wilhelm's honest gesture into English.

Barkley looked at Wilhelm and said, "Tell the Father, I got a bargain with God. I don't bother him with my prayers, and He don't bother me with His priests and Church!"

As they entered the hall with its smells of breakfast, Wilhelm mumbled softly, "Not the most hospitable people, the English."

Robert heard Wilhelm and stopped and looked him in the eye. "Barkley is no lover of the church, any church. Is it hard to blame the people when the self-serving clergy has betrayed them?"

"No, I am very accustomed to the views of Sergeant Barkley. His views are common, though rarely so openly stated. It was the disparaging comment regarding the holy father. It seemed so common as if it were the acceptable converse of a gentleman."

"Ah! You speak of Sir Gerard's 'papist' comment. You must consider, Father Wilhelm, that your holy father has, by Papal Bull, been inspiring and supporting plotters to kill English kings and Queen for over a century. Should you expect an English gentleman to call such a regicidal autocrat 'the holy father?' As he said, he meant no disrespect to you, Wilhelm. He takes my word and the word of Karl, that you are an honest man of God. Here is a table, sit. I will see to our breakfast."

Katharina sat down next to Wilhelm. Karl remained standing. "Let me help you, Robert. A man on a crutch should not be carrying a tray of food."

As they walked off, Karl quietly asked Robert, "Do you think Wilhelm is having second thoughts?"

Robert answered, "Father Wilhelm is a good man. His will is always to do what is right. And what other choice has he? He is now a hunted man by officers of his own emperor. His eyes are just opening to the world outside Vienna."

Robert made his way back, escorted by Karl, who was bearing a large tray with a loaf of bread, cheese, apples, pork, porridge and ale. Wilhelm hardly waited for him to be seated before he asked, "By what right did your King Henry VIII appoint himself head of the Church of England?"

Robert smiled. "It is still the custom in England for gentlemen to seek the Lord's blessing on the meal before partaking, would you ask the blessing father Wilhelm?"

Wilhelm blushed. "Yes of course. Bless these gifts, O Lord...."

When he finished, Katharina spoke up. "I would like to pray for Johann. It has taken us so long to be on our way. We must pray he is safe, and we reach him soon."

Wilhelm nodded. "Of course, we must remember Johann. Please pray, Katharina."

Katharina poured her heart into prayer. When she finished, she kept her head down, and her eyes closed, as she breathed a stray shaft of sunlight caught her face causing the remnants of a tear which she had wiped away to glisten and sparkle as through a prism. Wilhelm clenched her hands and softly said, "I shall never quit on you or Johann, I shall never leave you to right this injustice alone."

Robert, in no mood for an argument said, "Wilhelm, please let us eat. We can continue this debate later."

As the others attention turned to the food before them, Wilhelm's urgency to debate slowly left him. When they had sated their appetites, Robert looked stood and said, "Come, we have quarters. We must rest. Katharina, you will have an inside room. Karl, Wilhelm and I shall be outside your door."

Robert got up and started to limp off. Karl called out, "Robert, your crutch!"

"I can limp just as well without it."

Karl replied, "Do not forget the stairs that await you tomorrow. I will bring it along if you change your mind."

Settling into the quiet rooms the fatigue soon became apparent. In short order, the only sounds were light snores. Just before Robert slid off to sleep, a light knock on the door stirred him. Opening the door, a soldier stood outside with a field trunk. "Beggin' your pardon, Lieutenant Curtis but Captain Richard had me fetch your chest from the baggage room. 'Gonna be sent home, it was, not sold off like your ordinary soldier's, but seein' as you live, well, sir, here it is."

"Right. Well, just set it down here. And thank the Captain for me."

"Yes, sir. Sorry to be disturbin' you, sir."

Robert was about to return to his cot when he stopped and returned to the chest. He opened it up and dug through the contents, sighing a simple 'good' when he found what he was looking for. He looked at it thoughtfully, then he closed the chest, laid down and went to sleep.

An hour later, Robert was awake again. He opened the trunk and took out breeches, gray stockings and a blue cassock and headed for the door. Karl sat up and said, "Can't sleep?"

"Thought maybe a good washing and clean clothes would make me feel better. I want a word with Captain Richard as well."

"Give me a moment; I would like to speak with the boat captain, no telling what's been done to him."

Karl reached for the crutch and saw Robert shake his

head no. In the courtyard, Robert found a line of wash barrels. He stripped to the waist poured water over himself lathered a brush with lye soap and scrubbed himself red. After another rinse, he dressed in his clean clothes. He dropped his dirty clothes in the soapy water, stirred them around, pulled them out and gave them a good wringing before hanging them to dry.

When he was finished Karl remarked, "These look no cleaner than the others. Now, take me to the boat crew. We must know if they are willing to proceed downriver with us."

Robert and Karl found the boat crew comfortably quartered in the barracks, all but the captain sound asleep. As Karl and the boat captain spoke in German, Robert said, "If you can find your way back, Karl, I'll go on to see Captain Richard."

Karl nodded, and Robert was out the door.

Captain Richard was the second son of a viscount. He was well mannered and intelligent. The two had become close friends in the short months they had spent together. Robert trusted him. As Robert entered his room, Captain Richard appeared genuinely pleased to see him. "Well, Curtis, you just rise up like Lazarus from the tomb, and now you are off again with Sir Gerard's blessing! Please sit; tell me everything."

"And you are the second to say so!" Robert replied.

After he recounted his experiences, he then asked, "Tell me, Charles, was Barkley's the only report on my wounding?"

Captain Richard nodded. "Others saw you on the

ground. To a man, they took you for dead. Only Barkley saw you fall. Claims he heard a shot saw you fall and then saw Tilly's troops a hundred yards ahead. It happened fast; both companies had just emerged from cover, each surprised to see the other. Several volleys exchanged before each side returned to cover."

"Barkley did not mention that I was shot from behind?"

"Good God man, no! Is that so? No. There was no enemy to the rear or to the flank for that matter. Shot from behind, you say!"

"I saw them ahead. Last thing I remember. The ball pierced my helmet, took my scalp and some bone. Leg wound came in the melee after the skirmish, stepped on, I was."

Captain Richard stood up, his eyes boring down through the table. "Shot from behind? It makes no sense. No sense at all. And no one saw anything! Robbie I…"

"There is more. When I awoke, I was not alone among the living lying on the field. By the grace of God, I was silent. The moving and the groaning were all spiked. Murdered, every one of them. I dare not move lest I be among the dead. I did not see him, but he bent down and took my pistol before moving on."

Captain Richard looked up from the table and stared at the wall. "There was a flag of truce to recover the dead and wounded, though I do not know if the foul deed was done before the truce or after. How can I help you, Curtis?"

"We are to travel down river to Mannheim under

orders of Sir Gerard. I ask that you keep your wits about you if there are any rumors now that I have returned."

"What are you going to tell Sir Gerard?"

"He has told me my cousin Sir Geoffrey oversaw the recovery of the wounded. I don't know what more I shall say."

"You and Barkley have a history. The colonel has heard how you tolerate his insubordination. He means to instruct you on the matter."

"The man has a hatred of my uncle. He directs that at me, though I have always found him a capable soldier. Never took his words too seriously."

"Your uncle?"

"My uncle was made viscount for his strenuous collection of the king's ship tax. Never did understand why a man who hates the ship tax like Barkley does would volunteer to soldier on the proceeds of the very tax. Parliament will never fund this army."

"Damn French and their 'Divine Right of Kings,' poisoning monarchies everywhere. Thought we settled this years ago with parliament. So then, Curtis, eight tomorrow."

"Yes sir, good day Captain."

Robert rose and turned to leave. "Oh Curtis, is that priest coming with us in the morning?"

"Yes, sir, why do you ask?"

"Priest or monk, some papist came by yesterday under a flag of truce. Had a message he wanted to be taken to Colonel Vere. He visited Sir Gerard and left. Too many papists about for my taste."

CHAPTER 8
A HIGHER AUTHORITY

Robert was determined to climb the tall staircase of the bergfried. His wounded leg complained the most when bending; bearing weight when straight was no longer a problem. As they slowly climbed, Wilhelm looked at Robert and said in a low voice, "You never answered my question, 'What right did your King Henry VIII have to declare himself head of the church in England?'"

Robert said, "I will answer you with a question. By what right did the Bishop of Rome declare himself superior to the bishops and metropolitans who remained from the original twelve apostolic churches? Do not the Apostles and the Nicene Creeds declare us one holy and apostolic church? Our Saint Peter never claimed authority as a pope, but then he was a humble servant of God. Must I teach you your own history? It was an arrogant Bishop of Rome, Damasus, who in the year 366 first put forth this foolish idea which was rejected by the church, it was never accepted! Only the demise of the councils and the fight against Islam reduced the opposition to the Metropolitan of the Orthodox Church. His opposition was easy for your arrogant bishop to overcome; he simply excommunicated him!"

Wilhelm fumed and replied, "Your Henry VIII was never a priest, never a bishop, how can such a man be head of the church?"

"The King sees his authority as the 'defender of the faith.' He did not establish the faith; he seeks only to defend and preserve. Our king sits as head of our church to preserve the ancient practice of our faith, to mediate differences in peace, to see that the reformation in England proceeds without violence and civil war. He is aided by our Archbishop of Canterbury who speaks for the clergy and the parliament who speaks for the people. Though I profess sympathy for those who argue the body of Christ, the church itself should determine its governance, choosing its leaders by the call of the congregation."

"Even more anarchy! You must know that your reformation in England became convenient for Henry in the divorce of his lawfully wed wife."

"Queen Catherine was well loved and well treated. Henry wanted an heir for the peaceful transition of the kingdom upon his passing. Such cases were not unusual among monarchs, but the pope refused to Henry what he granted to others—for political favoritism, not for pastoral truth. If Henry meant it for evil, God granted it for our good and Christ's church in England is all the better for it. Truly, many suffered pain and died the martyr's death, but from their blood, a more perfect church did grow! England had time to reform carefully, our doctrinal differences debated. We have sought to preserve the solid core of truth of our faith and be faithful to traditions beneficial to true worship while placing the full authority of doctrinal truth in the Holy Scriptures. Only doctrine founded upon Scripture can bind the Church. We rely upon the Holy Ghost and our God-given ability to reason to interpret Scripture and understand our Maker's revelation."

"You would have me believe that there exists no debate within the Roman Catholic Church. The councils, the colleges, the…"

"All can be denied by the fallible man you grant infallibility!"

"His authority comes from God!"

"His authority comes from an election from bought cardinals. God speaks through his Holy Word; it is the only reliable authority untainted by sinful men!"

Wilhelm began, "The council…" and then trailed off.

Robert laughed. "You were going to say the Council of Trent and the end of the abuses, but you have acknowledged the lack of any real change."

Robert's face turned serious, and he challenged Wilhelm in Latin. "One last question of authority, father.

By what authority does the pope deny holy communion, deny Christian burial, and deny eternal life with our Lord in heaven above to those who not only profess but live lives of faith in our Lord, who love Him and bare their souls to Him in prayer? I speak of people like Karl and Johann and Katharina. Any man who would presume such authority to deny them access to Christ has forfeited his calling as pastor to our Lord's sheep!"

Wilhelm climbed in silence.

Captain Richard turned around when he reached the Colonel's quarters. "If you two are quite through, the Colonel is waiting."

Captain Richard went in first and announced their presence.

Colonel Herbert commanded, "Have the priest wait outside, the others may attend."

As they entered the room, Colonel Herbert looked up from his desk. "Ah, Lieutenant Curtis, come in; everything is prepared. I have a letter for Sir Horace Vere, and safe conduct passes for the boat, boat crew, and your party. I have requested that you be returned to the active rolls in rank. Pity I can't keep you here, we will soon need every man to defend this garrison. But if not you, someone must carry dispatches to Mannheim. So be it."

"I will do my duty as you command."

Turning to Karl, Sir Gerard said, "I wrote to my Commander, Colonel Horace Vere of your offer. Tell me, Herr Schroeder, do you believe you can sail more boats past the Count of Tilly. Won't he be more careful next time?"

Karl smiled. "I believe so, and if not by boat, there will always be another way."

"You said some friends seek to help us, can we trust them? Are they resourceful?

Karl nodded. "Some are powerful, and some are resourceful, but all are trustworthy."

"What of this Spanish army we hear so much of, any sign of it?"

"It will not be permitted to march across France but will sail to Spanish Netherlands and march east. Like you, Sir Gerard, I have yet to hear of its presence. We have watchers in the Netherlands who will report its approach."

"Watchers in Spanish Netherlands? Good. Very Good. Herr Schroeder, I look forward to meeting you again. God speed on your journey; I pray for your son's release."

Sir Gerard then ordered, "Have the priest come in."

Once Wilhelm was in the room, the colonel said, "You're a wanted man, father. It's clear the emperor's people don't trust you, the question is, can we? I had a visitor the day before you arrived from Eberbach. A clerical visitor."

Wilhelm spoke up. "An Abbot by the name Don Pedro. We saw him returning up the Neckar before we came down. Yes, I know the man. He travels with the Count of Tilly and the army of Flanders. He and two others assign priests and magistrates in the recovered lands."

Sir Gerard studied Wilhelm closely and said, "He came under a flag of truce. He had a message for Colonel Vere. He says his letter is from the emperor and the pope. All

English soldiers are guaranteed safe passage and provisions on our way to the United Netherlands if we abandon the Palatinate. Further, if we deliver all magisterial and church records to the same Don Pedro, there will be no action or retaliation against the citizens or buildings in the garrisoned cities."

Captain Richard, Robert, and Karl said nothing. Sir Girard pointed to a satchel on the desk. "It's all in my report to Colonel Vere."

He turned back to Wilhelm and said, "As my visitor was leaving, he stopped and asked, 'You haven't taken in a runaway priest traveling with a young woman? If you find him, let us know. I will pay well for their return."

Karl spoke up. "He is one of the men we suspect is behind the unrecorded arrest of my son. Don Pedro is no man of God. He is not one to be trusted."

Sir Gerard saw the anger flash in Karl's eyes. "Herr Schroeder, Karl, may I call you Karl? I am not in the habit of chasing the enemies of my enemy."

Turning to Charles Richard he said, "Captain, see to it our friends are fully provisioned and safely escorted as far as cannon range."

"Yes, Colonel, all is prepared."

"God speed. And Curtis, give my regards to Sir Horace."

After leaving the bergfreid, Robert gathered his clothes from the line and carried them into his room. Karl had gone to meet the boat captain, Katharina was in the courtyard, and Wilhelm was seated on his cot. Robert opened his box and put his spare clothes inside.

Before closing it, he reached down and brought out a large, leather-bound volume. Looking at it he asked, "Wilhelm, how well do you know the Bible?"

Wilhelm looked up. "Reading the Bible was never really encouraged in Vienna, but I could never get enough. I would study it when I should have been reading the church fathers. I think I know the Bible well."

"Did you commit verses to memory."

"Of course! How could I not?"

"Take my Bible; it is the English language Bible authorized by King James. It will help you to learn English. Read the verses you remember to learn the English words."

"I can't take your Bible, Robert, it must be very valuable."

"I can get another."

"It is dangerous to be caught with a Bible; they are only permitted in the Church or the monastery."

"Then don't get caught with it! Besides, you can always claim not to speak English."

"Yes, I can use it to learn English. A Bible! Thank you, Robert, thank you. And thank you for challenging me in Latin and not German or French in the bergfreid. I will consider your words."

"Let's hope Karl does not speak Latin. Come, we must make our way to the boat."

As they entered the courtyard, Captain Richard was walking towards them. "You have everything then? Good, let me see you safely to the boat."

Robert asked, "Captain, is the garrison kept well out

of sight? I see but a handful of men from the regiment."

Captain Richard replied, "We are lightly manned indeed. We play a waiting game with the Count of Tilly. He waits outside of cannon range. We believe he desires to force us to surrender the cities we garrison and leave the continent. He will not engage us yet. He dangles an honorable withdrawal, no reckless adventure to inflame the English people. We both wait for armies. We cannot withstand his assault and the Spanish Army coming to intercept. We await reinforcements from the protestant princes to the north."

"Do we control the river and the bank between here and Mannheim?"

"We only block boat and ship passage by us as far as our cannon can fire. When Tilly attacks, it will not be from the river. He will come upon us from the hills above the castle and across the old bridge. We English sit in our castles and wait while the Count of Tilly captures cities held by the Dutch and Frederick V. So long as he thinks he can keep England out of this war, he will let us sit."

"So, he has not yet cut off all supplies?"

"Look at the market stalls; they grow fewer by the day. He has begun to send his message."

Robert and Captain Richard made their way through Heidelberg down to the city wall, out the river gate and down to the wharf. The boat captain and his crew were directing soldiers carrying grain bags now filled with sand into the boat and placing them around the inside of the hull and nearly head high around the helmsman's station. When they were finished with the sandbags, the soldiers returned with half of the grain and other cargo which Colonel Herbert ordered to be carried down to Mannheim.

Karl was speaking with the visibly agitated boat captain. The captain threw up his arms and stomped off into the hold of the boat. Karl walked over to Robert and Captain Richard and without pleasantries began, "The boat Captain will not leave here in daylight. He wants a company of soldiers to escort the boat from ashore. He has just learned Count Tilly's forces control the riverbank just out of range of the castle cannons."

Captain Richard nodded. "It is true. Heidelberg is surrounded, as is Mannheim. That is why these provisions must get through to Colonel Vere's men at Mannheim. We do not have enough men to secure the river bank on even one shore. You outwitted Tilly's army coming here…"

Karl did not let him finish. "We caught them by surprise! Even then, they nearly caught us. Now they know we are here; they will be watching for us, waiting to make us pay."

Captain Richard sighed. "We are outnumbered. We wait behind stone walls for reinforcements. The Dutch have retreated in hopes of reforming and returning. Frederick garrisons many villages to delay Count Tilly's armies. That is our strategy. We buy time. Ask the captain if he would rather stay here and face the siege that will certainly come."

When the boat captain returned, Karl spoke with him.

The two men could be seen studying the river. The captain threw some chaff into the wind and watched it fly. Once it settled on the water, they followed its progress in the current. Both men could be seen nodding before the boat captain went ashore.

Karl came back and said, "The current remains strong, and if the night wind holds direction, it should be favorable. Mannheim is but ten miles downstream. With three more men at oars, the captain thinks we can make Mannheim in two hours of hard rowing and sailing. He favors waiting until three o'clock in the morning. Tilly's watchman should be at their most weary. Robert, you, Wilhelm and I shall be at oars."

Captain Richard looked at Robert. "Everyone should get some rest until then. Robert, come with me, perhaps I can find an Arquebus or two as well."

Robert followed Captain Richard to the armory where Sergeant Barkley was seated outside the locked door. Barkley rose when Captain Richard approached and said, "Sergeant, draw me two pistols for Lieutenant Curtis, and an arquebus or two if they remain."

"Aye, Captain, two Cuirassier pistols and any odd arquebus," Barkley acknowledged as he unlocked and entered the armory. He was back a few minutes later with the pistols, an arquebus and the armor of a cuirassier. He placed them on the table and said, "This armor was just turned in. Someone must have found it on the field and seein' as you're back from the dead, so to speak, lieutenant, I am thinking it may be yours."

Robert looked at his breastplate and backplate armor

and said, "My helmet wasn't back there was it?"

"No sir, just the armor."

Robert smiled. "Of course not, the hole in the back would tell too much a story."

"Beggin' your pardon sir?"

"Never mind sergeant, draw out powder, ball and match for these."

"Yes, Captain, powder, ball and match."

Captain Richard said, "I must say goodbye to you here Curtis. I can't say how pleased I was to learn you are still with us my friend. Sad that we must part once more. Careful Robbie. God speed my friend."

"I'll be back soon enough, captain. 'Couldn't leave you to face what's waiting for you short-handed. Just keep an eye on the sergeant here, that food is for our men not to be pilfered by a smuggler."

Barkley said nothing.

CHAPTER 9
RUNNING THE GAUNTLET

The rain began after sunset and continued through the stormy black night. At a little past two in the early morning, Wilhelm and Katharina silently followed Karl and Robert slogging through the cold and wet strects of the city, the wind-driven rain cut at their faces and fingers as they clutched their cloaks tight against them. Once aboard the boat, Katharina was led to the safety of the hold, and the tarp pulled over to provide a modicum of protection from the weather. The arquebus was left with the boat captain in the shelter of the pilot station. Robert asked to see Wilhelm's pistol and said, "Keep the match lit and the powder dry."

Wilhelm prayed for the cold rain to continue and keep any of Count Tilly's sentries under shelter. The crew let go the lines, and the captain said to Robert, Karl, and Wilhelm, "Remember, follow the stroke of my crewman. We will start off easy, but you must keep up!"

Wilhelm finished praying and said softly, "The weather will certainly hide us."

Karl replied, "And hide the channel and any river boom from the view of the captain as well."

"River boom? Wilhelm asked.

"There may be no boom tower between Mannheim and us, but surely a chain or boom float could be stretched across the river to entrap us. They are not likely to rely on a warning snare; they will try and block us."

Wilhelm returned to his prayers.

The heavy rain swelled the river, and the current was now running much faster, so much so that the captain decided not to risk raising the sail. The men pulled easily into the current, and the hull shuddered as it began to race downstream. In half an hour the boat safely rounded a bend, and the cannon of Heidelberg were out of range.

The captain fought to keep the boat on course, an experienced eye, knowledge of the river and excellent night vision all developed through years of experience prepared him for this night. Neither Robert nor Karl noticed the trim of the boat with the bow high before them until a bag of shot fell from Karl's belt and quickly slid to the stern of the boat. "Hold oars!" The captain shouted, and as the men took an unplanned rest, the lead oarsman recovered the shot and returned it to Karl with an angry growl.

When he was back in his seat, the captain ordered,

"Give way… together," and six men pulled on their oars in unison.

The men worked their oars in silence. Wilhelm was breathing heavily, but he knew he could not stop and determined to go on no matter the pain. The river began to narrow on them, the trees were but dark shadows with arms of black reaching towards them. "Give it all, men," the captain cried out, and the lead oar soon had doubled the pace. Wilhelm struggled to keep his oar in time, he felt cramps in his stomach and foul bile coming up his throat he prayed to God for strength to keep up, but his body was telling him it could not.

Suddenly the boat lurched up, the bow jumping like a trout chasing a fly. As quickly as the bow lurched, the entire boat began to spin sideways. The bow splashed down heavy into the current, water spilling over the gunwale and a grinding noise arose from the shuddering keel below them. The boat slid sideways into the current, slowly straightened and resumed its course downstream. The captain calmly said, "At an easy pace give way… together!"

Karl said the obvious. "Thank the Lord for the high water! We made it over the chain! I pray it was the only one!"

Katharina poked her frightened face from the hold. "All is well Katie, best you stay down there for now," Karl reassured her.

Wilhelm and Katharina exchanged smiles of relief and Katharina silently returned to the hold pulling the tarp back over her.

Whether it was his prayer, Katie's smile, or the adrenaline flowing through his veins, Wilhelm went back to pulling his oar with ease. The rain and the wind began to slacken, but the night remained dark and cold as the riverboat rounded the last bend, and the massive black towers and walls of Mannheim fortress came into view as a dark and foreboding shape against the deep gray of night.

The captain gave the order, "Hold water," as they neared the two boom towers on either side of the river. "Robert, give the password as I light the lantern and raise it."

The light of the simple lantern broke the darkness startling all that beheld it. As quickly as it was raised Robert was standing, calling out, "Theobald House! Theobald House! We come from Heidelberg with dispatches for Colonel Vere."

Out of the silence came the counter pass, "Herefordshire!"

Then the sound of chain ratcheting on an iron wheel and the command, "Hold water until the chain is lowered and then make your way to the wharf."

As Robert stood in the light of the lantern the loud crack that could only be an arquebus echoed across the water and splinters flew into his cloak. Robert dove into the hold as another blast and then third sent wood splinters flying. "I spy them!" shouted the captain. "Just upstream of the opposite boom tower," Immediately he fired and was soon followed by Karl and Wilhelm. Shots rang back and forth until the boom of a cannon sent mud, wood, and water showering from the opposite bank of the river. A second cannon blast left a gaping hole in the riverside trail, and the smoke slowly drifted away in silence.

As the boat tied up at the wharf, the captain of the guard said, "As the colonel is a light sleeper, I am certain he is now awake. This way."

After they passed through the massive gate in the fortress wall, they were shown to the guard duty room. A fire was burning in the fireplace; wall sconces kept the room well lit. A lantern on the table illuminated a water bucket and a dipping cup. The smell of warm bread made the stone and timber room feel warm and inviting. Two soldiers stood when the captain of the guard entered and when told to be at ease, stared at the wet and tired boatmen and travelers but soon directed their stares at the crucifix dangling from Wilhelm's neck.

"You say you have dispatches for Colonel Vere, first let me see your passes."

Robert removed the satchel from his shoulder, shook off the water and splinters, opened and removed the passes signed by Sir Gerard and gave them to the captain.

"Please, you may sit, there is fresh bread, water, and ale, no breakfast until after sunrise. Take off those wet cloaks let them dry near the fire. Ah! Lieutenant Curtis, I will let the colonel know you are here. I see you are to deliver the dispatches in person."

Turning to one of the soldiers, he said, "Sergeant, find quarters for our guests. A private and warm room for the young woman. Then have the quartermaster see to the provisions on the boat."

"Look lively, sergeant!"

"Yes sir, quarters for the guests and the quartermaster is to see to provisions on the boat."

After the captain of the guard followed his sergeant out of the room, the weary travelers settled into the warmth in silence. As Robert removed his cloak, he noticed two holes where a ball had gone through. He pulled out the splinters still tangled in the thick wool cloth and fell heavily into a chair, then straightened and massaged his injured leg. The boat captain and his crew immediately took a mug of ale and half a loaf of bread each, sat down and ate.

Wilhelm softly asked Katharina, "What can I get for you? Sit her by the fire and be warmed."

Katharina smiled at Wilhelm and said, "I am well, Wilhelm. I am strengthened knowing we draw closer to Johann and thank my maker that he has sent you, and Robert too, to help Papa and me."

Wilhelm smiled at her and she leaned over a kissed him on the cheek.

His face blushed slightly but, and neither drew away or feigned any embarrassment.

A half hour later, the captain of the guard returned and told Robert, "Colonel Vere will see you before officer call this morning. Can you, Herr Schroeder and your priest be prepared in an hour?"

Robert looked at Karl and then Wilhelm. Both nodded. Robert turned to the captain and said, "The colonel's urgency is appreciated. Have you found quarters for the boat crew and my party?"

"The sergeant will show you to quarters shortly. I must bid you good morning and be about my rounds."

Gray dawn greeted Robert, Karl, and Wilhelm as the captain of the guard led them atop the walls. They walked towards a tower in the corner of the fortress where the Neckar joined the Rhine. As they climbed the narrow circular staircase, Robert glanced out the tall, thin gun ports and was amazed at the visibility they provided and the unobstructed views up and down the Rhine river even on a dark and overcast day. Only one level up, they passed through a guard station with defensive gun ports trained on the stair tower below and entered a large hall with windows which also served as cannon stations on both the Rhine and Neckar. Colonel Sir Horace Vere, commander of the regiment English volunteers and a Dutch regiment of the United Netherlands, sat at a heavy oak desk.

Looking up he said, "Which of you is Lieutenant Curtis?"

Robert stood at attention and replied, "At your service, sir."

The colonel looked at him closely and said, "Yes. Sir Gerard reports that you carry dispatches for me. Well, let me see them, man!"

Robert stepped forward and gave his satchel to Colonel Vere and then stepped back into line with Karl and Wilhelm.

The colonel read the dispatches and occasionally looked up at the men before him before going back to documents on his desk. When he finished reading, he stood up and walked to a window looking north, down the Rhine river. He gazed out the window with his hands behind his back, and after nodding to his own thoughts, he turned and returned to the front of his desk.

"Herr Schroeder, Colonel Herbert recommends we help each other. Your offer of information from your watchers in the Spanish Netherlands and aid in supplying our garrisons is most generous. Only a fool would decline; however, I must be honest with you; my help does not extend beyond Frankenthal, not ten miles more down the Rhine. It is true, Mainz was in the hands of Frederick's armies not a month ago, but his forces have retreated, and I no longer know their location or strength."

Horace Vere liked to walk as he thought and spoke. Returning to the window, he continued, "We play a waiting game. A game of delay in hopes of reinforcements. A few soldiers in small strongholds, forcing Count Tilly to recover them one by one. I cannot be certain which strongholds we maintain."

Karl spoke up. "Then friendly watchers and providers of food are all the more important to your strategy."

"I can send you with passes to Frankenthal where you may have what you need for your journey to Mainz. My commander there, Sir John Burroughs, will provide you his best information, maps, and advice. I know not how else to aid your cause."

"And the company of Robert, that is, Lieutenant Curtis."

Looking at Robert, Vere replied, "Yes, if he is willing, you may have the services of Lieutenant Curtis."

"If I may ask sir," Robert began. "Karl, Herr Schroeder, is well known in the courts of the princes of Germany and indeed the continent. Might I suggest, colonel, that following our visit to Mainz, we continue north and confirm the arrival of reinforcements. Let Herr Schroeder employ his watchers and provide you information that..."

"I need facts, not rumors! Locations and movements of their forces. I need to know who commands and leads them. Are they disciplined and well fed? And if possible, I need to know their plans and their timing. This information must come to me quickly to be timely and useful. And this information must come secretly through countryside controlled by the forces of my enemies. This is no easy thing, Lieutenant!"

Karl stepped forward. "I have been considering such a plan for some time. No, it will not be easy, but I believe it can be done."

Vere nodded. "I will hear more of your plan later. Sit down with my adjutant, Captain Stock, he shall draw up your passes and we shall talk tomorrow."

Turning to Wilhelm, he said, "Father Hahn, you have been silent."

"I am here as a priest of Eberbach seeking justice for my people. I have given my word to Herr Schroeder and his daughter Katharina, who travels with us, to seek his release. I will never betray them."

"Father, I do not doubt your word to Herr Schroeder;

it is betraying my people that concerns me."

Karl strongly affirmed, "The Father is a hunted man by the emperor's officers; he has risked his life to help us. To whom would he go? He honors his vows to God; he has made no vows to the emperor."

"Your watchers are your friends and countrymen, Herr Schroeder; you must consider their risk," Colonel Vere replied.

Then turning to Wilhelm, he said, "I would have that all men of God serve only Him and leave governing to king and parliament."

Vere turned away and walked towards his window. "The captain will see you back to your quarters."

Outside of the colonel's office, down the circular staircase and now in the open courtyard, Wilhelm asked, "Colonel Vere, he is your commander?"

"Yes, Colonel Vere commands the twenty-two hundred English volunteers and another fifteen hundred German and allied Dutch soldiers in the Palatinate."

"And Sir Gerard and now I hear Sir John Burroughs are his subordinates?"

"Yes," Robert replied. "Why do you ask?"

"So, all English commanders are of the nobility?"

Robert stopped and turned to Wilhelm. "Colonel Horace Vere is a great soldier, perhaps only his brother surpassed him in fame in all of England. He was a commoner when he first rose to be a commander, and it is an injustice that he remains a knight with no title. Yes, like us he was a cavalier. He is the third son of a soldier. All the Vere's are soldiers, except his uncle who carries the family title, his older brother was knighted in the war against Spain in the Netherlands and made a baron. Colonel Horace Vere entered that war as a young man and was more heroic than his elders. I can only imagine that her highness Queen Elizabeth was too parsimonious to bestow lands and titles to two members of the same family; she chose the elder. After England and Spain agreed to terms, Sir Horace Vere continued the fight against the Spanish as a commander for the United Netherlands. Barons and Earls seek to serve under him; it is the surest path to General."

"He appears a most temperate man," Wilhelm offered.

"He is the best of men! When parliament would not raise an army for his majesty, King James, and James himself was reluctant to offend the King of Spain, Colonel Vere stepped forward to defend the crown of King James' daughter, Elizabeth, wife of Frederick the Fifth. The Colonel raised this regiment. His reputation could have filled many more regiments, but the king lacked the funds to pay even the one."

Wilhelm turned to Karl. "Did you know of this man?"

Karl smiled. "Yes, but more importantly, Count von Tilly knows him well. The count has surrendered to him in the past and knows not to come against him again without an overwhelming force."

Starting to walk again, Robert remarked, "Father Wilhelm, you have passed muster with a great man!"

CHAPTER 10
A MAN WITH AMBITIONS

Robert found the captain of the guard waiting in the courtyard outside of the officer's mess. "Fraulein Schroeder and your boat crew are inside at breakfast. You may join them and afterward rest awhile. I shall come for you, Lieutenant Curtis and Herr Schroeder, this afternoon and take you to the colonel's adjutant."

Robert was becoming accustomed to tense active nights followed by after breakfast exhaustion induced sleep. Not even the throbbing pain in his leg could keep him awake, so it took several nudges from Karl to bring him to a groggy consciousness.

"Robert, the adjutant is expecting us. He is certain to ask about my plans, but I will not tell him. I will not trust my people to a stranger. You must agree with me on this; do you understand?"

Robert stretched his back, rolled his head about his neck and sighed. "You have to trust someone. You made the offer to Colonel Vere."

"Vere has a reputation. Adjutants and aides are ambitious men. They pursue such positions out of self-interest, or so I have been told."

Robert sat up straight, his eyes now clear. "It is often the case, but also, often there is great loyalty. But I will follow your lead if you are concerned."

Robert and Karl found the captain waiting in the courtyard. "I hope you were able to get some rest. The adjutant, Captain Stock is most anxious to hear of your plans."

"Donald Stock?" Robert asked

"Yes, you know him?"

"I knew a Donald Stock at Cambridge, he was most well connected in the university and the church, I never thought he would join the army."

The men quickly made their way across the courtyard and into the fortress. Robert mumbled, "Not up in a tower I hope," as he carefully climbed the stairs.

"Only one flight, he is at the other end of the hall from Colonel Vere."

Robert clomped his way down the stone corridor, and the captain knocked on a heavy oak door. "Lieutenant Curtis and Herr Schroeder to see you."

As the captain opened the door, a black-robed figure was exiting a rear door and quickly closed it behind him.

The captain of the guard said, "Well, I will leave you here. If you need me, just ask any of the guards."

As Robert and Karl entered the room the man behind the desk rose. "Robert! It is you! Well come in man and have a seat. When I came from England assigned as Colonel Vere's adjutant, I was told a Lieutenant Curtis was missing and feared dead. It never occurred to me that it might be my Cambridge chum! I must say, Robbie, you look like ol' Jonah when the whale puked him up!"

Robert stood silent.

"You must take supper with me tonight, good food, not the open mess. Now tell me, what is this mission you are planning for the colonel?"

"Well, captain,"

"We're all friends here, Robbie. Call me Donald."

"I am sorry to disappoint you Donald, but it is merely his permission to aid the family that saved my life when I lay wounded on the battlefield. It is purely a local issue from the people of Eberbach seeking justice in Mainz. The good Colonel, the chivalrous man that he is, has agreed that I escort these good people safely through the English and Dutch lines. We are to keep our eyes open as we travel. You, no doubt will be told to restore me to the active list and draw up safe conduct passes."

Captain Stock eyed Karl's stony face suspiciously then turned to Robert, smiled and said, "Well, it is indeed a blessing to see my friend safe, and I am sure your documents will be completed with dispatch."

Robert asked, "Tell me, Donald, what brings a man with your prospects into the army? Several bishops come to mind who would gladly find you a vicarage or better."

"Robbie, you had your opportunities at Cambridge, but you never would commit yourself. Now it appears this is where the good Lord has placed me while a few opportunities develop for me in England. Service to the King is always an honorable endeavor."

Captain Stock stood up and said, "The offer for supper stands. I will see you at eight. That will be all."

As Robert and Karl were leaving, Captain Stock said, "Oh, Herr Schroeder, I hope you find your son Johann in good health."

Outside the room, Karl said, "I do not know this English word 'chum,' but you do not like this man."

"You cannot find a more ambitious, self-centered man in all of England. Loyalty? He does not know the word. No, you shall not trust your plans to him."

As they walked back through the stone corridor, Robert asked, "How will you communicate with Colonel Vere?"

Karl smiled. "I believe the colonel will be collecting tapestries for the ancestral home. I believe it is called Havering House in the Forrest of Essex. Perhaps, you too can learn to interpret a great masterpiece in cloth."

That evening, Robert called on Donald Stock in his quarters for supper. He was met by a servant in civilian clothes and offered a glass of wine while he waited for his school mate. The table was set for two with fine china and silver service. The suite of rooms, intended for senior a courtier, were graced with high ceilings and tall windows offering an excellent view facing south up the

Rhine River. Robert noticed a brass campaign signal lantern under a table at the foot of a tall window, which seemed out of place with the elegant silver candlesticks and sconces burning brightly throughout the room.

Captain Stock came out of the bedchamber and greeted Robert. "Robbie, punctual as ever ol' chum! I think I will join you in a taste of wine, one of the benefits of a campaign on the continent!"

"Donald, you seem to have set yourself up well for this war. Your timing could not have been better; the campaign tents never offered comforts like these."

"I made certain I quartered near the old man, an adjutant's prerogative it is. Just as it is to see everyone and everything before it goes into him."

"Well, of course, you will have no argument from me."

"Your German friend would not appear to share your view."

"Karl? Can you blame him for caution? You have heard his story. His son was seized in the night, there are no records of his arrest, and when a few questions are asked, innocent people are threatened, and now they are being hunted down. Certainly, Sir Horace will follow protocol in his dealings. But as I said, all that we asked of him was his aid in passing through to Mainz and my leave to travel with them."

Donald drank his wine, smiled and said, "And an offer of information was made."

Robert returned the smile. "Of Course. Right you are Donald. Herr Schroeder surprised even me with the offer. I believe the man seeks to curry favor by noting what troop movements he may encounter. Certainly, any passerby could help as much."

Still wearing his forced smile, Captain Stock said, "Sit down, Robert. Enjoy a good meal and let us catch up on old times."

Then to his servant, he said, "Andrew, you may serve us now."

Robert sat where directed and said, "What Donald? No orderly? You brought your own servant?"

Donald sat down and answered, "Why not be comfortable? You have my word on this Robert, this campaign will not last long, and better things will come from it."

Robert lifted his cup. "To his Majesty, King James!"

Donald replied, "To his Majesty the King."

"Tell me, Robbie, do you plan on a career in the army?"

"A career? It is only by the grace of God and the mercy of my German friends, as you call them, that I sit here today. No, I have no thoughts on any career, I only want to survive until tomorrow, and the next tomorrow as well."

"Robbie, a man with no direction, is weak. You squandered your opportunities at Cambridge, and now you squander an opportunity for redemption. I've read the reports about you. You could not maintain discipline among your men. You tolerate insolence. You have no pride, no backbone, and now you would have me believe you can somehow lead and protect this small band of

German outlaws?"

"Is this why you asked me here? To humiliate and offend?"

"You need to hear the truth! Good God man! Wake up! Listen to me; I can help you salvage the wreck of your career. It is not too late to be about something, to join with those who hold the future of England."

Robert's face grew serious. He stared into Donald's eyes. "What would you have me do?"

Donald sat back in his chair, smiled broadly, and said, "For now, just keep me informed. Certainly, there can be no harm in that. I am the colonel's adjutant."

Robert nodded. "We will speak tomorrow after the meeting with the colonel."

It was late before Robert returned to his quarters. He stopped, looked around and then lightly knocked on the adjacent door. Karl opened it, and Robert slid in.

"Is it safe to talk here?" Robert asked.

Karl nodded, and said. "Better than outside, but softly."

"He knows more than he lets on. I am to meet with him again after we speak to the colonel. We cannot trust him; therefore, I agreed to help him. He wants me to report to him everything we say or do for the colonel."

Karl nodded and thought for a moment. "You were wise to agree, it will help us get our information to the colonel if it goes through him. Yes, this can be a good thing."

"The information you send to the colonel, it will be in code, I fear the key may be compromised."

Karl smiled. "It is the best kind of code. The colonel will not need a key! But perhaps we can make one for your Captain Stock."

"We cannot be sure of him, but…"

"We will soon know where his loyalties lie. So, for now, each tapestry will contain two messages, one for the colonel and one for Captain Stock."

Robert shook his head. "You have put a lot of thought into this…"

Karl took out a pad of paper and began to write, without looking up he replied, "Divided loyalties are nothing new among the princes of the empire. The subtlety is giving the Captain information he may already know or have access to from von Tilly, but not good information the colonel requires. Now I will make two copies of this code key. You will nervously give one to Captain Stock after our meeting."

"Karl, you are taking great risk in this matter; you don't have to become involved."

The polished old man set down his pen looked up at Robert and smiled. "Robert, you speak of risk. What life is without risk? This war just has begun, and already you have noted the cost to peasants, villagers, soldiers, and families. You need to think less of avoiding risk and more of recognizing risk worth taking. I have seen that you are a young man with a good heart and a good mind to know what is right and what is wrong. I have seen a commitment to help Katharina and me in our effort to free Johann. I commend you for taking this risk but the injustice that has seen Johann taken in the middle of the night will not end even with his happy return. No, the injustice and intolerance towards our right to worship God as we believe will continue. Johann is not the end of our goal. His rescue is just the start of what we must do, and we will risk everything in this just cause."

"What was it that Luther said at last to the Diet of Worms, 'Here I stand. I can do no other.' Thank you for your advice. I will consider your words carefully. Good night Karl."

"Pray. Robert, never cease to pray. Good night."

CHAPTER 11
THE WATCHERS

Karl and Robert called on Colonel Vere early the next morning. Captain Stock was speaking with the colonel when they entered.

"Ah, Herr Schroeder and Lieutenant Curtis, good that you are here. My adjutant has drawn up the documents and passes as I promised. I hope they do you well. And Curtis you are returned to the rolls. You can thank Captain Stock for making that happen."

Turning to Stock, he said, "Thank you, captain, that will be all for now."

Colonel Vere waited for Donald Stock to close the door behind him before continuing. "Small world, Curtis, you and Stock being chums at Cambridge. Heard he wined and dined last night, the man rarely shows his face at the mess."

"Yes Colonel, I was quite surprised to find him here. Please let me say, he does not seem the man an experienced commander would choose as adjutant."

Vere looked closely at Robert before speaking. "He was ordered here by Lord Calvert himself, Secretary of State to King James. We are his volunteers; how could I refuse? Do you know him? Was he a pompous ass at Cambridge as well?"

"He knew the right people. He was bound for the church, very high placement. To my memory, he had no 'chums' among fellow students. There were rumors his brother is a Carmelite priest. Tight as thieves with one of the dons, a Howard Fitzhugh, high churchman, some thought him a closet Catholic."

"Mind you I don't object to training a nobleman. God knows I have been sent barons and earls, but a churchman and sent by the secretary. I don't like it. Smacks of eyes over my shoulders."

"Then you may like to hear what I have to say," Karl offered.

Colonel Vere turned to listen to Karl. "There must be many tapestries in Havering House. I am told it is a favorite of the King himself. Surely your time here will permit a few purchases on behalf of your uncle the baron. What wonderful stories have been told in the beauty woven into cloth. As I am a dealer in tapestries, I am always looking on behalf of my clients, and often I send small paper copies of tapestries that may be just what is sought. I have been known even to draw designs myself and commission the weaving. I can send you such drawings which will contain two stories, one for you and one for Captain Stock. Soon you will know his where his loyalties lie."

"Tapestries? Please go on Herr Schroeder."

"I am not alone. I have friends, 'watchers' as I said, and much more information than one man can see. I will give you this information for I want to rid the Palatine of the intolerance that our emperor has sent, and for certain, the Duke of Bavaria will be no friend of protestants."

Robert spoke. "Captain Stock is diligent in knowing what you know, colonel, and seeing everything that crosses your desk. He expects me to share with him all reports Karl or I send. I agreed to this, and after our meeting, I will give him a code key for the tapestries."

"But you, Colonel," Karl continued. "Will need no key and while the information that Captain Stock can verify with any of his outside friends will be accurate. Information regarding reinforcements from either the protestant north or the Catholic Spaniards, he will not see. Let me show you."

Karl unrolled a tapestry on the desk. "The border color identifies the location of the watcher. The flowers are armies, the leaves and stems indicate strength and direction of movement, but only flowers with green and brown stems are significant. A green stem alone has no meaning. The animals are the commanders, and the scene is the action. Mannheim is in the center; the Baltic is the top."

Colonel Vere replied, "A blue border court scene."

Karl explained, "This is your current situation. The court scene signifies negotiations and non-engagement. The blue border tells you the watcher is in the Palatinate. Now notice the small white rosebud with three leaves. White is the English forces. The stem is green and brown, so it signifies that this flower counts strength. One large and seven small leaves for seventeen thousand men, this includes General von Mansfeld and your Dutch support. Now note the purple violets on the green and brown stems. Purple identifies forces of the emperor, the boar in the field identifies the commander as Count Tilly. The leaves on the green and brown stems show his strength at nineteen thousand."

"Nineteen thousand? Our estimate is half that. He has a great advantage; why doesn't he act?"

Karl continued to explain, "Now, Count Tilly is the boar, Gonzalo Fernandez de Cordoba is the stag. You, sir, are the shepherd. I will place new commanders by their flowers in new tapestries. As for colors: yellow is Spain, white is England, purple is the emperor, orange is our Dutch friends from the United Netherlands, red the Danes, royal blue the Swedes, pink the northern princes and green, the Italians. The scenes are this: a court scene speaks of negotiations and unengaged forces, a castle speaks of siege, religious means reinforcements are en-route. Christ our Savior, they are coming to help you; the devil or hell they move against you. A pastoral scene is encamped forces with no indication of movement. A hunting scene denotes movement to battle in open field. A battle scene will tell you the casualties and results."

"Very Good, Herr Schroeder!"

Karl continued to point at the tapestry. "Now look at the leaves of the forces and strength flowers. The direction the top leaf points indicates the direction of movement. A bent top leaf tells you the force does not move. Now, colonel can you read this tapestry?"

Karl unrolled another tapestry atop the first.

Colonel Vere said, "A black border with a hunting scene It comes from the Protestant Union."

"Yes, Hesse Cassel. You see the stag at the bottom is de Cordoba, the yellow flower, his army, is in Hagenau waiting to intercept Christian of Brunswick, the bear, intending to prevent Christian's army, the pink flower, from linking with Count Ernst von Mansfeld, the hunting dog and the remnants of Frederick's army."

Colonel Vere pointed at the Tapestry. "And he is moving south. I see he has not yet arrived. The stallion is Ambrosio Spinola; he is still in Flanders. Moving here to the center, the white rose with three buds at the base of the castle is our position. It is three white buds for the three garrisons. And again, on a stem with one large and seven small leaves, for seventeen thousand men. I see the purple violets around us, the forces of Count Tilly, and I see some of Tilly's forces moving north. How would a watcher in Hesse Cassel know this?"

"My watchers share information; this watcher tells you Count Tilly has sent emissaries to the Spanish Netherlands, perhaps in preparation for the Spanish Army of Spinola."

Colonel Vere pointed at the tapestry. "You said there is

a key for others, those I may not trust. Please explain."

"Yes, there is a key which can be used to identify position and movements that friends of Count Tilly likely know. This key must be used to find a hidden focus that points to a very detailed code for the information we know they have. This code will take their eyes away from the obvious and have them counting knots, horns on stags and the direction of lay on the border. It is a simple truth that someone trained to see something will readily overlook what he might otherwise see."

Sir Horace chuckled. "Yes, I have commanders who can see only a strategy in which they have been trained. And you intend to provide this code to Captain Stock?"

"Indeed, Colonel, Robert will nervously provide a copy as if doing so is at great risk. I hope to provide you two services in doing this."

"Two? How so?"

"Well Colonel, first you will soon know the loyalty of Captain Stock, and if, as we fear, he is working against our success, he will pass it on to the Count's staff. How much better if von Tilly protects our couriers, so the tapestries are not intercepted? Also, it will provide the information we want our enemies to see."

Sir Horace looked up. "A good plan if he is working with our enemies in the field, it may not be as useful if he is working only with enemies in London."

"Yes Colonel, but are not the enemies in the field connected to their friends in the court of King James or Parliament?"

Sir Horace nodded.

"You must allow Captain Stock to find it. You will quickly learn his loyalty, and it will confirm to him that the code Robert provides is genuine."

"Yes, I will manufacture a distraction while he is in my office."

Karl added, "One last signal, if a shepherd is holding a lamb, it means I am coming to you carrying a message for your ears only. I will need a password recognized by your sentries."

"Of course," replied Vere. "I have such a password for emissaries from London; it is: 'verba veritas.' Beware, Captain Stock knows this password."

"For now, it is in his interest that you receive instructions from the court, but he will seek to discover its content."

"How can I get a message to you?"

Karl thought and then reached into waistcoat pocket. "Ask for a scene and I will prepare such a tapestry. If you must speak with me, pay my messenger with this coin. I shall know it when I see it."

Colonel Vere took the silver coin from Karl and looking at it he could see the likeness of Emperor Ferdinand with a gouge across his face.

A knock on the door broke the silence.

"Colonel, there is a visitor here. I think you should see."

The colonel opened the door. "Well Captain Stock, who is this important visitor?"

"A priest or a cleric, says he has a letter from the pope."

"I was just learning the finer points of tapestries from Herr Schroeder. Just a moment while I show him into my bedchamber to look at some new additions I have purchased for Havering House. Then you may fetch our papist friend and come through. Probably a papal bull against me to join the one he has issued against the king."

Karl rolled up the sample tapestries and tied them neatly with a blue ribbon. Captain Stock stared at the code sheet lying on the desk.

"Excuse me, Captain, I will soon be out of your way," Karl said smiling as he picked up the sheet, folded it neatly and handed it to Colonel Vere. "You'll be needing this Colonel," Karl said as he stepped through the door into Vere's bedchamber.

"Handsome indeed!" Karl said as he pointed to the tapestry in the next room, entered and closed the door.

Vere looked back at Donald Stock. "Look lively, then Captain! Show the padre in!"

A few minutes later Captain Stock returned with a black-robed visitor. "Colonel Vere this is Don, excuse me, Father Lorenzo. He carries a letter from his holiness the pope."

"Well come through then, deliver what you have brought me," the Colonel said impatiently holding out his hand.

Don Lorenzo extended an envelope crisscrossed with gold ribbon and sealed in a bright white embossed wax.

"Looks fine indeed, Lorenzo, though I am not one to recognize the pope's seal."

Don Lorenzo smiled "I can certainly swear that it is

indeed from his holiness' own hand."

As Colonel Vere opened the letter, Don Lorenzo continued. "The holy father is both a patient and a merciful man. He is ever prayerful for the repentance and joyful return to the holy church of all those who left in error, whether willful or misguided."

"This letter tells me no more than what has been said before. Sir Gerard has informed me of his visit by one Don Pedro with similar words. Let the people return to the Roman church and the kings and rulers blessed by him, and there will be no need of bloodshed."

"Colonel Vere, you have the promise of the pope, Christ's Vicar on earth. And I am sent to remind you that food still comes into your city. Merchants still trade, life is nearly normal. This is a sign of good faith. Why embroil your few men in the affairs of the emperor? Make use of the offer before you before it is too late."

"I see the emperor's army not far outside my walls, not the pope's."

"Is Ferdinand not the 'Holy Roman Emperor.' Crowned by the pope?"

"I do not care who placed the crown on his head; I care more for the numbers and skill of his soldiers. The Count of Tilly and I are well acquainted. I will deal with him. Is there anything else Don Lorenzo?"

"Just one small thing. I know you harbor a runaway priest who has taken up with a young woman, a siren and a seducer from Eberbach. We know they are here and ask you as a sign of good faith to send them back to resolve some local issues in Eberbach."

"Two emissaries seeking the return of this priest and a young woman, Is the Roman church and empire at risk from these two?"

"As I said, it is a small thing, a gesture that would be appreciated. A simple matter of the Emperor's justice."

"I am told it is the very injustice that they flee. Good day, Don Lorenzo. Captain Stock, please escort our visitor to the gate, then return here; I have some business for you to attend."

After Captain Stock left with Don Lorenzo, Colonel Vere said, "It seems Captain Stock took a good long look at the code sheet."

Robert replied, "I am certain I saw Don Lorenzo in his office yesterday morning. He was leaving through the rear door as we entered."

Karl came out of the bedchamber. "I do believe he will take the bait."

"Why this interest in the priest and your daughter?"

Karl nodded. "Yes, I believe these men sent to oversee the priests and clerics have gone too far. They are up to something. They have broken the agreement negotiated by the Archbishop of Mainz at the treaty or Ulm and do not want to be found out. Not even the emperor wants his protestant princes to re-enter the war when he believes it almost won."

After Stock left, Colonel Vere interpreted a third tapestry and was now confident he culd quickly read the information it presented. Sir Horace said, "Truly beautiful. Karl, I don't think I shall ever look at a tapestry the same ever again!"

When Donald Stock returned the colonel said, "Well Stock, what did you make of Don Lorenzo? Why so much interest in the priest and the woman?"

Stock eyed Karl carefully then replied, "As you have said, colonel, we play a waiting game. The Count of Tilly could blockade our forts at any time. How much food do we have? How long could we last once the siege begins? Perhaps a goodwill gesture can buy us time."

"Tell me, captain, what is our current estimate of Tilly's strength?"

"Our scouts estimate five thousand."

"And we are well fortified. No, Captain, I prefer to show good faith with the local people, our allies not our enemies."

Colonel Vere walked to the window and looked up the Rhine river valley. "But you have convinced me of one thing captain, like you, I will make better advantage of our time here. I have decided to engage Herr Schroeder to find high-quality tapestries for Havering House. You shall see to it his samples and purchases for me are not hindered."

"Certainly colonel."

"Now I understand you have documents and passes for Lieutenant Curtis."

"Yes, Colonel. This way Curtis, the documents are on my desk."

Karl and Robert followed Captain Stock out and down the stone corridor to his chambers. A satchel was waiting, and Donald handed it to Robert. "Everything is prepared. You may depart immediately."

Karl said, "I would like to make some purchases in the market before we leave."

"Go ahead; I will catch up with you. I would like a short word with Captain Stock regarding my pay."

With Karl gone, Robert nervously looked around and said, "We are to report on all movement of forces between here and Mainz. Also, anything we can learn from others on the move. The tapestries are coded. Here is a key. To read it, place the top figure on its match on the tapestry and the key will provide force strength and movements. Keep it well hidden. The colonel trusts no one looking over his shoulders."

Donald Stock studied the key. "Very clever indeed! So, Robbie, you finally commit!"

"This war is a waste of money and lives. We should not be here. I want to go home alive."

"Trust me, Robbie, there are many working to do just as you wish."

Robert returned to the quarters he shared with Karl and Wilhelm. "Is all well with you and Katharina? We will be leaving soon."

"Katie is sewing a tapestry. Fascinating how women can always find time for needlework."

"So now it's Katie?"

Wilhelm blushed. "She insists."

"I see you are reading the Bible."

"Yes, but I am confused. I read here a passage from Romans where Saint Paul asks if we should go on sinning so that grace may abound."

"I know the passage."

"Your English says, 'God forbid!' but the vulgate clearly says: 'May it not occur.'"

Robert smiled. "That is the beauty of the Bible in the language of the people. In England, both nobleman and peasant alike would object to the unreasonable by saying 'God forbid!' So now, Wilhelm when you learn English it will not merely be translated words, but the language of the people."

Wilhelm nodded.

"And Wilhelm, it was the study of Romans that led Martin Luther to understand the truth that underlays our reformation, that it is by grace we are saved, through faith. Please keep reading!"

CHAPTER 12
COUSIN SIR GEOFFREY

Karl returned from the market with fresh fruit, cheese, bread, and news. "Don Lorenzo did not leave Mannheim before stopping by several stalls in the market. He foolishly made no purchases. I am told several Roman Catholics in the city ask many questions of the soldiers, but their loyalty does not lie with Elector Frederick V. They are well known by the other shopkeepers who keep note of the strangers they speak to, especially those who do not buy."

"Watchers for the Count of Tilly," Robert replied.

"Yes, and they have one other friend, an English soldier, a messenger that comes from Frankenthal."

"Do they know this soldier's name?"

"No, but his armor shows it has felt the blow of a

sword on top of his right shoulder."

"The armor of a cuirassier?"

"It appears so."

Robert paused then said, "Colonel Vere tells me that all of the Rhine between here and Frankenthal is within cannon range of one fortress or the other. A daylight passage would be most safe."

"Yes. I believe Don Lorenzo now sees us as his resource and will certainly watch us but not hinder us."

Wilhelm had been listening silently. "If only he can convince Don Pedro and Maximillian von Greiffenclau to leave us be. I remember how they fought among themselves."

The passage to Frankanthal was a pleasant reminder of a peaceful past. The boat pulled away from the Mannheim wharf on the Neckar, and the crew pulled lightly on the oars as the current carried them into the wide Rhine River. The Captain unfurled the lateen sail, and they leisurely made their way down river. The walls of Frankenthal were immediately in view on the west bank of the river. Frankenthal did not house a massive mountainside castle like Heidelberg or even a city center fortress as did Mannheim. Frankenthal was a fortified city with strong walls topped with cannons all around. With Mannheim, the two cities anchored a safe crossing and kept the river free from any Imperial or Spanish boats. Passwords were exchanged and the boat tied up along the wharf close to the gate.

Robert presented their passes to the captain of the

guard who directed them to quarters while Sir John was notified of their presence. After a few minutes, Katharina, Wilhelm, and the boat crew settled in to wait as Robert and Karl made their call on the Commanding Officer.

The routine in Frankenthal under the command of Sir John Burroughs was similar to what the crew encountered in Heidelberg and Mannheim. Colonel Burroughs was an experienced soldier. Like his close friend and commander, Colonel Sir Horace Vere, a veteran of the long wars with Spain and in the low countries. He was known for strict discipline and brilliant strategy; his tenacity and determination were reflected in his loyalty to the king, his commander and his men. His men revered him in return.

As the captain of the guard led Robert and Karl to Sir John, Robert asked, "I understand my cousin, Sir Geoffrey Curtis is here. I want to look in on him before we leave."

"I will arrange for you to see him after your call on the colonel. Your cousin, is he? A strange thing about Sir Geoffrey…"

The conversation was interrupted by the sound of the chain from the boom tower and the loud retort of an arquebus firing. "Hold water and await inspection. Go no further upon pain of sinking!"

"Excuse me, lieutenant, I must see to the river action."

"We should like to accompany you, if we may."

"Very well, the river was reopened to trade traffic yesterday. Should be a busy day, Sir John will be keeping a keen eye on my men."

Karl asked, "The river is now open? The Rhine and the Neckar? For all traffic?"

"Open to what trade that the Count of Tilly will permit. The colonel believes it to be a negotiating ploy. It tells the northern princes that the Treaty of Ulm is working and is a reminder to us that we should leave while we can."

"Why did Sir John and Sir Horace agree?"

"Time, money and food. We collect the toll plus a tax for our service protecting trade. We look for food shipments, but if contraband is found we confiscate the boat and all that is aboard. Either way, we now have money to provision for a siege."

"That is where we intend to be of help," Karl replied.

Walking out on the wall above the wharf, a small flotilla of riverboats holds full and their cargoes covered by tarps, struggled to maintain their position, careful not to drift with the current into the floating boom across the river. Two small boats tended the ends of buoys which could be opened to form a narrow passage through the boom.

"Bring them alongside one at a time sergeant." The captain shouted. "Take your time, be thorough. Don't let them rush you. No reason to trust Count Tilly. Report on the cargo before you let them pass."

"Aye captain, one at a time, thorough search, collect the toll and report to you before they pass."

"Cannoneers keep a wary eye on your targets. Wait for my command to fire."

"And Sergeant, send Smyth to escort these gentlemen to Colonel Burroughs."

Entering Colonel Sir John Burroughs' Robert was immediately struck by the wall of books in the otherwise spartan chambers. The garrison commander could be seen watching the activity on the wharf. When he turned to welcome his visitors, Robert saw a middle-aged man with dark brown hair and intelligent eyes. His uniform impeccable and not a hair on his head or in his van dyke beard out of place. Robert remembered Colonel Burroughs reputation a brilliant strategist and learned man. Perhaps England's pre-eminent scholar-soldier.

"Lieutenant Curtis and Herr Schroeder, I presume. You may put Sir Horace's dispatches on the table."

With one last scan of the wharf, Sir John turned and studied the two men before him. "Been expecting you, gentlemen. Now let me see what Sir Horace has to say."

"Well, you are most fortunate. You should be able to continue downriver to Mainz if Tilly can be trusted. An ambitious plan, Herr Schroeder. Risky business, this network of watchers. Support, eh? Soldiers, we need soldiers from the princes! But food and provisions, whatever you can deliver. Good. And you Lieutenant Curtis, Sir Horace believes you can pass as a traitor. Risky business indeed!"

Robert asked, "Sir John, are there any garrisoned towns between here and Mainz? And what about further down river?"

"We barely hold this position on the west bank of the Rhine. No, you must go north of Mainz to find allies. The army of Duke Christian of Brunswick travels south. He hopes to join with the remainder of Frederick's army commanded by Ernst von Mansfeld. Tilly intends to keep us cut off from the north until Cordoba joins him and he can press us unhindered."

"And now that the Protestant Union has disbanded…"

"The princes disbanded the union to sue for peace at the fall of Mainz. Only Christian of Brunswick still fields an army in our cause. The Dutch are negotiating with Christian IV of Denmark, the price of King Gustav Adolphus of Sweden was too dear for the Prince of Orange to pay."

"Does not the Margrave of Brandenburg-Ansbach continue the cause?"

"The Margrave, Joachim Ernst, fights with the Dutch in the Spanish Netherlands alongside Prince Maurice of Orange. While together they keep the Army of Flanders of General de Cordoba in the Netherlands, he has been seriously weakened; we cannot rely on his support."

"Will there be no more support from the King in England?"

Sir John Burroughs sighed. "I am informed that the King's enthusiasm has waned. He supports his daughter Elizabeth, Frederick V's wife, for certain, but he opposed Frederick claiming the crown of Bohemia. He is counseled by his secretary, George Calvert to make an alliance with Spain by the marriage of Prince Charles to the Spanish Infanta Maria. In this, he hopes to counter to the French and seek neutrality with the Dutch and the German princes."

Robert answered in surprise. "Parliament would certainly not support such a reversal. How long have we fought the Spanish in the Spanish Netherlands? How many Spanish invasions have been attempted? The Dutch have been trusted allies and favorable trading partners. An alliance with Spain? Foolishness!"

Sir John smiled. "You are right that Parliament will abide no such alliance with the King of Spain, but neither is their heart in fighting for Frederick V who has also foolishly upset the balance between protestants and Catholics among the prince-electors to the empire. No, Lieutenant Curtis, parliament is not eager to expand this war."

"Then all hope is lost."

"No, not yet. If the combined armies of Christian of Brunswick and Ernst von Mansfeld reinforce us, we can hold much of the Lower Palatinate until the Danes or Swedes come in support of the Dutch and German protestants. We must know, are they coming? If we are reinforced, perhaps even Parliament and King James himself will recommit to the cause."

Karl nodded. "After Mainz, we will travel north."

The captain of the guard entered the room and bowed to Sir John. "The first barges were filled with salt, coal and linen. The fourth was said to be charcoal, but the barge was very low in the water with less than a full load. I sent the men aboard with shovels and found the bottom filled with iron bars. I am holding the barge. Colonel, Sir John, what are your orders?"

"Charcoal and iron, very good indeed! Commandeer

the barge and hold the crew for questioning. Send for the armorer. I believe there is a steel furnace in Frankenthal; if the Catholic League will not feed us, perhaps they will better arm us."

"Aye Colonel, we will make steel."

"That will be all captain. Wait, send Captain Sir Geoffrey Curtis up to me. I would see him at once."

"Aye Colonel, and good day to you sir."

Turning to Robert, Sir John said, "I understand you are a relation to Sir Geoffrey."

"Sir, he is a cousin and a Lord in Scotland, Baron of Cawmills."

"And you speak as an Englishman."

"The family lands and titles were divided between my grandfather and his brother. Sir Geoffrey's father was Baron of Cawmills in Scotland and my grandfather Barron of Tweedbridge in England. I am the nephew of the Viscount Curtis, Baron of Tweedbridge."

"Most unusual."

"It benefited both monarchies that there were no divided loyalties."

"Well Curtis, that is no longer an impediment."

"No Sir John, King James is now liege to both houses of Curtis."

The colonel nodded. "Right, Sir Geoffrey sees to communications with London, Colonel Vere, Colonel Herbert. And our allies. He will have the most current information on roads and safe travel. Ah, here he is. Come in, Sir Geoffrey. Your cousin requires your help."

"Cousin Robert! How pleased I am to see you well

and returned to service hardly the worse off!"

Sir Geoffrey was older than Robert, short with broad shoulders, wild red hair, and a wiry red beard. His cold blue eyes and furrowed brow betrayed the welcome of his words.

"And what would he and his foreign friends be needin' Sir John?"

"They will travel to Mainz and then north on the orders of the Commander, Colonel Sir Horace. A most important mission, Sir Geoffrey, they need maps, passwords, and information. Provide them anything they ask, food, weapons, clothes."

"Now then, Lieutenant Curtis and Herr Schroeder, I will let you make ready. God preserve you on your journey."

"This way cousin and Herr Schroeder," Sir Geoffrey said as he led them out of Sir John's chambers.

Robert asked as they entered the corridor, "Sir Gerard tells me the recovery of the wounded at the Neckar battle fell to you."

"Yes, that is true, but as I took charge of escorting the ambulatory back to our hospital wagons, I left my man Sharpe to look to those still lying on the battlefield. Good man, Sharpe. Very thorough. Took his time, he did. Only dead he found but recovered many weapons. Too bad he missed you, cousin."

"Yes, Sir Geoffrey, where your man failed, our Merciful Father in Heaven sent a priest, a papist yes, but a true priest to save me. A priest and a compassionate young Calvinist woman. It is now my honor to be of service to them."

Sir Geoffrey replied tersely, "And you have convinced Sir Horace that this rescue mission to Mainz can benefit us with these German 'watchers' eager for us to help them run the Catholic League out of the Palatine. I foresee just one more miserable failure in your lifetime of failures. But I shall do as I am commanded, cousin."

They entered Sir Geoffrey's anteroom where a cuirassier was pacing in front of a window overlooking the Rhine. "Ah, Sharpe! Good that you are here. Sir John directs us to prepare my cousin, Lieutenant Curtis and his German friend, Herr Schroeder to lead a party to Mainz and then proceed north unhindered by the Count of Tilly or the Catholic League. We are to prepare maps and provide what provisions they might need. You have traveled that way; we need to know safe cities or safe houses. We shall mark them on the maps we provide."

Sharpe turned away from the window and stood looking at Robert. He was tall and hardened, with eyes nearly as dark as his hair. The right shoulder of his half armor bore the distinct crease of a sword blow.

CHAPTER 13
MYSTERIES

Karl and Robert found Katharina and Wilhelm sitting in the shade of an inn oblivious to the mugs of beer sitting on the table in front of them. "No Will," Katie could be heard saying. "We can never earn our salvation. It must be God who first calls us. It is his Holy Ghost who opens our heart, and His grace is irresistible! It is by His grace alone that He calls us to Himself and we respond, to be other would allow us to puff up and say we found Him and came to Him, it was our own doing."

"But Katie…"

Karl interrupted. "Ah, Wilhelm, my Katie will make you a Calvinist yet!"

Wilhelm turned to Robert and said, "Robert, what do

you say on this matter? Surely, God is our judge and holds us responsible to obey Him. What need would there be for evangelists and priests, or the ordinances of the church?"

Smiling, Robert replied, "So now it is just Will, so much easier for an Englishman to say than Wilhelm!"

Sitting down and taking a good drink from one of the forgotten beer mugs, Robert wiped his mouth with his sleeve and answered, "Katie speaks of election, a peculiar doctrine of Calvinists. There is indeed Scripture in support of her argument and solid examples. Did not the prophet Jeremiah, speaking for God, say, 'Before I formed you in the womb, I knew you, and before you were born, I consecrated you; I appointed you prophets to the nations.' And Saint Paul said, 'But when He who set me apart when I was born, and who called me by His grace was pleased to reveal His Son to me, in order that I might preach Him among the Gentiles, I did not consult with anyone.'"

Wilhelm nodded. "Yes, yes. God in His sovereignty can do such things, and as you quote, Paul said it was to preach among the Gentiles. If God can simply call us to Himself, why the need to preach?"

"Let me speak for myself," Katie interjected. "Preaching carries the Word of God to men, it comes from the Holy Ghost and illuminates and softens the hearts of men. It is another wonderful grace of God that He chooses to work through His people. It is a gift to serve Him and see Him work His will in men and women."

Robert gave a big nod in approval. "You see now Father Wilhelm, that Katharina Schroeder too, is a priest of God! Does she not intercede on your behalf? This is the true work of the Church: brothers and sisters bringing the gospel of salvation to all men. The right doctrine and dogma will not bring you salvation, though these things are good and worthy pursuits. No, it is by scripture alone we are guided to grace alone, through faith alone in Christ alone to the glory of God alone."

Wilhelm rolled his eyes. "I have heard of the five SOLAS, thank you. But Robert, as you say, Scripture. Does not Saint Peter write? 'The Lord is not slow to fulfill his promise...but is patient toward you not wishing that any should perish, but that all should reach repentance.'"

Robert happily agreed, "Will, you do know your Bible! Yes, and in Timothy, Paul writes, 'God, who desires all people to be saved and come to the knowledge of the truth.' So, you ask, 'why are not all among the elect.' This is indeed a great mystery. God also said, 'Jacob I have loved, and Esau I have hated.' Is God unfair? If God is Holy and loving can He also be unjust? God forbid! Our Heavenly Father comes asking, not demanding. He knows our heart, and we shall never comprehend His mind in this matter. It remains a mystery, just like the Trinity, God in three persons is a mystery that we accept and know to be true."

Katharina put one hands over Wilhelm's and said softly, "Will, your calling, I believe, your election, is a gift not just of salvation to come, but salvation from every fear and doubt. You can know you are secure in your faith, sealed by God and His love for you."

Wilhelm looked down at the table in front of him. "It is true, I never felt worthy of God's salvation. My guilt and sin haunt me."

Katharina took both Wilhelm's hands into hers and answered, "Will, I know you love God and have the heart to serve Him. You must believe me, I know it is a very hard thing to let go of guilt, but we must."

The smile drained from Katie as she reflected on her words and after a brief silence continued, "Faith can make it happen. We must learn to just trust Him. Trust in His love. Yes, we must first trust God, then obedience will follow. It must follow from our love for God who first loved us."

Wilhelm sat silently.

Katharina said sighed softly. "I pray for you, Will. I know you are a man of deep faith and love of God. I pray you find peace and assurance of your faith."

Robert observing closely, realized the wisdom of Katie's words came from experience, an experience that must still weigh heavily on this very special young woman.

Karl did not recognize the pain behind his daughter's words, stepped behind Wilhelm and Robert, placed a hand on each man's shoulder and said, "I praise God that He has called you, Will, and you too, Robert, to this time and this good work He has set before you. Take heart and trust in the Lord."

Wilhelm looked up, smiled weakly and said, "We must

be seeing to the release of Johann. What news Robert? When do we leave?"

"Karl, can you talk to the boat captain? I believe the river is still the fastest and surely safest route to Mainz. We need to consider how we arrange an audience with the Archbishop, how we shall argue his cause and our plans after Mainz."

As Karl set off to talk to the boat captain, Robert saw the captain of the guard walking across the market square. Coming alongside the captain, Robert asked, "Just a word captain, I see your walk to be quite determined,"

"Walk along with me, Lieutenant, I am on my way to the steel furnace. The colonel will be expecting a report. Five tons of iron and charcoal, in three weeks, should yield five tons of steel. Imagine what defenses we can devise with cold hard steel!"

"Three weeks you say? I know nothing of such matters."

"Come along and learn. It is quite straight forward you know. Just need a good furnace and fuel to heat it."

"You can do that here?"

They arrived at a forge workshop at the city wall. Against the outer wall was a large oven with a massive chimney rising above it. A large pile of coal was heaped nearby. Robert saw men carrying iron bars into the upper chamber of the oven.

"They will lay a row of iron bars and then top it with charcoal. They will continue to stack, alternating the iron bars and charcoal until all the iron is in the furnace. This furnace is large enough for twelve tons of iron so that we can easily process all in one batch."

"All of this baked at once?"

"When the iron and charcoal are in the furnace, and the armorer and steelmaker add their salts, and then they will seal the top of the oven tightly with clay to hold the heat. The fire is set below in the lower chamber, the furnace, and fueled with coal. The iron and charcoal will bake for one week with a very hot fire from below. After a week, the oven will remain sealed and allowed to cool for two weeks."

"And then steel is removed?"

"Not good steel, but 'blister bars,' which still require refining. The blister bars must be welded and forged, then reformed, welded and forged at least three times again before a good quality shear steel is ready to be shaped and forged into bars, chains, swords or gun barrels."

"Gun barrels? How do they make that hole in the barrel?"

"You speak of the bore. The steel bar is flattened in the forge and shaped around a mandrel slightly smaller than the final bore. Once forged around the mandrel, it is welded and reamed to the proper bore."

"How did you come to know so much of steel and forging?"

"I enjoyed watching the work in the forge on my father's manor. You said you needed to speak to me; I'm sure it wasn't how to make steel."

Robert's face grew serious. "When I mentioned my

cousin, Sir Geoffrey, you started to say something before we were interrupted by the warning shot."

"Yes, probably nothing but it seemed strange to me. Our battalion was in the rear when the Neckar valley engagement took place. Word came down that a skirmish occurred and that we should collect all the wounded and stragglers. When we heard that an officer of the cuirassiers reported among the dead, I saw Sir Geoffrey lower his head and laugh to himself. The colonel saw too and asked what he found amusing. He replied, 'My pardon, sir, my mind was elsewhere, but please, allow me and my men attend to the wounded and stragglers, no need to slow the whole regiment, sir.'"

"I had heard my cousin was ordered to recover the wounded."

"Yes, he immediately summoned that strange man of his, a Mister Sharpe. He wears the armor of a cuirassier but is really just a courier."

"What do you know of Mister Sharpe, sir?"

"Quiet man, never speaks up. Don't know if he even has a mate in the regiment. Sharpe reports to your cousin. Understand he is both a scout and courier, always off somewhere. It seems only Sir Geoffrey knows for certain."

Pausing, the captain said. "Right, need to talk to the steelmaker, make sure he has enough coal and if all is in order."

"Yes sir, I will be leaving you to your duties. Thank you, sir."

Robert returned to the ratskeller where Katharina

and Wilhelm were still sitting with their beers before them.

Katie sighed and then said, "I was trying to explain to Will why protestants find the mass so abhorrent. I told him our Lord Jesus died once for the sins of all mankind and to put Him on the cross again, so to speak, is both presumptuous and cruel. He finds such objections surprising."

"Will and Katie? You must let me call you Katie or I shall certainly feel left out."

She replied, "Yes, Robert; you may call me Katie as well. Knowing how forward you are I will allow it."

Robert sat down beside Wilhelm and said, "My friend, the mass is not just cruel and presumptuous in recreating the death of Christ, but it has been used a cudgel to punish good Christian men and women your church elders have sought to persecute. The absurd reliquary mounted in a crucifix above priest or bishop of inquisition, containing only wine dipped communion bread but declared to be the Holy body and blood of our Savior, and a sign of His authority for the unholy proceedings held below. How can such abuse of the Eucharist not be found repulsive?"

Wilhelm answered, "Our Lord said, 'Take, this is my body broken for you."

"Yes, and He also said, 'Unless you eat the flesh of the Son of Man and drink His blood, you have no life in you.' He finished by saying, 'He who eats this bread will live forever.' And later He said, 'Do this in remembrance of me.' The Lord's Supper, like baptism, is an ordinance of the Church, a command given by our Lord for all believers. He speaks of Spiritual food and of communion between our Lord and a union with every member of His Church in all time."

Katie spoke in her soft but sure voice, "We are commanded to take the supper in remembrance of His sacrifice and great salvation. We are not to forget the price of our salvation but come together in humble confession of our sin and thankfulness for His grace and mercy which binds us all together in one great body, His Church. It offers not salvation but is a memory of the price our Savior paid."

"But even the Lutherans, I'm told, believe the elements are somehow the very body and blood of Christ," Will replied.

"I hold to the Anglican teaching of the 'real presence' of Christ in the elements, it is a mystery of how it occurs, but then so much of the Spirit is a mystery. The point remains that the presence of our Savior is not predicated on a repeated death of our Christ. He is no longer on the cross. He has ascended to Heaven and sits at the right of the Father where He shall reign forever, Glory be to His name!"

Wilhelm looked across to Katharina and then to Robert. "You almost convinced me. But I see an error in your arguments. Scripture can have only one meaning. You have described three interpretations of the elements of the Lord's Supper. The very flesh and blood of Christ, only bread and wine taken in memory, or some undefined spiritual presence. And this regarding a very command of Christ! No, my friends, only one can be right, and that is what the Roman Catholic Church does authoritatively, under the inspiration of the Holy Ghost. Since there can be only one truth, the Holy Church must be the one to teach what is true."

Karl returned with the boat captain. All eyes turned to him, and he said, "Good to find you all together, the captain is willing to take us on to Mainz but asks of our plans once we arrive. He will say he is delivering passengers afraid to travel by road and that he is seeking a cargo to continue down river. What business do we declare? And how do we arrange a meeting with the Archbishop? We must assume those who have worked so hard against this meeting will be waiting. The captain will be some days in arranging a cargo and can wait for us up to three days; then we are on our own."

"Will our pursuers be waiting in Mainz? Can we assume word has reached the Count of Tilly that our mission to provide information to Colonel Vere has been compromised?"

Wilhelm said, "Don Pedro and Maximilian Greiffenclau may not be of one accord with Don Lorenzo. The pope may be interested in the outcome of the war but the others, I fear, have different interests. No, we must prepare for treachery. If we can speak first with an official of the city, I believe I have the way to meet with Archbishop von Kronberg. But we can comfort knowing our short trip downriver should be safe."

After Karl left with the boat Captain and Robert made

his excuses to keep his appointment with Sir Geoffrey, Katie sat smiling warmly at Wilhelm. "I know the reason you are not convinced. For you do not believe only the Roman Church teaches the truth. You have said so yourself! You know the indulgences and corrupt practices taught and accepted were reformed at the Council of Trent, though with no real change. You know the pope accepts the different teachings of the Eastern Rite Catholics. No, Will, I understand why you hold back. All your life you believed serving God meant serving the Church. You have taken a vow as a priest. It tears at you. I know it does. But I know God loves you and your oaths of service are to Him not to a man in Rome. Know that I understand and will support you and pray for you. You have become very dear to me."

Katie got up walked behind Wilhelm and hugged him tightly.

Robert returned to his cousin's post and received the maps and passwords promised to him. As he got up to leave, Sir Geoffrey said "There has been news from home. Thought you should know. Your cousin, Jacob, the son of your uncle Viscount, Sir James, has died of fever. Sir James himself is very ill. It would seem your father is next in line for the Barony of Tweedbridge. Your father is saved from bankruptcy and debtors prison after all. And to think Sir James and your father have not spoken in years. Stay safe Robert you may yet receive the title... If you live."

"I have never considered such an event. Who would follow me in succession?"

Sir Geoffrey smiled. "Why me, of course. The Curtis estates would be united again, just as they should never have been divided."

By late afternoon everything was prepared, Robert, Karl, Wilhelm, and Katharina made their way back through the streets of Frankenthal, out the gate at the river wall and on to the wharf. The captain helped Katharina board. Karl followed and then stepped back on the stern deck to speak with the captain. Robert was carrying his campaign chest over the gangway when Wilhelm turned back and said, "Let me help you with that."

Both Robert and Wilhelm were on the gangplank when at a groaning sound, and a loud creak, Karl shouted: "Robert, Wilhelm jump! Jump! Now!"

Wilhelm dove into the boat landing on Katharina who clutched his head to her bosom while she wailed in fear and Robert fell onto the wharf as a large wine barrel swung across the gangway where the two men had been standing. The barrel swung across the boat and back over the wharf and smashed against the wall. Red wine bloodied the wall and wharf as the cargo hook swayed back and forth hanging from the loading boom. A handling line attached above the hook, hung severed, several feet from the hook. The other end of the line was cut just above the belaying cleat on a post beside the gate. As Wilhelm lay in Katharina's bosom feeling at once afraid and comforted, Karl saw the door in the gate was closing from the other side.

CHAPTER 14
MAINZ

The boat made steady progress down the Rhine. Grapes were being harvested on the steep hillside rising from the river, and the autumn sun provided a golden glimmer on the water. The soft breeze filled ambiance was disturbed by the tension of all on board. Karl voiced the obvious. "We must be wary at all times. Our pursuers may strike anywhere and at any time."

"It seems Captain Stock and Don Lorenzo cannot or will not protect us after all," Wilhelm began. "I fear Don Pedro and Maximilian Greiffenclau have other motives, be they land, titles or wealth."

"We cannot forget Robert's attacker. Perhaps it was he they tried to kill," Karl offered.

Robert replied, "It could be that the attack was meant for both Wilhelm and me. It seems those with a motive to kill me have ties to the three clerics pursuing Wilhelm and Katie. But how could they have been brought together?"

Karl stroked his chin. "Opportunity maybe? A common cause might bring together men who are working against Frederick, the Dutch and the protestants of Germany. But what is it that connects you, Robert, other than coincidence that these same men have a motive to see you dead?"

"I don't know, but we must assume that we are all now being hunted and unsafe by day or night, here on the river, in town or on the road."

The passengers settled into a troubled silence. Wilhelm reached into a bag and brought out the Bible Robert had given him. "I have been working on my English. I can read many of the verses I have memorized. Would you help me with my pronunciation?"

Robert looked up. "Of course! Please, read to us in English."

Wilhelm opened his Bible and leafed through the pages until he stopped in the Gospel of Luke. Clearing his throat Wilhelm read slowly and carefully, "They said to each other, 'Did not our hearts burn within us while He talked to us on the road, while He opened to us the Scriptures?"

Robert smiled broadly, shaking his head yes. He replied, "Very good my friend! Your accent is quite thick, but the words were clear and understood. Tell me, Will, why that verse?"

"It has been a favorite verse of mine since I first came across it while reading in my seminary cell at night. It speaks to me. God's very Word! It burns within my heart. I feel just as the disciples must have felt being taught the prophecies and promises of God by our Lord as they walked that dusty road to Emmaus."

Robert looked to the others and said, "Karl, Katie, there is no need to convince our brother Will on the saving grace of Jesus. God's Word speaks to his heart. The Holy Ghost has breathed the breath of life into his soul and will complete His good work in him; I am certain!"

Katie's face shown with love for Will, Karl nodded with a smile, and Will blushed.

Katie smiled brightly and said, "Read some more, Will, perhaps I can learn English with you."

Karl said, "Yes, say the verse in German and then English, Katie too, has a good knowledge of the Bible."

The adrenalin and tension each felt from the attempt on Will and Robert's lives in Frankenthal slowly drained away as first Will and then Katie recited verse after favorite verse in thick German-accented English, with Robert occasionally offering help with pronunciation. Soon the captain announced the sighting of the walls of Mainz. As they looked up, they could see the red sandstone towers of the five-hundred-year-old Mainz Cathedral.

Karl said, "Mainz, the home of Gutenberg, the man whose printing press helped give the Bible to the people."

"And the seat of the Prince-Elector Archbishop and

Archchancellor to the Emperor and prelate of the Roman Catholic Church over all of the Germans,"Wilhelm said.

Katie responded. "And the jailer of my brother Johann, Grant O God, that he is safe."

"And a deadly place for all of us," Robert reminded.

"We must be certain we are not handed over to Don Pedro or Maximilian Greiffenclau when we arrive. They are certainly waiting for us. They will recognize the boat and be waiting with orders from the Count of Tilly."

"If we come ashore before the city we will be seen. Likewise, if we sail past, we will be followed and watched."

The captain offered, "If I wanted to enter Mainz undetected, I would enter the Main River across from Mainz and sail up to Hochst. Is not Christian of Brunswick marching south towards Hochst as we speak? It would appear we seek refuge with Duke Christian's army and Don Pedro and Maximilian Greiffenclau would be foolish to attempt to follow. Once out of sight on the Main River you could find your way into Mainz by small boat and road."

Karl looked at Robert, and both men nodded. The captain continued. "I could make my entry into Mainz a couple of days behind you and wait as we agreed."

"Captain, please make for Hochst!"

Hochst was on the north side of the Main River at the confluence with the Wetterau River. Frankfort was on the Main River on the opposite shore of the Wetterau, which turned north into Hesse-Darmstadt while the Main continued Southeast, then east and wound its way to

Wurzberg and on to Schweinfurt. Traffic on the river was heavy, all the merchants expected the approach of Duke Christian, and the march of the Count of Tilly to cut off his planned joining with the remnants of Frederick's army led by Count von Mansfeld. A good profit could be made by staying and supplying the approaching armies, but the far safer bet was to leave before the fighting and pillaging.

Many of the boats carried refugees, those wealthy enough to travel, protestants seeking safety in the United Netherlands and the few Catholics who fled Mainz returning home from the Upper Palatine or Bavaria. The wharf at Hochst was chaotic, but the captain managed to tie up alongside another boat.

Karl ordered, "Stay here while I speak with a friend in the market. The captain will find a boat for our passage back onto the Rhine. If we head back down the Main River into the Rhine and beyond Mainz, we can enter the city by road."

An hour later, Karl returned. "I have sent a tapestry 'design' to Colonel Vere. Three armies are believed to be converging on Hochst but are still many days away. Christian of Brunswick is moving south from Hesse on the west side of the Wetterau. The Count of Tilly's main force is now north of the Main River heading west towards the Wetterau, and Ernst von Mansfeld's small army is in Darmstadt, holding the north of the Neckar above Colonel Vere's men, waiting for Christian's army to arrive. For now, the pressure will be off our English friends, but the Count of Tilly's men will be thick as thieves. His scouts watching every road for protestant soldiers."

"Will he be watching the roads west of Mainz?" Robert asked.

"He must be wary of any return of the Dutch from the United Netherlands. He will also watch boats coming upriver from Breda."

The boat captain made his way across gangplanks and enthusiastically jumped back aboard his boat. "I have made passage for you on a fast boat that will take you past Mainz this afternoon and turnaround after dark and drop you at a small brewer's pier between Mainz and Heidesheim am Rhine. From there you can walk in the northern gate early in the morning."

Wilhelm asked, "Will the daylight passage be safe for Katie?

"There will be much traffic in the afternoon, but anyone passing at night will be considered a smuggler or spy. That is why I have found a captain experienced in such matters. He knows how to 'disappear' after dark."

That afternoon saw Robert, Karl, Wilhelm, and Katharina seated close together in a small boat with four other passengers. Four men at oars supplemented the lateen-rigged sail. In the small hold, an unknown cargo was covered by a tarp. Everyone on board was warned not to approach the cargo on pain of being thrown overboard. The captain, dressed in the same black cloak as his crewmembers, had the look about of him of a man whose threats should be taken seriously.

Half an hour after departing Hochst, while the boat

threaded its way through the heavy river traffic, Robert noticed a man standing on the deck of a boat going up the Main River. He appeared to be studying each passing boat closely. As the boats, passed their eyes locked on each other. Robert immediately recognized the dark, cold eyes of Mr. Sharpe. He was not wearing his armor, but Robert was sure it was him. Robert watched as Sharpe could be seen pointing and arguing with the captain of his boat. It did not turn around but continued upstream to either Hochst or Frankfort.

They made the Rhine River across from Mainz less than an hour before sunset, and the boat turned north, downriver. Just after sunset they passed Heidsheim am Rhine and after a bend in the river put the town out of sight, the captain skillfully piloted the boat into a small channel shielded from the River by thick trees and underbrush. Once again Robert and his friends found themselves waiting in silence for the still darkness of the night. The chorus of frogs and insects the only sounds on the now quiet river.

The half-moon was high in the sky before the captain once again piloted the boat back on the river. The crew was well practiced in rowing silently. The boat ghosted by Heidsheim on the far side of the river, close to the bank and the protective cover and shadows of trees and bushes. The lights of Heidsheim disappeared as they rounded a bend, then they crossed back to the western side of the river and came upon an unlighted, small pier. The crew held the boat alongside as Karl jumped out first and signaled the others to follow, silently. Wilhelm helped

Katie, and once Robert, the last off, was standing on the pier, the boat was gone, silently sliding downriver with its remaining passengers and unknown cargo.

Karl led the group to the river road, and they walked about a half mile before coming to another road leading inland. Robert led them uphill, away from the river. Only after they were on the high road, above the river, where their voices could no longer carry across the water, did Robert speak. "We must walk another three miles to Mainz; we can take our time. Better that we arrive after sunrise to arouse less suspicion."

The weary travelers were waiting in the edge of the woods as the gate to Mainz slowly swung open just after sunrise. A sentry took his post in a small guardhouse just outside of the city gate.

Karl stood up and said, "Time to go."

As they approached the gate, the sentry took a position in front of the gate. He signaled them to stop and asked, "What is your business?"

Karl answered, "Travelers seeking an inn."

The sentry looked closely at Katharina and then Wilhelm and Robert. "Where do you come from and what is your business in Mainz?"

"We are traveling back from the north and seek to refresh ourselves as we travel south."

The sentry nodded and said, "Wait here," and stepped inside the gate.

The sentry returned with his captain who ordered, "You will come with me."

As they walked forward into the city behind the

captain, Wilhelm spoke up. "Captain, please read this sealed pass," as he took out an envelope and handed it the captain.

Surprised, the captain said, "What is this? A pass? Why didn't you say something sooner? Let me look at it."

While the captain opened and read the pass, Maximilian Greiffenclau walked up and said, "Thank you, captain! These are the people we seek. I can take them from here."

The captain of the guard read the pass and then said, "My pardon sir, how can I assist you?"

Greiffenclau spoke up. "I will take these people…"

The captain ignored him. "Father Hahn where can I escort you?"

"My friends and I desire an audience with the Elector Archbishop. Can you see we arrive safely?"

Greiffenclau tried again. "My father is the Archbishop's Auxiliary Bishop; I can take them…"

"Captain, I must insist on your personal escort. You alone are now accountable for our safety."

"I tell you, captain, I will take them…"

"Deacon Greiffenclau, if you have business with these people, you can take it up with the Elector Archbishop. This way Father Hahn and guests."

CHAPTER 15
THE ELECTOR ARCHBISHOP

Wilhelm, a pass signed by the emperor? You had this all along?" Katharina asked.

"Before I left Vienna, my father gave me a sealed letter and told me to present it if I found myself in trouble. I never read the letter or broke the seal."

Robert asked, "You must have known its content; it bore the emperor's seal. Why didn't you use it in Eberbach?"

"He started to but then put it away," Karl replied. "The clerk, Joseph Meyer, saw him. He told me Wilhelm was carrying a sealed letter."

"Karl, you knew? Yes, it is true. I did not believe I could trust the magistrate who acted against the protocols of the army, the emperor or treaties of the empire. No, I knew he was in league with my attackers and those who abducted Johann and threatened Katharina. Showing him the letter would only mean the end of me and Katharina as well."

"You waited to find an official with no attachment to our pursuers. You were very wise, my friend," said Karl.

The captain of the guard led them briskly through the ancient streets of Mainz, past the large homes and businesses of the wealthy merchant class with their shops facing the street and residences above. Large stone tablets, carved with family crests, stood in front of the tall half-timbered mansions. They passed many churches; church attendance was required in Mainz at least every Sunday. It seemed the city had as many churches as people, but indeed the city was crowded.

Karl explained, "You wonder about all of the large ornate churches? Donations of the elderly funded them. It was the practice in Mainz that the church would care for the elderly in their infirmity and final days in return for the gifting of the elderly or infirm person's full estate. For a citizen with no surviving family to care for them, this was the only option."

As they walked past the university, Karl recounted how the Reformation had come to Mainz. "Luther sent a letter to Archbishop Albert, but he was not convinced. After a while, Archbishop Albert became tolerant of Protestants, and they grew into an influential community. When Sebastian of Heusenstamm succeeded Albert as Archbishop-Elector, he was determined to root out all Protestant tendencies. His Auxiliary Bishop,

Michael of Helding ruthlessly led the purge. Archbishop Sebastian, a friend, and admirer of Erasmus called a provincial synod in Mainz with the support of the Archbishop of Trent, John of Isenburg-Grenzau. They sought to call the Catholic Church to a counter-reformation, indeed they carried their ideas to the Council of Trent, but when the Lutheran, Albert, Margrave of Brandenburg-Kulmbach attacked Mainz in 1552, Sebastian became unshakeable in his support of the doctrine, 'Whose realm, his religion,' which meant that the religion of the ruler dictated the religion of the ruled."

Wilhelm commented, "Fortunately, in Vienna, ruled by the Hapsburgs, our Catholic faith was stable, but in much of Germany…"

Karl nodded. "Indeed, there has been no stability since. This doctrine was accepted within the Holy Roman Empire in the Peace of Augsburg. The ruling Elector, Prince, Duke, Count, Margrave or Archbishop could dictate the religion of his state. This meant every city or state was either Roman Catholic or Lutheran and any other believer was a heretic, including Calvinists and especially Anabaptists. It also meant religious turmoil as the constant wars between the German states forced an ever back and forth change in religion as constant as the rising and falling of the tide. Only when Elector Frederick and other princes adopted Calvinism could our faith be practiced in the open."

"It is absurd to me," Robert replied.

"Apparently, it is not absurd to your English kings.

Have they not declared the Church of England the only church of the realm? Is not Sunday worship required, and the tithe as well?"

Wilhelm added, "And all Roman Catholic priests banned from the country."

Robert lowered his head and sighed. "And good Christian men and women martyred for standing on their faith."

The Prince Archbishop's palace was near the towering Mainz Cathedral. The captain of the guard made his presence known and insisted he would not leave Wilhelm and his friends until personally received by the Archbishop. Karl walked slowly through the large receiving room examining the large tapestries adorning the walls as the others waited nervously.

A door at the end of the hall swung open, a guard in ceremonial uniform stepped out and announced, "The Prince Elector Archbishop of Mainz, Johann Schweikard von Kronberg."

A man dressed in an elegant black coat, a white collar around his neck and a rich black cape over his shoulder with a large jeweled pectoral cross showing beneath the open mantle, entered the room. His immaculately groomed shoulder length hair and van dyke beard were white without a trace of gray or black and his blue eyes focused with intelligence at the group standing before him.

"Who bears a letter from our Emperor and demands an audience?"

Wilhelm stepped forward, bowed and kissed the ring

of the Archbishop. "Your Excellency, I am Father Wilhelm Hahn, here is the letter I bear."

Wilhelm gave the letter to the Archbishop and waited as he read it.

"Thank you, captain. You found it necessary to escort these people personally?"

"A deacon, one Maximilian Greiffenclau, had presented papers from the magistrate of Eberbach seeking the arrest of this man and woman. When they entered the north gate this morning, they were recognized, and I was about to give them into the custody of deacon Greiffenclau. But when I was shown the letter bearing the Emperor's seal, I determined I must see them here and let you judge between them."

"Maximilian Greiffenclau? The son of my Auxiliary Bishop, Georg Friederich von Greiffenclau?"

"I would not know the deacon or his father, your Excellency."

"You may return to your post, captain. You have done well."

"Father Hahn, I am obliged to see you. Please, come into my chamber. Your friends as well. I will hear your case."

As Karl walked over to join them, he asked, "Your Excellency, what has become of your Eden, Heaven on Earth, Tapestry?"

The Archbishop smiled. "Ah! Herr Schroeder, it has been too long! Yes, the garden tapestry is a favorite of mine as well. I have moved it to my private chambers."

Robert quietly followed the others into the room and

stood back by the door careful not to join the conversation. Inside this private study with the door closed behind him, the Archbishop's face turned serious, he turned to Wilhelm and asked, "What is so urgent that you could not resolve with the magistrate in Eberbach? And why did you wait until you were here in Mainz before presenting the Emperor's letter?'

"Your Excellency, I am here on behalf of this good woman, Fraulein Katharina Schroeder and her father, Karl, whom I surmise you know. Johann Schroeder, the Calvinist pastor of the church in Eberbach, was abducted without notice or any record of the magistrate or the army. When Katharina came to me to inquire as to where he was taken, her intent to minister to her brother until trial, I agreed out of Christian charity to find out what I could."

"Karl, I did not know you were a Calvinist, or that your son was a protestant pastor."

"We talked of tapestries and many other things, your excellency, but never my religious beliefs. I have always enjoyed serving you and found you to be a wise and righteous man, but yes, it is true. I hope we can still do business and enjoy our conversations."

"Quite so, I have always favored goodwill between protestants and the church. I am afraid the empire cannot survive if the balance of trust is disturbed. I also fear that this war may destroy that balance and lead to chaos, endless bloodshed and the destruction of Germany. I urged Ferdinand not to send the Count of Tilly's Army of Flanders into the Palatinate. I pray that sanity is restored before it is too late. I digress, please go on Father Hahn."

"I was told there were no records of his arrest. I was warned not to ask such questions in the future. When Katharina began asking questions in the city, she began to receive threats and attempts were made on both of our lives. We heard rumors of a prisoner taken to the dungeon of the Elector Archbishop of Mainz."

Katarina spoke softly. "Your Excellency, if my brother is here, I ask only to care for him until his trial. I trust God to protect him and see that justice is done, for I know he is innocent. Johann is a faithful servant of God, just as Father Wilhelm, who has been so honorable in all of his efforts."

Archbishop von Kronberg smiled at Katharina. "Child, be certain we will sort this out."

"Karl, what was all that business about deacon Greiffenclau?"

"Excellency, Wilhelm could tell you more of Maximilian Greiffenclau and his cohorts, Don Lorenzo, a papal envoy to the Count of Tilly and Don Pedro an Abbot from the Spanish Netherlands, but they have been pursuing us since we raised questions of my son's abduction."

Wilhelm continued. "Yes, your excellency, they were charged with assigning priests and magistrates in the cities and towns taken by the emperor's army. They assigned me to the church in Eberbach. I did not know them well as they kept to themselves, though they could often be seen arguing. I found it unusual that they appeared most interested in records of church lands taken after the days of Martin Luther. Ever since we fled Eberbach, they have pursued us aggressively and indeed had requested our arrest here in Mainz."

The Archbishop sighed, and then stood up and walked to his window looking out but his mind was elsewhere. He walked to the door, stopped and said, "Wait here."

He stepped outside the room and said to a guard, "Please send for the Auxiliary Bishop. I would see him at once."

He started back for the door and then stopped turned and said, "And for the head jailer as well."

When he returned, Karl said, "Your Excellency, you are the Archchancellor to the Emperor, you know that the abduction of protestants from a free city violates the Treaty of Ulm. Surely, the Emperor cannot be seen going back on his treaty, on his word as the Elected Emperor."

"My friend, you are not a diplomat. The Treaty of Ulm no longer binds the Emperor. The treaty was made with the Protestant Union, which no longer exists. The Union disbanded when they sued for peace at the fall of Mainz. And Eberbach may have been a free city once, but it accepted the protection of the Elector of the Palatinate when it chose to become protestant. No, my friend, it is now recovered territory of the Emperor. He has revoked Frederick's title and likely will give it to the Duke of Bavaria. The Duke will abide no Protestant Churches in his realm. All citizens will return to the mother faith of Rome or be expelled. I am afraid your son will not be permitted to pastor your church in Eberbach as long as it remains under the control of the emperor or his new chosen count."

Karl looked at Katharina and could find no words to respond.

"I am sorry for you, my friend. There was no need for this to happen. I warned Frederick against taking the crown, King of Bohemia. What was he thinking? It is true the Emperor had not visited there in years and that the people obtained the right of Protestant worship and yes, their nobles offered him the crown, but the title, King of Bohemia, belongs to the Emperor himself!"

Karl nodded. "I find the Church grows best where the ruler is absent."

"Well, I may argue that point, but it was most foolish for a Protestant Elector to challenge Emperor Ferdinand. He is not like Emperor Matthias or his brother Emperor Rudolf who was instrumental in my election here in Mainz. Both Rudolf and Matthais pursued conciliation with Protestant Electors and religious tolerance where the Protestant faith took hold throughout the empire. I have argued the same to Emperor Ferdinand, to no avail. He and his favored counselors seek to reimpose Catholicism by the sword. An imposed faith is no faith. But my voice is no longer heard. I fear even my auxiliary bishop seeks to fight a Catholic crusade here in Germany."

There was a knock on the door, and the guard announced, "Your Excellency, the Auxiliary Bishop, von Greiffenclau is here as you requested."

Georg Friederich von Greiffenclau-zu-Vollards was a small man, finely dressed and immaculately groomed. He paraded into the Archbishop Elector's office with his head up, filled with self-importance.

"Ah, Bishop Georg, please come in. These good Christians come from Eberbach in search of a brother said to be in my dungeon. His name is Johann Schroeder; I do not know what crime he is accused of, other than, perhaps being a Protestant pastor. Are you aware of this man?"

"Your Excellency, I do not recall..."

There was another knock on the door, the guard announced, "Your Excellency, the head jailer as you requested."

As the jailer nervously entered the room, the Archbishop said, "You were saying, Georg?"

"Yes, excellency I started to say, I do not recall the specific charges against this man, the magistrate is still drawing the charges in..."

"He is from Eberbach, the magistrate should never have sent him here," The Archbishop replied harshly.

To the jailer, he asked, "Do you know a prisoner named Johann Schroeder?"

"Yes, excellency, he has been here several weeks. He is kept separate from others."

"Why is he separate? Is he healthy?"

"He appears so, excellency, I was told to keep him alone and feed him well, he has important information."

"I will hear his case tomorrow. See that he is provided clean clothes and, no, you will permit his sister to provide him clean clothes and see to his preparation."

Bishop Greiffenclau spoke up. "Excellency, his case is

not ready, the papers…"

"Papers, yes, I understand there are no papers in Eberbach either."

Turning to Karl, he said, "Herr Schroeder, do I have your word as a Christian Gentleman to present your son here tomorrow at ten o'clock if I release him in your custody?"

"Yes, Excellency, you have my word."

"Jailer, you will release the prisoner, Johann Schroeder into the custody of this man, Herr Karl Schroeder, immediately. Is that understood?"

"Yes, Excellency."

"And Bishop Greiffenclau you will be prepared with the charges."

"But excellency…"

"That is all Georg."

"And Herr Schroeder, have him here presentable tomorrow at ten."

Turning to Katharina, he smiled softly and said, "Fraulein Schroeder, let me know if your brother has been mistreated in any way. Now go and remember me in your prayers."

As everyone followed the jailer out of the room, the Archbishop said, "Father Hahn, stay here. I would have a further word with you."

Wilhelm could not hide the surprise and concern from his face. He turned around and sheepishly replied, "Excellency, I am your servant."

Once the others had left the room, the Archbishop said, "I find your zealous actions on behalf of a man, a protestant pastor, most unusual. You appear to be well acquainted with Fraulein Schroeder, and the silent Englishman in your company."

"Englishman?"

"Well he cannot follow a simple conversation in German, and his boots appear those of an English soldier."

"Yes Excellency, we have come to know each other quite well. We have been together through perilous times, in hiding and through a dangerous journey. I have come to trust them well and will admit to a certain fondness."

"Have they discussed their Protestant beliefs with you?"

"Excellency, we have had respectful discussions and debates. We debate as brothers and sisters, followers of our Lord and Savior."

"Is this appropriate for an untested priest not schooled in such matters, unauthorized and unsupervised by your Bishop?"

"Excellency, I come to you as the prelate over Germany, there is no Bishop for Eberbach."

"I observed this fondness, and perhaps an attraction between you and Fraulein Schroeder. Has your desire for her influenced your actions?"

"Excellency, I must assure you she is most chaste, and there has been nothing inappropriate in our relationship. We are never alone anymore…"

"Anymore?"

"For a short while, we were alone in hiding until we

could arrange safe passage here. Excellency, you know her father, Herr Karl Schroeder is a good and righteous gentleman, and the silent Englishman is a priest, I mean…"

"What do you mean?"

"I mean, he was once a priest in England but has been disillusioned by the factions within the Church."

"The heretic English Church no doubt. Father Wilhelm, you make my case. I fear you may be losing your way. Come with me."

Wilhelm followed as the Archbishop led him out of the chamber down a magnificent hall lined with paintings and tapestries and through a heavy oak door. The hallway on the other side of the door was unadorned cold gray stone with only a few sconce torches to light the way. Halfway down the hall, the Archbishop pushed open a windowless door to reveal a small cell. The room had but one candle, a pitcher of water, a bowl, a small blanket and a crucifix on the wall. A small window, high on the wall, provided modest light near the ceiling.

"Father Hahn, you will stay here. You will meditate on your vows and your duty. Prayer, meditation, confession, and penance are good for the soul. We will speak again."

Wilhelm silently entered the room and the door shut behind him.

Wilhelm sat down on the floor, opened his bag, took out the Bible Robert had given him and began to read.

CHAPTER 16
THE PRISONER

The jailer led Karl, Robert, and Katharina out through the reception room to a small door behind the guard post. The hall behind the door sloped down towards daylight flowing through an iron gate. As they approached the gate, they saw a small walled-in courtyard. The austere yard was little more than a light well perhaps ten to twelve feet square surrounded on all sides by a ten-foot high wall. A solid oak door, strapped in steel was securely shut, barred and bolted at the far end. A bell hung above the door with a closed portal under it. A guard stood at attention inside the door.

Not exiting the gate, the jailer led them around the landing in front of the gate and down another dark

sloping hallway heading deep under the palace. Turning
the corner, they heard voices echoing incoherently up the
cold, dark, stone tunnel. A guard sat by a small table
outside another heavy iron strapped oak door. There was
a slit in the door at eye level that could be slid open. The
guard's post was lighted by a small ceiling window well.
Beside the door was a wooden rack lined with pistols. A
large ring of keys hung beside it.

As the head jailer began to descend the hallway, the
guard very quickly stood up and slid the panel closed
across the small window. The head jailer, irritated, said,
"Heiko, must you listen to his incessant noise?"

"Captain, it helps make the time pass. He is loud
because his interrogator has just left, called away by a
deacon waving a paper."

"Did you read this paper? What was it? Who signed it?"

"No sir, the interrogator heard the demands of the
deacon and came immediately. They both left without a
word."

The jailer turned to Karl and said, "You will wait here.
I will bring the prisoner and escort you out."

"Open the door, Heiko, your entertainer will no
longer keep you awake."

Muffled sounds became apparent as the heavy door
creaked open. The distinct sound of the doxology being
sung broke through the dark hall.

As the song finished a loud voice called out, "Gunther,
has the pain lessened, my brother? Pray with me
Gunther, pray all of you, my brothers! Was not the good
King David, a man after God's own heart, unjustly

pursued and persecuted before he saw the salvation of the Lord? Even so, David praised God and sang to Him, 'Wait on the Lord, be of good courage, and He shall strengthen your heart! Take courage and wait on the Lord!'"

"That's enough, Johann, you can pray for the others after your trial tomorrow. You will be released to your father until then."

"Papa? My papa is here? I am to be released?"

"Keep praying, heretic, you still face trial by the Archbishop tomorrow morning."

Heiko turned the key to open the cell door. As it creaked open voices began to shout, "Remember me, brother Johann." "Pray for me pastor." "Brother Johann, I will pray that the Lord Himself be your defender!"

As Johann's footsteps echoed on the stone floor, a chorus of voices arose joyfully singing. "Praise God from whom all blessings flow..."

As Johann came to the door at the guard station, he shouted, "Brothers, we are brothers forever in the Lord. It is written, 'Remain confident of this, I will see the goodness of the Lord in the land of the living!' Wait on the Lord my friends, wait on the Lord."

Smiling at Heiko, Johann said, "I will remember your son in my prayers. Be of good courage brother." The head jailer looked disapprovingly, but Heiko did not attempt to hide the peace that came across his face.

As Johann emerged from the jail corridor, Katharina rushed up to hug him, her eyes filled with tears. Karl was smiling broader and brighter than Robert had ever seen.

"My son, you are well. Tell me Johann is this a prison or a church?"

Johann looked puzzled. "Father, is not this world a prison of sin? Did not our Lord come to set the prisoner free? Is not the Church called to minister to the prisoner? Then said with a smile, what pastor does not long for his congregation to linger and listen? Father, I am content to preach the Word wherever I am sent."

Katharina sobbed, "Johann, I have missed you so much. I could not bear not knowing how you were. Did you not miss us at all?"

Johann bent over and kissed his sister's forehead. "Of course I missed you. I prayed that we all be reunited soon. But I did not fear, for I know the Lord is good and His mercy endures forever."

Karl put his arms around his son and daughter. "First, we take you to the bath house. Katie will buy you new clothes. Then we will discuss your trial tomorrow. Come, there is much to prepare."

As they followed the head jailer up the tunnel to the small courtyard, Johann asked, "Who is this man you have brought along?"

Karl answered in French, "This is Robert Curtis, a brother from England who helped us on our way."

Reaching out and clasping Robert's forearm, he said, "I am Johann. Thank you, brother."

Robert replied, "It is I who am indebted to your sister Katharina and Father Wilhelm Hahn. They saved my life."

Johann looked to Katharina. "Father Wilhelm Hahn?"

Karl said, "You shall hear all, but first you shall cleanse

yourself of that unbearable odor."

Robert sniffing, added, "I think we all could do with a bath!"

They stopped at the heavy gate in the prison courtyard long enough to ask the head jailer the way to the nearest bathhouse and stepped out into the warm autumn sunshine. Walking the peaceful streets of Mainz seemed unnatural after all they had been through. Karl insisted on stopping to buy new clothes for Johann and then looking at Katie's dress declared she would have a new one as well, or better two! Brother and sister walked hand in hand chatting about his treatment. "Katie, truly, I am fine. They kept me strong believing I would lead them to secret documents, deeds, and grants from the reformation. Of course, I know nothing of such things."

As they left the shops and walked towards the bathhouse, Katharina stopped and said, "Wilhelm has not joined us. He should have joined us by now. I fear something may have happened to him."

Karl nodded. "The rest of you go and have a good soak. I will check on Wilhelm and meet you at the bathhouse."

Back at the palace, Karl asked the attendant, "The priest that came earlier with us, the man with the pass signed by the Emperor, where has he gone?"

The attendant eyed Karl coldly. "He has not left the palace. I believe he is a guest of his Excellency, the Archbishop."

"I would like to get word to him and tell him where we will be staying."

"I'm afraid that will not be possible. He is to receive no visitors."

"Just a simple note…"

"Sir, his excellency has made it quite clear, his guest is not to be disturbed under any circumstances. Good day sir."

Karl walked back to the bathhouse and found Robert and Johann deep in conversation. They spoke as two old friends. Johann was questioning Robert as Karl joined them. "And the three of them pursued you to Heidelberg, Mannheim, and Frankenthal, and now one, Greiffenclau, you say, is here in Mainz?"

Karl interjected, "Yes, and we now learn he is the son of the Auxiliary Bishop; a man determined to return all of Germany to the Roman Church, by the sword if necessary. Tell me, Johann, who interrogated you?"

"Truly, father, I do not know. He was a young man, but someone else stood behind the door as I was questioned. This other man never spoke, but I know he was there listening. Perhaps you can ask the guard, Heiko, he is a good man. His son was wounded in battle and suffers from a fever. I pray for him; you should pray for his as well, my father."

"I will pray for the son of Heiko, but it will be hard to speak with your guard."

"He works the days. We can catch him leaving at sunset."

"Perhaps tomorrow. Did your interrogator ask anything specific?"

"Yes, he, was most interested in the old abbey. He

asked what became of the lands and vineyards. I answered the ancient and wealthy, Eberbach Abbey is on the Rhine and still in possession of the Cistercian Brothers, the little abbey on the hill above Eberbach is now the orphanage and home for the weak elderly. I do not know for certain who owns the abbey now, but the gardens grow vegetables, and the pastures feed cattle, sheep, and chickens. I told him the small vineyard and winery sell the wine to supplement the needs that cannot be provided by the garden. He insisted the vineyards had been sold off and the winery and all the field and lands are now the property of the church, but he demanded the records. I told him to take his questions to the magistrate or Elector Frederick."

Karl slid his head under the warm water of the bath and slowly emerged, the water running down his white hair. He took some soap and washed the dust from his tired body and the grease from his hair and beard.

"Who did you go to meet the night that you were taken?"

"Why it was Joseph Meyer, the magistrate's clerk. He said he needed to collaborate on the records so the three Catholic clerics would leave us in peace. But when I arrived at the church, it was the deacon Greiffenclau, and the Spanish Abbot waiting with a detail of soldiers and I was marched here."

"It is now moot. They were trying to establish their ownership in advance of the new Elector of the Palatinate. The Emperor has determined to grant the title Elector to the Duke of Bavaria. Already our Protestant brothers are fleeing the lands he granted him. He has issued an edict; there shall no longer be a Protestant church in his realm. Convert to Catholicism, leave or be expelled. I'm afraid you cannot return to our church in Eberbach."

"Father we must help them. These are dangerous times; they need us."

The men finished their baths, dressed in clean clothes and waited at the ratskeller for Katharina to join them. When she arrived, her still damp, braided blonde hair, laid heavy under her white linen coif, atop the white lace collar of her new high neck deep blue bodice dress. The long virago sleeves and skirts identified her as a woman of wealth and influence in cosmopolitan Mainz. But her new clothes, rosy red cheeks, and fresh, wholesome appearance could not mask the worry in her eyes.

Johann immediately rose and greeted his sister with a warm hug. "Katie, God has answered our prayers! Isn't He good? You worry about your friend father Wilhelm. We will find him. We will not leave without him. Now sit down with us and let all the people of Mainz be jealous of me, father and Robert honored to enjoy the company of such a beautiful woman."

Katie kissed Johann on the cheek and sat down. "Hans, you know that I find no flattery in your talk of beauty."

"Yes, your bashful smiles only make your face to shine brighter."

Karl reached over and gently rubbed Katie's back. "We will call on the Archbishop again tomorrow. He is a wise man and knows that the Emperor will hold him accountable for Wilhelm's safety. No, I believe the Archbishop's concerns are pastoral. He sees a young priest in need of guidance. We will speak to Johann's jailer, Heicko, but I do not believe Wilhelm is in danger other than a time of correction, meditation, and penance."

Karl stood up. "Johann, take Katie and Robert to the Crown and Crook Ratskeller across from the Archbishop's palace. I will join you there for supper. I have some important friends. I must see about a new tapestry."

A figure in black caught Robert's eye. "We have company. Mister Sharpe has followed us. I will go back into the bath as if I forgot something and then on the ratskeller. Johann, take Katie directly there. Karl, be careful he does not identify your contact. We will see who he chooses to follow."

Karl replied, "I don't like leaving you alone. It may not be safe."

"I carry my sword."

"All the same, I would light the match for your pistol."

"Not while I can be observed. You all go on. I won't be long."

The shadows of dusk darkened the streets and doorways of the city as Robert walked off towards the bathhouse. Karl strode off towards the market and Johann led Katie to the ratskeller. People were about the streets making their way home or to the brightly lit ratskellers. The stillness of the evening carried the soft conversations of contentment brought about by the end of another day and the anticipation of dinner conversation with friends and family.

Robert scanned the streets and alleys as he walked, looking in the shadows for a form, a silhouette that might be Mister Sharpe. His mind drifted. It was the first time he had been alone since his rescue by Wilhelm and Katharina. He felt a stranger in a strange city; looking at a world new to him. He was a long way from Cambridge and the drama of the English Reformation working its way harshly through the English church. His unhappy life in Berwick-Upon-Tweed was also a foggy memory, the feuds of his father and his uncle. *Did my uncle buy my place at Cambridge and indeed the army commission out of love for me, his nephew, or to spite his brother?* And Robert's short time in the army, how strange it has all been. He was shocked and appalled by what he had seen in war but felt warm bonds for Charles Richard and many other officers and soldiers he had come to know and respect.

Robert passed a lantern atop a large pole outside of the bathhouse when his senses awakened his wandering mind. It was a smell. The distinct smell of burning gun match cord. Turning towards the alley beside the bathhouse, Robert saw the red glow of ember shrouded in the middle of a black silhouette. He instinctively ran for the entrance just as he heard the loud retort of a pistol. He felt the large round ball pass behind the back of his neck as he made his way through the door. As a cuirassier, Robert knew that even a sophisticated eight-shot revolver had to be rotated manually and the pan powdered before re-firing, he had time, but not much.

His pistol match still unlit, Robert rushed out of the door and around the corner drawing his sword as he ran. Pain screamed from his injured leg, but it did not slow his run. Sharpe dropped his pistol, drew his sword and met Robert's charge. The sound of clashing steel and grunting men could be heard as the two men went at each other blow for blow. The mysterious mister Sharpe may have been an experienced fighter, but as an assassin, he chose to kill by ambush or from behind, a straight up fight was not his choice. Robert was not a professional soldier, but a man enraged, fighting for his life and the fury within him unleashed savagery unknown to a conscious man.

The two men fought on in the dark alley. Sharpe came after Robert with a high cut towards Robert's shoulder, Robert instinctively turned and successfully parried the blow, as he kept turning, he spun and slashed Sharpe across his side. As Robert's sword was tearing through Sharpe's tunic and flesh, Sharpe's parried sword came down on the back of Robert's right leg.

Sharpe grasped his side, eyes opened wide in fear, as he felt the warm blood flowing from the wound. He stepped back as Robert's leg weakened and Robert's injured knee went to the ground. Standing on one leg and one knee, Robert drew back on his sword to deliver another blow. Sharpe lunged away from Robert's slash, turned and stumbled off into the darkness.

CHAPTER 17
THE TRIAL

At the first crow of the cock, in the darkness of early morning, Wilhelm heard a light rap on his door before it creaked and slowly opened. A weary figure holding a candle stepped in. The barefoot old man wearing a simple wool tunic with a crude wooden cross hanging from a leather strap around his neck, softly said, "Arise, Father Wilhelm, you shall assist me at mass."

"Your Excellency, I am your servant."

"I pray you sought the Lord in prayer and meditation?"

"I did, excellency. It has been some time since I was free of distraction and waited on the Lord."

"Archbishop Electors are no different in their need to separate from distractions and focus on the will of our

Lord. That is why I still find peace in the monk's cell. It reminds me of who I am and who I serve. I was by your side Father Hahn, in the cell beside yours. I have prayed for you, my son. I prayed that our Lord speaks in your meditations and hears your prayers."

"I am humbled, excellency. Thank you for your prayers."

"Come, it is time to worship!"

Wilhelm followed the Archbishop down the cold stone hallway to a door at the end. Entering the room Wilhelm found himself in the sacristy of the Elector Archbishop's chapel. The Archbishop pointed to a row of black cassocks and white albs. After purifying his fingers, Wilhelm dutifully found a cassock that fell to his ankles. Next, he put on the amice, a small rectangular linen cloth over his shoulders, to protect the long white alb which he then donned over the cassock and accepted the narrow green silk stole with a gold cross embroidered on the bottom of each side handed to him by the Archbishop. Placing the stole around his neck, Wilhelm took a simple rope cincture and knotted it around his waist. Wilhelm helped the Archbishop into a purple Chasuble fringed in gold over his alb and stole. The Archbishop placed the silver chain of a large silver pectoral cross around his neck and finally pinned a Zucchetto, or skull cap on the crown of his head. All the while the two priests repeated the ancient words of preparation for the mass.

When all was prepared, they entered the small but beautifully adorned private chapel of the Elector Archbishop. The small congregation included a young priest, the Archbishop's attendants, and servants, several cooks, two guards in uniform and several humbly dressed outside servants. Missing were any courtiers, dignitaries and the Auxiliary Bishop. The Archbishop and Father Wilhelm proceeded through the ancient Latin liturgy so familiar to both men.

In his homily, the Archbishop preached with evident conviction and love from First Corinthians chapter six on the Apostle Paul's admonition to bring cases against brothers only before the church for righteous judgment. He reminded his small congregation, "The unrighteous outside of the church are unfit to judge and will not inherit the Kingdom of God." Repeating from memory, he cataloged their sin. "Do not be deceived: neither the sexually immoral, nor idolaters, nor adulterers, ...nor thieves will inherit the Kingdom of God. And such were some of you. But you were washed, you were sanctified, you were justified in the name of the Lord Jesus Christ and by the Spirit of God."

Pausing before closing, he looked at the congregation before him, people he clearly loved. Then slowly and softly he admonished. "My children flee from sexual immorality, or do you not know that your body is the temple of the Holy Spirit within you, whom you have from God? You and I are not our own, for we were bought with a price. So, glorify God in your body. Do not find yourself in judgment before our heavenly Father or me."

As the two men carefully returned their vestments to their prepared place in the sacristy, the Archbishop said,

"Father, you may borrow the cassock. And now, please join me for breakfast."

"I am honored excellency."

"It is this small congregation of faithful men with whom I share my most fervent homilies. They are always the first to hear the fruit of my meditations. They are good men of sound hearts and faith whose attendance is not compelled. They are not here to be seen, like many who only come to the cathedral when I officiate."

"We are commanded by our Lord to make disciples, excellency."

"What are your thoughts on the homily, Father Hahn?"

"Your homily should be repeated in the cathedral where those who need to hear such an admonition might attend. Or better, an instruction to bishops and priest of our church. You could start with my father, a bishop with sons and daughters. The hardworking, faithful men you disciple are not likely to foul their lives in sexual immorality."

They reached the Archbishop's apartment and entered the lavishly appointed chambers. A table was set, and servants stood waiting. "Another setting, Peter, Father Hahn will be joining me."

"Yes, Excellency."

Immediately another chair and setting were set out. The two men sat and continued their conversation. "How quick we are to direct the call to righteousness to some other sinner who needs to hear! Sexual immorality tempts all men, and I suspect all women as well. My prayers and meditations last night were for you Father

Hahn, a young and compassionate priest perhaps being drawn away from your vows by an attractive young woman. You would not be the first."

"Excellency, I too meditated on Paul's letters last night. But it was the letter to the Galatians. You worry that I am attracted to the young lady, Katharina Schroeder is her name. It is true; I am attracted to her strong faith and works of mercy. Though she and her father and brother are Calvinist Protestants, their love and zeal for our Lord are real. I considered the dogma of our church that all those who are outside of the church will in no way enter into heaven. I cannot reconcile this teaching with lives I see these good Christian people living…"

"You call them Christian. The pope is the head of the Christ's Church on earth; the Church is His body. If you are not in the Church you are not in Christ, you are not Christian, and you will not receive the promise of His salvation."

"Excellency, I know the teaching. But as I read Galatians, I was reminded how the Apostle Paul corrected Saint Peter when he sought to appease the Judaizers by placing burdens of the law on Gentile believers. Saint Peter humbled himself; he accepted the correction, and the Gentile believers were welcomed into the Church. They were accepted by their faith alone. Indeed, the evidence of their faith was shown in the fruits of the Spirit. The Holy Spirit of God lived in them and changed their lives."

The Archbishop put down the thick slice of bread he

had cut and replied, "Do you say that the rites, traditions, and doctrine of the church do not define the church and are of no value?"

"Not so excellence. Would you not agree that our Lord has never required a perfect understanding of religion by His flock? Do we not declare members of the Church the faithful? Faithful to whom? Faithful to God!"

"And to His Church."

"Yes, excellency, and to His Church, His body whom they become in faith. Excellency, did not the Church identify the essential beliefs many years ago and capture them in creeds? Both the Apostles Creed, first employed as the Baptismal creed of the Church and later the Nicene Creed which forever established our belief in the Trinity? Who established the creeds? Why it was the worldwide church. The creeds, all based upon Holy Scripture, remain the test of orthodoxy. To this day they are accepted in the East, in the Roman Catholic Church and among the Protestants, both Lutheran, and Calvinist. Is not requiring more than the creed the same as well intended Judaizers requiring more than faith?"

"The Church has learned much since the early councils. Others have gone their own way…"

"Excellency, would not a worldwide council open to all who profess Christ and hold to the creeds of orthodoxy provide a better hope for the Church than open warfare between people who profess to be Christian?"

The Archbishop laughed lightly. "Father, I commend your good heart. This war is not about reuniting the

Church even if I concede both sides are the Church. It is about powerful men, rulers with scores to settle. O some may say theirs is a Holy cause, but it is more about Emperors, Kings, and Princes extending their borders and possessions. I fear that the Church is now dependent on the whims and weapons of the rulers it crowns."

Wilhelm sat up straight and looked into the Archbishop's eyes. "Forcing Protestants and Catholics into separate Kingdoms will not restore Catholicism or reunite the Church. It will only further divide us, and we will only grow further apart. I fear we try the very heart of our God and Father."

The Archbishop listened respectfully and warmly replied, "The reign of Christendom has failed. The days when the Church and King reigned as one are behind us. I do not believe even the Prince Archbishops will withstand the flooding tide. Father Hahn, your Church needs you. I may not yet be convinced that our Protestant friends are brothers and sisters with us fully in the Body of Christ, but they are our friends and neighbors and deserving of tolerance and respect. Perhaps someday we can be in communion together. You can work with me in our Roman Catholic Church. Work with me for peace in our land. Stay with me another day. Pray and consider what I ask. Pray for me. I will hear your confession this evening, and we shall talk again tomorrow. My duties of state await me."

The Archbishop stood up and patted Wilhelm on the shoulder, and he silently left the room.

Robert limped towards the breakfast table leaning heavily on a crutch Karl found for him. Katharina's concern was evident as she got up as he approached and insisted on helping him into his seat. "You are in pain, poor man! I thank God that he saved you once again. I could not bear the grief if we were to lose you. Johann, please see to a good breakfast for our dear friend."

Robert replied, "Truly the Lord is good. Once again, my attacker's aim was off. And his blade, though it hit my old wound did not cut me at all. I am certain I fared better than he."

Turning to Karl, he asked, "Were you able to find him?"

Karl shook his head. "The trail of blood ended at the alley. Whether by horse or carriage, he managed to escape. I have asked my friends in the market to make inquiries, but this man, Mr. Sharpe, is not well known in Mainz. It is best if you not venture out alone. Please go nowhere without me or Johann or Wilhelm."

"You appear confident that Johann and Wilhelm will both be free to leave with us," Robert remarked.

"The Archbishop is a just man; you heard how Greiffenclau fumbled, he has no proper reason to hold Johann, we are now in his jurisdiction, not Eberbach. I trust he will see through the schemes of Greiffenclau, Don Pedro and Don Lorenzo. As for Father Wilhelm, the Archbishop will surely see the same goodness and compassion that we know of him. No, he will not impose his authority over him, rather he will appeal to his sense of duty and devotion as a priest. The decision to return with us or stay in service to the Archbishop will fall on Wilhelm himself. He will not find it an easy decision."

Katharina said, "He has kept his promise so far..."

"Once Johann is released, he has no further obligation; he can return to..."

Robert was interrupted by Karl. "Likely not to Eberbach, he is considered a traitor there, but somewhere the Archbishop can arrange, somewhere he will not be tempted by an attractive young woman."

Robert nodded. "I pray he finds answers in prayer and the Bible I gave him."

Johann had returned with a generous breakfast for Robert and sat down beside him.

"We must consider where we go and what we do," Karl said. Then turning to Johann, he mentioned, "You cannot return to Eberbach, Johann. The Emperor will name the Duke of Bavaria, the new Elector of the Palatinate. The Duke has expelled all protestants who refuse to return to the Roman Catholic Church. It will not be safe for Katharina or me either."

Johann looked up from his meal and said, "There will be many people forced to leave. Many women and little children. Where will they go? What will they do? Who will lead them? Who will protect them along the way? Is this not our mission? Our duty? Papa, you know many people. You can move about despite the war and the armies. You must make the arrangements. We must help God's people escape this persecution and lead them to safe pasture."

"First we must take you to the Elector Archbishop's

court. Robert, it is not safe to leave you here alone. Can you walk or shall I order a carriage?"

Robert looked at the crude crutch beside his chair and sighed. "I've become quite skilled with the crutch and as much as I try it seems I cannot leave it behind. No need for the carriage; I can walk."

Karl and Johann led the group across the square to the Elector Archbishop's palace and into the court. Johann surrendered himself to a court guard and was led off to the accused's box. Karl and Katharina were led to the defendant's table, and Robert found a seat in the gallery. The court was a large well-lit room several stories tall with a massive wood beamed ceiling and stone columns resplendent in frescos of the saints and Bible scenes. At the far end, the throne wall was paneled in wood all of which was carved. A massive throne carved from black walnut dominated the end of the room. Above the throne was an oversized coat of arms, a red shield with two six-spoked silver wheels one diagonally above the other connected by a silver cross.

When the Elector Archbishop Johann von Kronberg was announced, everyone rose from their seat, kneeled and bowed until he was seated on his judgment throne. The crier then called, "Uncharged prisoner Johann Schroeder."

"I am Johann Schroeder."

The bailiff continued. "Who brings charges against prisoner Johann Schroeder?"

Maximilian Greiffenclau rose and answered; "The magistrate of Eberbach sends Johann Schroeder to Mainz charged with…"

The Elector Archbishop interrupted him and asked, "Are there no prisons in Eberbach?"

"Excellency, the magistrate determined that the case was best tried outside of Eberbach…"

"Has not the Count von Tilly recovered Eberbach without a fight and established a peaceful transition? Have the people of Eberbach resisted by force?"

"No excellency, but it was determined…"

"Please bring me the warrant for Johann Schroeder's arrest."

"Excellency, I do not have a warrant but…"

"Where was the prisoner arrested?"

"He was taken into custody in Eberbach, excellency."

"How long has he been a prisoner in Mainz?"

"It is nearly a month excellency. We have been…"

"Sit down deacon Greiffenclau. Johann Schroeder, tell me of your arrest."

Johann stood and said, "Excellency, I am, or was, the pastor of Eberbach. When the emperor's army declared the city under the authority of the Count von Tilly and the only church permitted was now the Roman Catholic church, I cooperated when asked to provide all church records. I was asked for additional records, but I truthfully responded that I had made available every known record. One night I was sent a message asking me to come to the church. When I arrived, I was taken into custody and marched under guard here."

"You were not taken before the magistrate of Eberbach and charged?"

"No excellency. I was taken here and imprisoned where I have been confined to a solitary cell."

Karl stood up and said, "Excellency, if I may add to his answer?"

The Elector Archbishop looked at Karl thoughtfully then said, "I will hear Karl Schroeder, father of the accused."

"Thank you, Excellency. The night Johann was taken I went to the magistrate when Johann did not return home and asked if there were any reports concerning my son. He denied any report existed. I visited him daily and inquired, daily he denied any reports. The Roman Catholic priest who was with us yesterday can attest to this. He too inquired on behalf of my daughter and me. If you summon him, he will so testify."

"Father Wilhelm Hahn is my guest. His testimony is not required. You may be seated, Herr Schroeder."

The Elector Archbishop turned his attention to deacon Greiffenclau. "Deacon Greiffenclau stand up and hear me. Do not think that because your father is the Auxiliary Bishop of Mainz that my prison is available for your personal use. Sit down."

The turning to Johann he said, "The prisoner, Johann Schroeder, has not been charged with any crime in Mainz and any crime he may have committed in Eberbach should have been tried in Eberbach. Further, he was brought here improperly and lacking a magistrate's request from Eberbach for his return. He is released."

Pausing a moment, he then said to his clerk, "Notify the head jailer that no man may be imprisoned without a signed, written warrant. Also command him to provide me a listing of all new prisoners and their charges, daily."

He then arose, and immediately everyone in the court kneeled as he left.

CHAPTER 18
CHOOSING SIDES

Wilhelm was in his cell reading the English Bible Robert had given him when he heard a gentle knock on the door before it slowly opened. The Archbishop entered, he was wearing a modest black cassock and black skull cap and carried a small stool which he set down against the wall. "Father, I will hear your confession."

Wilhelm closed the Bible and bowed to the Archbishop. He crossed himself and then said, "Forgive me excellency for I have sinned. It has been a month since my last confession. I have accepted an English Bible given to me to learn English as I read passages I remember. I confess that reading a Bible other than the Vulgate of the Church, university or monastery is forbidden. I confess that I find comfort in the power of the Holy Scriptures as this Bible brings to memory passages that have touched me in the past."

"Passages from Galatians from which you spoke this morning?"

"Yes, Excellency."

"Why do you learn English?"

"My companion, the English priest speaks little German; his French is difficult though his Latin is quite good. He is a good man, excellency, though troubled in his spirit. He tells me the language of a people speaks to their understanding of God's revelation. The English translation is not a word for word translation as is the Vulgate but sometimes expresses itself in the idioms of the people. Is it not a good thing for people to hear the Word of God in their own language? Such a reading of Scripture had never occurred to me."

"Holy Scripture must be interpreted, and it is the role of the church to instruct the people in what is necessary to live as God demands."

"Excellency, it is a pastoral duty as you yourself performed this morning in your homily expounding on Scripture. Is it not helpful for the sheep of your pasture to have heard the Word before you expound?"

"You have more to confess. There is a woman."

"I confess I have feelings for the woman, Fraulein Katharina Schroeder, unlike feelings for any other woman I have ever known. Though she has remained chaste, I confess I enjoy her company. I confess I think of her often and even see her in my dreams. I confess that when I held her while protecting her when we under attack coming here, I was more pleased than afraid of our attackers."

"It is common for a priest to be attracted to a beautiful woman. But you must not act upon your attraction. Your relationship should never be more than pastoral, but as a protestant, she is not of our flock to shepherd. She is outside the church, and your relationship can be no more than tolerance of a neighbor. Do not be tempted to a physical relationship. Have you not condemned your father to me as an example of corruption and expediency? You must consider your vow, Father Wilhelm, are you keeping your vows made to God?"

"I meditate on my vows day and night. They tear at my very heart."

"Father Wilhelm, in your crusade to help free this protestant pastor you have aligned yourself with protestants at war with the true church. You espouse dangerous ideas. Confess that you have strayed from the faith and renew your vows of obedience, the church, and the Holy Father. Then join me in serving His flock."

Wilhelm sat in silence staring at the crucifix on the wall across from him. After several minutes words slowly came to him. "Excellency, I confess that I have not obeyed all of the dogmas of the Holy Father and what has been taught to me. But I do not confess espousing views outside of our Christian faith that has been handed down to us through generations, from the apostles and patriarchs, the councils and even many of the doctors of the church. Did not our faith grow through inspiration and debate blessed by the Holy Spirit? Tell me, excellency, do you agree with every bull of every pope? Our new pope, Gregory XV, what was his first act? He made his young nephew a cardinal and his assistant. He named his brother Captain General of the Church. Both he made Dukes and another nephew a prince. Is this to benefit the church?"

"You did not mention the one million gold ducats he sent to Emperor Ferdinand to fund his war against the protestants. But you forget, Father, that the bulls of the Pope, like the celebrant of the sacraments, are no less effective in the case of a sinful celebrant but are effective because of the work of the Holy Spirit."

"Truly, excellency, I have never known a bishop as humble and righteous as you. The wisdom of your words speaks to my heart. I see in your tolerance, a love for all of God's people and the heart of a servant of Christ."

"Stay with me, Father Wilhelm, the church needs men filled with the love of God. I am old, and I am looking for good men, good priests to carry on His work."

"Excellency, I fear I am not ready. I worry for my friends, for Johann and Robert. I need more time. Tell me, Excellency, if I go, am I still a priest?"

"Father Wilhelm, I will not keep you if it is your will to leave. The man Johann Schroeder has been set free. And I do not take your priesthood from you. You made a vow; only you can say if you still honor your vow to Him."

"I will consider your words excellency. Will you pray

for me, excellency?"

"Certainly, my son, 'Heavenly Father speak to your servant Wilhelm, make your will known to him and bless him today and always, in Thy Holy name I pray. Amen.'"

"I will leave you now, Father Wilhelm, the door is open for you to leave and for you to return. God bless you, my son."

The crude bench loudly screeched as it was dragged against the rough stone floor. "Forgive me," Robert apologized. "I must put my feet up and rest my leg a bit."

Karl, Johann, and Katharina smiled. Karl continued. "My friends warn me that we must move on soon, things are happening fast. Christian of Brunswick is thought to be moving quickly south to reinforce Frederick and then join the English and Dutch in the Neckar Valley before the Spanish army arrives. The Count of Tilly will try and stop them. I have sent a tapestry design to Colonel Vere. I hope that the crude drawing due to the rush will not raise the suspicions of Captain Stock."

"We must wait for Father Wilhelm. We cannot abandon him," Katharina replied earnestly.

Karl nodded. "We will first know of Father Wilhelm's safety. I have made inquiries."

"What do your friends say of Mister Sharpe? Is he still here? Is he badly wounded? Dead? Robert asked.

"He has not been seen since before his attack on you. He is likely being tended nearby. I heard that your mister Sharpe is known to visit Auxiliary Bishop Greiffenclau often in the company of young Greiffenclau and the priest Don Lorenzo from Rome. On one occasion, a poorly disguised English gentleman accompanied him."

"Captain Donald Stock, no doubt," Robert commented.

"Quite possibly," Karl affirmed.

"Could Sharpe be at Auxiliary Bishop Greiffenclau's residence?"

"Not likely, too dangerous. Word might get to the Elector Archbishop. No, it is more likely someone close to Bishop Greiffenclau is sheltering Mister Sharpe. Or he may be dead. My friends continue to seek information, discreetly."

"Papa, I would like to meet Heiko, the jailer this evening and pray for his son. He is a godly man, and I cannot leave without repaying his kindness. Do you think we can find bread and wine for communion and perhaps some oil to anoint his son with the laying on of hands?"

"Yes, perhaps Katharina will go with you and pray as well."

Karl turned to Robert and said, "Can I trust you to stay in the inn and avoid trouble for one evening. I must meet someone tonight."

A familiar voice replied from behind him. "I will keep our friend Robert out of trouble tonight. Can't I be away for one night without him finding trouble?"

Katherina jumped up. "Wilhelm! You're safe! I, we, were so worried! God is good! He has sent you back to us!"

Running to him she hugged him tight with tears of joy in the corners of her eyes. Finally freeing him from her hug, she pointed to Johann. "Father Wilhelm, this is my brother, Johann. He is free! Elector Archbishop von Kronberg is a just and merciful man and has found that Johann was taken without cause."

Hugging Wilhelm tighter, she said, "I am so happy you are returned to us unharmed!"

"Pastor Schroeder, I am pleased to meet you at last and so very happy that you have found justice. Your dear sister has told me so much about you."

"Please, call me Johann. And my thank you, Father Hahn, for taking up my sister's cause."

Wilhelm smiled and then turned to Katharina. "Truly, Katie, Archbishop von Kronberg is more than a just man, he is truly a man of God and has given me godly counsel and much to consider…perhaps if Robert could move that leg of his from the bench, a man could sit down and enjoy a beer with his friends."

Gingerly sliding his leg from the bench, Robert said, "You must tell us everything."

"There is not much to tell. I was shown to a monk's cell and told to meditate and pray. In the morning I assisted the archbishop in a small early morning mass, attended by household staff and several young priests. We met again this afternoon when he asked me to stay with him and work for peace. He did not take the English Bible you gave me, Robert, and he made it clear I could stay or go and if I left, I could return. He is a remarkable man, humble, wise and patient. I am certain he desires peace above all things and freedom to worship for Catholics and Protestants alike."

Turning his attention to Robert's leg, he asked, "It was only a night and a day, Robert, what happened to you?"

"I got the better of Mister Sharpe after his shot missed."

Karl stood up and said, "I will be going now. Don't look for me before breakfast."

Johann stood and said, "Come along sister, we go pray for the wounded son of my jailer."

After the others left Robert said, "Well, don't just sit there come along. I need your German tongue to help me find Mister Sharpe."

Wilhelm stood up with a puzzled look on his face and said, "Are you certain?"

Seeing the determination in Robert's eyes, he stood and said, "Where do we start?"

"Surgeons. We start with the surgeons. Sharpe is wounded. I slashed him deeply. I am sure of it. We find a surgeon who treated a sword wound last night. A wounded stranger, possibly English. One willing to help another stranger looking for his friend."

"And this friend has asked a priest for help?"

"I need to find him. How many more attempts can I survive?"

"You think it was Sharpe who shot you from behind?"

"He knows Captain Stock, Don Lorenzo and your deacon Greiffenclau, strange company for an Englishman. We know he is following us. And don't forget the attempt when we left Frankenthal. I intend to find him before he can try again."

"Then we start with the surgeons."

As Robert and Wilhelm were leaving the inn, pointing to Robert, Wilhelm asked the innkeeper if he could recommend a surgeon to look at his friend's leg. Within moments the innkeeper recommended three surgeons and gave directions to a nearby street where he could find them and others as well. Robert smiled at the German love of order. The surgeons all kept surgeries on a single block of the same street.

Father Hahn put on his best pastoral face as he patiently asked surgeon after surgeon if they had treated a sword wound the night before to an unfortunate stranger, brutally attacked before he could safely meet his friend. The answer was always the same; there was no wounded patient last night. When the last surgeon gave the same answer, Wilhelm asked, "Are there any other surgeons in Mainz not on this street?" The impatient surgeon answered, No, all practicing surgeons of the guild are here." Wilhelm turned around to leave when the man said, "but there is also the army surgeon at the barracks and the charity surgeon."

"Charity surgeon? Wilhelm asked.

"Doctor Waldheim. He tends the church orphanage, poor house, old age hospice, and the prison."

"Thank you, sir, you have been most helpful. God Bless."

Outside on the street, Wilhelm asked, "Which one should we try first."

Robert shot back, "Certainly the Archbishop has delegated oversight of the charity surgeon just as he has the prison. Greiffenclau treats the prison as his private jail; the charity surgeon is likely one of his men. But after today's trial, and the new reports of all prisoners, Greiffenclau is unlikely to use the prison itself. So even if the surgeon treated him, he is now somewhere else and the surgeon unlikely to speak honestly."

"Three possibilities occur to me," Wilhelm replied. "Either he is at the old age hospice, the home of the charity surgeon or in the house of Greiffenclau."

"Johann's friend, Heiko, would know the prison surgeon. Either way, finding Sharpe will be difficult."

Wilhelm nodded. "Let's see if Johann has returned."

As they walked through the streets of Mainz, Robert asked Wilhelm, "Will you go back?"

"To Eberbach?"

"To the church, to the Archbishop... to the priesthood."

"Not until I know."

Robert stopped walking and looked closely at Wilhelm. "What is it you don't know?"

Wilhelm cast his eyes down before him and mumbled, "There is so much I don't know. I made a vow, but I fear it was based on a lie. A vow to God I will honor, but I did not see the honor in the church, not until I met the Archbishop. Yet I see the same honor and truth in Karl and Katie. And Katie I don't know if..."

"You don't know if your feelings for her go beyond pastoral love."

"The Archbishop asked the same question. He could look into my soul, such a wise and righteous man."

"He is wise because he knows the way of men and the

heart of God."

Wilhelm nodded, and both men continued in silence. As they passed a convent, Wilhelm stopped pointed and looked at Robert. "What do you think?"

"I'll let you do the talking."

Walking over to the heavy door, Wilhelm pulled the cord on the bell. After a short time, the door creaked open, and a nun peaked out. Wilhelm wasted no time. "I hope I am not disturbing your prayers or works of mercy, sister, I will only take a few minutes of your time. I am helping this man find his friend, a stranger in our land, who did not arrive for a meeting last night. We fear he may have been set upon by robbers or injured. As your convent is known to nurse and minister to the unfortunate, I ask if anyone, someone from the outside required your works of mercy last night."

"Last night, why not here, but one of the sisters, Sister Margaret, was with Doctor Waldheim at the church hospice when he was called away to tend someone. She offered to go with him, but he declined. Most unusual for him. He has come to rely on our sisters to tend to patients. He finds cleaning, bandaging and sitting with patients tedious work."

"Did the sister say where he went or who it was who called upon him?"

"She said it was a priest that came, one she did not recognize. But he was with a prison guard. Sorry, I cannot say any more, and sister Margaret is in her prayers."

"Thank you, sister. We shall not keep you any longer."

After the heavy door shut, Robert said, "We must find the doctor. He will know if Sharpe lives and where he is."

Wilhelm replied, "We must convince Johann to take us to Heiko, he would know the doctor and where he lives. Heiko would know if we can trust the doctor with the truth."

"Time," Robert replied. "I do not want to give Sharpe another day. We must move quickly."

CHAPTER 19
A LESSON LEARNED

Karl waited in a well-appointed anteroom. The ceilings were high and brightly painted white between the dark oak beams. The walls were also clean white between the colorful tapestries. Embroidered window curtains hung to the floor, their reds and greens shining like silk. A large crystal chandelier, wall sconces, and a candelabra told visitors that no expense was spared providing an elegant, well-lighted room. Fine furniture, including a large walnut desk centered on an imported Persian rug and an imposing chair, projected the power of its owner.

Moses Bersheim entered the room, walked briskly to Karl and welcomed him warmly. "Karl, welcome my friend! I have heard the good news. Your son is free. The

Prince Elector Archbishop is a just man, and he is angry that the prison has been used without his knowledge. The auxiliary bishop Greiffenclau has denied knowledge of the imprisonment and begs the Elector Archbishop forgive his son's youthful indiscretion. You can be sure there will be reforms. We will all be better for your efforts."

"Yes, he is a good man. Matters are not as settled in the Palatinate. The treaty of Ulm is ignored. Cities are being garrisoned, and armies are marching. I fear the war will certainly spread throughout the German principalities, the Dutch Republic and the entire continent."

Moses nodded. "Yes, you must know that even the Elector Archbishop who speaks so eloquently of peace, is now building a new fortress on Jacobsberg Hill on the site of the old Benedictine Abbey to protect the entrance to the city. The Protestant Union and the Dutch took the city once; he will not allow it to fall again now that the Count of Tilly has returned it to him."

Moses Paused, put his fingertips together under his chin and said, "You have not come to gossip, what brings you here today my friend?"

Karl straightened up in his chair. "Gerhardt, the tapestry dealer, tells me we have similar aims and may be of help to each other. My people in Eberbach and all the Palatine face hardship and perhaps expulsion from our homes by the armies and the supporters of the Emperor. The Count of Tilly's army is mostly Spanish or from Flanders, the Spanish Netherlands. Another Spanish army has been bought and paid for by the Emperor and will soon arrive. Christian of Brunswick marches south; it said Christian IV of Denmark-Norway might march south as well. This war will grow. I provide information to the remaining English and Dutch Garrisons in the hope they can hold and not allow the Emperor and his supporters to expel all protestants from the Palatine. There is not an ounce of tolerance in Ferdinand II. His Spanish and many of his German allies are no more tolerant of Jews than Protestants. Does not the inquisition continue to this day in Spain and the Spanish Netherlands?"

"Moses lowered his head and sighed. "It is true. There are fewer and fewer tolerant princes. My family came here when expelled from Frankfurt many years ago. The Duke of Bavaria who schemes to take the Palatinate is a fervent Catholic and intolerant of any other religion, though he has sought loans from my people in the past. Of course, I will work with you and share information."

"When I leave Mainz, I will travel north and learn what Christian of Brunswick and other Protestant princes are planning. I will observe their movements and estimate their strength. But you must agree with me, the current prospects for the Palatine do not look good. I fear the garrisons will be insufficient to hold against the Count of Tilly. At best, Christian IV of Denmark-Norway or Gustav of Sweden may return it to Frederick V someday."

Karl took a breath and said, "Tell me, Moses, how do I prepare my people to leave their homes and property in the face of an invasion?"

The room fell silent; only the ticking of the mechanical clock on the mantel could be heard. Moses answered, "We Jews are strangers in this land. We have a homeland, a promised land which will someday be ours again. We have learned not to become attached to where we are, a place, land or property. We don't hold tight onto these; we can let them go. We have learned to accept that God is leading us on to our final home, our promised land."

We Jews do not buy farms, fields or property. I do not own this house. I rent and keep my assets liquid. They can move with me when needed. The Dutch were tolerant the short time they held the city, and the Elector Archbishop is tolerant as well. But who knows who will follow him? Tell your people that they should begin selling their property to Catholic friends if they have treated them well. A poor price is better than a forced sale or seizure. Frederick V may recover his lands and castles if Christian IV or King Gustav Adolphus restore him, but your people will not be so fortunate."

"I would tell your people to hold tightly to your better possessions. Hold onto your family, friends, community, and traditions. Traditions can make any new place home! Carry these with you wherever you go. Keep these, and you will survive; indeed, you will thrive, for these are the better gifts and possessions. Your pastors and leaders must teach this – better; they must live it and show it."

Karl nodded yes. "There is wisdom in your words, my friend."

Moses continued. "Know also that despair and disappointment will travel with you. Loved ones will die unjustly. Bad things – disastrous things will happen, but still, there is a comfort to know you are on your journey to Beulah, the promised land of which we see shadowy glimpses, visions of hope, visions of love, an awareness that still, despite all else, still, we matter to God."

Karl spoke softly. "Your people have been treated unjustly by those calling themselves Christian. I see now it was not only Catholics but protestants as well. Indeed, Martin Luther never sought forgiveness for the vicious attack he made against Jews when your Jewish leaders did not follow his reformation. I pray those times are behind us, but I fear it is a sickness that will not soon be cured."

Moses replied, "It goes back millennia. We do not see it ending any time soon. But we can find hope in friendship and trust. Friends have a gift of tolerance."

"Now, Karl, tell me how your information is shared."

Robert and Wilhelm found Johann sitting with Katharina at the inn. Katharina gave Wilhelm a bright smile and scolded, "Where have you two been? You had me worried!"

Wilhelm replied, "Robert is determined to find his attacker. We have been talking to the doctors and the sisters in the convent. The doctor to the prison was called away last night. Johann, can we see Heiko? He would know the prison doctor and where he lives."

Katharina interrupted. "Is this safe? Papa knows who

to talk to. He knows who can be trusted. Robert, you are hurt and walk in pain. And you, Wilhelm, you are a priest! What if you are attacked? What do you know of fighting?"

"We are not safe as long as Mr. Sharpe is alive," Robert said firmly. "We must act quickly while we have an advantage. He is gravely wounded."

Johann nodded. "Come. We will go to Heiko's house. His wife will know how to contact him."

Johann rose from his seat, kissed his sister's forehead and said, "Stay here. Say a prayer for us. And trust God."

Heiko lived in a small two-room apartment above a printer's shop. The apartment was carved out of the former warehouse, behind the great press and storerooms of paper and ink. It was situated at the rear of the building which afforded a small fireplace for heat and cooking. Crude though it was, a warmth was immediately apparent when Johann, Wilhelm, and Robert were invited in. It looked and felt welcoming and peaceful.

"You are back so soon Pastor Johann," Heiko's wife said when she saw them. "Our son rests comfortably since your prayers. I am afraid my husband has gone off to work."

Johann smiled. "May God's blessing keep your house in peace, and may all of your prayers be answered. I have come because it is urgent that these good men find the prison doctor. I have come to ask you how we can speak with Heiko at the prison."

"The prison doctor is a vile man. You do not want

him! No, spent your money on one of the doctors of the guild."

Johann replied, "We must find him. We seek a man he treated last night. A scoundrel of a man who tried to kill my friend. Heiko could tell us where to find him and if the doctor is in league with those who jailed me and attacked my friends."

"The guard at the alley gate will not open the door for strangers; only for guards bringing prisoners. Even for me, he will not open the door. If I pay him, he might send a message to Heiko. Better, I know where the doctor lives. It is not far. My son sleeps, if we go quickly, I will show you."

As she spoke, she was out the door walking past the stacks of paper towards the stairs in front of the printing press. At the bottom of the stair she shouted, "Hans, I am off for a few minutes if Claus wakens tell him all is well. I will return shortly."

A voice somewhere in the back replied, "God speed."

In the street, she walked briskly. "We are fortunate. Our landlord is a good man."

She turned at the corner and walked up the street towards the Archbishop's palace. She turned down the alley leading behind the palace. Near the prison gate, she stopped at a ratskeller across the street and pointed. "He lives there on the second floor. Ask for him inside. I will not enter; it is a place of drunk guards and soldiers. And women who please them."

Johann said, "Thank you. You have been most helpful. If I can, I will come again to pray with you. But know whether I can return or not; I will forever hold you, Heiko and your son in my prayers."

"Thank you, Pastor Johann, forgive me; I must return to my son." She left as briskly as she came.

The men entered the tavern and were struck by the smell of stale beer, vomit, and urine. In the dim light, they could see men slumped over tables with mugs of beer. They heard coarse laughter and profanity punctuated by loud thumps as mugs found the tables. Looking around, Robert noticed two women sitting against the far wall, one with a breast exposed from the dirty white blouse of her dirndl. Both sat waiting with disinterested faces. He continued to scan the room until he saw a man at a small table near the end of the bar. Robert nudged Wilhelm and pointed.

Wilhelm walked over and spoke to the man. He could see the man shake his head. Their conversation continued. The man's hand gestures made it clear to Robert that Wilhelm was not getting answers. The man called and waved to another who stumbled over and spoke with Wilhelm. Finally, Wilhelm walked back to Robert and Johann and said, "Let's go. The Doctor is not here. He is probably at the orphanage or the infirmary. He did bring a patient here last night. They say the doctor sent for the dead cart and the man was carried off in the early hours of this morning."

Robert asked, "Did they see the man the doctor brought in?"

"He said the man wore the boots of an English soldier. They say the body was covered when it was carried out to the dead cart. Paupers and strangers are buried outside the city. There is no service for them. The man does not know who drove the dead cart. He says it is not a job one holds for a long time."

"Your attacker is dead then, Robert?" Johann asked.

"Ask him the doctor's room. I will see for myself."

"But he was most emphatic…"

"All the more reason! His room number or I will check every room in this inn or brothel or whatever its nature."

Wilhelm went back to the wiry little man at the desk. Their voices grew louder and angrier. Wilhelm pounded his fist on the table, and it split in two. The little man rose up, looked at Robert and Johann then sat down again and said "fumpf."

Wilhelm signaled to Robert, and the three of them ran up the stairs to room five. The hallway was narrow, and floors creaked as they stomped their way towards room five. Wilhelm stopped and was about to knock when Robert came past him and flew the door open. The cramped, dirty surgery was empty. Bloody sheets were piled beside a narrow cot. Unwashed surgical instruments were scattered across a table next to the cot.

Johann opened the door to an adjoining room to find a bedchamber and sitting room. The bed was unmade, but the empty room was otherwise tidy. At the far end of the bedchamber was another door that opened onto the hall. It too was unlocked. Robert following Johann then ran to the window and looked down onto the alley to see a man walking briskly away. There was no way of knowing if he had come from the inn or was just passing by. He wore a black coat over brown breeches, common dress for Mainz.

Returning to the surgery, he saw Wilhelm holding one of the bloody sheets. "The blood has not fully dried. He must be dead. He could not have escaped our entrance."

Robert replied, "Perhaps, perhaps not. Let's return to the inn. Maybe Karl has heard something."

Coming down the stairs, Robert stopped in front of the little man, reached into his pocket and dropped a coin on the broken table. Outside he breathed deeply of the fresh air.

CHAPTER 20
SEPARATE WAYS

I will be glad to leave this place," Robert said. "But are you sure it is safe for Wilhelm, Johann, and Katharina to return to Eberbach?"

Karl put down his beer and nodded. "The Count of Tilly has divided his army; half has moved west to defend Hagenau in the Alsace from Frederick's army under Ernst von Mansfeld, the remainder awaits Christian of Brunswick. Besides, Johann's release will be a warning to the magistrate. My servant Werner can be trusted. He will know everything that is happening in Eberbach. Remember, we still have many friends there."

"Friends like Joseph Meyer, who led Greiffenclau's men to you?"

Karl frowned. "Yes, he seems to be playing both sides.

He gave me a small warning, but no, he cannot be trusted. He will seek our trust, but he must be handled carefully."

"We are on fool's errand, Karl. We know Tilly will soon march his united army north to block Christian of Brunswick from reinforcing Frederick's weak army. There is no heart left in the protestant princes to commit, and Christian IV of Denmark-Norway shows no sign of marching south, he worries more about Gustav Adolphus of Sweden. No, I am more concerned with this alliance between this man Sharpe and his friends Greiffenclau, Don Pedro and Don Lorenzo. Just what is our friend Captain Stock's interest? Does he seek personal gain? Money? Or is he a traitor?"

"Robert, you insist Sharpe was badly wounded, there is no evidence he is still alive. Even if he lives, he cannot follow. The movements you state are urgent. What are the numbers of Tilly? Or Christian of Brunswick or Frederick for that matter. And still no word of the third Spanish Army. No, we must go on. Captain Stock is not going anywhere, and the Colonel has his suspicions."

Karl took a bite of food from his plate. "Johann, you must prepare the sheep of your flock to leave Eberbach. If Frederick and his allies cannot secure the Palatinate and he is replaced by the Duke of Bavaria, who is at this moment making his case to the emperor, it will be untenable to remain. The Emperor has already given Duke Maximilian temporary sovereignty in the Upper Palatinate, but he most desires Frederick's title, to become a Prince-Elector. We must listen to the advice of

Moses Bersheim and sell what we can."

"Let me help," Wilhelm responded. "But first," pointing to the Palace across the square from the inn. "Let me see the Elector-Archbishop before we leave. I must tell him about my decision. I owe him that much."

"See him if you must, Wilhelm, but go quickly. I need to arrange your transportation."

"Papa, must we go separate ways? Let us all travel together. Robert is in no condition to be traveling about the countryside."

"Katie, you have been strong since this business began. You must remain strong while Johann prepares our people. Wilhelm will return with you; he has proven himself strong and loyal. He will help. Robert and I must go. Armies are moving, the real war for the Palatinate will be upon us soon. The victims of this war will not be only soldiers. No, there will be upheaval, destruction, pillaging, lost crops and perhaps starvation. You must help your brother prepare our people! Think of the children! Consider the innocent! Robert and I will join you when we can."

Wilhelm rose from the table and said, "I go now. I will join you here when I return."

Robert stood up and limped over to Wilhelm. He grasped Wilhelm's shoulders and said, "Brother priest, I know you struggle to seeks God's will and to walk in His ways, trust that your heart is true. Trust that He is leading you. If the Archbishop is half the man of God you believe him to be, he will see this as well."

Wilhelm managed a small smile then turned and

strode across the square.

Once Wilhelm's presence was made known to the Archbishop, he was quickly shown into the ante-room. "Father Hahn, I had hoped to see you again," the Archbishop spoke as Wilhelm entered.

"Your Excellency, I have come to give you my decision. My time with you helped me to see where our Lord is leading me."

"Prayer and fasting, father, they are true nourishment to the soul. Your face tells me your decision is hard for you to share with me. Best to be out with it, my son."

Wilhelm fumbled with his words. "Truly, excellency, no one has touched me as you, and I would find great honor and comfort serving here with you, but..."

The Archbishop smiled, and said, "But."

"But I believe I am called to return to Eberbach. Armies advance, war is coming and with it, a hardship for the people. Excellency, I do not know if Catholics remain in Eberbach or if some protestants will return to the church. But I do know the good people of Eberbach will need shepherds. I intend to return to Eberbach with Pastor Johann Schroeder and together see to the needs of all of God's people. I no longer believe this war is between Protestants and Catholics, but between princes, kings and emperors whose true desire is for lands and titles and money. Reconciliation within the body of Christ will not come by the sword, but by breaking down the walls that divide us. Only love and service can break down the wall of suspicion and hate."

"So, father, you ally yourself with Pastor Schroeder to

heal the schism of the Church? Two men?"

Archbishop, I cannot be accountable for others, but for me, I will by the grace of God, do what I can."

"Do you renounce your priesthood, your pope and your church?"

"Certainly not excellency! I am called to the priesthood! I shall not renounce my priesthood even if the church renounces me!"

The Archbishop studied Wilhelm as he stood before him, honest and open. He dipped a quill pen in ink and began to write. Pausing for a moment, he looked once more at the humble man before him and continued to write. Setting the pen down he folded the letter, let a few drops of candle wax fall on it and sealed it with his signet ring. He then offered the letter to Wilhelm.

"Take this letter with you. I have ordained you the priest of Eberbach and the Archbishop's Vicar General, governor of all church properties in Eberbach: abbeys, hospitals, workhouses, and ministries. You have the authority to act in my name as the prelate to the Germans. You will report to me on the execution of your duties. You shall act for the mercies of the people of Eberbach. I also have your letter of safe conduct from the emperor. Let your light so shine to the people of Eberbach that they may see your goods deeds and praise our Father in heaven. Go with my blessings and pass my good will to Pastor Schroeder."

"Excellency, I don't know what to say, I am at a loss..."

"Father Hahn, you have your ordination, now go and

serve the Lord. God speed."

As Wilhelm turned to leave the room, Prince Elector Archbishop von Kronberg called out, "Remember, you are to keep me informed."

"Yes, Excellency. Thank you, Excellency, for putting your trust in me."

"My trust is in the Lord!"

Karl and Robert disembarked the boat at the head of navigation of the Wettenau River. Their voyage east from Mainz had been uneventful, though Robert had no rest, constantly scanning every passing boat and every man on horseback looking for the elusive Mr. Sharpe. Karl rented two riding horses and a pack horse for the ride to Hersfeld in Hesse Cassel. They expertly loaded Robert's chest and the many carefully wrapped tapestries and rode northeast towards the Weser River.

Robert was glad to be off the river; the autumn breezes were funneled over the cold river water by the steep cliffs that ran against the river bank. The trees were now changing to shades of yellow and orange, not yet the bright red of full color. The nights and early mornings chilled and aggravated the wounds on his leg. Karl led their way into the Hersfeld market where he met with his watchers, two dealers in dyes. Once the shop was empty of other customers, the older, a man named Martin, nodded towards Robert.

"He is one of us," Karl said. "What news of Christian the Younger?

"Duke Christian of Brunswick, Bishop of Halberstadt

and now General of his own army?"

Karl nodded. "We have come from Mainz where we heard Christian of Brunswick audaciously opposed the Mainz accord calling the gathered protestant princes cowards and backsliders. With but a year fighting the Spanish and serving in the army of Prince Maurice of Orange, he insisted he would continue the fight."

"We had heard he was fiery and intemperate," Martin replied. "Indeed his badgering had its effect, for he has money and our young Lutheran Bishop of Halberstadt is about raising an army. Since returning from Mainz after the dissolution of the Protestant Union in May, he scours Brunswick and Westphalia for men, arms and horses, to continue the cause along with Ernst von Mansfeld's remnant of Frederick V's army and Georg Friedrich, Margrave of Baden Durlach's small force. With the help of the Dutch Republic and God above, they would save the Reformation in Germany. A true cavalry officer, he spends as heavily on horses as men. His new army is estimated to number ten thousand men and was last reported making its way south towards Munden, where the Weser forks."

Karl nodded. "Yes, it would seem Prince Maurice has made a disciple! It was Maurice who persuaded Frederick V to accept the crown of Bohemia and brought this war upon us. But tell me, Martin, how can I gain an audience with the determined young Christian of Brunswick?"

"He will meet with anyone willing to support his cause with men, money or information. I know someone he trusts. Someone who will provide you a letter of introduction."

"That would be most helpful," Karl replied. "And turning to the young man said, "Now Hans, I will need a tapestry sketch carried to Mannheim ..."

Robert sensed Karl was uneasy meeting with the stranger. Both his silence and the steel in his stare made it clear Karl was weighing the risks as they walked. "You trust Martin? Robert asked.

"Yes, none the less..."

"None the less you do not like it," Robert replied.

"I also trusted Joseph Meyer. These are hard times. Men's loyalties change."

They arrived at the inn. Martin directed them to and found a table near the fire. "Warm your leg," Karl said. "I will bring you bread, stew, and beer."

Robert watched as Karl made his way to the innkeeper. The short, fat man, nodded as Karl made his order. Then the innkeeper looked to the far corner of the inn. Karl turned his head, and he stared at a man in a brown cloak and hat sitting alone. Turning back to the innkeeper, he exchanged a few words and returned with the beer.

Putting one mug of beer on the table, he said, "Our friend is here. You sit, I will make contact. It is better I go alone and that he knows I have company."

Robert slid around the table to keep the stranger in front of him. He reached for the pistol in his belt and placed it on the table next to his mug. He took a full drink of his beer and fixed his attention on the man in the dark cloak who watched as Karl made his way towards him.

Karl stopped in front of the man, and after unheard words, slid out a chair and sat down. As Robert watched, the innkeeper delivered a loaf of bread and two bowls of steaming stew. Without taking his eyes off the two men in the far corner, Robert broke off a piece of bread, dipped it in the stew and ate. Across the room, Karl and the man in the brown cloak stood, reached across the table and slapped hands together. Then Karl made his way back to Robert, sat down, and drank his beer.

"And?" Robert asked.

Karl opened his fist and showed Robert the coin in his hand. "Don't spend it. It is our pass to the young Duke Christian. Now, I intend to eat."

"You are certain?"

Karl watched as the man in the brown cloak left the inn. "He is Sophie's gatekeeper. The Queen Mother of Denmark and Norway and the wealthiest woman in Northern Europe. Her money is funding her grandson's army. Christian's funds come mostly from his Bishopric's estates."

"Sophie of Mecklenburg-Gustrow? Mother of Queen Anne of England? Grandmother of Elizabeth Duchess of Palatine?" Robert asked, his eyes open wide. "I heard she was in exile on some small Danish Island after her regency over ..."

"She was regent of the Duchies Schleswig-Holstein until Christian IV was of age. She fought with the Regency Council who would not allow her participation in governing Denmark and Norway. The government never accepted her, and she was exiled to the Nykobing Palace on Falster Island. She is a shrewd and most resourceful woman. She manages the estates and has become quite wealthy from both the lands and in money lending. Even King Christian IV regularly borrows from his mother."

Karl tasted the stew. Not particularly tasty, but warm and filling. After another drink from his mug, he wiped his mouth on his sleeve and continued.

"She is most unhappy with her son-in-law, James I, chasing after the Spanish Infanta, Maria Anna, so soon after the death of Queen Anne. She believes his dream of an alliance with Spain to become the peace broker of Europe is a fool's errand. James plays a dangerous game against his Danish, German and Dutch allies. Now Sophie's children and grandchildren rule most of Northern Europe. She will not sit idly by while Christian IV argues with his council in Copenhagen. She will keep the Hapsburg's engaged while the kings and princes of Northern Europe prepare for the continental war that is inevitable. The balance between Catholic and Protestant, between the Hapsburgs and all the other noble families of Europe, has been tipped. She sees it as clearly as the Prince Archbishop-Elector of Mainz, but she sees no hope for peace at all."

Robert sat back in his chair and scratched at the stubble of his beard. "I suppose we travel to Munden to meet Christian the Younger. But I would like an audience with Queen Sophie. I fear James' game is being played in the Palatinate with deadly consequences for our English forces."

"Winter will soon be upon us. We now hear Christian of Brunswick will winter his army where he is camped in Westphalia and train and organize his paid mercenaries. Later we could travel the Weser to Bremen and then ride the one hundred miles to the Baltic and cross over to Falster. But you are right in thinking Queen Sophie knows what to expect. Surely, she has ears and watchers of her own in the palaces of Northern Europe."

"And the court of King James as well, I would wager."

"Robert you are developing a skill for this work!"

CHAPTER 21
THE EBERBACH GUILTY

W ilhelm questioned Johann on every aspect of ministering to the people of Eberbach. They discussed the hospital, the orphanage, the workhouse and the home for the old. They talked of raising funds for the ministries, the small vineyard and winery, the grist mill and the abandoned abbey. They spoke of the people in the work of the Church, their strengths and shortcomings. Their discussion reflected optimism and hope, with an urgency to get about the humbling task of serving the needs of a people gripped with fear for the future. Good people who loved their families honored God and cared for their fellow villagers. There were no theological debates, no doctrinal disputes or arguments over authority. They were as two brothers with a shared mission to serve as priests of Eberbach.

Katharina saw something different in Wilhelm; he was just as warm, just as compassionate and just as determined as before. But clearly, he was different. She pondered all that happened in the months she had known him. But seeing him forge a friendship, no it was more than that, Wilhelm found a kindred spirit in Johann, and he found his place in life, an assurance in his calling to serve God. He was whole. Hope filled his soul, and it lifted him as he walked into his new calling. And Katharina loved him all the more.

As they entered Eberbach, Katharina wanted to stop at their home in the city. "You may go home, but first things first. Johann, come with me to the magistrate's office."

Wilhelm and Johann entered the office together, the assistant, Joseph Meyer was surprised to see them, but said in an attempt at authority, "What brings you to the magistrate's office?"

Wilhelm loudly announced, "I come with my ordination and seal as Vicar General to the Prince Elector Archbishop of Mainz, I demand an audience with the magistrate to relieve him of all duties that his excellency has granted me as Prelate of the Germans."

Joseph Meyer slowly rose, total confusion on his face. Before he could move from behind his desk, the door behind him opened and the magistrate stepped out. "An ordination as Vicar General is that what I heard to…"

Wilhelm looked at the stunned magistrate and said, "To me, Father Wilhelm Hahn. Magistrate, you are

informed that as Vicar General I have been ordained as
Roman Catholic Pastor to Eberbach and Vicar General of
all church properties, ministries, and duties. These
include the hospital, orphanage, workhouse, old home,
and the estates that support them including the vineyard,
fields, winery, grist mill and dairy. If there are others that
provide service to the people of Eberbach that are held in
common by the city, they too shall be administered by
me as Vicar General."

Handing the sealed ordination to the magistrate, he
said quietly, "Read."

The magistrate still in shock took the paper and read
it.

"Do you understand?"

The magistrate looked up and said, "What duties
remain with the magistrate, Vicar General Hahn?"

"You may call me Father Wilhelm. You will maintain
the duties of state. You shall collect the taxes and enforce
the laws of the city and Elector. But you will collect no
taxes from estates and property under the administration
of the Vicar General. I shall review your activities and
give a full report of them to the Prince Elector
Archbishop."

The magistrate smiled and said, "And for whom shall I
collect taxes, Elector Frederick or the Emperor?"

"You shall collect taxes due to the lawful overlord of
Eberbach," Wilhelm replied. Then he smiled and said, "To
the royal who comes to collect them."

The magistrate nodded. Wilhelm then asked, "I must
share this ordination with Count Tilly's representatives,

Don Lorenzo, Don Pedro, and Deacon Greiffenclau. Where can I find them?"

"Moved on Vicar General, er, Father Wilhelm."

"Have they left a priest?"

"A Spaniard, Father Diaz."

"Does this priest speak German?"

"No matter. He speaks the mass in Latin, and no one attends."

"I shall make my office in the church. If you have no further questions, I go there now."

As Wilhelm was leaving, he turned and said, "I should also tell you, magistrate, that I carry a pass signed by the emperor. Know also that Pastor Schroeder and his sister, Katharina have returned with me. The Prince Elector Archbishop of Mainz has removed all charges and accusations against them. I would view any harassment towards them with extreme displeasure. The citizens of Eberbach will share equally in the ministrations of the Vicar General, and the practice of religion, Roman Catholic or Protestant shall be encouraged for the general welfare of our city and for the glory of our Lord."

"Yes, Father Wilhelm, and welcome home Pastor Johann and my regards to Fraulein Schroeder."

It was only a short walk across the square to the rathaus, the city hall where the burgermeister and the city aldermen warmly welcomed Johann. Johann embraced them and introduced Father Wilhelm. "Father Wilhelm has, at great risk to his person, secured my release after my unlawful arrest and imprisonment in the Palace at Mainz. He has stood by my dear sister Katharina and father. He is a good man, a true man of God. He has been ordained Vicar General by the Prince Elector Archbishop of Mainz of all church properties in Eberbach and Pastor of the Roman Catholic Church. Together, he and I will minister to our city, fairly and equitably to all, Protestant and Catholic alike. Elders, these are hard times. You know the magistrate sits across the street empowered by the Emperor and backed by the Count of Tilly's soldiers. Know also that armies are being raised in the north intending to recover the Palatinate in the name of Frederick the fifth."

"Yes, we have heard such rumors, but there has been very different talk as to progress," the burgermeister replied. "Since the Army of Flanders has left, the people wonder who is in charge."

"We advise you to heed whichever prince or army enters our city. But expect repeated taxes and seizures and plundering. The new armies are often poorly paid mercenaries. Hide all food and valuables, but not everything, that would raise alarms. Do not share your plans with the magistrate or his assistant Joseph Meyer."

"Certainly not the magistrate, Johann, but Joseph?"

"Joseph betrayed my father and sister; he cannot be trusted. And now Father Wilhelm and I will see to the workhouse, orphanage, hospital and old age home. But tell me, what of the priests Don Pedro and Don Lorenzo and the deacon Greiffenclau?"

"They spent most of their time at the abbey, vineyard, and winery. 'Assuring good management.' they insisted. Left two days ago without a word. We assume they follow Tilly's army."

"Friends we have much to prepare for. But let it be known, both Protestant and Catholics will worship at the church. And pray we have the winter to prepare for what is coming!"

As they walked out of the city hall, Wilhelm commented, "We must find a safe place for food at the abbey. Someplace out of sight of the magistrate."

Johann answered, "Yes, but getting it there in secret is the problem."

Katharina was troubled going home. The house seemed so large and empty, but it was the smell that told her she was home. She had forgotten the scent of her perfume upon her clothes and bed linens, the smell of the hearth and the cooking pots, the aroma of spices and the bread baked in the wood-fired oven. It was the familiar smell of the Schroeder household. The rooms and furnishings were just as she remembered them, yet she realized her life was now so different. A deep melancholy descended on her as she went into her room. There was no smell of Wilhelm or of Robert or the cabin or the inns they visited. She realized that she could not walk back into her past; she had found something she did not know she was seeking, a desire and a need deep within her heart. But it could never be. She loved a good man, such a warm and compassionate man, but she must not encourage him or permit him to love her. She felt no need to let his religion stand between them. She was confident he could be persuaded to convert. No, something far worse stood between them, the secret that she kept hidden from everyone else and the guilt that secret carried.

Karl's servant, Werner watched her come in and followed her up the stairs. "Miss Katharina, you are home. Is all well? Is Johann with you? Your father sent word you were returning. Please, let me find something for you to eat."

Katharina did not turn to face Werner; she knew of his ability to read her face. She replied softly, "Thank you, Werner. I will come down in a few minutes after I have emptied my bag. Yes, Johann and the priest, Father Wilhelm have come with me. They should be here soon. They wanted to attend to some business first."

"Very well, mistress. It is so very good to see you home again and well. I will leave you to your settling in."

Werner did not need to see the tears in Katharina's eyes to know his young mistress was troubled.

Katharina asked, "Werner, did my father say when he would return?"

Werner stopped on the stairs and replied, "He expects to be away some weeks, mistress. Come down when you can, a good meal and some wine to help you recover from your journey."

Katharina wiped the tears from her eyes and set about emptying her bag. She went to the window and watched as Johann and Wilhelm walked across the square. *Work,* she thought, *I must work all the harder to atone for what I have done. Perhaps, someday God will forgive me. But father and Johann must never know; it would break their hearts. And Wilhelm, I could never bring dishonor on his name.*

Downstairs in the pleasant room below, Katharina made her way towards the fireplace. Werner had placed several logs on the fire to warm up the room and take the away the autumn chill. She pensively gazed upon the portraits adorning the walls. The large painting of her father in his most expensive clothes proclaimed the successful and confident merchant that he was. On each side were handsome portraits of Johann and Katharina. She had always been amazed at how well the paintings captured her family, not just the unmistakable accuracy depicted, but somehow the personality, smile or demeanor of each family member was preserved forever on the canvas. On the mantel was a small, more primitive painting of a young woman both strong and serious.

Werner had quietly entered the room and walked beside Katharina. "How your father regrets not having a better portrait of your mother. This portrait hardly does her justice. She was beautiful in face and spirit, and oh, what love she had for all of you."

"I can barely remember her face, but her soft voice and gentleness still linger." Katharina said softly, her eyes still fixed on the small portrait.

"You were very young, mistress when she passed. Too soon, she was gone. Far too soon. But these portraits, they captured each of you so well. What a blessing that young Dutch painter from Delft came to Eberbach. No one will forget you, your brother or father. They but need to glance at these, and you will all be remembered."

Katharina stood silent. Werner turned back to the kitchen and said, "Come I have hot soup and bread, and fine wine, unlike what you drank in who knows what ratskeller. It is such a pleasure to have you here again mistress."

Johann and Wilhelm came through the door. Johann shouted, "Werner! Is that hot soup I smell? Two large bowls my friend and bread too, for me and our friend Wilhelm!"

"Pastor Johann!" Werner replied. "You are home safe! Come, sit, sit both of you. The house has come back to life and is a home again! Hot soup, yes, and bread and a bottle of our outstanding wine."

Johann and Wilhelm continued their conversation. "Hiding the provisions is one thing, but moving them to and from the hiding place multiplies the risk. And then we must consider who we can trust, who must know of our plan."

Wilhelm thought and replied, "Johann, not everyone needs to know everything. We deal with each farmer separately. We tell each only what he needs to know concerning when and where to leave what we shall hide. We keep the hiding place and how we move the goods a secret."

Johann nodded. "Yes. And we shall need a wagon and horses. We need to find someplace where traffic is expected, and yet is unlikely to store provisions. Someplace that will not be thoroughly searched."

"Certainly, no house, barn or warehouse will do. But I have an idea…"

Katharina sat silently watching as Johann and Wilhelm continued their conversation, seeing for herself what had been evident to others. Listening, seeing but not hearing a word said. She saw the acceptance and trust Wilhelm had acquired. She saw that he had entered their world and become closer than community. He was now family. She had welcomed him when, what now seems so long ago, he first offered his help; she allowed him into her world, and she would never be able to let him leave it. She knew she loved him and did not have the strength to send him away. How could she end the guilt that bore down on her? The sins had been committed; they could never be undone.

CHAPTER 22
EBERBACH COMES TOGETHER

Farmers and merchants in Eberbach immediately saw the benefit of agreeing to the plan explained to them by Johann and Wilhelm. The plan was both simple and effective; only the one market week's supply would be openly available, the rest hidden in two ways. Each farmer or merchant would hide half of the remaining inventory in a location known only to him and his selected family members or servants. The other half would be picked up at a prearranged place and hidden communally by Johann and Wilhelm. The market would appear normal to any buyers, the magistrate and visitors. A system of receipts was made to account for the goods they accepted and sealed under the authority of the Vicar General.

Johann and Wilhelm told no one who would make the pickup or where it would be stored. No one else knew that the straw beds in the hospital and orphanage were now filled with sacks of grain surrounded by straw, the same hospital now caring for a leper. The abbey, winery, and dairy all held secret places for storing the community's provisions. A dry cistern held casks of wine and other goods. A false bottom held water deep enough to accept the wooden pail hung above it. Empty wine barrels, hollow to a tap, were filled with dry goods. The more Johann and Wilhelm viewed, inventoried and tested, the more hiding places became available.

No one person knew where all the provisions were hidden. The farmers and merchants kept their hiding places to themselves as did Johann and Wilhelm. Immediately the leaders of Eberbach felt more confident, more in control of their future. But there was more to do.

As Johann and Wilhelm stowed a night's delivery, Johann said, "Our flock needs more than sustenance. The people of Eberbach must learn to trust and care for one another."

Wilhelm nodded. "Yes. Johann, I know the city fathers want to welcome you, their beloved pastor back to their city. I think I can make that possible."

That night Wilhelm composed an edict as Vicar General for the Eberbach Church. "After a thorough search of the records of Eberbach Church, I have determined that this Church was built to Glorify God not man, order or prelate. Therefore, the citizens of

Eberbach shall not be coerced by any church or state to a favored religion. So long as God is glorified, and His will sought, believers shall have access to the Church of Eberhart for worship and the free practice of religion. As a sign of this order, both Catholic and Reformed worship services will commence this next Lord's day."

Showing the edict to Johann, Wilhelm asked, "Can we do this, brother?"

"Does not the creed acknowledge, 'One holy, catholic and apostolic church?' Why not here in Eberbach?"

"Brother, if we are to unite the people, we must build on what unites us. We are united in our love for God and His children. We are united in the Holy Scripture, the creeds and much of ancient tradition. There is little difference in the liturgy, acts of mercy, indeed the very practice of religion. Let our citizens see this. Let our worship be at once together and separate."

Wilhelm's face brightened. "Let our separate liturgies coincide, yes they speak to one another like bells in a tower! But brother let our homilies and sermons be as one!"

"Scripture as well! And I have in mind the first homily. I would have the people of Eberbach recognize this new man, nay, this new neighbor who sees to their welfare!"

The burgermeister and aldermen quickly acted declaring that Sunday a day of thanksgiving for the safe return of their pastor and the welcoming of the Catholic Vicar General of Eberhart. The magistrate was less impressed with the edict but could not object. The Spanish priest was appalled and wanted no part of tolerance to any protestant heretic. Wilhelm argued, "Father, you cannot change a man's heart by the sword. If God speaks through the Roman Catholic Church, let the protestants hear our worship. They will not otherwise enter your church."

The Spanish priest held his tongue; it was too early to challenge this new Vicar General. Finally, Wilhelm said, "The magistrate will be at mass, I shall preside and you, father, will assist me."

The Spaniard softly replied, "It is my duty to attend mass daily. I shall assist you this Lord's Day."

For the first time since the army of Count Tilly entered Eberbach when the bells of the church rang to call the faithful to worship, the church filled. The people of Eberbach had recovered something they had lost, something they had always taken for granted but now found precious. Faces brightened with broad smiles found a full voice when the organ began to play old familiar hymns.

After the call to worship, Pastor Johann stood with outstretched arms and loudly addressed his congregation. "Good people of Eberbach. Friends! How good it is to praise our God! We come here to worship and adore our Savior and true King! Welcome, all! And welcome to our brother, Father Wilhelm Hahn, Vicar General of Eberbach, by the authority of the Prince Elector Archbishop Schweikhartd von Kronberg of Mainz. The good Father Wilhelm, already known to you for his many deeds of mercy and dedicated to justice and the well-being of our city has decreed that all who abide by the ancient creeds of the Holy catholic and apostolic faith may worship in the church of Eberbach. Know then, brothers and sisters, that we have agreed that our worship should be together as faithful followers of Christ but separate regarding our religion. So, as we worship here today, Father Wilhelm will celebrate mass in the transept chapel. I beg that no one here is found forced into the protestant faith. Any whose true heart lies in the Roman Church, please join Father Wilhelm at mass."

Johann turned to his right and said, "May God bless and inspire your worship, Father Wilhelm. We begin!"

Father Wilhelm followed by the Spanish priest entered the small chapel with his loud voice reciting Psalm 42 in Latin. "Introibo ad altar Dei, ad Deum qui laetificat iuventutem meam, (I go to the altar of God, the God who gives joy to my youth)." He then made the sign of the cross, and continued in Latin, "Our help is in the name of the Lord."

The Spanish priest responded in Latin, "Who made heaven and earth."

While this took place, Johann opened his service in prayer, the whole congregation listening with Wilhelm's voice in the background reciting psalms in Latin. Back and forth voices could be heard, Johann's, loud in the sanctuary and Father Wilhelm's echoing from the chapel, hymns countering the Kyrie and Gloria. The two servants of God found unity when leading both congregations in the Nicene Creed and the Lord's prayer. Both read the same scriptures for the day. When the time came for the sermon, protestants and Catholics alike, were surprised to see Father Wilhelm walk to the main altar and join Pastor Schroeder. Johann began, "Our lesson today comes from the Gospel of Luke, the story of the Good Samaritan."

Looking first to his small Catholic congregation, Wilhelm retold the story dramatically with passion. Visibly upset that any man, let alone a priest of God could walk by someone so desperately in need of help. He spoke tenderly of the Samaritan who stopped aided and cared for the beaten man. He explained, "There are two very different men in this parable, the priest and Samaritan. The priest gave his life to serving God. He researched the law for the way to righteousness. The Samaritan had little knowledge of the law. Perhaps he should have searched it as diligently as the priest. But God judged these men not on how they searched the law or what they knew. God judged them by their heart. He saw what flowed from each man's heart; one, a legalistic observance of rules and rituals, (now it is a noble thing to seek knowledge of God's law), the other with eyes that saw a need and a heart moved to serve. Jesus tells us that the greater of these is the heart to serve others before self."

Then Johann began. He challenged both congregations, "What is the lesson for us my friends? What would our Savior have us to do? Our Lord Jesus has told us what He desires for us. He would have each us be the true neighbor, even the Samaritan, the man of another religion who shows mercy under Grace. Friends, there is one here today who is that true neighbor, and we must become more like him as well. A humble man. A man whose religion may seem different to us, but is it not our Lord and Savior that he loves and serves? I speak of our friend and true neighbor Father Wilhelm Hahn who shows us his love and kind his works of mercy. Friends, brothers and sisters, God calls us to love Him and to love our neighbor as ourselves."

Father Wilhelm stood his eyes down to hide the tears in his eyes. Finally, he straightened up and said, "Brother Schroeder is far too generous in his remarks. But this is a true saying as we come to the table of our Lord, 'If any man has not forgiven his brother he is commanded by our Lord first to seek out his brother, confess his trespasses against him and them come and eat the body and drink the blood of our dear Lord Jesus with a clean heart and soul.' Amen."

The Spanish priest stared in disgust at Father Wilhelm standing alongside the heretic and his heart was filled with hate.

As Wilhelm went to serve his small following, Johann led his congregation in communion. As Katharina came forward, she crossed her arms in front of her. Seeing her arms crossed, the bread and wine were not offered, but instead, Johann placed his hand on her shoulder, and he blessed her saying, "Sister, may God bless you and keep you this day and forever. Amen."

Later that day when Johann found himself alone with her, he asked, "Katie, you did not take communion this morning, is all well with you."

"Brother, indeed, there is something which weighs on

my heart, but I am yet unable to speak of it with you."

"Please know there is nothing you need fear telling me, yet I understand you may be reluctant. Still, confession is good for the soul, spend time with the Lord, tell Him what upsets you so. He loves you and as he has forgiven you already and sees you righteous in His sight; he will provide comfort to your soul."

"Brother, I have sought His forgiveness many times, yet still I grieve."

"Katie, you cannot hold onto guilt. Whatever you hold tight inside of you must be released. That is why we confess our sins to those we have wronged, it provides release, and God pours out His grace."

"I will consider your words brother. Thank you. I know that you speak in love."

Katie knew she must tell someone of her guilt, someone trustworthy who could intercede for her with God. If it were anything else, she would confess to Wilhelm, but not this sin. No, she could not share this with him; there was too much pain. But who?

One morning while Johann and Wilhelm were visiting the hospital, orphanage and old abbey, Katharina knocked meekly on the door to the church office. The Spanish priest opened it and stared silently at the young woman standing before him. "Father, I am Katharina Schroeder and…"

"I know who you are. You are a sister to Pastor Schroeder. I know Father Wilhelm resides at your house."

"Your German is very good, Father, I have heard it said you do not speak our language."

"When no one speaks to you, no one welcomes you, why speak? I find it more rewarding to listen."

"Will you listen to me Father, I would have someone hear my confession."

The Spanish priest stared at Katharina for a moment and said, "Come in. I will listen."

Katharina went into the office and sat in a chair the priest pointed towards. "There is a sin in my life that weighs heavy on my soul. I have confessed to God, but still, I bear only guilt and shame. Even my brother counsels me that confession to the wronged or an intercessor is good for the soul."

"And what is it you would confess?"

Katharina determined that too many years of keeping her secret had passed; she took a deep breath and said, "I have permitted a man to paint me undressed, fully nude, in a most shocking painting. He flattered me with praise for my beauty and assurance that it was my innocence that he would capture in a true masterpiece. I was young and naïve, but I knew better. I was brought up to be a virtuous woman. It was wrong; it was…:

"You pause, there is more. Tell me all."

"Yes. Several years ago, a young painter came to Eberbach. A Dutchman. His paintings were so true as to be as clear a picture as one looking in a mirror. He painted portraits of all the leading men of our city. My father paid for him to paint his portrait and one of my brother and one of me. They hang in our home to this day. He stayed in our city for some time, and I came to trust him; his gift must have come from God."

"I am aware of these Dutch painters. They earn their living off the vanity of wealthy merchants and city elders. Please go on."

"The young man stayed in our house. My portrait was the last to be painted. My father was busy with his work, and my brother was gone most of the day. After he finished my portrait, he begged me to let him paint me in a special work, one that would make him a master. It was unlike the portraits for a commission. He called it art, not merchandise. He convinced me that masters were painting truth found in ancient mythology, paintings of the muses and gods. He called me a Venus and one whose beauty was spiritual more than physical. He said I smiled like no other woman he had ever seen, but it would find its perfection with my naked body as God created me. I agreed to his request; no one would know. It was an honor, I was assured so. But when I was unable to undress fully, he came to me and held me tight. He kissed me and undressed me. He loved me, and I did not stop him. And now my face and naked body are somewhere, and I have become an object of lust to men I will never know."

Katharina began to weep. "I have prayed to God for His forgiveness, but the guilt and shame will not go away. Father, please tell me that God has forgiven me."

The priest snorted as he began, "You, a heretic come to me, a priest of the true church? You can receive no forgiveness of this sin as you are outside of the faith. You are a heretic and a whore. You are bound for hell where all whores belong. First leave the heresy your brother teaches, return to the Roman Church and perhaps with penance and true obedience you can make a confession to a priest. No get out of my sight, filthy woman!"

Katharina wailed as she made her way out. "You will say nothing to Father Wilhelm…"

"I make no bargains with whoring heretics. Get out!"

CHAPTER 23
BISHOP, DUKE, AND GENERAL

Robert and Karl learned that Christian the Younger had moved down the Weser River, north to Hoxster, where he commanded the hospitality of the Prince-Abbot of the Abbey at Corvey. As much as he complained, Robert found himself once more on a boat moving slowly downriver. Leaves were turning from yellow and orange to the deep red of late autumn. The weather, however, was cooperating, with gentle winds and sunny days. The still air bore the strong scent of wood fires as they passed villages and castles.

Robert's attention remained fixed on each passing boat, and every rider passed along the road running beside the river. "Still looking for Sharpe?" Karl asked.

"Never hurts to keep an eye open when an enemy may

be about."

Karl nodded. "I believe you sleep with an open eye, friend!"

"Tell me, Karl, what awaits at the Abbey?"

Karl replied to Robert, "The Abbey remains an independent Benedictine state surrounded by the Lutheran Westphalia. The Prince-Abbot shrewdly maintains his seat in the Reichstag as a member of the College of Princes, having invited three noble families of Hoxster to share power through an arranged Protestant Assembly."

His eyes followed Robert's as he scanned another boat. "The Abbey had once been a member of the Hanseatic League and had long competed in trade with the nearby town of Hoxster. The Prince-Abbot had no choice but to cooperate with his protestant neighbors."

Satisfied all was well, Robert turned back to Karl and heard him continue. "The large and wealthy Abbey provides a fine headquarters for Christian the Younger to organize and train his newly formed army. Expect a large, sumptuous palace. It is noted for its fine library. It offers comfort for the young general and his officers. Food and forage are plentiful for his men and cavalry horses."

Robert replied, "Tell me about Christian. I hear he is hot headed."

"He has the impatience of youth. But he has demonstrated both bravery and skill in the service of Maurice, Prince of Orange. He is a most unusual man, very ambitious, as the third son of Duke Henry Julius of

Brunswick, he knew he would have to make his own way in the world. He was educated in Helmstedt, guided by his uncle King Christian IV of Denmark-Norway and earned the admiration of his grandmother the Dowager Queen Sophie."

"Apparently, enough so that she is funding his army."

"He earned the title of Duke when his brother, Rudolf, died and Christian became the administrator of the Halberstadt Bishopric. The position provides little in the way funds, and though the Catholic Church does not recognize the title transferring to a Lutheran, the Lutheran presence makes it real. Queen Sophie admires both his zeal and determination. She was never one to abide the cautious advice of councilors that slow the decisions of her son, King Christian IV."

"Which led to her exile."

"In truth, her exile has only made her strength grow and, also, a very wealthy woman. But as for Christian the Younger, he has taken his Bishopric to heart and is a fervent Lutheran."

"No wife?"

Karl smiled. "He is but twenty-one years old and has shown no interest in the diplomacy of marriage. He cares only for taking the war back to the Emperor and protecting the free practice of his Lutheran faith."

Robert turned to Karl and said, "How do you know all these details on so many people?"

Karl laughed. "So many princes and dukes competing for symbols of wealth and influence. They keep my family fed and my house prosperous. Cold castle and palace walls have much room for tapestries! I must learn who my customers are, what is important to them and to who they listen. And of course, I have my watchers who keep me abreast. With constant warfare, titles and positions change. I simply strive to stay current."

Arriving at the Abbey, Karl presented a letter and showed the coin he was given in Hersfeld. The sentry left and returned with the Captain of the Guard. "Show me the coin," he commanded. Karl handed the Captain the coin. The soldier held it close and scrutinized it. Handing it back to Karl he said, "You have a letter?"

Karl gave him the sealed letter and said, "It tells his Grace, the reason we request an audience."

"Follow me."

Karl and Robert were led to a waiting room in the palace. Karl circled the room examining the rich tapestries on the walls. Pointing to one he said, "I once sold this one to the burgermeister of Bremen. Well, the Prince-Abbot has an eye for quality."

"What? Robert remarked a prince in Germany who has not bought from you?"

"Not yet, but he will! I'd wager he will," Karl replied.

"A good Calvinist like you offering a wager? Your righteousness is slipping to my eye!"

"We'll keep that between us. My son and daughter would heartily disapprove!"

A door opened, and a servant appeared. "This way gentlemen. The Duke will see you now."

Robert and Karl were led through succeeding rooms, all facing the west, coming at last to a lavish library room lined with leather-bound books with gilded titles. Several tables were in the center of the room, each having a lamp, paper, pen, and inkwell. Seated in a cushioned chair along the window was a motionless Duke Christian of Brunswick-Luneberg. Across from him an artist was dabbing paint on a large canvas firmly held in a gilded easel. His eyes were focused on the painting before him, a brush in his right hand and a colorful palette in his left.

Without turning, the youthful and handsome young man spoke. "You bear one of my grandmother's rare coins. Thus, she tells me I should hear you. Your letter speaks of sharing information. I have lately returned from the disastrous meeting in Mainz. I know what allies remain. What can you tell me that I don't know or more to the point that I need to know?"

"Your grace," Karl began. "We have established a network of watchers in support of Colonel Vere..."

The young Duke continued to oeld his pose and replied, "Yes, the Englishman. In Mannheim. I know of him; Prince Maurice of Orange always speaks highly of him and his two fellow colonels."

Karl was accustomed to speaking to nobles whose attention seemed elsewhere. "The English hold the central Rhine and the entrance to the Neckar river. They hide in their strongholds as the Count of Tilly rages through the Palatinate taking city, village and garrison, one at a time. General von Mansfeld's army remains to the east, and the Spanish Army of de Cordoba harasses Prince Maurice and the western Rhine."

"Yes, yes, all of this I know."

Karl ignored the irritation in the Duke's voice. "But do you know the true strength of each force? Where it camps and when marches? Is this not useful? Your scouts may give you a day or two eyes forward and diplomats, well, your Grace understands the advice of diplomats from your meetings in Mainz."

Christian, turned away from his portrait painter and looked at Robert and Karl. "What is it you want from me?"

Robert interrupted in French, "If I may, your Grace..."

Christian bellowed in perfect English, "Your French is terrible! That of an Englishman! Spare us all. I understand English; my aunt was your late Queen Anne."

"Thank you, your Grace. Your English allies are determined to fight, but their position is precarious. The full forces of the Emperor are determined to keep Frederick from returning to the Palatine. And there are bedeviling events in the English court. The Spanish hold back for now in the hope that the English army withdraws, and their fortresses recaptured without the cost of a single man. Time, your Grace, time is everything. Re-enforcement can keep your English allies in the fight before the Spanish, and the Emperor lose patience, or King James loses his resolve."

"Certainly, King James would not desert the cause of his daughter, cousin Elizabeth?"

"I fear with the death of my late queen, your aunt, he may now love the benefits of an alliance with the Spanish and Emperor Ferdinand more than his daughter. She is a strong woman, and she will find her way."

Christian turned to the artist. "Jan, that will be all for today. I will find time to sit, perhaps tomorrow."

The artist put down his brush and palette, bowed to Christian and walked out of the room. Duke Christian walked over to the unfinished portrait and said, "A fine likeness, would you not agree?"

"Very fine indeed, your grace," Karl replied.

Robert listened in frustration. *Why do men in authority always change the subject when they are called to make a hard decision? An honest man would say, 'I need time to think.'*

Duke Christian continued, "Once again, my grandmother insisted I sit. She chose Jan. Jan van Ravestyn of Delft. She claims I am the only true warrior among her children and grandchildren and wants this to remind her of me…just in case. I think it is really to show her displeasure with my uncle Christian IV."

The young Duke paused staring at the picture softly said. "It is amazing to capture one so clearly." Again, he paused, then said, "I find the sitting so difficult. I have so much to do. Men to train, leaders to find. Never let them talk you into such vanity as a portrait!"

Karl smiled. "I would agree, your grace, for I found the experience much as you describe."

"Really, Herr Schroeder? You sat for a portrait? Who painted you?"

"Another Dutchman from Delft. He took commissions from all our town elders. A young man, Adriane van de Venne."

"Van de Venne? I know of him. He painted many of the

officers of Prince Maurice of Orange. I would never leave him alone with my wife our daughter! The man is a scoundrel and a rake! He fled when they discovered his dalliances with young wives."

Karl's face displayed his shock.

"He painted your wife or perhaps a daughter, Herr Schroeder?"

Karl regained his composure. "My daughter, your grace, but she is a virtuous young woman. Not one to suffer the flattery of such a man."

Duke Christian ended the conversation. "Yes, well, I must meet with my officers." Turning to Robert he added, "Englishman,"

"Your Grace?"

"What is your name?"

"Robert Curtis, your Grace."

"Robert Curtis, you and Herr Schroeder shall join me at my table this evening. I will consider what you ask."

When summoned that evening for dinner, a servant dressed in a military-style uniform led Robert and Karl through the same long row of rooms, past the grand entrance with its elegant staircase, to the opposite wing of the palace. They passed through lavish halls of state and a large dining hall. Behind the grand dining hall, the servant opened a door revealing an intimate dining room for twelve. Men in formal uniforms stood around the table murmuring in small groups. Soon after Robert and Karl entered, another servant opened the door at the far end of the room and announced, "Gentlemen, his grace Christian, Duke of Brunswick-Luneberg and Bishop of

Halberstadt."

Each man came to attention and bowed as Christian entered the room. "Please, Gentlemen, be seated," the Duke said moving to the head of the table. Each man stood behind his chair and waited for the Duke to sit before taking their seat.

"Another fine day, gentlemen! Fine indeed, but we have much to accomplish and little time. Now lets us give thanks to our Lord."

Bishop Christian blessed the food and then reached for a goblet of wine before him. Pointing to Karl and Robert, seated at the far end of the table, he said, "I have asked two guests to join us. They come with news from our English allies in the Palatine. But first let us eat"

After dinner, Duke Christian rose and said, "Now we will hear from our guests."

As all eyes focused on Robert and Karl, Christian sat down and continued, "They come from the Palatine with a plea from the Commander of our English allies for immediate relief from the Army of Count Tilly. The English wait behind the strong walls and fortresses of Heidelberg, Mannheim, and Frankenthal. Gentlemen, what is your counsel?"

A white-haired man looked to the left and right at his fellow officers, then spoke. "General, the English have stone walls to protect them, and no doubt have gathered grain and wine for the winter. Your army is yet in need of training. The pikemen are inexperienced farmers, peasants, your Grace, and tradesman. They must be drilled and learn to fight as one. Your cavalry includes many fine horsemen, many from noble families, but they too require training and coordination."

"Thank you, Colonel. Quartermaster, what do you say?

A portly middle-aged man, too large for his uniform answered, "General, we still acquire carts for baggage and provisions. We need more cannons, and we have no large siege cannons, general. We train and prepare to fight in the field, which is your favored strategy, looking for opportunities to engage smaller forces on ground that favors us. The grain store is not full, nor the wine. We still procure weapons and winter clothes, General, many of the men came with only threadbare clothes, lacking proper boots and winter coats. Provisions will be difficult to find in the Palatine as all crops were harvested and for certain, hidden away."

"What of grain and fodder for my horses," Christian asked.

"We have fodder and some grain, but not the carts sufficient to transport it."

Another officer spoke. "With your permission, General, the horses are not battle ready. They must be trained for the blast of the cannon and noise, smell and din of gunfire. They must be calm in the confusion and responsive only to their rider. Every horse must be so trained, even the baggage cart horses, for we shall not find battle ready replacement horses in the field."

"Thank you, gentlemen, you have been most honest. Adjutant, I have not heard from you."

The officer seated to his right, silent throughout the

report, lifted his head and answered softly, "An attack in winter would be truly bold, and audacity has its rewards. If you consider, general, the reward and the risk, what is to be gained by hasty action? The English will not withdraw before spring. They can safely winter behind strong walls. Surely the Count of Tilly will soon quarter his army as well. In early spring when the ground is firm, we will be trained and strong. We will have full provisions and will find no need to pillage the very people we seek to save, the subjects of Elector Frederick and your cousin Elizabeth."

Christian nodded, rose from his chair and said, "I thank God for the wise and capable leaders our Lord has provided me."

The adjutant responded, "Your grace, I speak for all of your staff and men when I say it is we who are honored to serve you. May God give you strength, and may He favor you in the victory against all of those who would deny us freedom to serve Him in accordance with His will."

Christian smiled and said, "You are most kind. Now permit me to advise our friends privately."

Once the room was empty, Christian walked over to Robert and Karl. He carried a pitcher of wine and refilled their cups. Returning the pitcher to a silver tray and lifting his goblet, he asked softly, "Is there any argument against the counsel of my officer's? No, you know they speak the truth. Tell your Commander we come in the spring when we are strong and battle ready. Tell him we agree to share information and welcome what your eyes and watchers can tell us. Herr Schroeder, the man who gave you the coin will be your contact. You know where to find him."

Karl nodded. "Yes, your grace, I will make the arrangements."

Robert asked, "Your grace, can we expect help from your uncle, King Christian IV of Denmark-Norway?"

Christian examined Robert closely before answering. "I cannot speak for King Christian, but I know that his council cautions him. He will not act if King Gustav Adolphus of Sweden does not join the cause. My uncle fears Gustav more than the Emperor. Neither wants to make the first move. Neither will leave his lands on the Baltic unprotected against the other."

Robert was surprised by his direct response but could not hide the disappointment in his face. Christian's face softened. "My friend I can afford to be true to my heart, my estate is small, my father Duke Heinrich Julius the ruling Duke and my brother Prince Frederick Ulrich are far greater in wealth and power, and King Christian and kinsman protect our lands on all sides. I do not fight for glory or lands. I fight to save the reformation! It is the intention of the pope and his client emperor and kings to exterminate any opposition to his authority. There has been no change in Rome. Their last council brought no reforms, though there were some who truly sought them. The Scripture is still hidden and forbidden. The people are not taught; they cannot question. They are to do as they are told; they stand and listen to the foreign babel of unlearned priests and submit to a corrupt and entitled clergy. The new pope is no different than the one our great Pastor Luther embarrassed. He gives estates, power and wealth to his family and sends gold to kill our new Church. God is testing us Mister Curtis; testing us to see if we have the faith to stand for His truth. He sends His grace, but His grace cost him greatly. His grace was costly, we too must be willing to pay."

Robert bowed to Christian saying, "I now see what your officers see, your Grace. And I pray God to bless you as an instrument of His will. O that my own King James had your heart."

Karl also bowed and said, "Your grace, we will take your message to Colonel Vere in Mannheim. I will speak to your man in Hersfeld on the way and arrange contacts. We will leave in the morning."

Robert made a glance with furrowed brow towards Karl before turning to the young Duke. "If you please, your Grace, I have one more request. We have uncovered a conspiracy among the allies in the Palatine. There are some among the English who meet and share information with a papal representative and a Spanish Abbot who travel with Count Tilly. They have conspired against Herr Schroeder's son, a pastor in Eberbach, his daughter and a priest who asked too many questions. These same men, for some unknown reason, collude with an Englishman, who has made several attempts on my life. I am merely a lieutenant of cuirassiers, and I am at a loss for a motive. But I fear we have stumbled upon a foul plot against Colonel Vere and the English forces. Your grace, the Dowager Queen Sophie has friends in the English court I would seek her counsel on this matter. With powerful lords urging our King to arrange a marriage with his son the Prince of Wales to the Spanish Infanta Maria, I fear there are divided loyalties. I could not stomach a traitor giving up your allies before your army marches south."

"Your King James plays a dangerous game with the Spanish. It is long suspected his loyalties are divided and he has little heart in the war to restore his daughter, Countess Elizabeth and Elector Frederick. Perhaps there is some urgency to your request."

Duke Christian paused and then said, "Your Colonel Vere knows you are here?"

"He knows we seek the support of the princes of the North and information on King Christian's intentions. He sees his position as precarious."

Duke Christian put his hand in a pocket and took out a coin. "This is the coin that brought you here. Take it to the Dowager Queen."

Robert took the coin and eyed Karl. "I will go to Falster at once."

"My grandmother visits my mother, the Dowager Countess of Brunswick in the palace of my brother, Frederick Ulrich, Prince of Brunswick-Wolfenbuttel and a ruling Duke of Brunswick."

"Your grace, I was told, forgive me for being so bold, that she was exiled to the Nykoping Palace on Falster Island…"

"Grandmother is no one's prisoner! It is true uncle Christian's council has made her unwelcome in the state affairs of Denmark, but she travels freely and provides welcome advice and funds to our family. She is too cunning and far too wealthy to be held isolated on a small island. She intends soon to visit Bremen where she can trade with all of Europe."

Christian clasped Robert's shoulder and laughed. "Lieutenant Curtis, you are indeed a bold and forward fellow! My grandmother will favor you very much. I tell you this, never underestimate her! And if your English Commanders withdraw, you come back to me. I will find you a place in my cavalry."

They walked briskly back to their room in the opposite wing of the palace paying no attention to the majestic and ornate rooms through which they passed. Once he was satisfied that they were alone and out of earshot of Christian or his staff, Karl anxiously confronted Robert. "Our mission is complete, we should return at once to Mannheim and report our information to Colonel Vere."

"You are anxious to return home. You worry about Katie. I saw it in your eyes when the Dutch painter's past was mentioned. You forget that we have not uncovered the plotters, their connection to the Don Lorenzo and Don Pedro. And who does Sharpe work for? Why the attempts on my life and the connection to Wilhelm and Katie. I too, am anxious to return to my friends, to stand beside Captain Charles, to stand with Sir Gerard Herbert in Heidelberg. No, Karl, we need contacts in the English court; Queen Sophie can help. When will I have such an opportunity?"

"But Robert, be reasonable..."

"Send a tapestry drawing, that will tell him all we have learned. If you insist on returning, I will go on alone!"

Karl snorted. "Very well, I see you are hard headed and obstinate. I dare not leave you to roam alone; you know little German, and your French accent is unbearable. You would only get yourself killed, and Katie would never forgive me."

Robert said, "So you are coming?"

Karl sighed. "Of course I am coming."

Robert laughed. "You had better; you lost the wager. I saw no tapestry sold. And in a palace with so much uncovered wall space!"

"A wager is it? We haven't departed yet!"

CHAPTER 24
THE HARZ MOUNTAIN INCIDENT

The next morning Karl approached Duke Christian with a request for two good riding horses. As payment, he offered up a beautiful tapestry and opened a few for selection. "A tapestry for your grandmother, a gift in return for the portrait, perhaps."

"Yes," Christian replied. "I can purchase more horses, that is fair."

Christian chose a large, exquisite court scene suitable for the Nykoping Palace.

Karl smiled. "Beautiful your grace! Such an eye you have!"

Karl sighed. "However, and I am embarrassed to say this ... I had hoped you would choose another. This one is, well, it is rather expensive. Does your grandmother have an appreciation for the best? I could find a lesser quality…"

"Lesser quality for Queen Sophie, are you mad?"

"Your grace is quite correct, perhaps a small amount in addition to the horses, say ten gold ducats?"

"The horses and seven gold ducats no more," the Duke replied.

Karl nodded. "In return for your gracious hospitality, seven gold ducats it is."

Christian was admiring the bright colors and fine detail of the tapestry. Karl offered, "Shall I deliver it to her on our visit? I can carry any letters you wish."

"Yes, please. I will write to her. My servant will take you to the stables, and you may choose among horses the stablemaster permits. Then return for the tapestry and my letter."

An hour later Robert and Karl rode out of Corvey Abbey on fine mounts intended for cavalry officers. This time it was Karl's turn to smile. "That should be a lesson, my young friend. Never claim a wager before it is due!"

"You have done this before, I see. Tell me, was the tapestry truly an expensive one?"

Robert nodded. "I only displayed my highest quality. That is why I suggested a gift to his grandmother, Queen Sophie. I knew he would not agree to lesser quality. She would never approve of anything but the best. And we need funds for this journey."

"And a fine profit as well, no doubt."

"I am a businessman, Robert!"

Looking back at the draft horse carrying the rolls of tapestries, Robert continued, "So we carry our bank account behind us. Very well done indeed! How pleasant to be astride a fine mount! And we can ride back to Mannheim."

They crossed the Wesser River at Hoxter took the road east to Nordheim, across the Leine River, where they found the road to Osterode at the base of the Harz Mountains. They rode to the inn on the market square, Karl instructed the servant, "Stable the horses but leave the rolls on the draught horse for now." Turning to Robert, he said." I will make a call on the Duke of Brunswick-Oster."

Robert smiled. "We stop for a sales call?"

Karl walked into the inn alongside Robert, his eyes looking for the innkeeper as he spoke. "We spend the night here. Tomorrow we take the road through the Harz mountains to Goslar. It's a long ride with but one village near the summit. From Goslar, it is but a day's ride to Wolfensbuttel. I must speak to a friend who watches travelers around and through the Harz mountains."

Up in their room, Karl said, "We will meet for supper when I return."

"I will stretch my legs in the meantime. Tell me Karl, how many Brunswick Dukes are there?"

Karl laughed. "Now you understand how strong my market is! So many princes, dukes, and bishops, each with their castle and palace. But to answer your question, two Brunswick families divide and combine land, the dominant house of Welf, Christian, his father and his brother, and the house of Guelph. The eldest son inherits the ruling title in the college of princes and the younger sons share lesser family titles and smaller estates."

"And they get along?"

"The two families get along, but there is strife in the mountains. The mountains have been mined for centuries, and the two families share access to the Harz mountains with the free imperial city of Lutter am Barenberge. The Dukes of Brunswick-Luneburg had ruled the city in the past and have never accepted the Imperial status granted to the city, and now with war, and Christian raising an army, I expect tensions are quite high."

"Well, you better be off. See that you can lighten the load of that poor draft horse before we start up the mountain."

"I shall do my best. Care to make another wager?"

"Nay, I have learned my lesson!"

After Karl left, Robert went for a walk through the town. It was like so many other German towns; a castle tower commanded the high ground, tower gates in the wall that could be lowered across the roads and defended in case of attack. The church and the half-timbered town hall dominated the market square with the inn and shops, also half-timbered, lining the perimeter of the market. Robert strolled trying to read German on signs above shops, matching the words with the universal picture signs. His peripheral vision caught a dark cloaked man matching his steps on the opposite side of the square. As he stopped and turned to look, the figure turned his back to Robert and disappeared through a doorway. *Probably nothing,* he thought, *Just someone about the market. Who would know we are here?*

At supper over roast pork, apples, cabbage, and beer, Karl shared with Robert what he had learned. "There were no troop movements in the area, but relations between the burghers of Lutter and Duke Christian's family were completely severed. Dowager Queen Sophie's visit and Christian's army were viewed as harbingers of an imminent attack. I will certainly forego any stops there. They also tell me a stranger has been wandering the market for several days. He buys only beer and light meals. He speaks to no one."

"I believe I saw him this afternoon. He seemed to shadow my walk through the market. When I turned, I was unable to get a good look at him. You don't suppose…"

"No, probably not. His habits are more likely those of a thief, choosing his mark. The mountains provide many opportunities to surprise a merchant in the thick forest."

"Would he be so obvious?"

"Not all observe as my watchers."

Robert smiled as he lifted his mug. "Is the horse any lighter?"

Karl nodded. "Of course! And my money bag a bit heavier!"

"All the better that we keep swords and pistols at the ready."

In the morning they set out up the mountain towards the village of Clausthal. The grade was steep, and the road snaked back and forth to gain elevation. The city below was in and out of view for an hour before they entered the dense forest. The autumn sun overhead, barely peaked through the dense canopy of oaks still clutching dead brown leaves. The stillness and the silence were broken only by the hoofs of the horses which brought a chill up Robert's back. Memories of lying face down in the field beside the Neckar River returned. The smell of grass and gunpowder and the stinging of briars on his bloodied hands and arms returned as he closed his eyes reflexively recounting the blackness.

His mount began to stray from alongside Karl who called out, "Robert, are you still with us?"

Opening his eyes, he gave his mount a nudge to catch up when the sound of a pistol shot loudly broke the spell. Again, the shot missed his back which moments ago was a slow, easy target. Robert reached for his pistol and pulled his horse to the right from where the shooting had rung out. The horse reared, spooked by the gunfire, its front hooves pawing at the air as it danced and pranced a pirouette and would neither settle nor respond. Robert swung himself from his mount and raced on foot into the forest.

Stopping and listening, his eyes scanned the woods. *There…to the right…breaking branches…a man on horseback riding off.* He raced towards him, and as the rider came into the clear, he fired. The man on horseback lurched forward but kept riding and disappeared into the woods.

Karl nudged his horse to a faster pace, the draught horse, tethered behind, obediently kept up. Robert grabbed the bridle of his horse, gently ran his hand down the frightened animal's neck, calmed him and remounted. He followed behind Karl, staying close to the side of the road. At Clausthal, Karl inquired at the inn if any single, dark cloaked rider had passed. "No one sir, and most every rider wears a dark cloak now days. Thieves are about, and finely dressed gentlemen and merchants make ripe plundering," the innkeeper replied staring at Karl's richly embroidered green wool riding cloak.

"Indeed," Karl replied. "As I have now learned. But keep an eye for this one, he may be wounded from his attack on us this morning."

After a brief meal and a beer, Karl and Robert were on the road once more. "Very likely a bandit, just as the innkeeper said," Karl began.

"A bandit? Who shoots first? And it is me who is his target?" Robert questioned.

"It is better you were his target. God protects you, Robert, you have more lives than a barn cat, my young friend!"

Robert looked at Karl sternly. "I would rather not put the good Lord to the test. And I am not convinced."

Karl replied, "You saw the man casing the town. The pack horse follows me, and you rode behind as a guard. Likely he meant first to remove my protection. Your garb is drab while mine is, I now see, too fine for this road."

Robert was not satisfied. Now it was his turn to

change the subject. "Why are there no miners about? No wagons of ore on the road?"

"The mines have guarded roads, only one way in and one way out to the strongholds and copper and lead smelters near the base of the mountain. The mines and their ore are well guarded, and only those in the employ of the Duke or the Free city owners may enter or leave. This road serves as a passage over the mountain and to the few woodsman and farmers hereabout. I chose this way as the fastest route to Wolfenbuttel."

"Did tell anyone our intended route?" Robert asked.

"No, only to the inn-keeper and my watcher know that Wolfenbuttel is our destination. As we departed so quickly and with trade goods, our route was easy to deduce."

Robert replied, "The inn-keeper? Well, I don't think our attacker would be so foolish as to come against us again today. All the same, I will keep both eyes open. I have been wrong before... Karl, you surprise me. The inn-keeper? Never trust an inn-keeper!"

Karl took the reprimand to heart. "Yes. I shall make further inquiries when we get to Goslar. Yes, it was foolish of me; who better to give information to a bandit about wealthy travelers. A few coins and a stranger is betrayed." Both men rode in silence as they continuously scanned the woods around them.

Goslar was just the same as Osterode, its twin facing east rather than west. The inn-keeper feigned surprise that an attack would occur on the road from Osterode. "Most alarming, sir! God be praised you were not

injured! No, we cannot have bandits on our road. Please
know this, I will make a report to the Duke myself! No
need for you to delay your travels. I'm sure you have
important and urgent business at…where did you say
you were heading?"

Karl replied, "I didn't. We travel east to Halberstadt
and beyond. You are certain you saw no lone rider in
brown come down the mountain?"

"Riders in brown, sir? Many riders in brown, but no
lone rider today. No, gentlemen, we pride ourselves on
the safety of this road. A gentleman and merchant can
expect a safe crossing. No more troubling yourselves,
gentlemen, it will be investigated. You can assure all that
the Goslar to Osterode road is safe! Have your dinner
and a good sleep. Go in safety tomorrow."

Once in their room, Karl began to speak. Robert
shook his head no and said, "I would stretch my legs after
so long a ride. Care to join me?"

Outside the room in the market now empty as the sun
was setting behind the mountain behind them, Robert
said, "Do you suppose the inn-keepers are in league?"

"It is possible. Clearly, he lied. It could be a lucrative
business with the bandits. The Mountain is a frontier of
different principalities and the free city. With the troubles
between the Duke and the city of Lutter, and travelers
avoiding possible conflict, it is most opportune."

"Profitable and effective so long as news of the trouble
does not leave the mountain. Tell me, Karl, your watcher
made no warning? That doesn't trouble you?"

"No. He made no warning, and after Joseph Meyer's

betrayal I see old loyalties betrayed."

Robert turned to Karl and asked, "Does Joseph Meyer know the identity of any of your watchers? If one of your watchers has turned, how much would he know? What damage could one false friend do?"

Karl looked ahead in silence.

CHAPTER 25
THE MATRIARCH
OF THE NORTH

To the east of Goslar, the craggy, wooded, Harz mountains quickly gave way to a flat, fertile, plain with wheat fields as far as the eye could see. Whatever minerals were mined from the Harz mountains could not surpass the agricultural richness of the Brunswick heartland. Peasants were busy gathering the harvest. The road was crowded with carts carrying the sheaves of wheat to winnowing sites and gristmills along the Oker River from where the grain could be shipped all over Northern Europe and the Baltic.

The city of Wolfenbuttel, the historic home of the Princes of Brunswick-Wolfenbuttel, arose before them. A new, Renaissance city with a high tower climbing from the majestic castle, commanded the view. As they rode closer, the city arose, alabaster white in the late afternoon sun, growing up from a verdant, green oasis in the middle of the Oker River surrounded by a waving sea of golden wheat.

"Almost magical, would you not agree, Robert?"

"Indeed, it is a vision of wealth and abundance! The city arises from the middle of the river from such green and lush land. I have seen none like it."

"Christian the Younger's grandfather, Duke Julius of Brunswick-Luneburg rebuilt the city as we see it now. He opened the Oker River to navigation to ship the wealth of the land by water north as well as road south."

"An inspired effort to be sure," Robert replied.

"He hired a Dutch canal builder to improve the waterways and build warehouses on new canals. A true man of vision and learning it is here he placed his great Ducal library ... and music! Perhaps you shall be privileged to hear the works of the Kapellmeister, Michael Praetorius, a man after your own heart. His music includes the most stirring hymns, and he longs to bring Catholics and Protestants back together in worship."

"Praetorius here? I have heard his work performed in the King's College Choir of Cambridge. I do miss music that praises the majesty of our Lord and God. His nativity celebration, 'Lo How a Rose Ere Blooming,' will remain with me forever. I shall very much like to hear his work."

On Karl's advice, the two rode directly to the castle where Robert presented his coin and a letter addressed to the Dowager Queen Sophie to the guard. They were admitted to the courtyard and told to wait. Half an hour later a uniformed servant returned and said, "The Queen Dowager Sophie will see you in the morning. She invites you to stable your horses and remain as her guests overnight. If you gentlemen follow me, your horses and goods will be stabled."

They followed to the wing of the castle housing courtiers and those having business with the Duke. Opening the door to the room the servant said, "All guests are welcome to super at the banquet hall. The Duke takes his food and drink there and enjoys stories, tales, and games with his guests. There will be no shortage of beer, wine, and merriment long into the night."

The servant then looked into Robert's face and continued, "Your business is with the Dowager Queen Sophie. I know from the coin that Duke Christian sends you. I would advise you then, that she does not approve of her grandson's drinking parties. Your cause is better served if you take your meal in your room. I can arrange it if you wish."

Karl answered, "That would suit us best as we are tired from our journey and desire most of all to be refreshed when we meet her highness in the morning… tell me, my friend and I would be most interested in hearing the Kapellmeister Praetorius. Will there be music available."

"I am sorry, but the Kapellmeister has recently passed. A replacement has not yet been named. Though music is always to be heard in the church on the Lord's Day. Is there anything else?"

"No, thank you. That will be all."

"Very good gentlemen. I will come for you in the morning," and the servant turned and left.

Once they were alone, Karl said, "I am told that Duke Frederick Ulrich is known to be given to drink. The man will be drunk when he arrives and carried away drunk sometime later. His mother, the Duchess Elizabeth of Denmark makes all decisions of state with the advice of her mother, the Queen Dowager Sophie."

"Your watchers do keep you informed! Tell me, is not the Duke married? What of his wife?"

The Duke's wife, Anna Sophia, is the daughter of the Elector of Brandenburg. They have no children, and the Duke is seeking a divorce; she often travels to Schoningen where she busies herself with a new school."

"You are saying, Karl, that he is Duke in name only and with no heir, his title will pass to one of his brothers or cousins."

"That is what I am saying, and the Dowager Queen Sophie and the Duke's mother, Elizabeth will have Duke Henry Julius' ear in all that occurs here."

The next morning Robert and Karl were led through the castle public rooms up the grand staircase and down to the far end of the castle. A servant opened the door as they approached revealing the private chambers of Queen Sophie. Two women sat beside a small table with letters opened on a small writing tray with quill and ink. Both women were resplendent in brocade and gowns. The elder, Queen Sophie, sat with the grace of a queen upon her throne. Her brocade coif surrounded her elderly but still attractive face with pearls embroidered upon the borders and a jeweled tiara sewn into the crown. The cap covered her ears and hair, no doubt, now gray. Her chin and jaw rested in clean white ruffles rising from the high collar of her red velvet and gold and jewel-encrusted brocade gown. A large gold cross encrusted with rubies hung from her neck, below a large brooch bearing the coats of arms of the House of Mecklenburg-Schwerin and the House of Oldenburg. She maintained much of the beauty of her youth which was complemented by her grace and the wisdom in her bright blue eyes. Wordlessly, she watched them enter, neither her eyes nor body language betraying her thoughts. The Dowager Duchess of Brunswick, Elizabeth of Denmark, was talking softly. "I shall tell the ambassador from Brandenburg their proposal is premature. The Duchess is secure and happy. She finds her work with the new school most fulfilling."

"Yes, quite correct. Thank you, Elizabeth, now I must hear what my dear grandson Christian the Younger of Brunswick finds so urgent."

Elizabeth arose and said, "Shall I leave you then?"

"No, my dear, stay and hear. I would have your opinion as well."

Looking at Karl and Robert, Sophie said, "You come from the Palatine and bear Duke Christian's coin. What is it you seek?"

Karl, responding honestly to what his eyes beheld said, "Your majesty…"

"I am no longer Queen of Denmark-Norway, you may call me 'your highness.'"

"Thank you, your highness, we came north in the service of Colonel Vere, Commander of the English forces in the Palatine. His small forces are besieged in Heidelberg, Mannheim, and Frankenthal. Duke Christian has received us but has determined to wait until spring when his army will be fully equipped and trained…"

"You have your answer then, why do you come to me?"

Robert spoke. "I am told you speak English. It is at my request, your highness…"

"It is no longer often I hear English, but please proceed."

"Your Highness, we have strong reason to believe there is a conspiracy afoot within the English regiments. Conspiracy with priests sent by the Pope and by the Spanish court."

"I would be surprised to hear if there were no conspiracy. There is a war, and state interests are involved."

"Truly it is so, Highness. I am told you are well acquainted with the intrigues of the English court and might share your knowledge so that the support of the English regiments not be lost. Surely, there is the Danish ambassador and others from the north in the English court…"

"I have no say in the affairs of my son Christian IV, his council has seen to that. You are English; why do you come to me?"

"Your Highness, I am not a gentleman of the court. I am but Lieutenant of Cuirassiers. I hold no title, though my uncle is Baron of Tweedbridge recently made Viscount Curtis. Yet several attempts have been made upon my life and on lives of Herr Schroeder's son and daughter. Priests and deacons from the Vatican and the Spanish Netherlands are acting in league with Englishmen in service to officers of the English Regiment. You see, your highness, my interests are at once personal and honorable. As a loyal subject of the King and a Protestant by faith, I am determined to find the truth in this conspiracy, to aid my Commander Sir Horace Vere and get word back to the court. If my findings do not reach the right ears at the court, all is still lost. I am aware of the factions but not the loyalties of King James' court. Who can I trust? Who would send traitors to our regiment? Who is working against the English support of Elector Frederick and Countess Elizabeth? Who is bending the ear of the King that he wavers back and forth like waves upon the shore?"

Queen Sophie looked intently at the passionate young officer standing before her. She sat silently tapping her fingers on the writing table beside her. Elizabeth also watched Sophie, knowing the next words must come from her. Sophie held up the small coin and letter from Christian. Finally, she said, "You bring a gift from Christian. I would like to see it if I may. He is a bold and audacious young man, I urge him to appreciate the finer things of a noble nature, art and music, science and of course worship. In that, at least he excels. Bring me the tapestry this afternoon, and we will talk some more."

Robert and Karl bowed and slowly walked out of the room. When they reached the door, Queen Sophie said, "Lieutenant Curtis, I am told you enjoy the music of the late Kapellmeister Praetorius. Please join me this evening to hear some of his works in the music room. I too am most fond of his uplifting music. Herr Schroeder, you may attend as well."

"Yes, Highness. You are most graceful. Thank you."

After leaving their audience with the Queen Dowager, Robert and Karl left the castle in search of clothes more respectable for a royal evening event. When they returned, a servant was waiting to escort them back to Queen Sophie's apartment. Stopping only to gather the tapestry, they followed behind the servant to the same apartment they entered earlier. Entering, they noticed a small man with graying hair and the modest dress of a clerk, holding what appeared to be a ledger book. Neither the Dowager Queen nor Duchess Elizabeth was present. The servant told them to wait while Queen Sophie was informed of their presence. The man turned and watched Karl and Robert enter then silently returned to his thoughts.

A few minutes later Queen Sophie was announced. She walked in briskly and said, "Konrad, did you bring what I asked."

The little man replied, "Yes your highness."

"The money my son the King borrowed from me to lend to the King of England; what was the amount in pounds sterling?"

Konrad opened the ledger and replied, "Fifty thousand English pounds sterling, your highness."

"Has it been delivered?"

"It is being sent as we speak. Your Highness."

"Thank you, Konrad, that is all for now."

The little man stood up, bowed to Queen Sophie and backed out of the room.

The queen turned to Robert and Karl. "Konrad brings with him the Royal Danish reports from the English court. We count it as interest against my son's loans. These reports go back to before my daughter Anne's marriage to King James in Scotland. We are prudent and deliberate people."

"Interest that Christian's Council does not know, your highness?"

Queen Sophie continued, "King Christian IV and I considered it some risk to allow young Princess Anne to marry King James of Scotland, but we knew Queen Elizabeth in England had no heir. Who else would she choose but a King, a Protestant and a Stuart?"

"Your wisdom is renowned all through Europe, your highness," Karl replied.

"Oh, we knew it some risk to send Anne to Scotland-a poor and dreary land. No money, no power, the Scots have but their whiskey to keep them warm in their cold, stony land, ever wet and miserable land – whiskey and growing warmth in the Protestant faith.

Robert and Karl remained silent. The queen turned to them as if returning from a distant memory and said in a perfunctory manner, "You come from my Grandson, Christian the Younger who gathers an army at my expense. You see my commitment to our cause. Your King James, Robert, has been a most undependable ally. Still, I risk my money and influence."

She continued. "King James has been outwitted at every turn by the Count Gondomar, the Spanish ambassador to England. Until now, my son in-in-law has permitted only volunteers paid for by others to fund Colonel Sir Horace Vere's regiment, the Dutch, the Elector Palatinate or the benevolence of clearer thinking English nobles. He has kept responsibility away from himself. He called the parliament only because of his dire need for revenue. He claims support for our cause but will not give enough funding in fear of upsetting the Spanish."

"That is the dilemma," Robert replied.

Queen Sophie tried to maintain her calm discourse, but her rising emotions were not be hidden. "He is a man frozen by his divided loyalties. He is a fool who believes he can be the great peacemaker on the continent, at one time championing his son-in-law Frederick V and preventing a full Spanish invasion of Germany through an alliance with Spain by marriage, a foolish notion to which even my daughter agreed to under the influence of her Catholic friends. He has been openly hostile to Frederick's ambassador, Count Dohna and ambassador Buwinckhausen of the Protestant Union."

Queen Sophie's face turned red her eyes hardened to a steely blue. "He has squandered his opportunities; the invasion has begun, and the Hapsburgs will bring to the rest of the continent what they have done in Bohemia where the reign of the native-born and historic aristocracy has been brought to its end. The Reformation, and the protestant people of Bohemia, ill-served by their leaders, lie bleeding at the feet of their Austrian conquerors. Shall all the houses of Europe be taken by the sword and given to papists pledging fealty to the Hapsburgs? Shall Protestant worship, free thought and long-ruling houses of Europe be crushed under the Hapsburg boot?"

The queen paused. Robert did not know if he was expected to reply, his mouth opened…

Sophie looked at him, once again composed and regal, and said, "We cannot permit treachery within the English regiment to proceed unopposed. What of Colonel Vere? Why does he not report the treachery himself?"

Robert replied, "Officers are ordered to his staff that he does not know or trust by a court official sympathetic to Spain. He is a soldier, your highness, not a politician."

"No doubt you speak of Lord Calvert. No, we must stop it if we can. You ask for my help. It is a dangerous time in the English court. You are aware of the factions, but King James' opening of parliament has only added to the instability. Who to trust, you ask? Better to question who among our supporters still survives?"

"Your Highness, I trust Colonel Vere who has sent us on this mission. He is an honorable man and the most gallant soldier in England…"

"I know the allegiances of Sir Horace Vere, but you Robert, I have searched into the house of Curtis. Your uncle the Viscount is so despised in Berwick that he cannot walk down the street in safety. And your cousin, Sir Geoffrey is believed a Catholic and a perhaps a plotter. And you, Robert, educated as a priest, have no parish and serve under a commission bought by your uncle. Am I to trust you, Lieutenant Curtis?"

Robert stood stunned and slowly replied, "All that you have said is true your Highness. But I am resolved as never before to protect the Protestant faith we enjoy in the reformation. England is no safer from the malice of the Catholic intent to destroy our faith than the Germans, the Dutch, the Bohemians, the Danes, and the Swedes. We are all at war."

Karl began to say, "I have found Robert Curtis to be…"

Queen Sophie waved her hand to dismiss his comments and said, "I have formed my own opinion. I believe Lieutenant Curtis has joined the cause. Now as to the English court, there is much danger. The former network of watchers established by Sir Robert Cecil has wasted away. Few are watching the plotters. Lord Calvert, Secretary of State, may be loyal to the King, but as we know, he favors the alliance by marriage with Spain, and he is most friendly with the Catholic Aristocracy. The newly titled Viscount St. Albans, Lord Chancellor Francis Bacon, has recently been found guilty of bribery and his voice against Spain lost. The King's favorite, the Marquess of Buckingham, George Villiers, sways back and forth with the king's position of the day. He is a man of no skill, no intellect and no morality. The new Lord Chancellor, John Williams, Bishop of Lincoln, a man of the Church in title only, is new to the court and has no friends and no known loyalties. James' chosen speaker of Parliament, Sir Edward Coke, has passed not a single bill and instead pursues vengeance against his enemies and has lost favor with the King and nobles and members of parliament as well. No, our only hope is with the Archbishop of Canterbury, George Abbott, I have heard there is a complaint against him about a hunting accident, but the King will not hear of it. He is a true friend of our cause and close to the court. Yes, he is the only man you can trust to use your information effectively."

Karl spoke. "I see the wisdom of my friend Robert in seeking your audience, your highness, truly you are a wise matriarch to our people."

"I have heard of your watchers, Herr Schroeder, I am pleased to see them used for more than selling tapestries. Now show me the gift my grandson sends."

The finest tapestry Karl had brought was unrolled before the Queen Dowager. She walked around it carefully studying the craftsmanship, the detail and the colors, she finally said, "It is indeed a fine tapestry. I am pleased with my grandson's gift. Tell me, Herr Schroeder, did Christian choose this himself?"

"Indeed, your highness he chose it from those I presented."

"And you presented only the best."

"I would not allow an earnest young man to choose other than the best for a Queen of your grace and refinement."

The Queen smiled and said, "I hope you gentleman dress in a more presentable fashion this evening. Good day."

Karl bowed and motioned for Robert to do the same. Both men backed out of the room.

That evening, Robert and Karl joined the royal party for an evening of music. Rather than be led to the lavish music room, they were brought to the castle chapel. In the great chapel, unadorned white columns rose majestically to support the vaulted ceiling. At the far end of the chapel behind the altar was a magnificent stained-glass window soaring from the altar to the vaulted ceiling. Even in the dark of night, lighted only by candles, the vibrant colors and symmetry declared the majesty of God. The raised altar table, covered in white, displayed only an open Bible and a single gold cross. To the right of the altar was a canopied pulpit ten steps above the floor declaring the importance of the spoken Word of God. A small orchestra was seated in front of the altar, a choir of twenty sat in their stall facing the organist seated at his bench.

Robert and Karl were seated in the rear of the royal box. They stood as the organ announced the arrival of the royal party, the Queen Dowager, Sophie, her daughter Elizabeth, the Dowager Duchess of Brunswick and a tall young man not yet bearded dressed in a uniform of a gold trimmed and multi-buttoned, red coat and white breeches, a blue sash and starburst emblem with the arms of Denmark-Norway.

Robert and Karl bowed as the royal party arrived. Queen Sophie smiled and said, "Herr Schroeder, Lieutenant Curtis, you have met my daughter Dowager Duchess Elizabeth, this is my grandson Christian, the Prince Elect of Denmark-Norway."

Both men bowed and said, "Your Highness, it is an honor to meet you."

The young prince replied, "I am visiting my uncles in Brunswick and grandmother has dragged me away from uncle Frederick's banquet hall for the evening. Papa insists I always listen to grandmother. He will be asking me for her letters when I return. I must make these tiresome visits to my uncles just to hear her wisdom."

The prince paused. Robert and Karl stood awkwardly unable to respond before the prince continued. "You shall join us for wine and refreshments following the music."

"We are indeed honored, your highness."

Over an hour of music was performed. The new Kapellmeister led but one or two of his own pieces, diplomatically choosing the grand music of his beloved predecessor, Michael Praetorius. The choir sang along with the orchestra alternating with organ pieces and concertos. When he finished with a hymn sing, the Queen Dowager rose to her feet followed by the Dowager Duchess and Prince. The entire assembly of guests and performers rose to sing along. Queen Sophie's splendid soprano voice could be heard joyfully praising

God. Robert noticed a small tear form in the queen's eye. As the hymn ended, she lightly dabbed the tear with a handkerchief before turning and smiling at her guests.

CHAPTER 26
THE GUEST

Katharina was still sobbing when she arrived home. Her red face was streaked with tears. Her white linen coif dislodged from her head, hung around her neck and her blonde hair was tangled in her wet fingers, plastered against her forehead by her hands cupped over her face. When she heard Werner call out, "Is that you Fraulein Katie," she wailed loudly and ran up the stairs to her room.

Alarmed, Werner followed her upstairs and cautiously peeked into her room. Katharina was sprawled on her bed with her face buried in a pillow, crying and shaking uncontrollably. Werner slowly entered the room, knelt beside the bed and placed a hand on her shoulder. "Katie, dear Katie! What has happened? Please, whatever it is you are safe here. Tell me what has upset you so much. Are you hurt? Is it Johann? Is Johann safe? Please, I am here to help. What has happened?"

Werner looked at her and saw no wounds, no blood, no disheveled clothes other than the coif which had fallen from her head. Katharina continued to cry. She sobbed out the words, "It is not Johann. Go away! Leave me alone! I've ruined everything. There is nothing you can do!"

Werner sighed and gently rubbed her shoulders and back. "Katie, you are the daughter I never had. You know I love you. When your father is away, it is my duty to protect you. Haven't I always been there for you? Now tell me what troubles you so?"

"Go away! There is nothing you can do. Should I tell my troubles to a servant? Is that why my father pays you, to follow me into my bedroom? Now go away!"

Werner replied softly, "Is this the first time I've sat by your bedside? Have I not comforted you since you were a little girl? Haven't I sung you back to sleep after a nightmare? Haven't I listened as you said your prayers? Have I not prayed over you as you slept? What is so terrible that this time is different?"

"I am no longer a little girl. I am a woman. I make my own decisions, I need no counsel from a servant."

"Katie, we never outgrow the need for counsel. You still seek the counsel of your papa and Johann. I will not let your words hurt me. You know I am not a servant, but a guest of my great friend, your father. He still seeks my counsel and support, as I seek his, that is what adults do."

Katharina stopped sobbing. "You have been a guest in this house all these years? Not a servant, though devoted you are?"

"It is true. I am a guest, but I seek to serve your papa, Johann and you. Your father took me in when I was in need. He helped me change my life. I am not embarrassed to say I was a great sinner who found grace and mercy. I also found friendship, trust, and love. Your father has never asked me to leave and refused every offer I make to move on. He tells me we are brothers and as brothers, we are of the same family."

Katharina stopped crying and sat up. "Werner, you have always been a righteous and loving man. I cannot imagine you ever doing anything shameful."

Werner stood up and reached for a chair which he drew next to the bed. He sat down, reached for Katharina's hands and held them softly. He smiled at her and said, "It is only by God's grace and the mercy of your papa that I appear to be the man you say is righteous and loving. I am a sinner, and I have done terrible things! Things that would shock you!"

"Shock me, Werner? What things have you done that would shock me?"

"Katie, first wash your face, fix your hair and coif, then come downstairs. I will warm some cider. It is time you heard my story."

When Katie came back downstairs, a warm cup of cider was waiting for her. Werner pulled out a chair at the table for her and motioned for her to sit. He moved across the table and sat down across from her. His eyes met hers, and he began, "You may not remember that before the Elector, Frederick V proclaimed himself a Calvinist and therefore all of the Palatine Calvinist, our church and pastor were Lutheran. Now to most people, there is little difference between Protestants. What most notice is that we no longer have a bishop and we elect lay leaders like your father to oversee our congregation. It is our local leaders who call our pastor and watch over the ministry. Your brother, a fine young man, studied at Heidelberg University where he trained as a Calvinist Pastor, was called and so he leads us so ably today. But before him, there was a Lutheran, Pastor Schwarzkopf, a man who chose to remain a Lutheran, and so moved on. Now Pastor Schwarzkopf was an old man, and not a gifted preacher, but he hung on to one thing better than any Calvinist. He preached grace, grace, and grace. Now I do not say Johann does not teach grace, for certain, he does. But grace to a Calvinist is mixed with a strong admonition to live an upright life. Does not Johann remind us to be holy because God is holy? And this also is true. But the greater truth lies in grace. We must clutch to God's grace because we will always miss the mark of righteousness and the devil lies in wait as an accuser using guilt to deprive us of fully loving and serving our Lord. To be sure, there are other differences, but they matter only to theologians…"

"Werner, you promised to tell me *your* story."

"And so, I did. But I can only tell my story because God's grace enfolded me, saved me and gives me hope to live for Him and one day see Him face to face. In my youth, I was a proud and arrogant man. Somehow, I convinced a wonderful young woman to marry me. She was much like you, Katie, sweet, loving, faithful and hardworking. I was unworthy of her love. We lived on a small farm outside of Eberbach with a few dairy cows and chickens. We sold milk, cheese, and eggs in the market. With hard work, we earned enough to get by. I would rise early in the morning to milk the cows and then return home for breakfast. Together we would tend to the cheese then I would take whatever eggs, milk, and cheese we had ready to the market and she would stay home and churn butter. Well, I began to stay in the town after the market closed and drink beer in the ratskeller, too much beer. Heidi begged me to come straight home, but I did not listen to her. I enjoyed sharing stories with men at the ratskeller. Even after she told me we were to have a child, I continued to stay late drinking with my friends. One night…"

Werner paused, lowered his face and closed his eyes in tears. Katharina sat in silence.

He went on softly trying hard not to cry as he spoke. "One night I did not go home. I lay in the mud all night passed out drunk. When I woke, the smell of fire was strong in the air. I arose and stumbled home, all the while the smell of fire getting stronger. As I came up the path to our farm, I could see the smoldering embers of the barn. I stumbled into the house which was still standing and called out her name. She did not answer. I searched, but she was not there. I ran back to the barn and there, and there…"

Werner bowed once more. When he looked up, he wiped the tears from his eyes and said, "I found her charred body among the embers, a blackened lantern at her feet. When I did not return, she went to the barn to milk the cows I should have milked, and somehow the lantern was knocked over, and the straw caught fire."

"You must have been devasted by grief!"

"That is not the worst. I blamed her! Why did she carelessly let the lantern fall over? Why didn't she wait for me? In my heart, I knew it was my fault. She begged me to come home. She longed for a happy home. She was carrying our baby!"

"You felt guilty."

"I was guilty. Who would deny it? But I was to sink even lower. I buried my wife and sold the farm. I could not stay there. The guilt was overwhelming. And then, even worse, I drank away all the money. When I spent my last coin, and the innkeeper would serve me no longer, in a drunken stupor I tried to burn down the ratskeller. The magistrate arrested me before any damage was done and I stayed in jail for two years. In all that time I had only three visitors, Pastor Schwarzkopf, and Karl Schroeder. Your papa brought me here the day I was released, and I have stayed here ever since."

"You mentioned three visitors in jail."

"It was in the Eberbach jail that I met Jesus. He poured out His grace on me and loved me. He has never left me, and I know He never will."

Werner gazed at Katharina with an open-hearted, loving smile. "Jesus knows. He loves you. His grace will suffice. Now, Katie, what troubles your heart?"

Katie began to cry again, but the words slowly came out. "I have done a most terrible thing, and the guilt will not leave me. Johann told me confession was good for the soul, so I sought out someone to hear my confession, someone who did not know me and would keep my secret safe."

"And this person…"

"I went to the Spanish priest, he agreed to hear my confession, but when I told him all that I had done, he declared me a heretic bound for hell and not worthy of the rite of confession. Worse, he said he knows Johann and Wilhelm and that my guilt is not bound to remain secret with him. He called me a whore and heretic and demanded I leave. He hates us, I am certain, and he will destroy the honor of our family. I have sinned greatly, and now father and Johann will be dishonored as well."

"Katie, you underestimate the love of your papa and brother. They will always love you. Nothing you have done or could do will ever make them ashamed of you. Now you must tell them before they hear from another. They will listen in love with grace. Trust them and trust our God to make His grace known to overflowing."

"You do not ask my sin?"

"No, Katie, I pray for your release."

Katie was sitting silently at the table across from Werner when Johann and Wilhelm returned. Her eyes were now dry and the faint smile on her lips sweetened the softness showing in her eyes. The spell was broken when she heard the loud voices of her brother and

Wilhelm. She called out, "Johann, it is good you are home we must speak. I must warn you about the Spanish priest!"

Johann replied, "The Spanish priest? Warn me?"

Katie spoke firmly. "He intends to harm you and papa with what he has learned. I made a foolish mistake, I confessed to him…Remember I spoke to you about confession? I thought he would hear my confession and help me heal. I thought you and papa need never know what I have I done. He listened but did not forgive. He has condemned me to hell and will not hold secret what I told him."

Wilhelm, aghast, said, "He did what? What did he tell you?"

"After he heard my confession, he said that as I am outside the church and a heretic, what he has heard is not a true confession. Until I repent of my heresy and return to the Roman Catholic faith, only then will he again hear my confession. He called me a whore and a heretic and demanded I leave. I am sure he intends to destroy our family. He threatens you, Johann, and papa too!"

Wilhelm, still indignant, replied, "He is no true priest of God! Such evil by one ordained to intercede for God's children! I will not allow this!"

Johann said, "Katie, nothing you have done is outside the love and mercy of God. It will be well. Please do not trouble yourself; only God above can love you more than papa or me. You will never shame us."

"You must hear what I have done, what has troubled me since I was but fifteen years old. Wilhelm, you should hear from me as well, rather than from your priest."

Werner had been sitting silently; he stood up and said quietly, "Please excuse me, I must go, I am off to the market." And left.

When Katie was finished, Johann said, "Katie, God's word reassures us, 'If we confess our sins, He is faithful and just to forgive us our sins and to cleanse us from all unrighteousness.' You can rest in the promise of God."

Wilhelm placed his hand on her shoulder and prayed, "God the Father of mercies, through the death and resurrection of His Son has reconciled the world to Himself and sent the Holy Spirit among us for the forgiveness of sins; through the ministry of the Church may God give you pardon and peace, and I absolve you from your sins in the name of the Father, the Son, and the Holy Spirit. Amen"

The tears that flooded Katie's eyes spoke of relief from years of guilt. Katie was free.

CHAPTER 27
SUBVERSION

The Eberbach market was busy. With the end of autumn approaching, the fruit stalls were limited to late apples and the last of the table grapes. Root vegetables, pickled vegetables, stone ground wheat flour, and rye attracted the most buyers. The dairy and meat vendors would soon close their stalls and sell only from their shops.

Werner was placing his order with the butcher when Joseph Meyer came alongside him. When the butcher went to cut the meat of Werner's order, Joseph whispered, "I need to get word to Karl."

Werner said nothing. Joseph tried again. "He must know what the priest and the burgermeister are doing. Johann will be betrayed. They must be warned."

Werner replied, "Have you not betrayed Karl yourself?"

"I warned him as soon as I could; I had no choice. They were on to me. You must believe me. I told Karl that Katharina was found out and would be arrested. They must flee at once."

"You led them to the cabin."

"I delayed them as long as I could. Was it not long enough for them to escape?"

"Why do you just come to me now?"

"Would you have believed me if I came sooner? I am ashamed of what I have done. They found out, they…I am not like you Werner; I still have a family and reputation to protect. But now Johann and Katharina have returned, and they are once again in danger."

The butcher was returning with the carefully wrapped pork roast. Werner said softly, "We will talk later. I will let you know when." Then to the butcher, he said, "Is the account up to date?"

The butcher replied, "Yes, yes, you can pay me at the end of the week, just as always. Good day, Werner."

As Werner was leaving, Joseph could be heard saying, "Just the sausages today…"

The room was small but comfortable. Flames of a small fire danced slowly to the beat of quiet crackles as bits of red coals fell into the embers. A woman sat by a small table graced by a single candlestick, silently knitting. Her husband dozed in his heavy cushioned wooden chair. The quiet autumn night was disturbed by the frantic clucking of chickens.

Joseph Meyer sighed, opened his eyes, got up and went to the window. The moonless black night was impenetrable from inside the cozy cottage. "Something is bothering the chickens. I think I will go outside and look around. I won't be long."

Joseph lit a small lantern and took his crossbow from its peg by the door. He drew back the bow and put a bolt on the shaft and went outside. Holding the lantern in front, he made his way across the grassy compound to the chicken house. His coop was protected in a small shed, so much the better to protect his birds in the cold winter. Joseph opened the door and swung the lantern inside. His chickens were still alert but seemed to be settling down. There was no sign of a fox or anything else. Satisfied that the chickens were unharmed, he left the shed and turned to close and bolt the door behind him. It was then he felt the blade of a knife against his throat.

"Say not a word. Put down the crossbow. Do not try me for I am a man with nothing left to lose."

Joseph carefully put the crossbow on the ground beside his feet. The voice now said, "Now go back behind the shed, and walk towards the woods. Not a word."

The men made their way to the back of the shed and into the woods behind it. Fifty yards into the woods Werner lowered his knife and said, "I will hear your message to Karl."

Joseph exhaled deeply and said, "Werner, it is you! You did not need to abduct me at the point of a knife. I would have come to you, just as I did at the market."

"As we have discussed, your history with my good friend Karl is not reliable. Why should I trust you now? Tell me first why you betrayed Karl and Katharina, then I will hear your message."

"The priest, Don Pedro and the new magistrate they were looking for records. They tried to find when property changed hands, who owned what land and for how long; who paid taxes, how much they paid, and how much rents and produce came from each parcel."

"Yes, we know all of this. They pestered Johann for his records as well."

"They did not find everything they were looking for, but the priest, Don Pedro, is clever with numbers. He found that the highest producing parcels were not the highest taxed and that I paid no taxes on my cottage."

"He discovered you were taking bribes and cheating on your taxes."

"Yes, and he said I must help them or be jailed and lose my position."

"What help did he seek?"

"He said the burgermeister informed them that I was close to Karl. He had seen us together often, but our conversations stopped when he approached or became too general for the intensity he observed. He believed I knew where Katharina and the missing priest were hiding. He threatened my family! Such a thing! A priest threatening an innocent wife and children! I had no choice! I tried to warn Karl, I slipped away for a moment and warned him! Ask Karl, it is true, I swear it!"

Werner snorted. "I am no man to judge you. What is your message?"

"I have heard the burgermesiter, the new magistrate and the Spanish priest talking. They are preparing letters. They request the Count of Tilly to garrison troops in Eberbach until Don Gonzalo de Cordoba's army arrives. They send letters that Johann and Father Wilhelm preach insurrection and are hiding provisions that the armies of the Emperor will need. They send letters to Don Lorenzo, bishops and the Elector-Archbishop of Mainz that Father Wilhelm permits apostacy in the Church of Eberbach. They say they have information to destroy the Schroeder heretics in the eyes of the people."

"You are sure the burgermeister has joined them?"

"There is no doubt. He has cast his lot fully with the Catholics."

"I will take your message to Karl. But just as you find yourself in the debt of Don Pedro and the new magistrate, you must remain loyal to Karl and Eberbach. If you betray us again…"

"I know I must play along with the magistrate, but my loyalty is with Karl and Eberbach. I beg forgiveness for not telling Karl everything before; there was no time. He must forgive me. You, Werner, must forgive me…"

"Karl is a forgiving man, perhaps…But now go back to your wife and children. Say nothing of our meeting to anyone. I will contact you when our communication path is set up. We must not be seen together."

"I will tell no one."

"The burgermeister is with them?"

"Werner, I know how we can handle him, but I wait to hear from you."

Father Wilhelm was sitting pensively in the cold church office when the Spanish priest came in. "Good morning, father, he said as the Spaniard walked by.

"Good morning." He replied as he kept walking.

"Father, a word with you, if you please."

The Spaniard sighed and turned around. "If you must. I have much to do today."

"Yes, undoubtedly busy with your large congregation. I heard you had someone come by yesterday asking you to hear a confession. I also heard you agreed to listen but then refused the rite of absolution."

The Spaniard's face flushed. "There can be no forgiveness outside of the church. Have you forgotten that Father Hahn, or is it just one more rite tossed aside for your heretic friends?"

Wilhelm asked, "Father, when Dinah, the daughter of the patriarch Jacob and his wife Leah was seduced and raped by Prince Shechem, who did God punish? Remember, Father, that Dinah went to Shechem on her own accord and against her father's will. What was God's punishment?"

The Spaniard replied, "Dinah was only a young maiden, and Shechem forced..."

Wilhelm argued, "Dinah was indeed a young maiden, just as the woman who came to you seeking peace and forgiveness was also just a young maiden. You believe her outside the church. What did Saint Francis teach us about those outside the church but 'preach the gospel at all times, if necessary, use words.' You did not receive this woman with love. You say she is outside the church, yet her heart is earnest for God, she holds to the same ancient creeds that you and I hold. The prince of the land determines the church of his subjects. Would you condemn his subjects to hell for the religion of the Prince-Elector?"

The Spanish priest replied, "It is not my decision, or yours. The pope has declared…"

"The pope, a man, a sinful man full of pride and thirsty for power and wealth, he decides? A sinful man cannot be wrong?"

"It is not the man. It is the papacy, given first to Saint Peter and then to every man chosen by God that succeeds him."

"Have they indeed been chosen by God?"

"Father Hahn you may ask your questions, and God have mercy on your soul! Your heresy will soon be found out. I wash my hands of you! I will not join in the apostasy you bring to Eberbach. I will not assist you in the mass. I will not minister to any heretic until they repent and seek wholeheartedly to return to the Roman Catholic faith.

"I sent letters to the Tribunal of the Holy Office of the Inquisition for the Spanish Netherlands to send investigators here to Eberbach seeking their help in removing you and your heretic pastor. The feeble witted Archbishop of Mainz cannot protect you for long.

"You can ask your questions to the Inquisition Father

Hahn when they arrive with the Spanish army. I will speak with you no more."

The stable behind Karl's house provided a dry respite from the cold autumn rain. The four fine riding horses were quiet, ignoring the soft conversation between Werner and Joseph Meyer. "There has been a reply to the magistrate's request. The Count of Tilly will garrison Eberbach, the magistrate has been told to prepare to quarter five hundred infantry and arquebusiers, perhaps more. The burgermeister has been told to begin identifying houses to occupy. You can be sure Karl's house will be on the list."

Werner nodded. "Did they say when the soldiers will arrive?"

"They march in two weeks. The Abbott, Don Pedro and the priest, Don Lorenzo will come within a few days to ensure all is prepared and to investigate the complaints of the Spanish priest. They know Father Hahn carries both the ordination as Vicar General of Eberbach and a safe conduct pass from the emperor. They are concerned the Spanish priest lacks the skills of diplomacy."

"You heard all of this in the magistrate's office?"

"I keep a cup to listen against the wall. It is quite thin."

"What can you tell me about the Abbott Don Pedro and the priest, Don Lorenzo?"

"I thought you knew all about them. The Abbott sends his reports to a Spaniard. I have seen letters dispatched in a diplomatic pouch. They were addressed to a Count Gondomar, whoever he is. Don Lorenzo sends his dispatches to the Vatican."

"Do you know the contents of these dispatches?"

"They were sealed when I saw them. I do not know their contents. I suspect they deal with the English regiments. I have heard them discuss 'their English friend,' quite often."

Werner thought for a moment and then said, "Do you think you can arrange for the burgermeister to meet with the magistrate and Spanish priest during Sunday worship? Also, that his family not to be present as well?"

"I think I can convince the burgermeister to meet with the magistrate and priest. I will suggest they plan the quartering while the people are at church and mention perhaps his wife's cold might keep her away from unnecessary questions."

"Good. Joseph, I am sending word to Karl to return and meet with you quickly. I will talk to Johann and Karl about perhaps moving some of the hidden food. We must not allow the burgermeister to give up what he knows."

Joseph nodded. "It might be justice if the burgermeister was himself caught hiding not only his food but city funds as well."

"You can arrange that?"

"It will be my pleasure."

Sunday morning as Werner accompanied Johann, Katharina, and Wilhelm as they walked across the market square to the church, his eyes scanned the four towers and low walls around the city. They passed the open, ungated archway to the wharves and quays along the Neckar River which made Eberbach prosperous as a trading city. He imagined how this pleasant city would soon change as Spanish soldiers gated the river entrance and manned the watchtowers. Johann noticed Werner's eyes wandering over the city walls and towers and said softly, "I know Werner, we must prepare our people. I believe that God will provide."

Johann preached a sermon based on the gospel of Matthew 10:16: "Behold I am sending you as sheep among wolves, so be as wise as snakes and as innocent as doves."

At the end of his sermon he charged his congregation, "I believe the rumors many have heard are true. The Count of Tilly will garrison Eberbach and winter five hundred to one thousand soldiers in our city. It is at the request of our magistrate with the approval of the burgermeister that they will come. They will quarter among us in our homes. We will be charged with providing food and drink as well as beds and firewood to keep them warm. We can no longer hope and pray that it will not happen; we must prepare. Never leave your wife or daughter alone with the soldiers. Daughters must spend the night in their parent's bedrooms. We must feed the soldiers as we feed ourselves. Show them hospitality and respect. A normal store of food should be seen in the storerooms. Our abundance must be kept secret. You must know who you can trust, for as we meet here today in worship our burgermeister plans with Count Tilly's appointed magistrate in choosing among our houses for quarters. Trust only he who moved your provisions to deliver them once more. Brothers and sisters, we have one final week to prepare. God make us wise as serpents and gentle as doves."

Robert and Karl were riding south and when they arrived at Darmstadt. Werner's message was delivered to Karl along with the news that Count Tilly had blockaded access to Heidelberg and siege works were being prepared in the hills above the castle and in front of the old bridge across the Neckar. Robert thought out loud, "Word of King James' loan from Christian IV of Denmark-Norway must have reached Spain, and the Count of Tilly has been ordered to increase pressure on the English regiment."

"I will send a tapestry design to Colonel Vere about the garrisoning of Eberbach. We must get back there while we can still enter the city freely. With Don Pedro and Don Lorenzo returning to Eberbach, I fear for the safety of Johann, Katharina, and Wilhelm."

"It appears too late for me to rejoin the regiment. My heart lies with Captain Richard and Colonel Herbert. Surely we can stop first at Manheim and speak with Colonel Vere."

This time it was Karl who shook his head no. "No Robert, time is short, we can get word to him, and will be able to provide him better information outside of the English garrisons."

"He must be warned of the Don Pedro and Don Lorenzo connections and finding the identity of "their English friend."

"Colonel Vere knows Don Lorenzo represents the pope and suspects Captain Stock cannot be trusted. We can pass along this report, but we must proceed to Eberbach at great speed, where we can watch Count Tilly's movements. Heidelberg is under growing siege. How much longer before Mannheim? We can still provide intelligence. If we are trapped in Mannheim, what then?

Robert thought and then replied, "We go first to Eberbach, but then I must rejoin my commander in Mannheim."

Two days later Robert and Karl rode through the unguarded gate of Eberbach. Men in the markets doffed their hats as Karl rode by. Women curtsied and said "Welcome home Herr Schroeder. The burgermeister led the magistrate out the door and pointed.

Robert surprised said, "I have seen nobility receive a less cordial welcome."

Karl smiled and said, "Just old friends and neighbors."

Werner appeared just as the pair reached Karl's house and came forward to hold the horses as the men dismounted. "Your safe return is an answer to prayer! Katharina will be most happy to see you. Johann and Father Wilhelm as well. Come in. Please come in, I have been expecting you."

As Karl followed Werner into the house, he heard Werner say, "You received my note, my friend?"

"Yes, any news on the soldiers?"

"Joseph keeps me informed, I think we can trust him…we must trust him, but I will let you decide."

Then nodding at Karl, he said, "Already, he is on his way, and the magistrate and burgermeister are watching."

Joseph Meyer walked stiffly up to Karl. "Herr Schroeder, it is good you are home. You are to make your house available to the commander of the garrison here at Eberbach."

"Garrison, Herr Meyer? What garrison?" Karl answered loudly as if annoyed.

"The Count of Tilly has chosen Eberbach to garrison nearly a thousand soldiers for the winter and perhaps longer. Your family will be permitted to stay and prepare meals and make the stay comfortable for a senior officer. These are your instructions."

Joseph presented Karl sealed letters, and said softly, "The second is everything I have heard concerning the Spanish commander.

Karl opened the first letter and palmed the second. As he read, Joseph said softly, "I convinced the magistrate you were the man to house him graciously. Perhaps he will become comfortable in your presence."

When Karl finished reading the letter, he said loudly, "I will provide hospitality owed to such a distinguished officer of the King of Spain's Army of Flanders."

Joseph bowed and said softly, "We will speak later."

Karl responded loudly, "Thank you, Herr Schroeder, I have my orders."

Robert followed Karl and Werner into the house. Immediately Katie rushed to her father, threw her arms around him, kissed him and cried, "Oh papa! I am so very glad you are here at last. I must tell you everything…"

CHAPTER 28
THE COMMANDER

All the stalls had been cleared from the town square to make room for the gathering company of pikemen and company of arquebusiers, infantry components of the occupying Tercio of the Army of Flanders. The mixed nationality companies of Flemish, Dutch, Belgian and Spanish soldiers marched into the square calling out to any woman they passed, laughing, shoving, backslapping and lacking any discipline in their drill giving the appearance of a large band of thugs rather than the seasoned and victorious soldiers they were. The officers leading columns rode ahead unconcerned with the undisciplined behavior of their men. They rode to the far end of the town square, dismounted their horses and made their way to the city hall now showing the flags of the Emperor and the King of Spain.

As the square filled with nearly eight hundred men, a hundred horses and fifty wagons, the stench of unkempt men, animals, manure, and urine drove all but the most curious townsman behind the closed doors and windows of his home. Joseph Meyer was not so privileged; he walked beside the adjutant with his lists as they directed sergeants to lead groups of men to their assigned houses. By late afternoon all the soldiers had been escorted off, the horses taken to newly built stables and a small guard detailed to watch the wagons and baggage carts until their contents were securely stored. Soldiers could be seen coming in pairs to draw the baggage of their officers and slipping into the ratskeller for a beer. For the first time in decades, the four towers of Eberbach were manned and guards patrolled atop the city walls. Not a woman of Eberbach could be seen.

Joseph Meyer rapped sharply on the Schroeder house door. When Karl answered, he took study of a young man in his early thirties, sandy hair and brown eyes with helmet, armor and a fine sword hanging from an ornate leather and gilt belt. Joseph introduced Karl to Major Antonin Ryskamp, the new Commander of the Army of Flanders Garrison at Eberbach. Karl bowed slightly and said, "Welcome to my home Major Ryskamp we will endeavor to make your stay here comfortable."

Joseph said, "Major this is Karl Schroeder, a leading merchant in Eberbach. Karl, please see to the major's things," as he pointed to a bag."

Karl reached down and took the major's bag. "Please

let me show you to your room, or quarters if you prefer," and led him into the house.

Inside Karl continued. "There is a large bedroom on the first floor which you may find convenient. We will share what food we have with you and will arrange meals to meet your schedule."

As they passed through the comfortable sitting room and dining room, the major said, "I will require these rooms to conduct my business."

"Certainly major, they are for your use only."

Karl placed the bag in the large bedroom. Major Ryskamp said, "This will do," and returned to the sitting room. He stopped to look at the portraits on the mantel and said, "How many others live in this house?"

Karl answered, "Besides me, there are my son and daughter and three others."

Still staring at Katharina's portrait, he asked, "Three others?"

"Yes, there is my close friend, Werner, who helps me with cooking and chores, there is the new priest, the Archbishop of Mainz's Vicar General, Father Wilhelm Hahn, and there is my business associate, Robert Curtis."

"What is your business, Herr Schroeder?"

"I deal in fine tapestries."

"Do you now? I come from Ghent. We pride ourselves in the finest tapestry weavers in Europe."

"Indeed, major, I have dealt in many tapestries from Ghent."

Turning to Karl, the major fixed his gaze on him and said, "I will dine at eight. Please send your man Werner for my baggage. Here is a chit to give to the quartermaster, he will retrieve it from the cart. Now, I wish to be alone."

At eight o'clock that evening, Werner knocked lightly before entering the dining room just off the kitchen and carried a tray of food to the table. "Would you prefer wine or beer with your meal, Major?"

"Beer. You are?"

"Werner, major."

"Yes, tell me Werner where are Herr Schroeder and his family?"

Werner replied, "They take their meal in the kitchen."

Major Ryskamp looked at the dinner tray and said, "Ask Herr Schroeder and his household to join me."

At the dinner table, Major Ryskamp thanked Karl and said, "I will be with you through the winter at least, perhaps longer. You have shown me kindness and hospitality, and that is much more pleasant than a fine room and no company. So long as you permit me to conduct my business as commander of the garrison in privacy and unimpeded, there is no reason we cannot enjoy our company outside of my military obligations. Now please, Herr Schroeder, Karl, introduce me to the others."

Major Ryskamp was surprised to learn that Johann was the protestant pastor, turning his gaze from Katharina, he asked Wilhelm. "So tell me, Vicar General…"

"Please call me Father Wilhelm."

"Tell me, Father Wilhelm, why do you share a house

with protestants and indeed the protestant pastor?"

"To be sure, Major Ryskamp, until you arrived the magistrate, a Spanish priest and I were the only confessing Roman Catholics in Eberbach. My ordination as Vicar General by the Elector-Archbishop of Mainz was to ensure peace in the city as change is inevitable. The purpose of the Archbishop is to see justice, mercy, and tolerance for the people of the city. He wishes to win hearts and minds through common faith rather than resentment and hate through the drawn sword."

"And do you find any converts, Father?"

"I find openness and hospitality, major."

"Yes, if their hospitality appears genuine."

Once again turning his eyes from the silent Katharina, he asked Robert in French, "You are a business acquaintance of Herr Schroeder? Your accent is unusual, how long will you be staying in Eberbach?

Robert answered, "My family trades wool in Berwick, my cousin serves in the English regiment in Frankenthal and wrote saying this is a good time to buy tapestries. He is too constrained to conduct business himself, so I came…"

Major Ryskamp laughed. "He may soon be even more constrained. So, you find this war a business opportunity."

"We must make the most of every opportunity wherever we find it, major."

"Now, here is an honest man! Only a merchant or a son without inheritance could speak so boldly!"

Robert asked, "I hope to visit my cousin soon, major,

do you believe I can enter and leave Frankenthal safely?"

"I would not tarry long. That is all I can say on the subject."

A new normal settled upon Eberbach. The market reopened with the stalls of grain, flour, meats, vegetables, and wine. Selection and quantity were enough to feed the city that day was displayed. Beer was available from brewers and in the ratskellers. The buildings looked the same, but the people were somehow different. Women were rarely seen and never without a husband, father or brother. Pleasantries were exchanged in passing and in the market, but they seemed less cheerful. The citizens felt the eyes of the guards in the towers or the soldiers milling about watching them. Certain ratskellers were frequented only by soldiers speaking Spanish, Dutch or French. The new normal was guarded.

Few people took note when a small boat tied up alongside the quay, and two robed clerics stepped onto the pier. Don Lorenzo and Don Pedro made their way to the magistrate's office. It was not long before the Spanish priest went to meet them. An hour later, Werner observed Joseph going across the street to the city hall and escorting the burgermeister back to the magistrate's office. When he returned, Joseph came out and swept the dirt from the entrance to the magistrate's office and left the broom alongside the right side of the door. Later, the Spanish priest walked to the church and sat down in the office across from Wilhelm. The priest said nothing but opened a journal and began to write.

That night Werner waited for Joseph Meyer behind his shed. Joseph reported, "They argued. The Spanish priest wants Father Wilhelm arrested and held for the Inquisition. The two Dons will not allow it. The Elector Archbishop has the support of the College of Princes, if not the Emperor, and the case against Father Wilhelm has not been documented. They believe the confession Katharina made to the Spanish priest can be used to persuade Johann and Wilhelm and Karl too, if necessary, to cooperate when the collection is ordered."

"Collection?" Werner asked.

"Yes. Major Ryskamp has been ordered to provide provisions for one regiment in addition to what he needs for his garrison."

"When is this collection to begin?"

"The major has said he would make all decisions regarding his duties to the Army of Flanders. He has acknowledged that his men monitor the provisions where they are quartered. He waits until provisions must be replaced. He contends that he must maintain peace and sufficient provisions for his own men as his first priority, while he investigates and plans how and when he will proceed."

As Werner was about to leave Joseph said, "One last thing; Don Lorenzo and Don Pedro do not know the Englishman is in your house. The major has not mentioned him. It would be good if he arouses no suspicion and is not seen in the city."

"The burgermeister. Will he support this collection?

How much does he know?"

"He suspects Johann and Wilhelm have hidden provisions but does not know where. Don't worry about the burgermeister. When the time comes…"

"Thank you, Joseph, Karl thanks you for the risk you take."

"We are all at risk. To do nothing is certain peril."

When Werner returned home, he caught a glimpse of Karl and Major Ryskamp enjoying a bottle of Schnapps in the sitting room before a low fire. "I tell you, Herr Schroeder…"

"Please, Karl."

"I will tell you, Karl, my friend, I am glad you found this bottle tonight, it relaxes me. Such a day!"

"The duties of command must weigh heavy on your shoulders, major."

"The Count Tilly's staff officers, not a real soldier among them! They leave me no discretion. They make demands; they do not read my reports. And civilians, these priests! They pretend to be diplomats and, and … well, they think they are in command."

"Everyone wants something, but you are responsible, you will be held accountable!"

"Yes, and if there is trouble, I will have not one friend among them!"

"You have done well by our city, my friend, we are safe, we are warm, and we are fed. By God's grace, we should have just enough for your garrison to be fed through the winter. You have been most honorable. Tell me major, do you tire of war? Does the military life wear upon you or your family? Perhaps your wife and children?"

"Tire of it? It is not something I can allow. No, the army has been my opportunity. I chose it. The right victory will bring me recognition and reward. That is all I have. Wife? No. Children, I acknowledge none. They will come after my reward after my title has been awarded. No, now is not the time to be held back by a clinging woman. Why take a wife when I can take another man's wife when I need her?"

Karl's face tightened. The major continued, "Does that surprise you, my friend? You have much to learn of armies at war."

Karl stood up. "Major, I must retire. I travel tomorrow with Robert to view some tapestries. The hospital looks to sell from the old abbey to purchase more food for the sick."

"The hospital runs low on provisions?"

"Yes, major, it depends on donations and tithes from the church, but the townspeople have less to give."

"Very well. But let me give you a pass. It may be needed to re-enter the city."

Karl went upstairs where Werner was waiting in his room.

The next morning Karl and Robert set out for the hospital just after breakfast. The hospital was half a mile outside of the city walls in what once was an abbey. The chapel, barns, winery, and fields appeared old, tired and worn. The monastery cells and common rooms now functioned to shelter, care for and feed the sick. Across the field was the workhouse now used to shelter orphans and the elderly with no family to care for them. The hospital chapel sat on a high hill overlooking the city to the right and vineyards covering the hillside going down to the Neckar River below. The church tower provided a clear view in all directions for miles around.

The Deacon overseeing the hospital, orphanage and elder's home was waiting on the front steps for Karl and Robert when arrived. Karl called out to him as he dismounted his horse. "Someday I will surprise you!"

The deacon replied, "Not before you become invisible!"

Karl said as they walked inside, "You would do well to keep your sharp lookout, I have news."

"Soldiers will be coming for our provisions soon?"

"As you say. Eberbach will be called upon to feed more than the garrison; indeed, they seek provisions for another full regiment. I have told the commander you already run short, but I do not believe this will shield you."

"We will be ready."

"I have asked Werner to employ Joseph Werner to help him in resupplying the people. I do not want anyone in the city to know of your plans and methods. It is far too dangerous."

The deacon replied, "You fear someone may talk and yet you now trust Joseph Meyer?"

"I fear torture or threat of torture to wives and children. There will be no compassion. As for Joseph, he has proven himself at great risk."

The deacon nodded. "I have further dispersed the provisions, in small caches of one wagon load. It will lessen the chance of any patient or resident knowing our hiding places."

"Very good. Can you find a place for my friend Robert to stay for a while? The priest Don Lorenzo and the abbot Don Pedro have returned, we do not want them to know of Robert's presence."

The deacon looked at Robert and said, "Yes, I will find somewhere for him. Someplace where he cannot speak to patients and residents. His accent is suspicious."

A small bell rang inside the chapel, and a voice called down. "Deacon, a rider from Eberbach approaches… Werner comes at full gallop. .."

Karl ran to his horse. "Robert we must get back!"

That morning Werner was sitting in his room beside the window overlooking the market square. He watched as Joseph Meyer stepped out and swept the steps. When he finished, he left the broom on the left side of the door. Immediately Werner got up and went to the butcher's stall in the market. The butcher said, "You're here early today Werner."

"I've noticed your selection seems to be becoming smaller. A pork loin cut into chops please."

As the butcher went to cut the order, Joseph came alongside Werner and whispered, "Don Lorenzo and Don Pedro ride out to the hospital today. They have heard that Johann and Father Wilhelm have spent much time there."

"Any news on the provisions search?"

"The major has ordered his men to begin discreet searches. The Spanish priest insists Father Wilhelm and Johann are plotting something against the emperor."

"Meddlesome fool."

"What was that you asked?" The butcher said as he returned

"I said, 'Bring some sausages too.' Joseph is here as well."

When Werner returned to the house, Katharina was in the kitchen. "Where is Johann?" He asked.

"Johann was called to pray for Frau Schmidt. She has a fever and is bedridden. Wilhelm went with him."

"I must ride out to the hospital. I shall not be away long."

Major Ryskamp watched from his chair in the sitting room as Werner left. He stood up went to the window and watched Werner ride away. The major paced about the room nervously.

Twenty minutes passed, and he went into the kitchen. "Fraulein Katharina, are you baking? It smells so wonderful! I had to come and see. Perhaps you will share a small taste with me?"

"It is just bread, Major Ryskamp. It will not be ready for some time."

"Worth waiting for, I am sure! I thought we might have a conversation. I am not busy now. Can we talk while you bake?"

Katharina replied, "You are our guest, major, I will listen if you allow me to continue my chores."

"Certainly, I would not interfere with your baking;

please go on. Tell me, Katharina, you have no gentleman callers?

"Please major, such a personal question! I will not discuss such things!"

The major came close to where she was bent over the table wiping away flour. When she tried to stand up straight, the major was behind her and put his arms around her waist. He put his face against the back of her head and kissed her neck. "Your perfume is even more inviting than the aroma of the baking bread. I find you enchanting, and finally, we are alone!"

"Please major. Please let me go."

"You are a beautiful woman Katharina. We can enjoy our time together. I know how to bring pleasure to a woman. Such pleasure! No one else need know."

"You misjudge me, major, please sir, let me go."

The major slid his hands up over her chest and tightened his grip on her, his mouth beside her ear and said, "Katie, I know what kind of woman you are. I will not be the first. A previous lover carries your nude portrait. I will only take what you willfully gave him. You will enjoy it, we both will and when I leave there will be no regrets."

"My father—"

"Your father will be at the hospital all day with Robert. Your brother and the priest are gone, and Werner too rode off to the hospital. We are alone, and I will have you."

Katharina screamed, and Ryskamp immediately cupped his left hand over her mouth, his left arm forcing her head against his shoulder. He pushed her hard against the table, his right arm holding her arms down trapped at her side pinned against the table. Her body pressed tight against his. Katharina's red, teary eyes opened wide in fear, and she struggled to free herself from his grip. She was hopelessly trapped unable to move.

Major Ryskamp did not notice the door swing open or see Karl charging towards Katie's attacker from behind. Karl grabbed the major's collar and pulled him off Katie. As Karl pulled his head, Major Ryskamp, released Katie, swung his body around and hit Karl on the side of the head. Surprise and anger glowed from each man as they faced off. Karl lunged at Ryskamp who drew a knife from the sheath on his side. Karl caught his hand before Ryskamp could slash him, and he drove the major against the wall. As they struggled for control of the knife, sweat flowed from each man's face. Neither man spoke, but their grunts and groans betrayed two men fighting with all their strength and drowned out the cries and sobs of Katie.

Karl's face ground into Ryskamp's as they inhaled each other's breath. With a grimace of exertion, the major sharply and forcefully brought his knee up into Karl's groin. Karl groaned and weakened just enough for the younger man to break free and throw Karl off him simultaneously slashing with his knife. Karl's eyes widened, and he fell to his knees clutching his chest.

Katie's scream shook the house. Major Ryskamp stood frozen for a moment undecided as to strike Karl once more or grab Katharina. Robert heard her scream in the stable where he had just unsaddled the horses. He drew his sword as he raced to the house. He never stopped until Major Ryskamp was dead, eyes wide open in disbelief, blood still dripping from his mouth after his last hopeless gasp, his body hanging on Robert's sword driven to the hilt through body and wall.

CHAPTER 29
ESCAPE

Katie tore open Karl's doublet, his vest, and shirt to uncover his wound. She stanched the blood loss while Robert ripped the sleeves from his shirt to wrap the wound tight. "More bandages!" he shouted.

Katie rushed off only to return with an armful of clean blouses. "Stay with us Karl!" he shouted. "Katie, talk to him. Keep him awake."

Katie pulled her father up against her, seated on the floor, her back against the wall and held his head in her arms. "Papa, don't you leave me. Don't you leave me papa. If you love me, papa, you will not leave me! Oh, God, save my papa. He is a good man, a godly man. Oh Lord save him and preserve him. Do you hear me, papa?

Talk to me!"

Karl said, softly, "Katie, my child, my love. Hold me. It is in God's hands. Hold me, Katie. I feel so tired…"

Robert knelt beside Karl and said, "Karl we cannot stay here. Katie cannot stay—it is not safe. We must get you out of here before Major Ryskamp is missed. We need you. You must have your wits about you, man! Can you ride? Or a cart perhaps?"

Werner came in as Robert was speaking. "What happened here?"

"The major has wounded Karl; we must get him to safety before the major is missed."

Karl looked up. "The boat. I go by boat with all the tapestries. Werner, you bring Katie, Johann, and Robert by horse to Mannheim."

Werner said, "Robert knows the way. I will stay here and with Joseph see what they do."

Karl insisted. "It will not be safe…"

Werner replied, "When has what we do ever been safe? No, I have the least to lose. I will follow after."

Werner turned to Katie. "Fetch your brother and Father Wilhelm, tell them they must return at once. Then go to the boat Captain, tell him we must make a night voyage. He will understand. I must get word to Joseph Meyer."

Once Katie and Werner left, Robert sat next to Karl. "Rest my friend. I will bolt the front door and close the curtains. We will show no lights as if the major retired early. I must do something with the body."

Karl looked at Robert and said, "Thank you, Robert.

Thank you. You saved me, and you saved Katie."

Robert asked, "Surely I am not and never was worthy of being a priest of God. I am nothing but a selfish and sinful man."

"You are a compassionate priest, a godly man… faithful to others and God."

"I just ran a man through!"

"God is sovereign. It was His will."

Robert kissed Karl's forehead. "He has blessed me by just knowing you, my friend."

Robert got up braced his foot against the wall and pulled his sword out. As the major's body slid down the wall, Karl said, "Bring me paper and pen from the sitting room."

Robert closed the curtains, bolted the door and returned with the pen, paper, and ink. Karl said, "Go pack our bags while I write."

When Robert came down Pastor Johann Schroeder, and Father Wilhelm Hahn were kneeling with hands on Karl's head praying for God's healing, comfort, and strength. They called Katie to them and prayed for her, thanking God for protecting her. Karl looked up and said, "There is much to do. Johann, gather all of our tapestries, we must get them into the cart. Save an old.one of lesser quality to roll me in. Katie put together bags, gather everything of value, money, jewels, but not too much to carry in saddle bags. And Wilhelm, I have a task for you. When we leave, I have written a confession, an account of what happened. I have written it in German, French, and Spanish, so all will understand. I want you to post it on the church door as you ride out of the city."

"Your confession? Me, ride out of the city?"

"Father, you are a good man, a good priest. But you cannot stay here. Your enemies will condemn you with all of us. No, you must come. God is not finished with you yet. And yes, a confession, I will read it: 'The body of Major Antonin Ryskamp can be found in the kitchen of my house where he died in an altercation which arose yesterday when I came upon him forcing himself on my daughter Katharina. It was the major who first drew his weapon and drew first blood. I stand on my honor as a father and gentleman not to leave such behavior unchallenged. I could not standby and permit such debauched behavior in my home directed at my daughter. The villain in this affair is the Spanish priest who violated the sanctity of any Christian priesthood by slandering my daughter to the major and others on what was shared with him in holy confession. Citizens of Eberbach do not let yourself be party to this injustice. Have faith in God for the strength to resist the evil occupation of our city. Karl Schroeder'"

Robert said, "Karl why do you not say I killed the man. You are innocent in his death though you had every right to attack him."

"I do not seek credit or glory in the major's death. There is no need to put you, a stranger and my guest at risk. No, you too, are under my protection, and we will see you safely to Mannheim or wherever God directs your path. No, my friend, the statement is accurate, and there is no need to implicate you or anyone else. Isn't one man repeatedly shooting at you enough?"

Werner spoke. "There is time for this later. Johann, Katie, Wilhelm, and Robert must leave immediately. They can delay no longer. I will get Karl and the tapestries to the boat and then post the confession early tomorrow morning. I will be its discover and make sure it is read and heard by our citizens and not destroyed by the priests or magistrate. Go north, if asked at the gate say you are visiting the sick at the hospital. Ask the deacon to ferry you and your horses across the river and ride to Mannheim. The deacon will not betray you. He will tell any who ask that your rode quickly north. Do not delay ride now!"

Karl nodded. "Do as he says. God willing, we will meet in Mannheim. From there we will get Father Wilhelm safely to Mainz where I can sell the tapestries and then look ahead. Werner, you must follow, my friend. Do not overstay your welcome in Eberbach!"

Werner replied, "We still have friends, Joseph and I, the deacon, and there are the watchers. We have eyes and ears. Don't worry about us, Karl. As soon as it is dark, I will take you to the boat. Now kiss your father Katie and Johann and be off!"

William walked over to the body of Major Ryskamp knelt, crossed himself and gave the major last rites.

Four hours later it was dark. Karl lit one small candle and set it in the sitting room. He locked all the doors and moved to the stable where he filled a cart with rolled tapestries. He and Karl waited another hour before Joseph Meyer helped him roll Karl in a rug and lift him into the cart. Werner led the cart slowly through the quiet streets of Eberbach to the river gate. The guard questioned him, "What is your business on the quay?"

Werner answered, "Just delivering rugs and tapestries to the boat for shipment."

The guard walked over and looked in the cart lifted his lantern and said, "Rugs and Tapestries. Go ahead."

The boat captain was waiting. He carefully assisted Werner in loading the rolls of tapestries onto the boat, slipped his lines and was immediately underway downriver. Werner returned through the gate with the empty cart and back to the stable, unhitched the horse and waited for dawn.

Robert, Wilhelm, Johann, and Katie were safely across the Neckar river less than an hour after leaving Eberbach. A rider met them at the other side, one of Karl's watchers who recognized the signal from the old abbey chapel tower. "I'll have you safely in Mannheim in less than six hours," he confidently affirmed. "Count Tilly has sent most of his army to winter quarters. He knows the English are going nowhere before spring. He watches only the main roads from the cities. A good dark night will be our friend!"

The party quickly fell into a column of twos. Johann and the watcher led, Katie and Wilhelm followed them, and Robert followed at a distance behind, his sword on his side and two pistols on his belt. Katie had not said a word since leaving Eberbach. Her downcast eyes made it clear to Wilhelm she was distraught. "Katie, it is over, you are safe. Your father will soon join us in Mannheim. You can breathe deeply and thank God for your salvation."

"Is it over, Wilhelm? What I have done will not be forgotten. My guilt nearly cost papa his life. No, it is not over. It will never be over."

"Katie, you cannot hold onto this guilt. You are not to blame for what has happened. You have confessed a sin that was not yours. It was his sin. He seduced an innocent young woman. Stop blaming yourself."

Katie shook her head no. "Sin has a price. There must be atonement. God is holding me accountable for my weakness."

"Do not blame God for the evil in this world! He has atoned for your sin by the death on the cross of our Savior and Lord Jesus Christ! Even so, any small error on your part has been absolved. God calls you to faith, faith that He is, and He is a rewarder of those who follow Him. No Katie, holding onto guilt is like keeping Christ on the cross, suffering and dying for no reason."

Katie was quiet; her teary eyes still downcast. Finally, she said softly, "Do you forgive me, Wilhelm? Do I repulse you with me filthy past?"

Wilhelm reached over and took the bridle of Katie's horse in his hand stopping both. He sat up in his saddle beside her and said, "Look at me. Look at me!"

Katie looked up, and Wilhelm said boldly, "Katharina Schroeder, I have known no other woman like you. Forgive you? I have never loved any woman as I love you."

Wilhelm dropped the reins of Katie's horse, turned his horse, and they rode on in silence.

Sometime after midnight, the boat approached Count Tilly's boom across the Neckar River three miles upriver from Heidelberg. The Captain came alongside it and raised his lantern. He waited patiently as a small boat rowed out from the guard post on the riverbank. The guard called out to the Captain, "Your pass."

The Captain held up a paper, and the small boat came alongside. The guard said as he took the pass, "You are on your way early, what is your cargo and destination?"

The captain said, "Rugs and tapestries. Mainz."

The guard read the pass. "No passengers? I see your pass says Army of Flanders passengers and provisions to Eberbach. Nothing here about rugs."

The Captain said, "An army cannot eat rugs and tapestries, but they can be traded for provisions in Mainz."

The guard held his lantern over the side of the boat. "Unroll that one."

The captain unrolled a tapestry and brought it close to the light."

"Supposin' that would bring a good price indeed. How do you intend to get past the cannon at Heidelberg?"

"The changing of the guard will be a little sloppy tonight."

"Will it now? Well, good luck then. Food is getting a little thin at the outposts." He signaled with his lantern and the chain across the river was lowered.

At Heidelberg, the Captain produced the passes Sir George Herbert and Colonel Vere provided Robert and

Karl, and after a cursory inspection and the learning current password, he proceeded to Mannheim. Johann, Katharina, and Wilhelm were waiting for Karl when he arrived. A surgeon examined Karl and redressed his wounds. "The slash is long but not deep. He should rest.

"Where is Robert? We must see Colonel Vere at once," Karl said.

"Papa, Robert has already gone to meet with the Colonel. He asks that you rest," Johann replied.

The guard led Robert up the familiar stairs of the castle, but at the top, he turned right instead of left to the Colonel's office. When Robert hesitated the guard said, "I am taking you to Captain Stock, the Colonel's adjutant. You will wait there until the Colonel asks to see you."

Captain Stock was sitting at a table covered with maps and correspondence when Robert entered. "Robbie," Stock began. "You have been very busy! You and your German friend, Herr Schroeder out and about seeing the sights."

Robert replied, "We did our best for Colonel Vere. Is he available now? I want to give him a more detailed report."

"Sit down, Robbie." Stock's face turned serious. "Do you take me as a fool? It will be to your peril and the peril of your friends as well. I do not know what game you are playing, but it is over."

"Game? I play no games, I…."

"You gave me only half of the code. You tell only of the enemy troop movements and strength."

"Is not that the most valuable information? Is not knowledge of your enemy strategic?"

Captain Stock shot back, "Your mission was to report on relief for our regiment! You wandered all over the north and yet not a clue as to von Mansfelt's intentions or Christian IV…"

"Count von Mansfelt is detained, you know that, and Christian IV tarries in Copenhagen, also well known."

Stock shouted, "You were sent to Duke Christian of Brunswick! It is equally known he raises an army. You were in his lands! He is the key! Is he coming? When? What is his strength?"

Robert lowered his voice. "Spies. They are everywhere. We were followed. Every step we took was known. We chose to protect the most critical information. We took no unnecessary risk. We have what you ask. You will hear it with the Colonel. If it is his desire."

"So now you suspect me as a traitor?"

"We suspect everyone. It is to the Colonel we will make our report."

Stock sat back. "You say you were followed…"

"A man we have seen here before."

"Well, who is he, man? A name!"

"A Mister Sharpe. He has made at least three attempts on my life. Do you know him, Captain?"

"Sharpe, you say? Yes, I have heard of this man."

Captain Stock sat silently for a few moments and said, "It is time you make your report to Sir Horace."

Robert followed Donald Stock down the stone

corridor, their boots ringing their presence as they made their way. Captain Stock stopped in front of the heavy oak door to Colonel Vere's apartment, knocked once briskly and entered. "Colonel, Lieutenant Curtis has returned and will make his report."

"Not waiting, Robert tipped his hat in salute and said, "Colonel, Duke Christian of Brunswick has raised an army of ten thousand infantry and cavalry and marches here in the spring. He plans to join with the Count von Mansfeld and with your support, drive Count Tilly's Army of Flanders out of the Palatinate. King Christian IV of Denmark has agreed to loan King James the money he requested and is encouraged that his highness will stand with Elector Frederick and the protestant cause."

Colonel, Sir Horace Vere, looked surprised by Robert's hurried report in Captain Stock's presence, but quickly gained his composure. "Very well, Lieutenant, please come in. Tell me, Lieutenant, are there any other allies moving to our aid?"

Robert stepped forward into the room. "No colonel, the armies all seek winter quarters. The Army of Flanders is dispersing to garrison cities in the Palatinate. I have just come from Eberbach, now garrisoned with eight hundred men. It appears both sides wait for spring and re-enforcements."

The Colonel looked to Captain Stock. "Captain it seems your analysis of our situation was correct. We are here through the winter without relief. Proceed with our defense works, provisioning and training plans. And pass this intelligence to Colonel Herbert and Colonel

Burroughs. That will be all Captain."

Once Captain Stock's boots could be heard making their way down the stone corridor, Sir Horace asked, "Why the hasty report for Captain Stock?"

"Colonel, the man is no fool. He deduced he did not see all the intelligence. I needed to regain his trust."

"Sit down Lieutenant. Explain."

Robert sat down on a chair opposite the Colonel and spoke softly. "I told him we were followed, which is true, A Mister Sharpe, a man I believe connected with Captain Stock did indeed follow us and made several attempts on my life. I told Stock, we dare not risk such vital information if our mission had been betrayed, now, of course, it is safe to share, but I did not want him to know you had already received our report."

"You still suspect Captain Stock?" Vere asked.

"We know Stock is in league with the papal diplomat Don Lorenzo and the Spanish abbot Don Pedro. We believe he is passing information intended for the Spanish Ambassador to King James, a Count Gondomar, who directs the game against our King with the marriage negotiations for Prince Charles and the Infanta Maria.'

The colonel nodded. "How can I lead if my adjutant selected by my superior may be a traitor? I need proof."

Robert replied, "Let me inquire after Mister Sharpe. We crossed swords in Mainz, where I know I cut him; he managed to escape, and I do not know if he lives. But the proof may also be found in the court in England, the Queen Mother Sophie of Denmark-Norway is an ally and has offered up her contacts there."

Colonel Vere stood and walked to the window overlooking the Neckar and the Rhine. He stood with his hands behind his back, his eyes staring but his mind in thought. "I understand Herr Schroeder is badly wounded."

Robert replied, "At the hands of the garrison commander, a Major Ryskamp. Karl defended the honor of his daughter as any father would. I finished what Karl began. The major is dead and Karl's family safely here."

"And your papist priest?"

"He was most helpful in Mainz and has made a strong ally in the Elector Archbishop. But yes, he is here also. He can be trusted, Colonel. I would put my life in his hands."

The Colonel spoke to the window. "Nose around a bit for Mister Sharpe. Tell Herr Schroeder I would like to see him when he is up to it, to thank him. Tell Captain Stock to arrange it for tomorrow. That will be all lieutenant."

As Robert got up to leave, Sir Horace said, "Welcome back, Curtis. Well done."

CHAPTER 30
A SMUGGLER'S WORK

Robert walked back to Captain Stock's apartment and entered just as Sergeant Edward Barkley was leaving. "Barkley!" Robert said surprised to see him.

"Just leaving, Mister Curtis. Good to see you safe and in one piece."

"Wait for me; I would like to hear about our company at Heidelberg. This will only take a moment."

Robert turned to Captain Stock. "The colonel has asked to see Herr Schroeder tomorrow. You are to tell me the time."

Stock looked at a paper on his desk and said eleven o'clock. Anything else from the colonel?

Robert replied, "He had the same concerns regarding

my shadow. I will do some checking, and we will speak more of it later. You will know all that I learn."

"Very well, Robbie."

Robert closed the door behind him and walked down the corridor with Barkley who said, "Robbie is it?"

Ignoring the comment, Robert replied, "How do you know Captain Stock?"

"The captain was asking after Mister Sharpe, Sir"

Robert asked, "You know Sharpe then?"

"Aye, what if I do?"

"The man has made three attempts on my life. I cut him last time. In Mainz. Haven't seen him since."

Barkley replied, "So, you're thinkin' it was him who shot you along the Neckar. Thought it was but couldn't be sure. Too bad you didn't *finish* the job in Mainz."

"Donald Stock is no more a friend of mine, than you are, Barkley."

"Oh, so a workin' man and respectable sergeant ain't good enough for a high and mighty member of the Curtis family!"

Robert stopped and looked straight into Barkley's face. "I have put up with your insolence long enough! I know you are a capable man with great skill. You never soldiered, yet you are made a senior sergeant. You whine incessantly about the ship tax and burden the King places on the working man. Why are you here Edward Barkley? If not for soldiering why are you here?"

Barkley stared back at Robert and replied, "I have not seen Sharpe since you left Heidelberg. I missed him as much as I missed you."

Robert's voice grew loud and stern. "You took the stripes of a sergeant. A true sergeant is a leader, an example to both soldiers and officers. When will you understand we are soldiers, we serve the king and our senior officers. People depend on us for their very lives. It is time you put away your games. Your pub drinking friends are not here to listen to your flippant remarks."

Barkley stared a Robert for several seconds before answering, "Yes, I know Sharpe, known him for years. Evil man he is. Has no friends, no heart, no deed too foul for that one. It was him who sought me out, sayin' there was a need for a man with smugglin' skills. Someone who could get letters, packages and maybe people between England and the Dutch Republic, even Germany. Said they would make me a sergeant, all respectable and good money in it too."

Robert said, "They couldn't have found a better man for the job."

Barkley smiled. "Funny thing. It was your uncle, the Viscount who picked me for the job." Barkley turned serious. "Understand this, Mister Curtis, I may be a smuggler and against taxes what hurt the hard laborin' man, but I am an Englishman. And I am loyal!"

Robert nodded yes. "I always believed you a smuggler but not a thief. And a true Englishman."

Barkley smiled. His eyes brightened. Robert then added, "No more gibes of my commission bought and paid for. You're no more a soldier than I, Sergeant Barkley."

"It is a true saying, Mister Curtis. Though you now

look more the soldier to me than I reckoned."

Robert said, "Do we understand each other?"

With a nod Barkley replied, "Aye, sir, so we do."

"My friends can call me Robbie."

"Aye, Robbie it is. Barkley is what I answer to. Only my mother called me Edward; God rest her soul."

"So, tell me, you and Sharpe…"

"Sharpe was the outside man, the runner, enforcer. Did whatever was needed. Couldn't have a true soldier runnin' about the countryside. Knows the language, good at blendin' in. Never talked. Never needed anyone to talk to."

"So why go after me?"

"Makes no sense to me, Mister, er Robbie."

"So, Captain Stock gives the orders and…"

"Mostly Captain Stock, but your cousin, Sir Geoffrey, as well."

Robert, surprised, said, "Sir Geoffrey?" and then muttered, "and Uncle James."

Karl was asleep when Robert returned to the others at the guest quarters. Johann and Wilhelm were talking quietly, still weary from the stress filled day and long ride. "Has Karl arrived?"

Johann replied, "Yes, the surgeon has examined him and redressed his wounds. He is asleep. He is strong, and with God's grace he will recover."

Robert nodded. "Good. And Katie is still not speaking to you, Wilhelm? What has happened between you?"

"Katie sits beside Karl. Katie is fine. You know her

strong spirit."

Johann said, "She blames herself for what happened. She has always been sensitive to others."

"She tells us she intends to find a convent," Johann added.

Robert nodded. "Calvinists! You hold onto your guilt and accountability. You must see the fruit of the Spirit to ensure your election. You need to relearn from the Lutherans, to live in God's grace! God's saving grace is never earned; it is our ever-present comfort. Does Katie not abound with the fruit of Spirit? You let her assume the guilt and blame herself? Wilhelm, have you ever known a woman so rich in love and abounding in grace?"

Wilhelm lowered his eyes and said, "No. No, I have never known a woman with so rich a love."

Katie came out of Karl's room and seeing Robert said, "Papa is awake. He asks to see you, Robert."

Robert walked into the room as he said, "Come with me. You all need to hear this."

Karl was sitting up in bed, his face pale, nearly as white as the hair on his head, his blue eyes drained by pain. For the first time, he appeared an old man. Robert lied, "You look good, my friend, rested up and ready for another ride north."

Karl grunted. "Robert, you are a terrible liar. Now tell me, what has Colonel Vere to say?"

"He has received our reports and knows all that we know. But there is more. Donald Stock is suspicious. He figured we withheld information from him. I had to tell him we kept secret the movements of the allies because we were being followed. I learned Mister Sharpe has not been seen since he left to follow us. I also learned that Sharpe recruited my sergeant Barkley, remember him from Heidelberg? He is a lifelong smuggler and their man to move documents and people between here and England. Barkley is here. Tells me Sharpe is the outside man, makes the runs and does whatever nefarious deed required. An evil man, he says."

Robert paused and looked at the surprised faces of the others. "Rest today Karl, my friend. Take some food. The Colonel will see us again tomorrow at eleven. But know this, all of you. None of you can tarry here. You must move on. Surely your presence here will be reported and escape difficult. You do not want to be here once the siege begins."

Karl said, "Mainz. The tapestries will wait for us in Mainz where they can be sold for cash to take us to safety." Turning to Robert, he said, "Does Barkley say why Sharpe wants you dead?"

Robert shook his head. "No. Barkley, though a smuggler he is, is yet a loyal Englishman. He can help us. I believe the answer is in England."

The next morning Karl did look better. The food, wine and rest did much to restore the vitality that buoyed Karl. His eyes sparkled blue as he asked Robert to help him up. "Do you need a cane, old man?" Robert teased.

"To give you a good thrashing, impertinent Englishman," he retorted. As they slowly walked, Karl said, "So you intend to leave us and return to England?"

"I am still a lieutenant of cuirassiers, remember. My

duty is still to my commander and my king."

Captain Stock escorted Robert and Karl to Colonel Vere's apartment. Welcoming Karl, the Colonel said to Stock, "I want to thank Herr Schroeder for his efforts personally. But I need you to look into a few matters for me right now. First, see if there are any entries in the logs regarding a Mister Sharpe, and then find the reports on our provisions. I want to know how long we can continue at our current consumption, that is Heidelberg and Frankenthal as well."

"Yes, Colonel."

"Return as soon as you have the information."

Captain Stock closed the door as he left. His boots rang out against the stone floor as he walked briskly back to his apartment. "Sit down Herr Schroeder. I'm told you left a dead Flemish major in your house."

Karl sat down and replied, "Just as you say. The garrison commander. Eight hundred men, infantry and arquebusiers. A good intelligence opportunity shattered by his attack on my daughter. I was just getting him to talk…I can abide many things, but my daughter…"

Vere replied, "I would do the same if I were in your position, justice and honor demands it. But what of his plans did you learn."

"His men are quartered for the winter at least. He has orders to find provisions for a regiment in addition to his garrison. He sees the provisions held in houses, market, and larders insufficient and surmises, correctly that more is hidden. It is a dangerous game for the people of Eberbach. My son, Johann here, and the priest, Wilhelm organized the safekeeping of what we had gathered."

Colonel Vere nodded to Johann. "I am glad to see you safe and released from prison."

Johann said, "Thank you, Colonel, for aiding my father in my cause. I owe my freedom to you and to my friend Father Wilhelm who has won the influence of the Elector Archbishop."

"Has he now? Father Hahn? Very good then."

Robert interrupted. "Colonel, I have met a man from my company, a Sergeant Barkley, who knows the man Sharpe who followed us…"

"I am aware of Sergeant Barkley and the skills which he brings to our effort…"

Robert nodded. "Yes, Colonel, Barkley arranges the dispatch of messages and people to and from England. He…"

Vere interrupted. "I know of his skill in procuring what we need for the quartermaster, but you say dispatches and people?"

"He tells me Captain Stock directs his duties and sometimes my cousin Sir Geoffrey Curtis. Mister Sharpe was the outside man, the runner and …"

"So, Captain Stock is tied to this Mister Sharpe as well as Don Lorenzo and Don Pedro. And Sergeant Barkley is one of them."

"I am convinced Barkley is loyal, and only following orders. He has no love for Sharpe, hasn't seen him since I left Heidelberg, must have died after I cut him. Tell me Colonel, is Captain Stock in charge of dispatches?"

"Well, yes. But a civilian runner and a smuggler. Most

unusual. And why is sir Geoffrey involved?"

"Colonel it is well known the King's negotiations with Spain trouble many in parliament and among the court. Can there be any doubt schemes are afoot? And it is your men here in Germany that will suffer the consequence. The answers lie in England. You cannot trust Captain Stock with such dispatches—nor my cousin and nor perhaps my uncle who arranged Sergeant Barkley's enlistment. I have been given contacts. Let me go to England and find the traitor. I will return and report before the spring offensive."

Colonel Vere stood up and walked to his thinking window. "Herr Schroeder, is your watcher organization still intact?"

"Yes, Colonel. Stronger than ever."

"Tell me, Karl, if you were paid in advance for food and provisions, could you get them to my three garrisons? There would be a bonus upon delivery that might go towards the good people of Eberbach."

Karl took a deep breath and said, "It is true; food will be hard to come by. I am sure the Army of Flanders can be ruthless in acquiring what it needs and just as ruthless in stopping any supply to you. It will be difficult, but I think it can be done. I will take the request to my friends."

"Thank you, Karl, I know I can depend upon you. And tell me, Robert, how will you get to England and back?"

"Why with the help of our smuggler, Sergeant Barkley, if you can spare him."

"It will surely put Captain Stock on notice. Perhaps he

can still be played. Regardless, his communication path will be cut."

The Colonel thought and then continued. "He still has his papist Dons."

The Colonel returned and extending his hand to each said, "Gentlemen, proceed."

Robert smiled. "Thank you, Sir Horace. I will arrange to communicate through Karl's network."

"One last thing, it is not safe for your family here, Karl. A city under siege is no place for your daughter. I wish I could say other…"

"I understand Colonel. We must depart soon."

Less than an hour later, Sergeant Edward Barkley knocked on Robert's door. Upon entering, he said, "I have been ordered to report to you for a special assignment."

"Orders? From whom?"

"Captain Stock says they come from the top, the Colonel himself."

Robert nodded. "I'll wager Captain Stock was none too happy with that."

"He did seem a bit peeved, could not tell me much… said you'll tell me all I need to know. Where we goin' Mister Curtis?"

"First stop Mainz then on to England. That is if you can get six of us and our horses out of Mannheim unseen."

"England? I could use a good ale! Smuggled out or smuggled in. It's all the same. When are we leaving?"

"As soon as possible."

"Smugglers hours then. Middle of the last watch. We will meet at the stable at two tomorrow morning. Have your passes for the horses with you. Tell your friends dark clothes and cloaks with hoods. Dress 'em warm, Robbie, it will be a cold night."

It was indeed a cold late November night when Robert silently led Karl, Katie, Johann, and Wilhelm to the stable. Barkley was waiting to meet them. Robert presented the pass for their horses and one for Barkley. The guard nodded and went back to his blanket in the hay. Barkley reached into a sack and gave each person four squares cut from a blanket and four leather strips. "Tie a blanket patch under each hoof. Make sure it is tight. Don't need no horseshoes ringin' out on the paving stone."

When Barkley was satisfied that hooves were padded correctly, he said, "Lead your horses on foot. Not a word! Understand not a word until I say it is safe! Put your hoods on. There is a moon tonight, but the cold is our friend. Anyone about will stay close to their warming fire. Robbie, you follow last, herd any strays. It's time."

Barkley led the small group through the streets north to a small gate in the wall which opened onto the marshy wetland of grass, brush and scrub trees on the shifting sand and mud flats at the true confluence of the Neckar and Rhine, at the tip of the narrow peninsula on which Mannheim was built. The walls of the city obstructed any view from the piers and wharves of Mannheim. Outside the gate, the cold air was biting, moist, and pungent with the musty smell of rotting vegetation. A small path of crushed mussel and snail shells crunched under the hooves of the horses. Only the heavy breathing of the party gave notice to the people slowly making their way into the darkness, into the marsh.

The path led them into a thicket of small trees and brush and alongside a narrow canal where two flatboats, livestock barges, little more than rafts, were tied to the trees. Each barge had a large sweep oar at one end with a man seated patiently. Barkley silently led each horse and person onto a raft positioning each pair where he wanted them and whispered, "Hold 'em by the bridle. Don't let him move."

When everyone boarded safely with their horse, Barkley, on the first barge nodded to the oarsman, who lifted his oar from the sweep lock, shoved off and started down the canal. The oarsman of the second barge followed him silently.

When the barges entered the stream, the oarsman gave one last push of the oar against the bottom and dropped the oar back into its sweep lock. As the barges entered the current, a straight course was maintained with the sweeps of the long oar.

Out on the river, the top of the Mannheim wall came into sight. Warming fires could be seen from the guard towers. The lights of Ludwigshafen could be seen directly across the Rhine. The two barges slowly and silently made their way down the Rhine and around a bend into the darkness.

And as if guided by an invisible force the two barges entered a small estuary where people and horses stepped ashore onto a narrow path. Instantly the barges disappeared into the night, and Barkley said quietly as he removed the hoof pads and mounted his horse, "The road to Mainz."

CHAPTER 31
DECISIONS

The boat from Eberbach was moored at the far end of the wharf in Mainz. The captain welcomed Karl on board. All his tapestries were safe and dry. "Any difficulties along the way?" Karl asked.

"No more than usual," The captain replied.

"I bring you a proposition, my friend. Steady business with a good return and you would be helping our friends in Eberbach and our religious cause."

The captain replied, "A good return implies risk. What is the cargo?"

"Food. Grain, meat, oil, wine. Whatever can be bought and safely delivered to Frankenthal…"

"Frankenthal is little risk."

"And Mannheim…"

"A bit riskier, and next you will say, Heidelberg, even more risk."

"Yes, and also Eberbach, perhaps the most risk of all."

The captain smiled. "I have lived a good life; perhaps it is time for me to give back to our brothers and sisters and our friends who risk their lives for our right to worship according to our faith. It will be difficult to do alone. I will need support in moving provisions onshore. And information, I must know what awaits along the route."

Karl said, "I can arrange that. But is there food to be bought?"

The captain said, "Not here. Downriver, perhaps, away from the armies and the garrisons."

Karl pointed to his tapestries. "I will arrange to pick them up straight away."

Robert and Wilhelm were talking quietly and did not notice Karl return from the riverfront. "The tapestries are here; I must arrange for a cart and their safekeeping until they can be sold. I could use some help, where is Johann?"

"Johann has gone to visit his friend Heiko and see if his son has recovered."

Karl nodded. "And Katie, did she go as well?"

Wilhelm mumbled, "She finds my company uncomfortable. I shall soon be parting ways."

Karl was speechless for a moment and then said, "She finds your company uncomfortable? It must be something else. Wilhelm, your company, could not be more welcome and comforting. I don't understand."

Robert spoke. "Katie has been through a terrible ordeal. She believes she has brought it upon herself. She believes she can no longer join the company of men, other than you and Johann. She is afraid she will lead Wilhelm astray from his calling."

Karl replied, "I noticed she has been silent the last two days. She has always been so strong and resilient. A man dead. For certain it is a hard thing, but lead you, Wilhelm, astray?"

"Karl, I have just made my confession to my friend Robert, but I must confess to you that I have wounded Katie so dear to you and me as well. As we rode to Mannheim, I told Katie I have never loved a woman as I love her. I should not have been so bold. I know I am unworthy of her, but I did not mean... I did not intend...she hasn't spoken to me since. So, you see I must part ways and... and well, there are vows, duties... I did not mean to impose my love on her; truly I admire her loving spirit... her..."

Karl saw the pain on Wilhelm's face. "Wilhelm you have become family to my family. Stay. Stay for now. I know your intentions are honorable. Your leaving would only cause more pain. Stay. Let me talk to my Katie."

Karl walked off towards Katie's room. Robert spoke softly to Wilhelm. "My friend, you cannot run away to a monk's cell and hide. That is not serving God or anyone else. What troubles you, my friend is that Katie rightly understands your love. You have fallen in love with her. And why not? You are well suited. She is indeed a most loving person, selfless and kind. She is sweetness and light. She does not hide because she does not love you, she hides because she loves you just as you love her. Sadly, neither of you believe that God would permit you the joy of being loved."

"It can never be, I made a vow."

"Wilhelm you have been questioning those vows long before you realized your affection for Katie. You know the Church universal is more than Rome. You know Katie is as much a child of God and saint of the Church as you are. You can serve God outside the Catholic Church, and serving God is more than a clerical collar. Don't let that stop you from the blessings of marriage."

Wilhelm whispered, "But what if all my questioning was not spiritually motivated? What if my questioning was really to justify pursuing an attractive young woman, saintly though she is."

"My friend, answer a question. Do you believe God has called you to serve Him?"

"This is not helping. Of course, I believe God has called me. I strive with all my being to be worthy of this calling. It is a hard thing to love others more than yourself. It is hard, very hard and I work to this calling."

"And you love God?"

"Robert, you know I love God."

"Then listen, my friend, for I believe you do love God with all of your heart and all of your soul and all of your mind. I believe the same can be said of Katie. Remember the words of Saint Paul, 'For we know all things work together for good for those who love God and are called according to His purpose.'"

Robert put an arm around Wilhelm's shoulder. "This love you have for Katie and the love Katie has for you is of God's calling. Do not run-off. Stay. See if it is indeed God's will."

Wilhelm replied, "I thank you for trying to help. I will consider and pray."

Robert said, "You might consider this. Come to England with me, Katie too. It isn't safe here. Where can she go? Katie, Karl, Johann, none of them can go back to Eberbach. And the inquisition will catch up with you sooner or later. Come to England. We are still working out the reform of our church. You have much to teach."

"England? No. England? I am a priest! Priests are banned from England."

"Only priests practicing Roman rites. Consider it. Any true church of God would welcome you, Reformed, Lutheran or Anglican."

Robert found Barkley in the corner of the ratskeller, sat down across from him and set two steins of beer on the table. Barkley took a stein to replace the empty in front of him and said, "Your walkin' just fine. No more limp. A man on the run should not draw notice. A limp, a fancy hat, jewelry, or great embroidered coat even a fine horse is remembered when questions get asked."

Robert nodded. "You're right. My leg has healed, and I will remember to blend in. Like Mister Sharpe."

Barkley continued. "Pretty straight forward from here Robbie. Amsterdam. Just talked to your friend Karl's boat captain, Otto. Knows his ropes, he does. Fine chap, believe I can do business with him in the future."

"Otto? I never knew his name."

"Robert, you need to know people to trust them. Anyway, your friend Karl, a fox that one is, Karl plans to take his family to safety in Amsterdam. We shall go along. I know someone among the English exiles there…"

"English exiles?"

"Those what you high church call non-conformists. Puritans they are—a good number of them in Amsterdam. The city, aye, all the Dutch Republic is filling with fleeing protestants. Don't you know this? Not just English Puritans, but Lutherans, Calvinists, Anabaptists, French Huguenots, even Hussites. A tolerant people these Dutch. Even Jews are tolerated. To the Dutch, these people work hard, make no trouble and bring industry. Karl wants them all to be safe while he continues his work on behalf of the cause."

Robert nodded. "He is, as you say a sly fox and committed to the protestant cause as are his son and daughter in equal measure."

"You found yourself in good company with them. And the young lady, stunning she is, few like her to be found."

"Yes, she is beautiful…"

"Oh, I was referring to her sweetness of heart. Truly kind. Reminds me of my mother, she does, always worried about others, always put someone else before her. Me mum would say to me, 'Edward now you be good to the stranger and be sure they have what they need. The good book tells us so, says we never know the stranger we share with may be an angel of God above.

Tell me, Robbie, does the good book say that?"

"Yes, what your mother taught you is true. She was a true Christian lady."

"That is how I started in the smugglin' business. When me father died, there was never enough, and mum still gave what we had to anyone showin' up to our door. Smugglin' is honest work, truly! Let them who ain't strugglin' pay the taxes!"

Robert nodded. "Your mother taught you well. Amsterdam it is then."

"Aye, not a hard journey. But hard it will be for you to part with such friends."

CHAPTER 32
ENGLAND

Lambeth Palace was situated on the south bank of the River Thames, just across from Westminster Palace. It was an old building, acquired over four hundred years earlier to serve as the official residence of the Archbishop of Canterbury, since the days of Henry VIII, Primate of the Church of England. It's imposing red brick façade was fronted by a parish church, the Gothic, Saint Mary-at-Lambeth, and surrounded by a magnificent garden and orchard. The oldest wing was now the Chapel. At the northwest corner stood a high tower and sometimes prison, where the early reformer and Bible translator, John Wycliffe was held and tried for heresy. It was a building that survived the turmoil of the English Reformation and the changing royal dynasties.

Lambeth Palace grew with change, not so much

destroying the old as adding the new. The memory of the great Catholic Cardinals of England was memorialized at Lambeth, where they retained their influence upon the Anglican Church, and upon the protestant Primates that followed in their footsteps. Tradition survived in the Anglican Liturgy and remembered the ancient traditions of the Church but was now sung with grace and majesty in English. A new tradition occurred during the Gospel reading. The priest followed an open Bible carried to the center of the church for the gospel reading, a clear proclamation that Holy Scripture should be brought to the people, that the Bible belonged to the whole Church.

Robert could not be other than awed and humbled as he approached the guard at the door and requested an audience with the Archbishop. Edward Barkley noticed old figs on a tree beside the door and casually picked one. The guard responded as he did countless times before. "The Archbishop does not grant audiences unless arranged in advance by his secretary."

Then, glaring at Edward, he barked, "You would do well not to touch Cardinal Woolsey's tree. It is ancient and protected."

Barkley nibbled on the fig and said, "If protected means its fruit is left to rot."

Robert urgently replied, "I request an audience with the Archbishop's secretary."

The guard, now animated, raised his voice. "Requests for Appointment with the Archbishop's secretary are only accepted in writing from a Bishop of the Church of England."

"Surely there are exceptions…"

The guard looked at Robert and Edward Barkley and replied tersely, "Aye, from the King, his council, or the House of Lords. But save your effort, the Archbishop and his secretary are off to Cambridge for a fortnight."

"At the university then; which college would that be?"

"Good day sir." And the guard returned to the warming hut beside the door.

As they walked off, Robert said, "You could show a little respect."

"I show it when I receive it. How far is Cambridge?"

Robert sighed. "Sixty miles north."

At Magdalene College, Cambridge, Robert was warmly received by his tutor the Reverend Doctor Thomas Giddings. "Why Mister Curtis, come in! Good to see you again Robert. Sit and your friend?"

"Doctor Giddings, this is a comrade from Berwick-Upon-Tweed, Sergeant Edward Barkley."

"Welcome sergeant! Please sit. A comrade, Robert? Strange for a priest of the church. But these are strange times. Tell me, Father Curtis; I do not recall your parish or placement."

"I have no parish, no placement in the church. I am a soldier, a lieutenant of cuirassiers with English volunteers in the Palatine."

"No parish? No placement? And now a soldier? And whatever is a cuirassier?"

"A cavalry officer of pistols. And no Bishop would have me, so there you are."

"Too many questions, Robert, you always had too

many questions. No one knew what to make of you. You could never make up your mind on the right path in the church. But a soldier? And why are you here and not in Germany?"

"It is true I could not identify with one faction, I found truth among all of them and error, well, who has not erred? I am more swayed by the heart of the servant than the theology of the priest. This determination to martyr our brothers and sisters over what, jealousy of authority? The pope has unleashed the Holy Roman Emperor to crush every follower of the Reformation. Good people who love God are being driven from their homes or forced to renounce their faith at the end of a sword. I have recently come from Amsterdam where English puritans live in exile. Faithful Christians! Protestants and now exiled by our King and our faith. Pardon my questions reverend doctor, but where is God's truth and justice in this?"

Edward Barkley cleared his throat. "Robbie, perhaps you should tell him why we are here."

"Please excuse me. My friend is right. I am not here to argue; rather I find myself here in need of your help. I urgently require an audience with the Archbishop. Many lives depend on this audience."

"Your passion for the faith is commendable if only you would learn to channel it constructively. What is the purpose of this audience you find so urgent?"

"There is an evil scheme afoot to betray the English volunteer regiment in Germany. Without English support, the reformation could very well be crushed. I dare trust no one in the court to report this treachery other than the Archbishop. He can be trusted to hear the evidence we have gathered."

Doctor Giddings sat silently with his eyes closed. He breathed deeply, looked closely into Robert's face and replied, "The Archbishop has come to hear from Calvinists urging greater tolerance of the non-conformists, your puritan friends. For once the common enemy, the pope, and his emperor are drawing feuding protestants closer. Perhaps I could arrange an audience in the guise of your report on the Puritans in Amsterdam. You must make the most of this audience, do not badger the Archbishop. Archbishop Abbott is, as you know a tolerant man, himself a Calvinist with Puritan leanings."

"I shall be most diplomatic, Doctor Giddings."

"In the meantime, I shall provide you a pass to attend the conference. Perhaps listening might increase your faith and restore your hope in our Church. You received holy orders; you are a priest, Robert. You must learn discipline and perseverance to balance your passion. You have received no call because your questions are too difficult to ignore."

"You have always been a mentor to me, Doctor and I thank you for standing by me."

"Kings College chapel. Ten tomorrow morning. I will have your pass. Good day, Robert, good day sergeant."

As Robert got up to leave, he looked out of the window on the grounds below. He saw a man in luxurious robes, not the black frock of an academic. His eyes fixed on the man, and after a moment, he asked,

"Doctor Giddings, do you know that man?"

Giddings turned around to look and said, "Why yes, that is Count Gondomar, the Spanish Ambassador. He is a friend of Reverend Doctor Fitzhugh. That is Fitzhugh's apartment he enters. Strange that the Count would be here now. He certainly would not be welcome at the conference."

Barkley spoke up. "Another man joins them, a priest. A shoeless priest."

"That would be Father Simon Stock, a discalced Carmelite priest."

Robert asked, "A Carmelite priest here in Cambridge? In England? Simon Stock, you say?"

"Yes, most unusual. He is an Englishman but serves as a diplomat for Spain. He is often in the company of Count Gondomar."

Robert, trying hard to remember said, "I have seen them before. I am certain of it. Yes, now I remember. It was here in Cambridge just before I graduated. That's right. The court was right empty; we were rushing past Doctor Fitzhugh's apartment, well late for Chapel. The priest was leaving the room. I clearly saw Count Gondomar speaking with Fitzhugh and another great noble. I heard my companion, George Fox, God rest his soul, exclaim. "The don Howard Fitzhugh is certainly in lofty company, that is the Secretary of State, Lord Calvert, he entertains."

Surprised, Doctor Giddings said, "Lord Calvert was here? And he met with Doctor Fitzhugh? Why you would think he would have mentioned it. Howard Fitzhugh is not one so humble as to withhold such an honor. As vain a don can be, Fitzhugh exceeds all others! He trumpets his influence at every opportunity!"

Giddings paused and said, "Your friend, George Fox, you said God rest his soul."

Robert nodded. "Yes, shortly after we left Cambridge, George died. Killed by robbers is what I heard. A tragedy, truly, the man had a heart to serve God."

Robert sighed. "Come, Barkley. Ten tomorrow Doctor Giddings."

The early evening darkness of December found Robert and Barkley seated at a fireside table in a pub across from the college. As Barkley tried a second taste of the fare before him, he grumbled, "You ate here more than once? This was your favorite pub? The worst cook in the army could not produce a meal this vile!"

Taking a drink from his mug, he spat it out. "Worse than the food! You can stay here if you please, Robbie, with your happy memories and all, but I am off to find food. It has to get better away from the college."

Robert looked at the meal before him and nodded. "I remembered it was all so good, but I must have been daft. Let's go."

They made their way out into the cold still night. As they walked along a rider could be heard slowly approaching behind them. Both men instinctively made their way to the side of the road to let him pass. As the rider slowly made his way around them, Robert looked up at him, a habit since his days on the rivers. The rider made no note of him, his eyes on the street ahead.

Robert sprang alongside the horse and grasped the bridle as he shouted, "Sharpe!" Pulling back on the horse's head, the animal circled back, hoofs stomping in surprise. "It was you who murdered George Fox! Why! Why do you pursue me?"

Sharpe's eyes widened, he tried for a pistol at his side, but the uneven gait of the frightened horse caused his reach to miss. Robert held onto the bridle and with his other arm pulled on Sharpe's right shoulder. The horse was spinning and began to buck his rear legs. Barkley quickly came and took the bridle as Robert now pulled Sharpe from the horse with both hands. Seeing he had no escape from Robert's grasp, Sharpe dove onto Robert and both men went to the ground. Sharpe continued to claw for the pistol at his side. "Yes, I killed Fox. Easiest mark ever I had. Put up no struggle, not he. Churchman. Soft as a baby. I will be your death as well, Curtis, though you be the very devil's boy. Thought you dead when I shot you at the Neckar skirmish. Was certain when I heard Von Tilly ordered the spiking of the wounded on the battlefield, yet still, you live! Never before have I missed a mark. Aye, only the devil can account for your life."

Robert pinned Sharpe's arm to the ground out of reach of the pistol belt. "It is my God who shields me, and he will be your judge."

"There ain't no God, only the devil in this evil world! It is the devil I trust."

Robert shouted, "Why Fox? Why me?"

Sharpe's left hand found his boot and the dagger kept

there. As he swung his arm, Barkley's booted foot kicked it away. The force of the kick and the pull of the horse brought Barkley to the ground as well, losing the grip on the bridle but managing to hold a rein as he fell. The now free horse reared, slashing his hooves which came down on Sharpe's head. The horse continued to spin and buck. Again, and again Sharpe was struck, and his body absorbed blow after blow. Robert rolled away and was on his feet. Barkley, up before him, again grasped the bridle and stroked the frightened horse's neck. Over Robert's heavy breathing, Barkley could be heard softly calming the horse. Sharpe's bloodied and broken body lay silent in the manure covered street.

"I could have used your help a little earlier, Barkley!"

"We couldn't lose the horse. I came through when needed, and we have the horse."

"Sharpe was the threat, why do you worry after the horse?"

"Think Robbie! Sharpe is the runner. He was leaving Cambridge after we see Count Gondomar thick as thieves with his devil priests. He must be carrying letters, something. I fancy we will find them on this horse. Now help me get his body on the horse and…"

Robert stood up straight and looked around. "No. Leave the body where it lies. Find the knife and put it back in his boot. His wounds are as if thrown from his horse and trampled and the horse a runaway. Quickly we must get the horse out of sight and search. Then we let the horse free to wander the streets of Cambridge."

"Robbie, you may have the heart of a priest, but you

have the mind of an outlaw! Pity he never answered you. Perhaps you will never know his motive."

In the stable of their inn, Robert and Barkley silently went through every bag and bundle carried by Sharpe's horse. Finding nothing, Robert began to repack the saddlebags as they found them and was about to throw them back onto the horse when Barkley took off the saddle. The blanket slid with the saddle but did not fall to the ground. It was lashed onto the bottom of the saddle. He stared at the saddle blanket and gave it a tug. It held secure. Robert noticed Barkley shaking the saddle and joined him in undoing leather straps they found woven through the blanket to the underside of the saddle. As they undid the blanket lashings, two small leather pouches fell onto the ground. After carefully searching the saddle and bridle for others and confident they found what they were looking for, Barkley led the laden horse with the saddle slipped under its belly, outside and around the corner. He gave it a whip across the haunches, and the horse ran into the night. In the warmth of a pub, they opened the pouches to find a small key and letters to A, B, and C.

Archbishop George Abbott sat on the Bishop's throne in the Kings College Chapel listening to cleric after cleric petitioning for recognition or license to lead *his* church or *the* church into a particular reformed doctrine now widespread on the continent or style of worship appropriate to his sanctified convictions. The Archbishop looked like a man going through the motions, a judge who has heard the arguments before and knows the outcome is a foregone conclusion.

"Most Reverend and Honorable Archbishop Abbott, surely some license should be permitted for our country parishes, filled with simple but pious folk put off by popish excess foreign to plain folk, license to worship plainly, hearing the Word of God spoken to them by faithful priests and servants of the Lord. What need have they of incense and richly robed priests? What value of music more appropriate to the courts of royalty? Their minds are too dull for the lofty prayers and liturgy of readings from the Book of Common Prayer. Allow your priests to know their flock, to pastor and instruct them plainly, serve them the Eucharist without mystery and send them blessed into the hard world they know. Have we not removed Catholicism from our land? Let us remove every vestige that remains of that foul religion that never spoke to its flock, whose priests with their backs to their people spoke a foreign language and prospered a church only for entitled clerics."

The Archbishop responded, "Reverend Smythe, would you not lift your flock above their estate? Are they not entitled to blessings here and now, not hoping only for their heavenly reward? Are we not commanded, 'To ascribe to the Lord the glory due His name?' You suggest majesty and beauty are not due our God? Or should we discard every practice of the Roman Church because it is Roman? No majesty in music, no majesty in approaching the altar of our Lord? No fear coming into God's presence and His house of worship? Toss out every practice of the Roman Church—toss out works of mercy? Shutter the hospitals? House no widows or orphans? Shall we toss out prayer? Halt all baptisms? My Bible speaks of the beauty of His holiness. Can we not teach and share this beauty? And their minds too dull? Or is teaching the ancient truths and the creeds beyond your skill?   All that you asked has been considered before. License has been permitted in the liturgy, choices from the Book of Common Prayer, prerogatives in the order of worship, but shall there be no unity in the Church? Shall a worshipper find every other congregation as foreign? Thank you, Reverend Smythe, but I cannot take the personal desires of every country parson to the House of Lords for consideration."

Archbishop Abbott stood up and said, "I have come to listen for calls for unity within our protestant faith. The pope has funded and commanded his emperor to crush the Reformation which has liberated us from the tyranny of a pope who withholds Holy Scripture, grace and salvation from all but his too often corrupt clergy or those obedient without knowledge. Yet I hear only the same petitions. I shall take my meal and time of meditation, and you will reconvene at three this afternoon. I will not attend this afternoon, nor tomorrow. I grant you this time to come together and find one voice. But hear me, brothers, when I return to you for one final hearing, let there be only one voice I hear, one petition and all among you must agree to it."

The conferees stood stunned in silence as Archbishop Abbott departed. Once his grace had left, a loud buzz of animated conversation filled the chapel.

As Robert stood to leave a young priest tapped him on his shoulder and said, "His Grace the Archbishop will hear you now. Please come with me."

Robert followed into a small study where the Archbishop was seated, his robe and mitre on a chair nearby. "A friend tells me you have news of our brothers and sisters in Amsterdam and from the English volunteer regiments as well. Well, do come in, sit down. And tell me the news."

"Most Reverend and Honorable Archbishop, it as you say, I have recently returned from the Palatine by way of Amsterdam. Our Dutch neighbors tolerate our English brothers and sisters and they are permitted to worship and labor freely. But they have little dealings with their hosts and live as aliens in a strange land."

"Is language to hard a problem to overcome?"

"You grace it is more than language, more even then custom. They worship differently than their Dutch hosts, Calvinists mostly; and their faith teaches them to live differently, separately – and then there are the others. Lutherans and German and French Calvinists, even Anabaptists and Hussites – they all seek refuge in the Dutch Republic, most travel to Amsterdam. They fill the city with refugees. So many that they overwhelm the hospitality of the most earnest brother or sister. The English Puritans of Amsterdam long to return to England, but they will not forego their peculiar worship."

The Archbishop sighed. "Yes, some have gone to the wilderness of America to make their way in the new world. But are the times so desperate on the continent that protestants flee in such great numbers?"

"Your grace, they are indeed most desperate! When the Protestant Union dissolved under the Mainz Accord, few of the German princes continued the struggle against the emperor and his determination to crush the Reformation. Our English regiments are garrisoned in three cities, Heidelberg, Mannheim and Frankenthal. They are surrounded and harassed by Count Tilly and the Army of Flanders. It is known another Spanish Army moves north and General Wallenstein moves his Austrians west from Bohemia. The Dutch Republic continues its war with the Spanish Netherlands and has no men to spare. I have traveled through the German principalities and know only of Duke Christian of Brunswick raising an army, and he will not move before spring."

"You believe our brothers and sisters in faith are in mortal danger."

"I do, your grace, but even worse, I have learned of treachery within our regiments. I have evidence of a conspiracy involving a Vatican and a Spanish priest, the Spanish Ambassador, Count Gondomar and Englishmen here in Cambridge. I know the King seeks a marriage between Prince Charles and the Spanish Infanta Maria Anna which some use to pursue a more treacherous purpose, the very betrayal of our regiments with great loss of life. Forgive me, your grace, but I sought you out on the advice of the Dowager Queen Sophia, Queen mother of Denmark-Norway and of our own late Queen Anne. She sent me to you as one who is trusted in the court. A voice in the King's ear and a fair judge of the King's council."

"They tell me you are a priest, but you come as a soldier and a spy with a story of treachery and intrigue."

"Indeed, your grace, I am a priest without placement and found myself a soldier. My heart is to serve God. I desire above all else the unity of the Church, that all with a heart for our Lord and Savior, find common fellowship and worship in the universal truth of the holy catholic Church. I affirm the primacy of Scripture, the historic creeds, the practice of baptism, celebration of the Eucharist and works of mercy. Are not these truths and practices our true religion? Even as a soldier, I did not seek to become a spy. I have stumbled upon what I have, and only ask the questions a loyal Englishman would ask."

"You have evidence. More than hearsay?"

"I can report truthfully what has happened, what I have seen and what I have learned. And then, there are letters…"

CHAPTER 33
THE KEY

Edward Barkley was waiting for Robert when he returned. "The letters make no sense to me. I have not been blessed with your education, but never have I heard anyone, peasant or noble speak in such a difficult and disjointed way. Aye, they arc English words, even sentences, but in the end, they are gibberish."

"They are in code."

"Of course, they are in code, but such nonsense makes it obvious they are code. Is their code so weak that it cannot be disguised?"

"Perhaps they are confident the letters would never be intercepted, so the code is merely a safeguard against unfortunate discovery. A statement: 'You found this letter, but it will do you no good.'"

Robert thought for a moment and then continued, "But we found all of the letters, and we found them here, where the traitors meet. We know the senders from this end, and we know there are three recipients in the regiments. We must look for answers here."

Barkley nodded. "We must search Fitzhugh's apartment. He must have a cipher for the code."

"Perhaps the letters say where to find the box or door the key opens. Or it may be something has been sent ahead. Something that can only now be opened. We do not have much time to act. I am to go to London with the Archbishop in two days. You are coming with me."

Barkley nodded. "We have little time to find what we are looking for, and if we find it, we must be gone before it is discovered missing."

"We must find it, but we cannot take it with us. It would not only be noticed, but it would force them to change their plans. No, we must find it, learn what it means and leave it. We have two nights."

Barkley sighed. "We have another problem. They must know Sharpe is dead. Surely his horse has been recovered, and the letters and key are now known to be missing. Even if the saddle did slip or fall, I don't reckon them so daft as to believe the pouches could have come free. I expect they are planning for visitors."

Robert closed his eyes and stroked his bearded chin. "Perhaps…"

The following afternoon the Cambridge University Chancellor published a decree decrying poor interest by clerics, and faculty of the University in the historic events taking place. "All faculty are commanded to hear the final, universal petition to our primate Archbishop of Canterbury, and wise judge for answering the concerns of certain vicars and churchman for an acceptable and universal practice of our religion to be presented to His Royal Highness James I, King of England, Scotland, Ireland and Wales, by the Grace of God Head of the Church."

Robert took the notice to Edward Barkley. "Fitzhugh will march with the college of Magdalene to the conference. You must waste no time in entering his apartment and finding the cipher to the code, or a box or lock to match the key. Do not take what you find but carefully copy…"

"Surely you will come with me, Robbie?"

"I will follow Fitzhugh from a distance and watch."

"You see, Robbie, I can neither read nor write. Perhaps we should trade roles. Would it not be better if I follow Fitzhugh? He does not know me, but you…"

As soon as the robed dons of Magdalene College marched off in a column of twos, Edward walked by the apartment of Howard Fitzhugh and tried the door. As it slowly opened a man sprang from inside shouting, "Who goes there?"

"I am looking for Howard Fitzhugh, a kinsman. I was told this is his apartment."

"The don is not here. He is off to a conference with the college at Kings Chapel Trinity College. Now be on your way."

Barkley put his boot inside the door, and it closed against his foot. The man inside, now annoyed, opened it again. Barkley said, "I am new to this city, so many colleges and chapels. Be a gent, and show me the way."

"I cannot leave now; go ask someone else."

Edward did not remove his boot. "The court is empty, there is no one else about. Just come to the gate and point to the spire. It will be but a moment of your time, and I will speak well to my cousin on your behalf."

"Just to the gate. Come along then."

Edward followed along behind Fitzhugh's man. As they entered the arched portico of the gatehouse, the man lifted his arm to point when Edward clubbed the back of his head with the hilt of his dagger. Robert immediately appeared, and they dragged the unconscious man back to the apartment. Edward bound and gagged the guard as Robert began the search. A large desk in the tutor study looked across a half dozen chairs for students at a window facing the courtyard. Shelves of books lined the walls, and a small fireplace warmed the room from behind the desk. Robert quickly glanced in the adjoining bedchamber. It was furnished with a single canopied bed with embroidered bedcurtains, a large cushioned chair, a washbowl on a small table and a chamber pot beside it.

Returning to the study room, Robert said, "Put him on the bed. Make sure he cannot move, and no one can hear him. He is breathing I pray."

Barkley snorted. "Aye, he lives. He will not be a problem, just a bad headache when he awakes. I know my business."

Robert looked at all the books. "So easy to hide a coded cipher among the pages." He looked at the desk and noted one drawer with a keyhole. He pulled on the drawer as he reached for his key. The drawer opened easily. It was unlocked and contained only writing paper and quills. Again, he scanned the room and looked at an encased manuscript in a glass-topped box on the table by the window. Robert walked over and looked at an ancient and ornate text. It was a Celtic Bible opened to the gospel of Matthew chapter 16. Not the most ornate page in such an important and artistic hand copied and hand painted work, but in the margin was a vibrant depiction of the apostle Peter alongside the Latin text, 'I say to you, you are Peter, and upon this rock, I shall build my church…'

Robert had heard of these rare and beautiful Bibles but to see one up close, and here in the study of a Cambridge don. He looked closely at the intricate marquetry of the case; the front was inlaid with a lamb bearing a flag and shepherds crook. The sides bore crowns of thorns. Robert carefully picked up the box to look at the rear. It seemed the same as the front. There we no keyholes to be seen. Robert held the box in front of him pondering the beauty and significance of the precious book within. He noticed the box was deeper than the bottom of the book. He lifted the box higher to examine the depth, a side panel moved, nearly causing him to drop the precious artifact.

He carefully put the box back on the table and called, "Barkley, something strange here!"

With the precious Bible back on the table, Robert slid the side panel back revealing another panel bearing a keyhole. As Barkley watched, Robert fumbled to fit the key into the lock. The key fit securely, and Robert carefully turned it. He heard a click as the lock opened, but the side panel did not move. The box appeared unchanged. Both men looked all around the box; nothing was out of place. As Robert stared, Barkley reached down with both hands and lifted the glass lid from the box. Robert raised the Bible and saw a satin tab which lifted away a thin cover from a base compartment lined with velvet embossed with gold. Inside was a crucifix, a rosary and a folded piece of paper.

Robert sat in Fitzhugh's chair and copied what he read, nodding and mumbling to himself as he carefully recorded what he found. When he finished, he returned the paper to the base compartment, closed the case, locked it and slid back the side panel. Barkley took out the corner of his shirt and wiped the glass clean. "Don't need to look man-handled!"

Barkley went back to the bedchamber and shook the guard. There was no response. He took a flask of Scotch poured some on the face of the unconscious guard and placed the flask in his hand. He then ungagged and unbound him, and both he and Robert were immediately out the door.

Robert sat opposite the Archbishop in his regally appointed carriage, while Edward Barkley rode with the mounted guards. The Archbishop held the code cipher in one hand as he read each of the letters. Putting the letters back in a leather pouch he held up the key and asked Robert, "Nothing about this key strikes you as familiar, Mister Curtis?"

Robert shook his head. "No, your grace. Should it be?"

The Archbishop held the key in front of him at an angle. "Imagine if I held an identical gold key at the opposite angle…"

"Of course, Saint Peter's keys to the Kingdom of Heaven! The only proper key to open the 'gift' from the pope to Howard Fitzhugh!"

"Your visit was most timely. Count Gondomar carried a new code and new orders for the Vatican's agents. The priest, Don Pedro has delivered a similar box to one of these traitors in the Palatine with instructions to be followed once the siege begins. He withheld it until the proper time. I am surprised that Lorenzo and Fitzhugh did not fully trust their agents. As a precaution, he sent separate letters. But one man they do trust, and he was to receive the key."

"Then you will present the evidence to the King?"

"Oh, I can't. I am under investigation by the House of Lords, a canon law issue. An accidental hunting accident with the King. Archaic cannon law. It seems Clergy are barred from participation in the blood sports. I never knew! And there is the unfortunate issue of homicide. Sadly, a bolt from my crossbow cut down a new game warden, a man who was somewhere he should not have been."

"Who was this man? Why was he there?"

The Archbishop looked surprised but did not reply. Robert continued. "You were in the King's company, and a man killed as a result of being somewhere he should not have been, a man no one really knows and acts contrary to the common sense of a warden, and no one asks these questions? Do you not find this suspicious?"

"Hmm. Yes, well, as I was saying, I am set aside from any council to the King, but I will give this evidence to the King's favorite. This and the successful petition from the Calvinists and non-conformists."

"Favorable petition? I heard no two speakers petition alike. Many in contradiction to the others."

Archbishop smiled. "As I knew the case would be. I gave them an ultimatum which would lead them to exactly the petition I desired they make. There will never be agreement on one form of worship, one universal rite. Nor will there will be unanimity on every doctrine or dogma of the church. We are blessed that the Holy Spirit of God led our patriarchs to the ancient creeds of the faith. Even recognizing the Authority of Scripture alone, the tradition of the creeds and the reasoning of faithful men, doctors of the church will come to different conclusions on framing a theology to explain the mysteries of God. But beyond these three, Scripture, historic creeds and tradition, anything more than this is non-essential to orthodox, historical teaching of the church. Let those churches follow the non-essentials as they do, whether, Lutheran, Calvinist Reformed, non-conformist Puritan, even Hussite. No, there could be no agreement on the practice of religion, but all Protestants, all Reformed Christians can agree that the pope and the emperor are a threat to the Reformation everywhere and must be stopped."

"You carry a petition for the King to support the protestant cause on the continent.?"

The Archbishop smiled. "It is time the King fully commits to the cause. He will see he has the support of the people and all protestants in his realm. And he will learn that while Count Gondomar drags on a hopeless negotiation for the marriage of Charles and Maria, behind his back he schemes with English traitors to destroy the English regiment in the Palatine."

"And the King's favorite can be trusted?"

"Marquess Buckingham has had his fill of Lord Calvert and Count Gondomar. He has had enough of crypto Catholics and their schemes. No, he is with the parliament in favor of war."

Robert looked out the window at the English countryside. The bare trees, brown grass and gray skies of mid-December spoke to him of death. Without turning, he asked, "What will happen to the conspirators?"

"Why I surmise the English traitors will be tried and put to death. Count Gondomar is an ambassador. He will not be touched. He can only be sent home."

"And the priest, Simon Stock?"

"Maybe English by birth, but he is here as a Spaniard, an assistant to Count Gondomar. The King's authority cannot touch him."

Robert said softly to himself, "My friend. I cannot believe he is one of them. To think that I trusted him."

The guard at the door of Lambeth palace stood stoically at attention as Robert accompanied the Archbishop into his home. Edward Barkley made a point of pulling a fig from Cardinal Woolsey's fig tree which he then handed to the guard as he followed Robert and the Archbishop in.

"First an ale," the Archbishop said, to quench my dry throat from a long day's journey. Please, gentlemen, sit."

Turning to his servant, he said, "Three ales for a thirsty old man and his friends."

Robert asked, "Your grace, when shall we go to the Marques of Buckingham?"

Archbishop Abbott nodded. "I know the urgency you feel, Mister Curtis. But we do not go to Buckingham. We must wait for him to come to us. I have sent a letter ahead. We must wait."

Seeing the disappointment on Robert's face, George Abbott continued. "He is the King's favorite, always available to the King. He is a most remarkable man; you shall understand when you meet him. He has put the King's affection to good use. He is a most ambitious man, and now he accompanies the King in Council as well as games and affairs of state. There a few opportunities for him to leave the King's presence, even then he must seek royal approval."

"We may wait for months! And time…"

"Patience Mister Curtis! Buckingham is excells in receiving the royal favor of the king."

George Villiers, the Marques of Buckingham was indeed a most remarkable man. He appeared the following day, coming alone on horseback. He entered the palace with confidence born out of his sense of entitlement. His presence and appearance nothing less than stunning. His dress lavish, rich with gold embroidery, more costly than a year's profit of a vast estate. The cut of his clothes emphasized his perfect athletic body, the curve of his calves, the chiseled strength in his arms and shoulders and the flat trim stomach above his narrow waist all framed perfectly to be displayed like a classic Greek sculpture. But more attractive was his face, at one time beautiful in form and radiant with life—a face of warmth and charm which wore a playful smile of uninhibited fun. His words were sung as they crossed his lips; they assured one that this indeed was a true and refined gentleman.

"Archbishop, so delighted you have returned safely. Indeed, the souls of the King's subjects are secure in the sure hands of God's chosen shepherd! And these, your friends good and stout fellows they appear to me!"

"You do me great honor, Marques, this is Lieutenant Curtis and Sergeant Barkley, the men I mentioned in my letter."

For a moment Buckingham's eyes reflected serious study but quickly returned to their flattering sparkle. "Most splendid soldiers! Capable and true to his Majesty the King. Now, show me the gift you bring. Your letter mentioned a pearl of great value."

Archbishop Abbott opened the leather pouch and handed Buckingham the letters and the cipher sheet. He sat and read, his eyes going back and forth between papers. Finally, he looked up and said, "Truly a pearl of great value. We have them! And we have proof. Fitzhugh, Gondomar and the turncoat priest Simon Stock recruited and placed the three Captains, Charles Richard, Donald Stock, and Sir Geoffrey Curtis. Sharpe was the go-between."

"Sir Geoffrey, any relation to you, Lieutenant?"

"He is my cousin, a Curtis of Scotland; I am of the English family."

The Marques nodded. "A Roman Priest, Don Lorenzo is their master. Until now they merely reported on the English regiments, but now, they intend to act. Captain Richard has the other box and awaits the key and orders to open it. Donald Stock has informed me of a Catholic cell; he suspected Captain Curtis due to his familiarity with Sharpe. He did not know of Captain Richard, or the don, Howard Fitzhugh."

Robert interrupted. "Donald Stock reported to you?"

Buckingham replied, "He came to me when his brother first recruited him. Stock may love his brother, but he is a true Englishman-loyal to his king."

"Colonel Vere thinks him a traitor, as I did as well. We hid intelligence from him."

"Yes, he was frustrated that he never gained the confidence of Colonel Vere though he serves him faithfully. The late posting as adjutant, I had to convince Calvert, my mistake not to tell Vere. But here is their plan, at first cannon fire of the siege they are to arrange the death of their Colonels, instill disorder and insurrection to culminate in surrender."

Robert spoke. "There will be no support for the regiments until late spring. Duke Christian of Brunswick has raised ten thousand men, cavalry and infantry but he will not move until the roads are firm in the spring. He will join with the remainder of Count von Mansfeld's army before moving into the Palatine. Von Tilly will commence his siege early, starting with Heidelberg, before Duke Christian marches."

"You know this?" Buckingham asked.

"I have met with Christian. I know this is his plan though I urged him to move sooner. I also know of the loan made by King Christian IV to King James, but there will be no army coming from Denmark."

The Marques looked again through the letters. "He refers to other friends moving forward to take Prince Charles. A brood of vipers, these papists! But it is unclear what he means. It may be Fitzhugh bragging. The rack will get the truth from him."

The Marques looked at Robert. "You have outdone that old man Lord Calvert and all of his watchers. Truly grand work, Lieutenant! This will help me move him to retire."

"I have seen Lord Calvert meeting with Fitzhugh, Count Gondomar and the priest Simon Stock at Cambridge. You don't think..."

"No, the old fool has Catholic leanings and will not let go of his dream to align England and Spain and thereby to the Holy Roman Emperor, but he is in the end, a man of principle and loyal to the king. No, he, like the king, is courted by Gondomar and Simon Stock has designs to convert him to Catholicism, but they know they cannot turn him. No, Calvert has little time in left in office, he has lost the support of the Lords and parliament. He is shunned at court for his Spanish plan."

The Marques picked up the key and said, "This will never make its way to Heidelberg. There is nothing better than the trials of traitors to gain the attention of the king. And the proof of another cell, well that will steel his determination even more!"

Archbishop Abbott spoke. "There is still more. I have returned with a petition from the Calvinists, Puritans, and non-conformists. A most timely unanimous petition that the King does not forsake his support for the Protestant cause on the continent. There is not a Protestant vicar or cleric in his realm that withholds his support for this petition. He is the ordained a protector of the faith!"

"Yes, all comes into alignment, the Lords, the Parliament, the Church and the will of his people. I will gladly take this petition to his majesty."

The Marques stood up. "I must return, the king will expect his 'Steenie' at the ball this evening.
Tell me, Curtis, what at are your plans?"

"Sergeant Barkley and I are to rejoin our regiment in Heidelberg."

"Do take a leave. I will write to Colonel Vere all that we have learned. Stay in England. I may need you."

"As you wish, we shall go to our families in Berwick-Upon-Tweed. My uncle, Viscount Curtis can find us."

"Very good then, I shall be in contact. And Archbishop

Abbott, that hunting mishap, the King tires of your absence from court. I expect he will act soon on your behalf."

After the Marques of Buckingham left, Edward forwardly asked, "Steenie?"

The Archbishop replied, "His majesty's name for the Marques...the king sees the face of Saint Stephen, the face of an angel."

Edward nodded. "If ever I thought a man could be beautiful, Buckingham is that man."

CHAPTER 34
THE LORD OF MISRULE

Both Robert and Edward were anxious to return to Berwick-Upon-Tweed, three hundred and fifty long miles north of London. The thought of a hard, long ride through the December cold led Barkley to insist they find a ship going north and cut the time of the journey from two to three weeks to as little as four or five days. Barkley's effort paid off, and the next day they boarded a Dutch fluyt, a speedy cargo ship, in Rotherhithe and were making their way down the River Thames before noon. The ship had brought a cargo of wine and root vegetables from Holland to London and carried finely crafted furniture and porcelain to Berwick-Upon-Tweed, where it would load wool for Amsterdam. Though the weather cold and the seas choppy, the ship was solid, dry and warm.

Both men used the time to reflect on the events of the past months. Robert was now certain it was only his chance witnessing of the meeting in Howard Fitzhugh's Cambridge apartment that put the assassin Sharpe on his trail and cost the life of George Fox, an innocent man with a future of faithful service ahead of him. His Calvinist friends would insist it had all been ordained by God. Was such an acceptance any more comforting than the random death of a good and righteous man? Yes, God can use a tragedy to bring about good things, and it was indeed Robert's prayer that his friend had not died in vain, but this brought him no peace. Why did he survive, not one but at least three attempts on his life? A mystery of faith, Robert concluded one more mystery beyond understanding.

The weary soldiers arrived in Berwick-Upon-Tweed on December 24, 1621. Barkley said as they stepped onto the pier, "I'm off home, Robbie. How long must we wait for word? I am wantin' to return to the regiment."

"Return to soldiering, Barkley? Thought you might have had your fill. You know the men at Heidelberg will have no relief."

"Aye, I cannot leave them to their fate. And where shall I find you, Robbie, with your father or uncle?"

"Truly, I have questions for my uncle, and certainly news regarding Sir Geoffrey. But I go first to my father's house."

As Barkley walked off, Robert called, "Come tomorrow, my friend, as it is custom on Christmas. But after church!"

"Aye Robbie! And be ready to pay the piper!"

Robert found his father's house dark and empty. The neighbors told him his father had moved into the manor with his brother, Viscount Curtis. Robert hired a cart to haul his chest filled with armor, uniform, and clothes, and made his way up the hill overlooking the harbor to the great granite stone house on top.

A loud knock on the heavy door was answered immediately by a servant. "Master Curtis, welcome. Happy that you are here for Christmas. Your uncle the Viscount is with the others in the Great Hall. Please go directly; I will tend to your things. A room has been prepared for you." Entering the great hall, Katharina shouted out, "Robert! Oh, Robert, you have returned and for Christmas! God is so good! Look, Johann, Robert is here."

Katharina rushed to Robert and embraced him with a warm hug. Soon Johann joined the embrace. "My brother, it is indeed a blessing. Your family has shown us such hospitality!"

Katharina gushed, "If only Wilhelm and papa could be here now. It would be perfect!"

Robert asked, "Is there any news from Karl? Is Werner safe? And where is Wilhelm?"

Johann answered, "Werner and papa are safe. They send word through the watchers. I will go to join them, to lead our people to safety in Amsterdam."

"They will be welcome here as well," Robert replied.

"So it would appear, but it may be hard for them to

cross the sea. In the United Netherlands, they are closer to home and can follow events. And your English ways can be so different."

"And my brother priest, Wilhelm?"

Katharina answered, "He spends all his time at the hospital, the orphanage, and the widow's home. He is determined to minister where he is needed."

"He does not perform the mass, I pray?"

"No, he honors the law and the customs of your people. He serves by helping, listening and praying."

Robert asked, "Does he hide in his work? Surely, he will join us for Christmas worship tomorrow?"

Katharina pleaded, "Talk to him, Robert. He listens to you. He values your advice. He has even learned English from the Bible you gave him and practices all the time!"

An elderly man spoke up in the pause. "Can someone not gifted in French or German have a word?"

"Father, it is good to see you well, and here with uncle James. I went first to your house, but your neighbors said you live here now. And uncle James, I must thank you for the hospitality you show my friends."

Viscount Curtis nodded. "I have learned that these are family to you. They saved your life and took you in. Are they not my family as well? And my brother, who came to serve me in my illness. He has been such a blessing, I insisted he stay even as I have recovered—two old men who needed to be reminded of the meaning of family, and brotherhood. My house has never been so filled with joy! Welcome home, Robert!"

"Uncle James, and you as well, father, I bring news.

Hard news that should be for your ears alone. Friends, please excuse us for a few moments. Let me have a word, and then I will share with you my adventures."

Robert walked to the Viscount's study when his uncle called out, "Not that room Robert! No, come with me."

The Viscount led him to the receiving room and said, "What hard news, Robert?"

Taking a deep breath, he began. "Cousin, Sir Geoffrey, will soon be arrested and tried for treason. It is true, I am afraid, he provides information to the enemy. He intends to kill Colonel Sir John Burroughs and surrender the garrison. He is a member of a Catholic cell led by a Vatican priest and a Cambridge don. Barkley and I found the proof and delivered it to the Marques Buckingham who takes it to the king."

Viscount Curtis stepped back in disbelief and sat in a chair. "It is true I never much cared for Sir Geoffrey, but a traitor? A noble of the house of Curtis, a traitor to our king? He will bring disgrace and dishonor on our house."

Charles Curtis replied, "Is it not fortunate, brother, that it is a Curtis who brings this news to the king? Will he not see our loyalty at the pain of our own house?"

"Excuse me uncle, but what becomes of the titles and estates of traitors?"

"They are forfeit to the crown."

"I am certain, uncle, that the Marques of Buckingham will protect the Curtis' of Tweedbridge. But tell me, uncle, why did you send Sir Geoffrey's man, Sharpe, a man who three times tried to murder me, why send him to Edward Barkley?"

"A murderer? I did not know the man's character! No, I simply honored sir Geoffrey's request to recommend a man skilled in smuggling and procuring hard to find goods, goods where no man is concerned with their history. I knew Barkley was a smuggler. I have known it for years. He is good at his trade, but he only became proficient with my protection."

"You protected Barkley?"

"Even a smuggler has a limited number of beaches he can land, and there are only so many roads. No, I made sure the patrols never interfered with him."

Now Charles replied together with Robert, "Why?"

"On account of his mother. She was a saintly woman. Such a kind heart! Even as a widow I saw that she would have enough for herself and her son, but she could not say no to another in need. She gave away all that she had. She gave not just her money and her food; she gave time and service and love. Never did a woman love so many so well. She gave to me…she…she deserved to receive. If she would not keep what I provided, I let Edward provide what he could. Don't be fooled by his bluster, Edward was a good and loving son. And who has been hurt by his smuggling? The wealthy and comfortable paid their taxes; the poor only took what they needed."

Robert replied, "You knew. You knew all along."

After a pause, he continued. "You are right about Edward Barkley, he is a good man. I now count him among my dearest friends. He intends to return to his regiment and likely die with them."

"His mother would be proud of his sense of honor, but

you should not let him return!"

"It is only on the orders of the Marques of Buckingham that we await his permission to leave England. We may be called as witnesses in the trials."

"You too, Robert? Then I hope justice comes slowly and you remain safe!"

"Uncle, why did you buy my commission in the volunteers?"

"Your cousin's request for Barkley put it in my mind. I bought you time and an opportunity to find your calling. You may have the heart and the calling of a priest, but a soldier learns he must act! Too much thinking, Robert. You needed to learn to act!"

Wilhelm did not join the festive dinner that night. Robert left word to awaken him when father Hahn returned, and that Wilhelm was to wait to see Robert before retiring. It was past midnight on Christmas morning when an exhausted and worn Father Wilhelm Hahn finally returned to the manor house. Surprised to hear of Robert's return he warmly greeted his friend. "Robert! How good to see you brother! I did not know of your return. But here you are! In one piece! No new wounds, no more limping! Good to see you, my friend!"

"You missed a most wonderful and festive dinner, brother. Shame on you for hiding from those who love you."

"Robert, there is so much need! So much to do...I am sorry I could not leave sooner."

"You will come with us to church this morning. We will worship together; you can hear the familiar liturgy in

English, sung beautifully and the choir! I long to worship together once more!"

"Of course, Robert, I will worship with you. It will be a joy."

"And with my father and uncle and Johann and Katharina. We shall worship and then return to feast."

Robert paused, his face turned serious. "You look tired, my friend. I think it is not for long hours of service. I think your soul is still troubled. You question why you are here and not saying mass in Germany. Can we pray together, brother? Do you trust our Lord to answer you?"

"I do pray, Robert, just as I did in Mainz before we left, but my doubts remain."

"Still you are here. You are serving our Lord and ministering to the great need you have found. I learned that Sharpe tried three times to kill me, but God saved me. My friend, George Fox, a good and righteous priest, he killed easily. I learned it was because we witnessed a meeting of men I did not know. But you see God preserved me. I know he loved my friend, but he saved me, and I must walk the path He has chosen. Has not our Lord and Savior preserved you and set you on a new path as well? I only ask that you consider it. We will talk more, later. Indeed, I look forward to sharing so much with you my brother, and with Johann and Katie. Look how great is our God! I came home to find my father and uncle reconciled! Sleep friend. Rest and tomorrow rejoice with me!"

The next morning, Katie insisted on holding Robert's

and Wilhelm's hands as they walked to church. The old stone church in the center of Berwick-Upon-Tweed was filled as Viscount Curtis led his family and friends to his box at the front of the church just beneath the pulpit. Robert never remembered the church as festive and joyous as that Christmas morning. Fresh greens and hollies added to the colors of the altar cloth and the best vestments of the vicar. A choir in white robes echoed the liturgy sung by priest and congregation. Robert smiled as he saw tears of joy on so many faces, his father Charles and uncle James, Johann, Katie, and Wilhelm. As they followed the cross, the priest and the choir out in the recessional, he saw Sergeant Edward Barkley dressed in his best uniform singing powerfully at the aisle in the back row. Bowing as the cross passed him, he gazed over and nodded to Robert, who reached out for his hand as he passed. "A happy Christmas to you Sergeant Barkley. I expect you at the manor house for the feast."

Barkley smiled broadly. "No sergeants in the manor of the Viscount on Christmas, wouldn't be right!"

Robert smiled at his comrade and said, "Perhaps not a sergeant, but a friend!"

Katie hurried the group back along the road up the hill to the grand manor house. "Hurry, you must come quickly. I have a surprise. O what a surprise for a happy Christmas!"

Johann smiled. "You must listen to her. We must hurry, or she shall surely burst!"

They marched through the door, and Katie ran forward through the great hall and stopped at the door to

Viscount Curtis' study. "Everyone, please come near. Come closer. Here is my gift," she opened the door to reveal a large fresh cut evergreen tree standing in the center of the room with bright white candles sending soft white light on the green tree. "At home, we enjoy the tree after midnight worship service, it is so much more beautiful at night, but it would not be right to celebrate until after we worship God in His sanctuary."

Viscount Curtis replied, "We will still enjoy it come nightfall, but let us now feast!"

A servant appeared with a tray of wine and ale, even a bottle of good Scotch whiskey was set out. Wilhelm took a dram of Scotch whiskey and said in halting English, "I have never known so much love as I know today! To my brothers and sister!"

The toast echoed back, "Here, here! To my brothers and sister!"

The toasting continued throughout the feast when a loud pounding was heard on the front door. Viscount Curtis stood up. "That will be the 'Lord of Misrule,' let him enter and join the feast!"

Robert smiled and said as he rose to welcome the lord, "An English custom, the poor go about on Christmas day as lords of misrule, demanding the feast of the rich be shared. On Christmas day they cannot be turned away but welcomed to join in the joy of celebration and taste the feast of the wealthy."

As Robert finished his explanation, a loud voice bellowed, "Make a place at your table, Viscount Curtis, the Lord of Misrule is here!" Edward Barkley dressed in his former working clothes, the dark cloak of a smuggler stumbled into the room."

Robert yelled back, "It seems the lord has made a few stops before this good house! Come sit your lordship and join our celebration."

Barkley sat down lifted a mug of ale, leaned back to drink, and fell back passed out drunk. Robert eyed his friend and said, "Carry this lord up to one of the rooms, perhaps another lord of misrule will come and take his place!"

Wilhelm was laughing uncontrollably, Johann, Charles and Viscount James joined the laughter. Katie walked over behind Wilhelm, wrapped her arms around him and kissed the back of his neck. Crying tears of joy, she said, "Where there is love, all will be well, Wilhelm. All will be well."

ALSO BY DAVID MARTYN

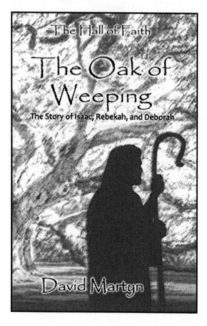

THE OAK OF WEEPING
The Story of Isaac, Rebekah, and Deborah

One of the great love stories of the Old Testament.

Available Now

THE PRAISE SINGER
A Disciple of Melchizedek

Available from Blue Forge Press
November 2019